C000151653

M4

Sword of the Spirit

Millennium Series

Staci Morrison

First published by Alanthia Publishing 2022

Copyright © 2022 by Staci Morrison

ISBN: 978-1-958113-01-1

First edition

For Bob, who has read every word in the series multiple times, believed in the big dream, and always loved the "Esmeralda" part of me. Without your encouragement and support, Alanthia would just be some cool series I wanted to write one day. I am tryly belssed to call you husband.

Thank you, Honey.

Table of Contents

Enter the Millennium

Welcome back! The reader will recall that years in the text are indicated with ME, Millennial Era, instead of BC or AD. Thus, 999 ME is 999 years into the Millennium.

Character names use a Hebrew construction, whereby 'ben' means child of, so Josiah ben Eamonn means Josiah son of Eamonn.

So, what is the Millennium, and when will it occur?

It is a prophetic time, the next great age. Our world today will not continue ad infinitum. At some point in the future, the Lord will appear in the Heavens and call His church to Himself. This global cataclysmic event is called the Rapture and sets off a series of events that will usher in the Tribulation, seven years of wars, famine, earthquakes, fire, and pestilence; hell on Earth. But in the end, the evil forces are defeated. The Lord returns to rule, ushering in the Millennium, one thousand years of paradise, a return to what was lost in Eden.

Series Notes

As the series progresses, we move deeper into the tale, often going on the "other side of the door". And while each book could technically be read as a stand alone, I do not suggest it. The breadth and depth of the story is fleshed out in vivid detail by reading the series in order. I am not big on recapping, but I do my best to anchor each part where appropriate. Sometimes I leave those things to the reader, as I think it adds some little tidbits to discover.

M4-Sword of the Spirit explores 998 ME, so while not techincally a prequel, this was unexplored in the previous novels. In typical fashion, we see our favorite characters, but we might meet them prior to the last novel, so when we meet Joanna and Ian in M4, they have not yet married. To help keep it all straight, I created a "Bonus Section" on alanthia.com that offers readers a timeline of events from the previous novels. If you like that sort of thing, check it out.

I am honored and humbled to have you back, so from the bottom of my heart, thank you. Take my hand; I am going to tell you an amazing tale.

Therefore put on the full armor of God, so that when the day of evil comes, you may be able to stand your ground, and after you have done everything, to stand.

—Ephesians 6:13

Part 1 - Thaddeus

March 21, 987 ME - (Two Years into Rebellion)

What Are You Looking At? - Thyatira Woods, Pennsylvania

"What are you looking at?" Thaddeus ben Todd growled across a campfire, backhanding a dribble of whiskey that leaked down his stubbled chin.

"I ain't looking at nothing," the man protested. But his bloodshot eyes narrowed over the flames, and he slurred, "I just thought maybe—"

"Don't think," Thaddeus said, turning away to hide his face. "You don't know anything. Leave me alone." Grabbing his battered knapsack, he heaved himself off an upturned bucket and staggered into the woods.

A hundred yards away from the vagabond's camp, he tripped over his own boots and caught himself on a tree. Resting his forehead against the bark, he wondered when they would ever stop saying, 'Hey, aren't you that guy?'

He wanted to howl at the moon and shout, "No, I never was! I wasn't that man. It was all a lie, just an illusion, a figment of your imagination, just a figment."

He ran his hand through his hair and grumbled, "What the hell kind of word is figment, anyway? That's a stupid word, like my stupid life."

Deciding he was not fit company, he walked for a time, weaving in the darkness and finishing the bottle. But the ground was uneven, and the whiskey finally did its work. He went down on one knee, no clue where he was. "Oh, how the mighty have fallen," he whispered, passing out in the dirt, using a fiddle head fern as a pillow.

Where Did That Come From?

When Thaddeus woke the next morning, his mouth tasted like a herd of cattle had passed through it. Sunlight broke through the canopy of trees, but fog covered the ground, coating everything, including him. His body hurt, from sleeping on the dirt or alcohol poisoning, he could not be sure which, not that he cared.

He sat up, scrubbing his face hard and dislodging a leaf from the itchy growth of a three-day beard. Picking a fleck of gunk out of his eye, he noticed an earthenware jug and wondered what he had been drinking. His canvas knapsack lay upended beside him, an extra pair of socks spilled onto the leaves, but the contents appeared to be undisturbed. He lifted a blanket puddled around his legs, perplexed because it wasn't his.

"Hello?" Thaddeus called, his voice cracked with sleep, rough with whiskey. "Anybody here?"

Nothing moved.

He examined the blanket for a name tag or other markings; there were none. But his clothes were dry where it covered him, which was good. Being damp was never pleasant, drunk or sober.

He stood up and gave the blanket a sharp flick. It shed the dew in a fine spray, growing instantly dry. Narrowing his brows, he scanned the area, suspecting the owner might want his blanket back, but saw no one.

Shrugging, he mumbled, "Well, you got yourself a blanket, Thad." With shaking hands, he folded it up, surprised at how lightweight and small it became, shrinking to little more than a deck of cards. With a rueful shake of his head, he crammed it in his back pocket and stumbled away from the camp to relieve his bladder.

Leaning against an enormous oak, his stomach flipped, and he expelled the swirling poison floating in his gut. He groaned, his mouth fouled with sickness, feeling the ominous throb of an eyeball headache coming on. Having no intention of sobering up, he stumbled back to his belonging and retrieved the jug. Pulling the cork, he gave a tentative sniff, curious what it might be. It wasn't whiskey, his current beverage of choice. With the remnants of bile burning his tonsils and his tongue stuck to the roof of his mouth, he figured the jug could not be worse.

Cool liquid bathed the back of his throat, sweet and clean. His liver rejoiced at something that was not alcohol, and it felt as if his dehydrated cells breathed a sigh of relief. With his Adam's apple bobbing in great convulsions, he drained the contents, suspending the empty jug over his mouth, letting the last drops splash his lips and grubby face.

Life surged through his veins, his vision cleared, and colors intensified, becoming vivid and surreal. The world seemed to shift as he watched the forest change from muted greens and browns into vibrant, fantastical hues. He stumbled backward in shock, tripped over a root, and fell hard on his rump.

Rubbing his eyes, he blinked in astonishment as the woods transformed into Eden, teaming with life, full of wonder. He detected the tangy scent of a wild cranberry bush, smelled the leaf mold and rich soil of the forest floor. A squirrel scampered up a tree, a robin called its mate, and a speckled fawn peeked around the trunk of the hulking oak to his left. A mink scuttled out of the shrubbery, stood on its hind legs, and regarded him with a quizzical expression.

Thaddeus met its ball bearing eyes, his own wide in stunned fascination.

A giggle caught his ear, and he swung around toward the source. "Hey!" he called. "Who's there?" But the thick woods absorbed his voice. No one answered.

His vision returned to normal. "What the hell?" he muttered, rubbing his eyes hard and deciding he really had to quit drinking; this was getting out of hand.

Scrambling to his feet with a habitual groan, he stilled, realizing he no longer hurt. He smacked his lips, testing, but his mouth tasted cool and clean. "What was in that jug?" he said aloud, intending to investigate, but when he looked around it was gone. "Oh, this is strange."

Certain he was experiencing some sort of alcohol induced delusion, his hand moved to his back pocket. The blanket was still there. He shook it out and examined it closer. To his untrained eye there was nothing noteworthy about its construction, but when he pulled on the fabric, it stretched and snapped back into place. It felt silky between his fingers, but the herringbone weave had strength. Giving it a sniff, he detected leaves, soil, and himself, which, if he were honest, was not pleasant. It appeared brown when he awoke, but against his shirt it took on a blue hue, almost blending. Testing a theory, he pressed the cloth against a tree trunk and watched the color change, becoming almost invisible. "What the hell?" he said to the empty air.

His stomach growled. Food... he needed food. When was the last time he ate? Yesterday? Had he eaten yesterday or just drank that bottle of whiskey? Whiskey. That was all. No wonder he was hungry.

Unbidden, a sweet voice called in his mind, 'Come down, Thad. Your food's ready. I made your favorite.'

He closed his eyes as the memory shredded his soul. "I miss you," he whispered into the silence. "I miss you." He swallowed a gurgling lump of grief and left the squashed fiddle head fern, intent on finding breakfast.

Now What?

Two hours later, Thaddeus dropped his backpack and took a seat on a boulder near a waterfall. He was lost, hopelessly and thoroughly lost. The irony of his situation did not escape his wry sense of the absurd, because he knew he was lost in more ways than one. With sullen resignation, he ate a handful of black raspberries instead of the eggs and toast was craving. He had never been much of a fruit eater but was pleasantly surprised at how delicious the berries tasted, and as a bonus, they gave his burning stomach something to process.

He leaned on his elbow and stared at the waterfall, not sure what to do next. Fine mist caught the late morning light, casting iridescent rainbows that seemed to dance in the breeze, reminding him of the surreal color explosion this morning. Sitting on the rock, peace surrounded him.

The pool below beckoned with unspoken invitation. He scratched his chest in absent contemplation, recognizing the need to bathe. He was grungy, and for the first time in weeks, became cognizant of how rotten he smelled. He supposed it came from being sober, which he was. As disgruntled as he might be about it, unless a liquor store manifested out of the trees, there was nothing to be done at the moment, so he may as well get clean.

The slope proved easy enough to navigate as he hopped from rock, to ledge, down to the pool at the base of the falls. Digging in his knapsack, he found a personal hygiene kit one of the do-gooders pressed on him last week. He'd taken it to get her to shut up and was now thankful he did. Unsnapping the little pouch, he unwrapped a toothbrush and toothpaste, shampoo, deodorant, soap, and a razor with a small mirror. But it would do little good if he bathed and redressed in his filthy clothes. A sample packet of laundry detergent floated around the bottom of his pack somewhere. He dug it from the depths and stared at it dubiously, having never hand washed an article of clothing in his life.

Getting naked out in the open was another thing, but he scanned his surroundings and after not seeing or hearing another soul in hours, felt certain he was alone. Shucking his boots and clothes, the air felt cool on his bare skin. He reached his arms over his head in a bone popping, spine aligning stretch, and braced himself for the chilly water. A small eddy near the bank hollowed out an ideal spot for washing his clothes. He threw them into the pool with a wet thwap and watched the jeans puff with air before taking up the dance with his shirt and socks. He sprinkled the detergent into the mix and watched with hypnotic leisure as the mountain stream agitated the clothing into a frothy foam. "Nature's own washing machine," he remarked.

Wading into the pool, he was gratified to find it bracing but not icy. With a deep breath, he went under, experiencing the sudden cessation of all sound. The crash of the falls muted, as he took a moment to enjoy the gentle pulse of energy against his bare skin. He looked up and saw he was surrounded by sunbeams that penetrated the water's surface in shafts of golden light. Sediment passed through them, glimmering like fairy dust, before disappearing into the dark. Running his fingers through his hair, small twigs and leaves loosened and floated away.

With a powerful thrust against the silty bottom, he broke the surface, taking a deep gulp of clean forest air. He swam for a bit, letting the pool cradle him, but decided if he was going to make it out of here before nightfall, he needed to finish bathing and washing his clothes.

The warm air created a comfortable contrast to the cool water beading over his body. His skin pebbled over a physique grown thin with neglect, like taut rawhide over 6' 6" of lean muscle. He weighed little more now than he had in high school when he was the All-Star power forward on his basketball team.

He soaped up and shaved with contemplative slowness, letting the steady fall of the water soothe his ears, appreciating the constancy of it. Noises bothered him, the sound of some-one eating being the worst. Don't slurp, smack, or crunch around Thaddeus. A rattle or a high-pitched squeal set him on edge, and gum chewing, whistling, and humming were strictly out of bounds.

With his body and his clothes washed, he draped the wet garments over a bush and stretched out on his wonder blan-ket, which had taken on the green hue of the mossy bank. He reckoned if anyone saw him sunning himself naked, he would roll himself up and ask for directions out of here.

Not that much waited for him back in civilization, other than a bottle of booze and oblivion. Neither appealed to him at the moment, so he laced his fingers behind his head and relaxed, thinking about absolutely nothing except the shape of the clouds. It was a skill, thinking about nothing, and he had grown quite adept at it, though it took practice, espe-cially for a mind such as his, or such as it had been before degenerating into a whiskey-soaked sponge. But that was the purpose, the primary reason for this bender, to turn off and forget, to disappear. If he drank enough, the world narrowed to nothing more than a spinning, rye-washed blur.

They would be looking for him, of that he did not doubt. Someone like him could not disappear without notice, but he managed well enough, if he discounted the occasional wanderer who recognized him. A cavalry man's cap and jacket, found at a veterans shelter, disguised him as one of the innumerable Alanthian Civil War's walking wounded. Only a month since the fighting ended, he blended among their ranks. No one questioned him, the war being a touchy topic. He served, though not fighting and bleeding on the battle field, but in another capacity, no less dangerous, and in the end, just as deadly.

A girl's voice broke his reverie. "Do you feel better now?"

He rolled up like a burrito, coming his feet with the blan-ket riding low on his hips. "You startled me!" he barked.

She covered her eyes and giggled, "You were naked."

Color rose up his neck. "It's not nice to sneak up on people."

"I didn't sneak up on you. I've been following you since this morning," she informed him, pulling a brown ringlet over her nose and watching it bounce back under her tug. Then she smiled, her blue eyes crinkling at the edges. "You seemed lost."

Thaddeus glared at her. "Why didn't you speak up? I am lost."

She hopped onto a rock, balancing on her tip toes. "You were grumpy, so I decided to wait until you weren't."

"Where am I?" Thaddeus asked, watching the little nymph.

"In the woods," she said, stating the obvious and jumping to another rock. Then she smiled over her shoulder. "Get dressed. Lunch will be ready soon."

His stomach growled loud enough they both heard it.

"Come on."

"Hey!" Thaddeus called. "What's your name, kid?"

"Esmeralda." She skipped off, her little dress swinging around her ankles.

He stared after her, realizing the clothes she wore blended with the surroundings like the blanket. One mystery solved. He pulled on his damp clothes and followed her into a world he did not know still existed in the Millennium.

Time Capsule

His grandfather told him stories about places like this, the way life used to be in Alanthia. After the Great Judgment, people lived in isolated, self-sufficient communities. For hundreds of years, peace and harmony reigned in little hamlets such as Thaddeus now found himself.

Esmeralda took his hand and pulled him toward a small wooden house with a blue door. "Come on. I told Mother you were coming."

Thaddeus ducked through the door frame, careful not to crack his head.

The young, apple-cheeked housewife smiled and said, "Welcome, come in. Esmie told me she was bringing a friend for lunch." She looked up at him. "Though you are taller than I expected."

He reached out a hand in greeting. "Thank you for having me, mistress. I'm Thaddeus." He did not give his full name, even in this remote village they might know it, and he did not wish to deal with the inevitable questions if they did.

"It is fine to meet you, Thaddeus. I'm Julianna. My husband, Claude, will be along shortly. Please have a seat." She gestured to a fine table and chairs in the small dining area connected to the kitchen.

The scent of fresh bread made his stomach growl. Esmeralda giggled, and they shared a smile. Out of the cabinet, she retrieved a jug that looked like the one he drank from this morning—second mystery solved. He gave a tentative sniff of the glass she poured him but did not drink, eying the curly headed imp. Julianna bustled around the kitchen, preparing what was obviously the big meal of the day, something he was grateful for. The tantalizing aromas drifting out of cook pots made his mouth water.

A man of the house entered and called, "Greetings, family." Spying Thaddeus, he nodded. "Well, hello and welcome. I'm Claude." His accent held a German twang, as did his wife's.

Thaddeus rose, extending a hand. "Thank you, sir. I'm Thaddeus."

Claude drew back in surprise. "My word, you are tall."

"Runs in the family," Thaddeus answered by rote.

"Claude, will you say grace?" Julianna asked setting out the meal.

The family bowed their heads, and Thaddeus followed suit, realizing he had not uttered a prayer in quite a while. Thankfully Claude was not long-winded,

Esmeralda sat beside Thaddeus as he dug into meatloaf, corn on the cob, fresh green beans, and soft white bread with salted butter. Heaven. Minding his manners, he thanked his hosts profusely between bites.

After the meal, he contemplated the water. He cast Esmeralda a dubious look and took a sip. Cool and refreshing, it flooded his mouth and washed down the rest of his lunch. Again, his vision changed, and he saw colors in a vivid and dazzling manner, though this time he was prepared. Julianna's hair sparkled golden brown with hints of blonde. Esmeralda's slate-blue eyes danced with mischief, the irises shifting and pulsing with the beat of her heart. He noticed the rich draperies, felt the soft cushion of his chair, and admired the elaborate tapestry above the fireplace. "You have a lovely home."

"Thank you, that is very kind," Julianna said and began clearing the dishes.

He wiped his lips with the napkin and sat back. "What is in that glass?" he asked in a voice that belied the contentment sweeping over him.

"Spring water, it runs through our village." Claude grinned.

Thaddeus nodded. "What is the name of this place?"

"Rephidim," Esmeralda piped up. "We make cloth here, the finest in the land. Father is a weaver. You should take him to the mill and show him around." Turning to Thaddeus, she added, "It is wondrous to behold."

"If you are so inclined, I would be happy to give you a tour," Claude offered.

"I would not want to keep you from your work, sir."

Claude waved away his concern. "Nonsense. We don't have many outsiders come to call, and the men at the mill would harass me for weeks if I let you get away without bringing you by."

Thaddeus rose. "All right."

"Well, come then, but watch your head," Claude said, leaving the house.

Thaddeus ducked through the doorway. "I always do."

Men from the village made their way across the open square, greeting each other and Claude with curious glances. Thaddeus garnered introductions to half the male population in the five-minute walk. The sounds of the mill reached them before they entered the gates, a bustling vast complex, though no loud banging of electrified machinery shattered the peace. Thaddeus smiled, his kind of place.

They stopped in the doorway to a small office. "Rexum, I'd like you to meet Thaddeus. He's here visiting, and I'm going to show him around."

A wizened man looked up from behind oversized glasses, his eyes magnified behind the thick lenses. They got even bigger when they saw Thaddeus. "You need a job, young fella? We got plenty of work around here." He picked up a short stack of papers and waved them in the air. "These came in today," he lamented to Claude. "It's a triple order from the Golden City. I don't know how we will meet this deadline."

Claude smiled. "We'll find a way, Rexum. We always do."

"Come on." Claude gave Thaddeus a stout pat on the back. "You're not afraid of spiders, are you?" As they moved down the narrow hallway, he said over his shoulder, "I suppose I should have asked that before I brought you down here."

"Spiders?" Thaddeus asked, wondering what spiders had to do with a textile mill.

Claude chuckled, "Spider silk, stronger than steel, a thousand times thinner than a human hair, waterproof, light, stretchy—welcome to Arachnid Weaving."

With a smile, he opened the door to the most amazing sight Thaddeus had ever seen. "This is the silk house," Claude said with a quiver of a laugh at Thaddeus' thunderstruck expression.

From floor to ceiling, rows of towers held twig boxes that housed millions of spiders. A steady rustling filled the room as workers went between the aisles. Thaddeus was not squeamish but thought a million spiders might give even the stoutest heart pause. He blinked, the blanket in his back pocket growing suddenly uncomfortable—mystery three solved. "I've never heard of such a thing," he breathed.

"Rexum's Great Grandfather, Hyrum ben Dirk, figured it out about a hundred years ago. He had one of these critters take up residence in his front window. His wife made him clean the web every morning, and he noticed how strong the fiber was. He got the idea, and everybody thought he was crazy… until it worked." Claude ushered Thaddeus inside. "The biggest challenge he had to overcome was getting the spider to produce silk for him without building a web. It wasn't efficient to wait for it to build it in the wild and knock it down, so he figured out how to train them."

Thaddeus did a double take. "You've got trained spiders?"

Claude nodded. "We sure do, look." He took down a cage and showed it to Thaddeus, a large black and yellow writing spider housed inside. "In here," Claude pointed to the top of the cage where a hole and tube sat, "this is where we drip nectar. When the spider sits on the silk collector," he tapped a silver metal cup below the cage, "the nectar releases and feeds it."

Thaddeus' eyes widened. "These spiders eat nectar, not bugs?"

"You have been living outside," Claude said with a cryptic shake of his head. "We're still blessed in Rephidim, Thaddeus. Animals and humans aren't killing each other here."

Thaddeus covered his eyes. "I should have come here sooner, Claude. They… my…" His voice caught, and he could not continue.

Weavers and Spinners

Claude's square jaw went rigid, recognizing his grief. "I'm sorry for your loss, Thaddeus."

"Thank you," Thaddeus said, appreciating the simple condolence came without probing questions. He regained his composure and cleared his throat. "Right then. Show me the rest because you definitely have my attention."

Giving a stoic nod of acceptance, Claude resumed the fascinating tour. Thaddeus listened and observed with rapt interest, entering a world and industry he previously never gave a moment's thought. From roving the silk and spinning the fibers into yarn, to dying and weaving, the self-contained complex turned spider silk into magic. Water, steam, and the skilled craftsmen's ingenuity drove it all.

Walking into the noisy weaving room, Thaddeus stared in awe at one of the magnificent machines, towering twenty feet in the air. "Tell me about this one."

Claude smiled and rested a hand on the wooden frame. "She is a beauty, is she not? We call her Tabitha. She is a jacquard loom." Claude gave Thaddeus a comprehensive explanation of the inner workings of Tabitha, which produced cloth of such detail and precision that he could barely grasp the complex nature of its operation.

The tour concluded in the finishing room and warehouse, where workers wrapped bolts of breathtaking fabric, entered the stock into inventory, and cataloged each for transport. Thaddeus ran a finger over an iridescent roll and asked, "Where do you ship it?"

"Once a quarter, we send what we have to the Golden City, a tenth as a gift and our tithe, the rest we sell to the royal court or the temple priests. In so doing, every man pays homage and makes his pilgrimage. The journey takes a year. The men bring back the next quarter's orders and trade merchandise they pick up on the way home."

"So, you do not sell any of this in Alanthia?" Thaddeus asked, genuinely curious.

Claude shook his head, a shadow crossing his face. "We trade a bit with the surrounding communities, but Hyrum instituted a policy when he founded the mill that holds today. Only those who remain in fellowship and obedience to the Iron King may purchase our fabric." He shrugged. "Thus, we send nearly all our output to the Golden Kingdom now."

Thaddeus stared at his boots, feeling his own personal failures.

"I suspect with the outcome of the war, that policy will hold indefinitely."

Thaddeus met Claude's eyes and knew the other man assumed he was a rebel soldier, exactly as Thaddeus intended by his disguise. But that was the extent of his deception. He did not want to lie to this man. "This has been an extraordinary tour, Claude. I thank you for taking your time today."

Claude tilted his head, studying Thaddeus intently. "It was my pleasure."

Thaddeus moved toward the exit, melancholy in his departure.

"If you are interested, Rexum does not make idle offers."

The sentence hung as the bustle of the mill continued around them. Thaddeus did not turn but studied the quaint village, heard the gurgle of rushing water and the constant clatter of machines. His heart pumped as an idea took root. Nothing worthy waited for him outside this hamlet. Loneliness, grief, and drunkenness seemed less appealing than they had the day before. A respite that did not involve hangovers might be in order.

He looked over his shoulder and said, "As long as I don't have to work in the spider room, I might take him up on it."

Three Meals and a Room

Last night, Thaddeus passed out drunk, using a fern for a pillow. Today, he was sober, employed, and holding paperwork that would garner him a room at Grandma Eve's Boarding House. Thaddeus knew better than anyone one day could completely change your life.

"You'll probably find Eve around back with her flowers. Just give her this, and she'll get you settled," Rexum said. "We will see you on Monday."

Thaddeus walked across the town square, smiling at the raucous game of tag the village children had going. He spotted a pale-yellow house with white trim, which looked promising, its front door bearing a shiny copper kick plate and a wreath of daisies and yellow chrysanthemums. The breeze lifted a decorative flag that read 'Grandma Eve's Boarding House' and featured a whimsical old lady bearing a pie. The tin roof gleamed in the sun, and Thaddeus thought with some contentment that it would sound nice in the rain. He stifled a yawn, imagining a feather down comforter and a soft bed. Idly running his hand along the white painted railing of a wrap-around porch, the eclectic assortment of cushioned rocking chairs invited neighbors to stop by for a visit.

He went around the side of the house in search of Grandma Eve, who turned out to be nothing like Thaddeus expected. Trim and wearing a colorful house dress that showed off a great pair of legs, she sashayed toward him with a friendly wave. Sparkling pale blue eyes smiled with the rest of her face as she introduced herself. "Hello, I'm Eve ben Medford."

"Good afternoon, Mrs. ben Medford. I'm Thaddeus. Rexum at the mill sent me over," he said, showing her the papers.

"Oh, do come in. I heard there was a new man in town. Welcome, welcome." She pulled off her gloves and stuffed them in her apron pocket, then took his elbow and ushered him into the mudroom.

Removing her soiled garden apron and rubber boots, she fastidiously picked up a stray blade of grass, flicking it into a wastebasket. "You'll come through here at night. I don't want grime from the mill tracked all over my clean floors. This will be yours." She gestured to an empty wooden cubby. "You can use any of the hooks to hang your coat, but Olaf likes the first one, so keep the peace and use one of the others."

Thaddeus checked his boots and unlaced them while she chatted. Long silver earrings dangled from her lobes, a faint head tremor causing them to shimmy and shake, even when she was still and silent, which was rarely. Thaddeus expected a round, gray-haired lady. Eve was not, and he suspected she still turned heads, despite being well into her seventies. She was browned from the garden sun, her hair, brown from a bottle.

"Come, come." She winked. "I'll show you around. There are six bedrooms, four up and two down. We eat in here."

He followed her into a spacious yellow kitchen with white cupboards that sported whimsical red knobs that looked like cherries. Plants thrived on windowsills and side tables, including a miniature lemon tree in full fruit. An oak table held seating for eight, and the air smelled like pie. Despite his huge lunch, Thaddeus' stomach growled.

"Breakfast at 7:00 am, lunch at 12:00 pm, and supper at 6:30 pm." She took in his height and the lean hollows of his face. "You have a cupboard, if you care to keep extra food, but I would prefer you not store it in your room." She gave him a pointed look, then nodded to the back door. "I do not allow alcohol."

He felt his color rise and wondered if he still reeked. It was probably oozing out of his pores. He covered his discomfort with a hollow cough and let the whirlwind of Eve ben Medford sweep him down the hall.

"There is a full bathroom here." Eve pushed open a six paneled door to a masculine themed space with heavy towel racks and a magazine stand beside the commode.

Thaddeus nodded and looked around. Everything was spotless, the air scented with lemon cleaner and beeswax polish. Multicolored rag rugs muted their footsteps as Eve continued the tour. From her rehearsed recitation, he could tell she had done it many times.

"Here's the community room," Eve said, stepping into a living area full of overstuffed chairs and sofas, covered in mismatched throw blankets and pillows. Floor to ceiling windows looked out on the porch, offering a pleasant view of the front yard and town square.

"Feel free to make use of the library, everyone shares." Eve narrowed a critical eye as if just noticing the novels and reference books stacked in haphazard piles around the crowded bookcase. "I need to have Barton make another shelf. Remind me to mention that at dinner tonight." Without a pause, or an explanation of who Barton was, she swept from the room.

At the base of the staircase, she stopped. "This is my curio cabinet, where I keep all my treasures." Her expression softened as she admired her trinkets. "The boys bring them back for me." By 'the boys', Thaddeus deduced she meant her tenants. From the exotic to the tacky, the cabinet held teacups, hand blown glass flowers, and painted seashells. "This one is new." She jingled a brass bell with a six-pointed star handle. "Krish just brought this back from the Golden City last week."

With an energy that belied her age, Eve sprinted up the steps to show Thaddeus his room. She informed him in a constant and pleasant chatter that the previous occupant left on pilgrimage and would not return for at least nine months.

The room, like the rest of the boarding house, was decorated in shades of gold and dark green, which contrasted nicely with the pale oak furniture and floors, creating a warm, welcoming environment. While not large, it suited his needs perfectly well, with a dresser, a nightstand, small bookcase, and a bed.

"I am sure Rexum explained our arrangement, three meals and your room as part of your wages. I present my invoice to the mill, so there is nothing for you to bother with." She winked. "It keeps it friendly in the house."

The corner of Thaddeus' mouth lifted. "I suppose it does."

"Certainly." Eve fluttered about, plumping pillows, and pulling open the Swiss dot curtains of his bedroom window. "You share a bathroom with the room next door, but Jamison is leaving this week for his pilgrimage, so you may have it to yourself for a time." In a friendly, businesslike manner, she reviewed the rules of the house, and in so doing, revealed she had seen it all.

When she finally left him, he sat on the edge of the bed, testing its springs, finding it firm and well-constructed. Even before lying down, he knew his feet would hang over the end, but that was normal. The down comforter obviously came from the mill, the faint sparkle revealing its origins.

He unpacked his battered knapsack, which took about three minutes. Never one to nap, the steady rhythm of the village beyond his window bore investigation, and he decided to go exploring.

Rephidim was organized around a main square with five rows extending outward. The largest building in town, other than the mill, was a white stuccoed church with a stunning steeple that soared toward the heavens. Water danced above a community fountain in the center of the square; its intricately carved base depicted scenes from the pilgrimage and Golden City. As he watched, the spray pattern changed, and the bubbling water morphed into a series of growing cascades. He figured the mechanism must be on a timer, powered by an underground spring or pipes, and though he could not be certain how it worked, he was thoroughly charmed by it.

The boarding house and the towns larger homes lined the square, and as he walked, he noticed the same blue and white limestone used in the fountain present in many of the homes and deduced they must quarry it nearby. Flowers grew in front yards; vegetables and fruit trees in back, with each row sharing a larger plot for various crops. He counted wheat, barley, soybeans, corn, and potatoes, as well as sunflowers, oats, and alfalfa. As he explored the fourth ring, where the houses were smaller and closer together, he saw young mothers hanging laundry and looking after younger children. They all possessed a healthy glow, most waved, some even calling him by name.

Life in a small town.

Workshops, barns, stables, and other commercial establishments completed the fifth ring, the rear of their properties extending to the edge of the dense Thyatira Woods. Thaddeus paused in front of an ancient livery stable, reading the ornate, weathered sign that advertised mounts, asses, and conveyances of the finest quality. Carriages and wagons filled the yard behind the stables, and compost piles of various stages of maturity lined the fence. A hand-painted sign read, 'Free for the hauling, don't take the steaming ones.' A pasture held a half a dozen grazing horses, with a small donkey patrolling the perimeter. It brayed a greeting as Thaddeus approached. He reached out and gave it a good scratch under its neck. The donkey made a contented bluster and rubbed his head, positioning Thaddeus' hand where he wanted it.

"*Guten tag*, may I help you?" asked a man from the rear of the stables. He wore a heavy leather apron over somber black work clothes and a battered straw hat that sported various equine nibble marks.

Thaddeus clicked his cheek at the donkey and turned. "Good afternoon."

Wise gray eyes regarded him through heavy lids as the proprietor approached, a slight hitch in his gait as he favored his left leg. "You would be the new man at the mill, the one staying at Eve's?"

Amused the village already knew his business, he nodded and extended a hand. "That would be me, name's Thaddeus."

Pulling off a work glove, he looked Thaddeus in the eye and said, "Ernst ben Otto at your service. Are you looking for a mount? We have an excellent mare that's come on the market if you are interested."

Thaddeus shook his head. "Not at the moment, sir. Just doing a bit of exploring before I settle in."

Vague disappointment registered on the man's craggy face, but he recovered quick enough and said, "*Ist* a fine day for exploring, to be sure." He gestured to the woods beyond the village. "Take today, once you start in the mill, you will be glad. Six days a week they run."

"So I have been told," Thaddeus replied with a wry smile.

Ernst's accent held a stronger German edge than most, though all the Rephidimites had it to varying degrees, rendering their w's to v's, and some of their s's and th's to soft z's. Though he only heard English spoken since arriving, he suspected the local accent was adopted decades or centuries before. Isolated communities often had their own speech patterns and cadence, some veering so far from standard English as to be nearly incomprehensible to outsiders.

"What brings you to Rephidim, Thaddeus?" Ernst asked with an equal measure of curiosity and suspicion. "We don't have many who find us these days."

"Looking for a change, and this seemed as good a place as any," Thaddeus evaded.

"Is a good place, not many like it left. Your generation has seen to that, yah?"

Thaddeus raised an eyebrow and shrugged. "Perhaps."

"Is no perhaps, *ist* fact." Ernst nodded, assured in his opinion. "The war was just a symptom, technology just an excuse. It is a heart issue. Even here, one or two every quarter do not return from the pilgrimage. Before, they all came back and lived content, no longer. The young people are lured away into the cities." Ernst's piercing eyes looked beyond Thaddeus' battered soldier's attire as he observed, "You have strong city about you."

"I've spent some time there."

Ernst cocked his head and seemed to consider his next words. "If I could give you a bit of advice?"

Thaddeus acquiesced with a nod.

"Whilst you are here, be here." Ernst's arms hung by his sides relaxed and nonthreatening. "Do not try to bring the city to Rephidim. Leave it where it belongs. If you miss it, go back."

Thaddeus knew there was nothing left for him to go back to, and the words of the old farrier ran true. "I thank you for your wise counsel, sir."

"Well, at least you have manners. Welcome to Rephidim, Thaddeus. Enjoy your stay."

Esmeralda materialized beside him, taking his hand, and startling him with her sudden presence. "Where did you come from?" He tried to pull away, but she held on.

"From home. Mother told me you were staying. I knew you would." Her slate-blue eyes seemed guileless and knowing as she smiled up at him.

Despite himself Thaddeus returned her smile. "And how did you know that, young lady?"

"Because I prayed about it this morning when I saw you sleeping," she said, swinging his hand as they walked.

"You did?" Thaddeus withdrew, uncomfortable at the thought of this innocent girl seeing him passed out in the dirt.

"Uh, huh." She paused outside a bakery and grinned up at him, an unruly ringlet falling over one eye. "You will like it here. It is a marvelous place."

"Marvelous?" Thaddeus suspected she guided him to the sweet shop on purpose. "Rephidim or this bakery?"

She batted long eyelashes at him. "Both."

"I suppose I owe you a treat and thanks for bringing me here."

"I will settle for a treat now. You can thank me later." Esmeralda pushed through the door, greeting the owners by name.

The smell of baking bread, cake, and chocolate hit him like a wave as he followed her inside. A young couple ran the shop, and Esmeralda crooned over the selections, artfully displayed in glass cases.

Armed with chocolate covered eclairs, they resumed their stroll. "Do you still have that blanket in your pocket?" She eyed the bag in wistful anticipation. "Because if you do, we can sit under my favorite tree and enjoy Heidi's eclairs. They are divine."

From her vocabulary, Thaddeus decided his initial estimation of her age at eight or nine was incorrect. "How old are you, Esmeralda?"

She reached in his back pocket and pulled out the blanket. "Twelve."

Thaddeus straightened a fluttering corner of the material and sat down, putting the eclairs between them. "You are awfully little for twelve."

Esmeralda shrugged, unconcerned. "I'll grow."

At twelve he was almost six feet tall. "I suppose you might."

"Sure I will, otherwise you would be way too tall for me." She dug into the bakery bag and handed him his treat.

"What?" Thaddeus asked with distracted interest, focused on the eclair. The first bite sent shivers of pleasure down his spine. Her next words chilled them.

"When we get married," she stated matter of fact, then lowered her voice to a conspiratorial whisper and added, "I've already seen you naked."

Thaddeus blinked in shock and horror. "Now look here, what is this crazy talk? You can't go around saying things like that. They will have me arrested."

"I won't tell anyone." She licked a fleck of chocolate from her upper lip. "That would be a terrible way to start our relationship."

Thaddeus dropped his half-finished éclair back in the bag and stood up, backing away from her. "Listen, kid. I don't know what you are talking about, but it needs to stop."

She waved him away. "I didn't mean right now. I'm twelve for goodness sakes."

"And I am twenty-seven! That is more than double your age," he said, his mouth hanging slack in astonishment.

"It won't matter when I grow up. Grandma Eve says age is just a number." She licked custard off her finger and shrugged. "Besides, the Lord is never wrong, and He told me today that one day you would be my husband." She smiled, in beatific innocence. "We both like eclairs. That's a good start."

He held up his hand. "Stop, right now. There is no start, there is no relationship, and I am not going to marry you." He ran his fingers through his hair, his voice ringing with conviction. "I will never marry anyone... ever again." He stalked across the square, retreating to the safety of his room.

Esmeralda watched him depart. Tall and lean, his long strides ate up the ground. She looked at the sky and said, "I hope by the time we get married, he's happier about it."

May 12, 987 ME (Six Weeks Later)

The Rhythm of Life

Thaddeus began work at Arachnid Weaving in the spinning room. He chose the assignment because he liked the sounds. Unlike the weaving room with its dissonant clatter, the consonance of the spinning mules proved soothing. Four times a minute, the large machines pulled and twisted spider silk roving into yarn. The return of the carriage wound the spun yarn onto spindles loaded with bobbins. The speed of the spin controlled the size of the yarn produced by the mules, the faster the spin, the finer and stronger the yarn. Arachnid Weaving operated four mules each with 1320 spindles. They color coded the bobbins by yarn weight, with each mule producing different types according to the manufacturing runs of the day.

Thaddeus started off as a doffer, responsible for removing full bobbins from the mules, replacing empty ones, and loading the yarn in rolling bins that a team of young boys transferred to the dye house. The work was monotonous and mind numbing; he loved it. His quick intelligence soon elevated him to minder, which meant he took charge of the mule and its operation. The rapid promotion was met with good-natured ribbing from the other men in the spinning room who teased that Thaddeus would be running the mill by year's end.

He could not deny, the entire manufacturing process intrigued him. Ever mindful of Ernst's advice to be present, he appreciated the skill of the craftsmen and spent his break times visiting each section, asking questions, and watching them work. The silk room still gave him the willies. They nicknamed the crowd that worked the floor Opies, after the genus of spider they tended, Argiope. Thaddeus thought them an odd group and noticed they all moved in a peculiar spider-like manner. The rovers were a fussy, exacting bunch, but the delicate work of extracting the spider silk into individual strands and preparing it for spinning required extraordinary attention to detail, their skills were rivaled only by the weavers. His group of spinners were the most raucous, and he soon discovered they were the liveliest and most fun-loving crew. The dyers were huge, grumpy men, the heat and humidity of the dye house enough to squelch even the cheeriest soul, though the magnificent colors they produced distinguished them as moody artists. The weavers were a mixed bag, combining the personalities and skills of all the crews into the final production.

Thaddeus settled into the mill's routine with alacrity, and found with the work, his thirst for oblivion faded. Though in the quiet of his room, his memories found him. So he avoided his lonely bed, often falling asleep in his comfortable chair in the common room, a book resting on his chest. His face lost the gaunt, sunken look he had when he first arrived, but his naturally lean body and the constant physical labor defied Eve's most ardent attempts to 'put some meat on his bones'.

Eve became a bright spot in his life, always ready with a laugh or a corny joke. She adored games and prodded him into playing cards with her most nights. The stakes ranged from drachmas to silly consequences the loser had to do, such as clucking like a chicken or wearing a colander on their head for the rest of the evening. She loved gags and put bars of soap in the showers that would not lather and served water with fake flies floating in the glass. She hid whoopee cushions under pillows and would hoot with laughter when some hapless boarder sat down. One of her nieces sent her a pair of glasses with eyeballs attached to springs, which she would slip on then act like nothing was amiss as her fake eyes bounced out of their sockets. In perpetual motion, she cleaned, sang, and talked to her boarders, or herself if no one was around.

Every night, she nodded off—sitting up. Thaddeus took great amusement watching her do it. Her eyes fluttered, growing heavy. Head bobbing came next, but she would never just go to bed, perhaps because she feared missing something. Finally, her chin would relax onto her chest, her breath coming in quiet little snores that would build, and build... until....

Thaddeus would elbow Barton. "Look, there she goes."

With one great, head-jerking, neck-snapping snore, Eve would wake herself up. Blinking innocently, as if nothing happened, she would say, "Good night, boys," and shuffle off to bed.

"Good night, Eve," they called after her, sharing amused grins.

Thaddeus always did the evening rounds, locking up. No one else bothered, but he had reason to lock the doors, even in Rephidim, which they all thought peculiar. But they did not press, simply let him find his way and place, in the household, and in town.

Three of Eve's tenants worked in the mill, Krish, the Opie, Hans, the weaver, and Olaf the dyer. The fourth man, Barton, was a woodworker who turned out spindles and rods for the mill and occasionally exquisitely crafted furniture. True to Eve's prediction, the remaining room in the boarding house sat empty, the former occupant on pilgrimage with no newcomer to take his place.

They spent Sundays in church, leaving the rest of the day free. Thaddeus struck up a friendship with Ernst, the stable proprietor. The old man was a natural storyteller, the region's resident historian, and an avid angler. After his first week at the mill, Ernst invited him out, and they struck a routine. Standing on the edge of the quiet banks, Thaddeus discovered the joy of fishing.

Eve promised to turn his catch into Sunday night supper, with the caveat that he cleaned the fish and join her in the kitchen. She talked so much, he didn't have to, but several weeks after arriving, he found he was curious about the place he had chosen to settle and asked, "So, if I have this right. At one point, Rephidim was part of a loose confederacy of three villages established soon after the Great Judgment, which are collectively referred to as Thyatira."

"Yes, that is correct. I have cousins over in Bezetha, which is where they quarry all the limestone you see around town. My cousin's wife is from a family of potters, they are quite famous. She made this for me." Eve held up a gorgeous, glazed bowl she often served potato salad in. Tonight, it held coleslaw.

"Bezetha is Rephidim's sister village?" Thaddeus asked, though he knew the answer.

Eve shrugged and turned back to the fish. "Somewhat. They are changing."

Thaddeus suppressed a grin. That was about as critical as Eve ever got. She took to heart the adage if you can't say something nice, say nothing at all. "The third village, Endor, no longer exists, right?"

"Mmm, yes." Eve moved to the sink to wash the corn-meal off her fingers. Then pointed at the stove. "Bring the oil up to temperature, Thaddeus."

Thaddeus shook his head in bemused resignation. No one in Rephidim ever talked about Endor. But earlier that day, fishing with Ernst, he broached the subject again. "What happened to the third village?"

Ernst's face made a nearly imperceptible flicker. Thaddeus had been trained to catch such tells. He caught it.

The older man looked across the river and said simply, "It is gone."

"Rephidim is the textile town. Bezetha is the quarry town. What was Endor?"

"Horses," Ernst said quietly and stared into the dense forest.

"What horses?"

Ernst turned. "You are such a city boy. You have not heard of the mighty horses of Endor? They are legend."

Thaddeus baited his hook and cast his lure into the still water with a plunk. Sensing he tread precarious ground, he asked, "What happened?"

Ernst made a sound of disgust. "They were judged, two decades ago. There is nothing left."

"And the horses?"

Ernst pointed into the Thyatira Woods, his face and words haunted. "If you have a clean heart, they may still come. Some say they are only legend."

"What about them was legendary?" Thaddeus asked.

Ernst waded into the river and said cryptically, "It does not matter, the Guardians are gone."

And with that, Thaddeus saw the subject was closed.

After supper, Thaddeus spotted Esmeralda across the square and ducked into Jake's Tavern where he knew she could not follow. He studiously avoided her, though she made it difficult. The morning after her startling declaration, he awoke with his blanket spread atop him and no memory of her sneaking into his room to put it there. She had the disconcerting talent of turning up, appearing out of nowhere, at his side. She never mentioned her lame-brained idea of marrying him again, but he was never easy in her presence and always made sure someone else had eyes on them.

Enjoying his root beer at the battered old bar, he sat in comfortable solitude with quiet conversations going on around him. He developed a reputation as a man who kept to himself, and the Rephidimites respected that. They left him alone, everyone except Esmeralda. She pestered, probed, and prodded him for information. Where did he grow up? Where did he go to school? What did he study? Who were his people? What was *her* name? She took his rebuffs in stride, never got her feelings hurt, and would disappear as quickly as she appeared; usually right before he lost his temper.

The village was blessed, an oasis in a kingdom fully embracing rebellion. Golden light shone, water ran pure and clean, and animals remained herbivores. The mill hummed along, producing the world's finest cloth. They went to church, celebrated holidays, and birthdays. In the evenings, they sat on front porches, hosted potluck dinners, and took in a broken, tired man, adopting him as one of their own.

However, it was not all light.

While he slept, nightmares crept under his door and destroyed the peace he fought so hard to reclaim by day. They dragged him kicking and screaming down a blood-spattered hallway, where no one heard his cries of pain, grief, and rage. Visions squeezed his heart in a vice of terror, forcing him back there. The nightmares refused to let him run away.

He came home from work and walked into his house, but immediately realized something was wrong, no one greeted him, no sounds came from the kitchen, and no one played in the backyard. Thaddeus called out into the hollow, emptiness of his sanctuary.

Always in the nightmare, he hoped it was not true, hoped the scene would be different, but it wasn't. The hardwood floor of the landing creaked under his weight as he detected the copper tang of blood. He flew upstairs, taking two steps at a time. He should not have rushed, should have turned, and run. He should have never gone around that corner and seen. But he could never unsee it, ever.

Utter desecration.

Because upstairs in the hallway outside their bedrooms, scattered like trash, lay the mutilated remains of his wife and two sons.

He woke with a wet pillowcase every morning.

And the great evil that stalked the edges of Rephidim, pushed the boundaries and waited.

December 2, 988 ME

Hoops

It took almost two years, but Thaddeus brought one thing from the city to Rephidim—basketball. It started innocently enough. One morning in late September, he made a fade away jump shot with a stray bobbin. The boys in the spinning room stared open mouthed as it sailed into the cart thirty feet away.

"Do it again!" Leo, the bobbin boy, shouted.

Thaddeus met his eyes, caught the bobbin Leo threw to him, feinted to the left, and shot. Perfect. This set off a frenzy of flying bobbins that sent Leo running for cover.

"Hey now!" The shop superintendent put a stop to the melee, but something broke free in Thaddeus with that shot—the game!

Throughout the morning, the boys sidled by, giving him curious looks. The normally sedate and stoic Thaddeus had a gleam in his eye they recognized, fun. At the noon break, they followed him across the square.

Leo, the brave one, asked, "Hey, Thaddeus, what was that back there with the bobbin?"

Thaddeus considered whether he should say but looking at the kid's disheveled red hair and eager expression, he reminded Thaddeus of Goofy Dave from his junior high basketball team, so he said, "That, young man, was a jump shot."

Leo's green eyes lit up. "What do you shoot at?"

Thaddeus continued his long-legged stride across the square. "A hoop. It was a basketball shot."

"Basketball?" Leo scratched his head. "You throw a ball in a basket?"

"Essentially, yes." Thaddeus shrugged. "It's a fun game."

Simon, Leo's brother, raced ahead of Thaddeus, walking backward. "You know how to play?"

Thaddeus thought of the endless hours he spent with a ball bouncing under his palm. "You might say that."

"Will you teach us?" Leo enthused.

"It would take some doing, but we don't have the equipment."

Simon pondered that. "We've got plenty of baskets, and Joe's got a ball his brother brought back from the Golden Kingdom last month."

"You could teach us now!" Leo shouted; all thoughts of lunch forgotten in his excitement.

"It doesn't work that way. Basketball would take a little planning." A grin broke over his square-jawed face. "Let me think about it."

That night, a crowd of boys gathered on Grandma Eve's front porch ready to plead their case. Joe held out his prized soccer ball and from the looks of it, Leo and Simon gathered every basket in the village for Thaddeus' perusal. Thaddeus accepted the ball, gave it a spin, and balanced it on the tip of his finger. The boys' eyes widened in amazement, and a chorus of, "Let me try!" erupted.

Under Thaddeus' supervision, the mill wove the nets, the blacksmiths fashioned the hoops, and the woodworkers made the posts and backboards. Mickey, Leo and Simon's father, went into Easton to procure the basketballs, and Jake, the owner of the tavern, offered the back corner of his property to serve as the court. With the site prepped and leveled, Ernst drove a wagon over to Bezetha, returning with bags of ground limestone and clay, the cement used for the court. By late November, they had what they needed.

Thaddeus arranged their first exhibition. Most of the village showed up to see what all the excitement was about, and Rephidim's new craze was born. The girls, not to be outdone by the boys, took an equal interest, everyone except Esmeralda. Despite himself, Thaddeus scanned the crowd, expecting to see her among the eager faces. Her absence came as a shock.

For him, she was as much a part of Rephidim as the mill, Ernst, and Eve. She sidled up beside him, pestering him with questions, laughing and telling him about whatever new book she was reading or new subject she was studying. Over the last two years they developed an odd friendship. But after the basketball exhibition, she simply and completely disappeared from his life. He had not realized how fond he had grown of her until she wasn't there.

Thaddeus kept his own council, but at the end of the second week, it was eating at him. Adopting a casual tone, he asked Eve, "Where's Esmeralda been?"

Eve looked up from her reading. "She's around. She came by yesterday."

Thaddeus stroked his chin and said, "Hmm, I haven't seen her."

Eve returned her attention to her book but added softly, "She's growing up, Thaddeus. Perhaps that crush she's always had on you has finally run its course."

It was the most personal observation she ever made to him, and he caught the significance. Not bothering to deny her words, he said, "One can only hope that it has."

"Can one?" She stood, for once ready to retire before she fell asleep in her chair. "I think to be loved by anyone is special, Thaddeus. You'd do well not to wish it away." She patted his shoulder. "Good night."

That night he dreamed *the* dream, but this time instead of Olivia's pretty face looking up at him in blood-soaked horror, it was Esmeralda's. Thaddeus sat bolt upright in bed, his chest heaving. His blanket, the one she had given him, was gone.

January 10, 989 ME

Peace Offering

Six weeks after the exhibition, Thaddeus felt like a nervous idiot, standing on the stoop of Julianna and Claude's house. He held a present, wrapped in pretty paper and tied with a bow of Eve's making.

Julianna opened the door. "Thaddeus, how nice of you to stop by. Please come in."

He ducked inside, embarrassed heat rushing up his neck. "I brought a birthday present for Esmeralda." The house smelled like cake and beef stew, which he knew were Esmeralda's favorite foods.

Julianna wiped her hands on her apron and said with an edge to her voice, "Well, *that* was thoughtful of you."

Her unspoken accusation made Thaddeus' spine stiffen. "It's just a book, something small." He glanced around the empty house and asked, "Is she here?"

Julianna pressed her lips into a thin line but gestured outside and said, "She's in the stable. Go have a word with her."

Thaddeus suddenly wanted to leave the present and go but knew this was something he had to do. "Thank you."

After the warmth of the house, the air felt cold on his face, matching the dread that settled in his gut. He did not understand why she dropped out of his life, nor could he have imagined he would miss her, but he did.

Inside the small stable, he found Esmeralda brushing the family's dappled mare, cooing nonsensical words, as her slender arms flexed with each long sure stroke. He took a moment just to look at her, realizing she had changed in the last few months. She told him she would grow, and she had, so had her wild curly mop of hair. "Esmeralda."

She stiffened. "What are you doing here?"

The wrapping paper suddenly grew clammy in his hands. He cleared his throat, feeling like a fool. "I brought you a birthday present."

Esmeralda rested her forehead against the horse's neck, not looking at him, then with a deep sigh turned around.

Thaddeus controlled a sharp intake of his own breath, his eyes widening. She had grown in more ways than just height. He glanced away and extended the present.

"Thank you." She took the package without touching his hand, fingering the pretty gold wrapping. "Grandma Eve made this bow."

Thaddeus regained his composure by executing a harassed male eye roll and said, "Boy, did she. She would not let me leave the house without it."

Esmeralda raised a sardonic eyebrow, giving him a knowing look. "She's like that."

Thaddeus nodded. "She is, she's a good woman. I'm fond of her. We're friends," he moistened his lips and added, "like we used to be."

Esmeralda made a hollow snort and said, "We've never been friends, Thaddeus."

"Don't be ridiculous, of course we are."

Esmeralda bit her bottom lip. "Did you invite Ernst to your basketball exhibition?"

"What does that have to do with anything?"

She swallowed thickly and drew her shoulders back. "Did you invite Grandma Eve?"

He wished she wouldn't stand like that, but he pushed that thought out of his head as understanding dawned. "Is that what this is all about? That I didn't personally invite you? I thought you'd be there."

"So, you invited your other friends, but you just expected that I would come?" A silver tear escaped her eye.

"Hey," he coaxed, closing the gap between them, "that was nothing."

She looked away, hugging the book to her chest, and whispered, "It was something to me."

He raised his hands helplessly, feeling like a heel. "I'm sorry, Esmeralda. If I had known—"

She turned her back on him, clapping a hand over her mouth, as her shoulders shook with silent tears. Thaddeus had never been good with crying females, and certainly not ones where he caused their tears. "Dammit," he swore quietly, frozen in place, not sure what to do. Finally, he said, "Happy birthday. I hope you like your present."

Neither said goodbye.

Striding across the yard, shame swamped him. Unintentional though it was, he could not deny, he had hurt her. With a sudden flash of anger, he slammed the gate and stormed off, muttering, "Ridiculous kid, overreacting to something as trivial as a basketball exhibition. When in the hell have I ever asked her to be by my side? She just is."

Grumbling about the moodiness of teenage girls, he entered the woods, wanting time alone. The January breeze stung his cheeks, chapping his lips, but he felt nothing until his anger abated. He ended up by the waterfall where she found him that first day. Sitting on the ledge, he buried his face in his hands, more shaken than he cared to admit. The stone under his rear end was hard, the limestone shelf cold. It seeped into his bones as he listened to the gray river falling over the rocks, seeing the hurt betrayal on Esmeralda's face repeatedly in his mind.

Normally, if he waited long enough, she would appear, plop down beside him, and start pestering. As she toyed with her springy curls and asked him a million questions, he would grumble at her because she forced him to remember who he was before he came to Rephidim; and most of the time, he was simply trying to forget. Esmeralda refused to let him, and that made him angry. The entire reason he settled here was to forget.

"What were their names?" she asked the last time they spoke in late November.

He spun. "I don't speak them."

"Tell me about them, then."

Thaddeus waited, he waited for the piercing pain, the overwhelming grief, and found that it did not come.

"Tell her about me." he heard Olivia whisper in his heart, *"tell her about the boys."*

He pushed the prompting away. "I can't."

Esmeralda stood, her hands on her hips, her slate-blue eyes flashing. "I think you can. You just won't."

Until today, those were the last words she spoke to him. They played over in his mind, *"You can, but you won't."* What the hell did she know? She couldn't possibly understand the magnitude of her questions, all her questions… But he knew without her constant probing, he would have become a shell, a living breathing shell, scooped out and empty inside, fighting dark memories, as if spider silk twined around his head, shrouding everything he had ever been.

That was why he missed Esmeralda.

In the intervening six weeks, no one asked him a single personal question, no one tried to penetrate the shell, and it was lonely in the darkness.

February 22, 989 ME

What's in a Name?

Thaddeus pushed through the underbrush, skirting a large puddle blocking the path to his boulder. Lately, this was where he spent most of his free time, staring at the waterfall, thinking. In the three months of Esmeralda's silence, he began a tentative exploration of his grief. Judiciously avoided for two years, once he breached the wall, he found he wanted to speak of his family. In the sitting room last week, he caught himself right before he said, "My wife used to do that." Then at breakfast this morning, he thought, "My boys liked pancakes." However, he guarded their memory too close, held his pain too tight, and the words trapped in his throat.

As he rounded the corner, he saw Esmeralda sitting there, on his rock. Today of all days, she was there. He moved beside her, his feet coming into her view. She glanced over at his boots but did not look up, nor did she speak.

They shared the waterfall in silence.

"Olivia, Jacob, Matthew, and Richard." His voice sounded raw. Their names cut his throat like shards of glass.

She looked at him then, a curl falling over her left eye. She tucked it behind her ear and waited.

"Richard was my brother." Best to start there, he thought.

"He was a soldier, killed in a jihadist raid a couple of days before the Civil War started. It was a trap, a set up. He died." His voice faltered. He heard his own desolation ringing off the rocks, and it made him angry. "But not before he took five of those scumbags out."

Esmeralda stared up at him as waves of grief crashed over his heart. She did not say a word, did not ask a question. Now that he was talking, she let him.

"Richard was a hell of a fighter, but they used an X420 gas grenade in a small bedroom, and it knocked him out. They shot him, while he lay unconscious." He looked unseeing at the river with his nose flaring. "His best friend was wounded, but he told me what happened."

Esmeralda hugged her knees to her chest, and looked up at him, her large eyes, the color of the pale sky, swam with compassion.

"I'm a lawyer, you see, by education and trade, that is, before I became a spinner," he scoffed.

"A lawyer?"

He nodded.

"What happened?" she asked, her voice barely above a whisper.

"After the September 11th terrorist attacks, my superiors in the Justice Department assigned me to an investigative unit. We were tracking the money, to find out who was behind the bombings at the Capitol and the assault on the Palace that killed Princess Alexa," he said through gritted teeth. "You can't hide that sort of money, not forever, and I was determined to make them pay for killing my brother.

"And I did! I found them." He flung his arms to the sky, like a champion on the field.

Esmeralda's brows shot up in surprise.

He looked down at her and sneered, "You should have seen me. I was something, full of pride and righteous vengeance. The press went nuts, plastering me on the front page of every newspaper in the kingdom. I lapped it up, every drop. I gave interviews, spouted rhetoric, and thought I was a hero, invincible."

He covered his eyes and squeezed his temples. "They started talking to me about my future in politics. There's big money in New York, Esmeralda, and I had their attention. Perfect candidate, martyred hero brother, basketball star, young, smart, good looking… with a… a… beautiful wife," he paused and swallowed, "and… twin sons."

Esmeralda scrambled to her feet, facing him, tears hovering in her eyes.

He exhaled hard. "They were murdered, by the same jihadists I so proudly proclaimed I destroyed. They should have just killed me. I was the one they wanted." He hissed, "But they don't operate that way."

Esmeralda put a hand on his bicep. "Thaddeus, it wasn't your fault."

He tensed, curling his fists. He had never spoken these words to anyone, nearly drank himself to death to avoid thinking them. "It was my fault. I made myself a target. If I hadn't been so damn cocksure and arrogant, maybe they would not…"

Esmeralda's voice shook, but she gripped his arm tight. "The Bible says it is the Lord who determines our days, from the moment we are conceived. Nothing you did caused their deaths."

He closed his eyes tightly, then said through a great rush of breath. "It was today. Two years ago today, I came home… and I found them, my wife and my two-year-old sons."

Esmeralda threw her arms around him and whispered into his heart, "Oh, Thaddeus, I'm so sorry."

Thaddeus froze, holding his body as still as a granite statue. With great effort, he accepted her hug, burying his face in her curly hair. A sound tore out of his soul, jagged and raw, as he writhed in agony on that rock, finally weeping for his family.

Until at last, it passed, and they stood together, quiet and still, as the tremors settled. At length, he managed to whisper, "Thank you, Esmeralda."

"That's what I'm here for, Thaddeus." Leaning back, she brushed a tear from his cheek. "Let's go. It's cold, and I told my mother you were coming over for supper."

Thaddeus gave a tremulous laugh, remembering the day they met, and feeling naked before her again.

August 3, 989 ME (6 months later)

The Boy Next Door

When Thaddeus entered Eve's kitchen, he registered a newcomer, a white-haired old man. When the stranger turned, the unlined face of a youth smiled in greeting. "I'm Ian ben Kole, nice to meet you."

Thaddeus blinked, unable to take his eyes off the man's shock of white hair. "Thaddeus ben Todd," he replied automatically. "Good to meet you." He pulled out his customary chair in the corner and settled down to supper with the rest of the men.

Eve bustled over, carrying a steaming bowl of green beans. "Sit down, Ian. You look hungry."

Ian grinned, showing upper and lower straight white teeth. "Ma'am, you'll be finding I am always hungry."

"Are you Irish?" Barton asked, dishing his plate.

"No," Ian said with a shake of his head. "It's just the regional accent I grew up around. A large migration of Irish horse breeders settled in our area, Galway, to be precise. Are you German?"

Everyone around the table laughed. "Point taken," Barton said, raising his glass of tea in a toast.

"I'm sure Eve told you the house rules, but I'll bet she forgot to mention dinner rule number one, don't smack your food around Thaddeus. He's particular about that." Hans, the weaver, confided to Ian.

Ian shared a look with Thaddeus. "That makes my skin crawl, too. I don't smack."

Thaddeus rubbed his chin in contemplation. "You play basketball?"

"I knew that would be the first thing you asked him," Olaf complained. "You're too late. He is joining the Dyers."

"He looks like a Woodworker to me." Barton held Ian's eyes. "You don't want to step foot in that mill, Ian, trust me, and we could use a hand in the shop." Barton glared at Thaddeus. "Besides, he's already loaded his team."

Thaddeus accepted the bowl of green beans and heaped a huge helping onto his plate. "I just understand the fundamentals of the game, unlike you ham handed Woodworkers."

"We haven't won a game this year. It's only fair if he joins us," Krish, the small Indian Opie, protested.

Barton took a bite of his roll. "Nobody wants to work with the damn spiders, Opie." Despite his bravado, Barton's aversion to the silk room was well known.

"Language!" Eve scolded, placing a platter of chicken in front of Ian. "Ignore them. They are obsessed with basketball."

"Obsessed is a mighty strong word, Grandma," Hans protested, taking a wing and a thigh off the platter.

"Call it what you want. I call them like I see them, and you lot are obsessed." Eve went back to the kitchen and began ladling gravy into a bowl. "There is scarcely another subject you men discuss around this table except basketball."

The corner of Thaddeus' mouth twitched. "You're just mad because I am not letting you cheat at cards every night."

Eve turned with a hand on her hip. "I do not cheat."

Olaf snorted, "You do, too."

Krish, who had been forced to cluck like a chicken last week, took Olaf's side. "No one wins as much as you do without cheating."

"I just have skills." She tilted her chin imperiously, her blue eyes dancing with mischief. "And you are a sore loser, Krish. Your chicken needs a lot of work."

Barton laughed. "Do it again, Krish."

"No way. I don't even eat chicken," Krish grumbled, chomping on a corn cob.

Barton turned to Ian. "It was the worst chicken imitation ever done in this house."

Ian had no such qualms about eating said topic of conversation and bit into a juicy breast. "Spiders, chicken clucking contests, and basketball? This ought to be fun."

After supper, they ushered Ian out the door to the court where the village men gathered on the long summer nights. Walking beside Thaddeus, Ian was almost as tall, with a lanky grace that started an immediate reprisal of the argument that raged over the dinner table. Which team would get him?

Rexum, too old to play, but the self-appointed commissioner of the Rephidim basketball league, stepped in. "Leave the man alone, for goodness sakes, where are your manners? He's been in town about four hours, and you horse's asses are making fools of us all. He might not even want to play."

Collective groans and protests erupted.

A tall, curly haired girl caught Ian's attention. With a quick cock of her head, she motioned for him to follow her behind the equipment shed. Ian looked around. With the crowd directing their attention toward Rexum, he took his chances and escaped.

"They get a little heated," the girl confided. "Don't pay them any attention. It's all in good fun."

"They are serious about their basketball, aren't they?" Ian laughed. "I have not played since before the war, so I might not even be any good." He reached out a hand and added, "I'm Ian ben Kole, by the way."

"Esmeralda ben Claude, at your service." She pushed herself off the wall and took his hand.

Energy traveled between them.

She drew back as if she had been shocked and gasped, "Are you a Gune?"

Ian's eyes widened, equally startled. "No…" Then studying her he asked, "What makes you say that?"

"Well, the Holy Spirit all over you, of course. I've never felt it on someone so strongly." Esmeralda craned her neck, looking deep into his eyes. "That's how you got that hair, isn't it?"

"How do you know that?" He took in her luminescent skin, the amazing abundance of curls that glimmered in the golden light, and her elegant form. "I think maybe you're the Gune."

Esmeralda giggled. "Don't I wish. Wouldn't that be fun? They are amazing, aren't they?"

Ian blinked rapidly. "You've met one?"

"Sure, a couple of times. She's really pretty, but she's kind of bossy." Esmeralda curled a long lock around her finger.

"Sounds like Jelena," Ian said matter of fact.

Esmeralda bounced with excitement. "Yes! You've met her too?"

Ian smiled, as kinship blossomed between them. "I have."

A chorus of calls reached their ears as the crowd discovered his absence. Recalled to her purpose, Esmeralda spoke quickly. "If you want to win, join the Spinners. If you are partial to the underdog, the Opies need all the help they can get. The Rovers argue over every call, and if you like following rules, that's the team for you. The Dyers are brutes, but they play the best defense and could use an outside shooter. The Weavers, that's my father's team, are currently in second place. If you are any good, they might just unseat the Spinners. The other teams are all stuck in the middle, but I guess it depends on what you do while you are here. They seem to forget that these days. Mother calls it basketball fever."

Olaf stomped around the corner. "Here he is," he called, then shot a pugnacious look at Esmeralda. "No recruiting! He can make his own choice without you batting your eyelashes at him."

Esmeralda took two steps toward the beefy dyer. "I did no such thing, Olaf. I gave him a moment to breathe."

Olaf grunted, conveying his deep skepticism, then gestured to Ian. "Come on, stranger. Let's see if you can actually shoot."

Ian followed, giving a bemused shake of his head. This was like no other assignment the Lord ever sent him on, but he had the distinct feeling he was going to enjoy himself.

Rexum stood at center court, blowing the silver whistle he was inordinately proud of and used to excess. "Listen up," he called, blinking his magnified eyes, "our new guest has just arrived. League rules state that you play for the team where you work," he paused and nodded toward Ian, "though I hope he will join us at the mill." The Woodworkers, Shopkeepers, and Smiths protested loudly. Rexum held up his hand, signaling silence. "He might not even want to play. Eve tells me he's just passing through."

All eyes turned to Ian, who rubbed the back of his neck, feeling the pressure. "I will stay as long as I'm able, though I go home to see my family every October. But I'll play while I am here, the Lord willing."

Thaddeus got his attention and threw him the ball. Ian snagged it with a large hand and began to dribble.

"Where's home?" someone called, obviously calculating the end of the season.

"A small town in Northern California," Ian answered to the collective groans of the crowd. With King Korah's construction projects and railways, Rephidim was a month's journey to Redding. Ian heard Esmeralda giggle and gave her a conspiratorial look. "I'll leave mid-September." He passed the ball back to Thaddeus.

Thaddeus recognized the skill behind the bounce pass and called, "You and me, one-on-one. Let's see what you got." He whipped a pass and grinned.

Ian caught the hard thrown ball and met Thaddeus' eyes directly. Blood surged through his veins—competition. Channeling Beau Landry, Ian said, "Where y'at, Thaddeus?"

"I'm about to take you to school, Whitey."

The basketball felt good under Ian's hands, the rhythm of the game pulsing with each dribble. "We'll see about that, Stilts."

The crowd erupted in laughter.

Thaddeus moved to center court and shouted, "What are the stakes, Eve?"

Ian joined him with the distinct feeling he might be clucking like a chicken before the night was over.

Instead, Eve called over the noise, "The winner gets first dibs on the bathroom."

"For now, or forever?" Thaddeus asked, sizing up his opponent.

"For the duration," she declared.

Thaddeus reached in and stole the bouncing ball. "I hope you like cold showers." He head feinted and drove past Ian, making an easy layup.

Ian sauntered over to the basket to retrieve the rebound as Thaddeus sprinted by with his arms open wide, a grin on his face.

"Oh, it's like that, huh?"

"School, welcome to school," Thaddeus taunted.

Ian took the basketball and began to play. He did not disappoint the crowd when his fade away jump shot from twenty feet hit nothing but net. Cheers echoed deep into the Thyatira Woods, as good-natured wagers were placed.

Esmeralda rooted them on equally, appreciating the spark of life that flared in Thaddeus as he faced his first serious competition since introducing the game. Thaddeus had two inches on Ian, a Collegiate Championship ring, and home court advantage where he practiced daily for the last ten months. But Ian ben Kole was nine years his junior with fresh legs, no lingering knee problems, and the Holy Spirit on his side.

It was a one-on-one for the ages.

Tied up, the winner of the next point, took possession of the bathroom. Sweat dripped off their noses and drenched their shirts. Neither man smiled, the trash talk gone silent as they both struggled for air. Adrenaline raged; the spirit of battle held them firmly in its grip. Thaddeus drove to the basket, going for the win. With the legs of a twenty-year-old, Ian blocked his shot, rejecting the ball so hard it whizzed into the hooting crowd.

Winded, Thaddeus rested his hands on his knees and bent over, accepting a towel from Eve, and wiping sweat out of his eyes.

Esmeralda handed Ian a cup of water.

He downed it in a single gulp, then looked up at her in wonder as the world shifted and colors changed, everything pulsing with life, vivid and vibrant. His breathing returned to normal as a wellspring of strength and energy surged through his tired body. "What?" he said in awe.

She gave him a knowing smile and whispered, "You need to win. He needs you to win."

Ian narrowed his eyes and truly saw Esmeralda. A faint sprinkling of freckles dusted her cheeks, big slate-blue eyes sparkled with mischief and something deeper, knowledge that went beyond her years. In a flash, he recognized it, another in communion with the Lord. It pulsed around her like an aura.

An understanding passed between them.

Ian nodded with resolution. "You got it, Curly."

Thaddeus moved to the sideline to inbound the ball, fatigued, his face red with exertion. But Ian saw it all in slow motion, the way Thaddeus favored his right knee, the stern set of his square jaw. This was more than a basketball game for bathroom rights. This man was one reason he was here, and if Thaddeus was going to hear the message, Ian had to win.

Thaddeus head faked to the right, but Ian read it, reached in, and stole the ball. Loping like a gazelle, Ian flew down the court, into the air, and slammed the ball through the hoop.

Amazed, the crowd erupted.

Ian jogged back, offering Thaddeus a hand. Thaddeus shook it vigorously, and Ian pulled him in for a good-natured, back-slapping hug.

"Good game, Whitey. I'll get you next time."

When the celebration calmed and the energy waned, Leo called out, "What was that, mister?"

They answered in unison, "A dunk."

Simon picked up the ball and tossed it to Thaddeus. "I guess he showed you something, yah?"

Thaddeus leveled Simon a look, one he used in the spinning room when the kid let his mouth get away from him. Without a word, he dribbled once, took two steps and spun, dunking the basketball backward behind his head. Then he walked off the court, leaving Leo, Simon, and the rest of Rephidim staring after him in open mouthed astonishment.

Ian caught up with him. "I don't mind cold showers. You got first dibs on the bathroom."

That night, a powerful friendship was born and a rivalry neither expected.

August 15, 989 ME

Playing with Fire

Two weeks later, Thaddeus glared across the square, growling as Esmeralda laid a hand on Ian's arm. Her husky laughter reached his ears, scorching him, and fanning the flames of his anger. A hot wind blew through the village, as Thaddeus ben Todd stormed across the green, determined to put a stop to this right now.

Esmeralda saw him bearing down on them like a raging bull and froze. "Uh oh, we've done it now," she said to Ian without moving her lips.

Ian followed her gaze, his body growing instantly alert, prepared for an imminent attack.

"What do you two think you are doing?" Thaddeus demanded.

Ian stepped in front of Esmeralda. "We are talking."

"It looks like more than that to me!" His eyes bore into Esmeralda. "Go home, young lady, before you get into trouble."

Esmeralda tried to step from behind Ian, but he blocked her way. She leaned around him and retorted, "You are the only one causing trouble, Thaddeus!"

"I will not have it!" he thundered.

She crossed her arms, and said through tight lips, "You'll not have what?"

Thaddeus' chest heaved. "I will not have you acting like a trollop in front of the whole town!"

Ian scowled. "Hey, now, that's uncalled for."

"You stay out of this!"

Ian took a step forward, his temper flaring. "I will not. You are out of line."

Venom poisoned Thaddeus' voice when he barked, "No, Ian, you are the one who is out of line. She is fourteen-years-old."

Ian resented the implication. "I know that. We are friends, who happen to share several mutual interests."

"I know what your interests are! I've seen the way you look at her." Thaddeus poked a finger in Ian's chest.

Esmeralda threw off Ian's restraining hand, jumping between them. "Stop it!" She grabbed Thaddeus' elbow and pulled. "Come on. You and I are going to discuss this rationally."

Thaddeus shot Ian a parting glare and turned, brimming with righteous indignation.

"What are you playing at?" she demanded, stomping across the square.

Curious eyes followed their exit.

"What am *I* playing at?" he laughed humorlessly. "That's rich! You, hanging all over him, batting your eyes, flirting!"

"I was not! We are friends out for a walk, until you came storming over, raving like a lunatic!" She stalked ahead, drawing them away from their audience. Several people came out of their houses to listen.

"There is one of us who has lost their mind, and it's not me," Thaddeus said in a low, menacing tone.

Esmeralda gave up trying to reason with him and whirled, thoroughly put out. "First, you call me a trollop, then you call *me* crazy? Ian and I are friends. I like him! Why is that so bad?"

"Because he is a man, Esmeralda!" A gust of wind blew his hair away from his face as his eyes blazed fire. "You do not understand what that is like, what men think, what they feel and want to do. It does not matter that you are little more than a child, it is a force beyond reason."

A bee buzzed her head, and she swatted at it in irritation. "I am not a child, Thaddeus."

He looked away in self-disgust. "I see that, but so does he, so does every man in this village."

Her voice shook with outrage and hurt. "I did not do anything wrong."

Thaddeus pinched the bridge of his nose and closed his eyes. "I know that, but you don't understand."

Little ticks of emotion flicked across her face as she fought to control her temper. "I understand much more than you give me credit for. I may be young, but I am not stupid."

"No, you're not, but you are naive and sheltered, and you are messing around with a grown man." He took a step toward her, intimidating her with his height, a fierce rebuke in his voice. "Don't play with fire, little girl, you just might get burned."

"I think there is one person on fire here." She spun on her heel and stalked away, calling over her shoulder, "And it's not me!"

You're Not the First

"It's not me either," Ian said from behind Thaddeus.

"You!" Thaddeus turned, raging against her words, raging at himself, and Ian. "You are the cause of this! Keep your eyes and your hands off her."

"Just exactly what are you accusing me of?" Ian snarled, his nose flaring in fury.

Thaddeus lifted his lip in a sneer. "I think you know."

"Go look in a mirror," Ian ground out.

Thaddeus turned crimson. "She is my friend, like my little sister. I am not a pedophile!"

"Neither am I, Thaddeus." His gentle rebuke diffused the situation.

"Unreal!" All the air seemed to go out of Thaddeus as he closed his eyes, deflating like a balloon. "I just made a gigantic fool of myself, didn't I?"

Ian cocked his head. "Yes, you did, but I daresay, you aren't the first man to do so, nor will you be the last."

Thaddeus looked around Rephidim, his haven, until now. He moistened his lips, dry in the hot wind. "Can I buy you a beer? I think I need one."

Ian thought Thaddeus needed a cold shower but wisely held his tongue. "Lead the way."

Curious onlookers followed their progress, but when it became apparent that they were not going to come to blows, interest waned. Jake's Tavern was a favorite spot for the mill workers after their shifts and games. Thaddeus did not frequent the place, in fact, since coming to Rephidim, he had not touched a drop of alcohol. The tavern was deserted this time of day, so Ian and Thaddeus had their choice of tables. Jake brought them each a large tankard of ale and left them in peace.

Thaddeus took a fortifying gulp and wiped his mouth with the back of his hand.

Ian raised his glass in salute. The cool amber lager burned his throat but settled nicely in the hollow spaces in his belly. He burped and grinned.

The corner of Thaddeus' mouth twitched, and he belched back.

"That was a pretty good one," Ian observed. "Hang on." He guzzled half his beer and let loose a window-shaking belch.

"Holy smokes, man. They heard that over in Endor."

"I can burp the alphabet, backwards and forwards." Ian grinned, relaxing into the padded bench, and digging into a bowl of pretzels.

"That's quite a skill. You make any money at it?"

Ian laughed, "As a matter-of-fact, yes. My friend Beau Landry bet some poor schlep twenty shekels that I could do it. Actually, come to think of it, he ran book on it, and we drank that entire thirty-six-hour pass on our take."

"He sounds like an excellent fellow to have around."

In his best bayou cadence, Ian replied, "Talk about, *mon frère*."

"Louisiana, huh?" Thaddeus took a sip of his beer. "Hang on, Landry from Louisiana?"

Ian nodded.

Thaddeus gave him a knowing look. "That's big money."

"Some of the biggest, but you wouldn't know it if you met him."

"Lenox is in a class by himself, Ian. I've met the old man." Thaddeus regarded Ian through fresh eyes, having taken him for one of the Civil War walking wounded who periodically found their way into Rephidim.

"I've never met Andrew ben Lenox, but I've met his daughter." Ian raised an eyebrow. "If he's anything like her, I can imagine that is one intimidating dude."

A shadow crossed Thaddeus' face, once the Golden Boy, he was well acquainted with the rich and powerful. "As I recall it, at the time he was trying to convince me to run for the legislature." Another pair of gentlemen came into the tavern, Thaddeus raised a hand in greeting.

"And now, you are a spinner," Ian remarked casually.

Thaddeus made an innocent, open-palmed gesture. "Purely by choice. How about you, Ian? Once a friend to one of the richest families in the world and now a drifter?"

Ian wiped beer from his mouth, contemplating. "I wouldn't categorize myself as a drifter exactly. I'd say I'm more like a traveling saint."

Thaddeus scoffed. "A saint?"

"It's what the Word calls somebody like me," Ian said with a shrug.

Thaddeus snorted, the alcohol loosening his tongue. "I never took too much stock in what Paul had to say."

Ian shook his head. "Maybe you should have a conversation with somebody about that."

Thaddeus put his elbows on the table and held up his forehead. "I've been contemplating doing exactly that. There's a new crew leaving for the Golden City in a couple of weeks. I've seriously considered joining them. After today, I'm thinking that might be a good idea."

Ian's eyes brightened, as if some truth had just been revealed. He nodded and said, "Thaddeus, I believe you are right."

Thaddeus drained his beer and motioned for another. Halfway through his second pint, he heaved a sigh and said, "She's just a kid, Ian. What the hell am I doing?"

"Seems to me, you're doing exactly what you are supposed to."

Thaddeus met Ian's eyes and swore, "I've never laid a hand on her, ever."

Ian raised his mug, acknowledging the truth in that statement. "I believe you."

"She's followed me around for the last two-and-a-half years. I don't know what would have happened if she hadn't brought me here. I was well on my way to killing myself."

He nodded at the booze. "I was half starved, out of my mind with grief, and then there she was, smiling at me, feeding me, pestering me with questions."

Ian gave him a knowing grin. "She asks a lot of questions."

Thaddeus rubbed his eyes and chuckled, "Yes, she does. It's part of that mind of hers. She is the most inquisitive person I have ever known. Ask her about anything. She's read every book in this village and beyond. Every quarter, the returning pilgrims bring her a crate, and she reads them all. Her mother told me she could read by the time she was two. I have no doubt about it."

Thaddeus studied the dancing bubbles in his beer, suddenly melancholy. "If you ask her about beer, she can not only tell you how to make it, but the origins of it, and what makes this beer golden and yours red. Then, she'll look up at you with those big blue eyes and tell you something about your own soul that you never even considered, and she'll be right."

Ian simply listened.

"She's funny, and she's smart, and I enjoy her company. I tried to run her off the first couple of years, but she wouldn't go. And when she did, I realized how much I missed her."

Ian nodded. "She is a special girl."

"That's just it, Ian, she's a girl. She's not a woman. Hell, she's not even a young woman. I'm fifteen years her senior, and I've had a wife and two sons. My sons would be closer in age to her than I am." He took a long drink. "I've got to get out of here."

Ian rubbed his chin and nodded. "Yes, Thaddeus, you do."

"A year will not be long enough." Thaddeus closed his eyes and sighed, "Three years isn't long enough."

"The Iron King has His own timing." Ian settled back against the bench, relaxing. He accomplished at least one thing the Lord sent him to do in Rephidim. "I think the pilgrimage is a good start."

Thaddeus nodded, his course set. "The Spinners are still going to win the championship, with or without me."

The conversation took a decidedly male turn, and the two dispossessed gentlemen enjoyed their beers and each other's company. However, Thaddeus knew he had to leave, and his heart, which had only just begun to heal, tore wide open, again.

September 2, 989 ME

Goodbye, Kid

Thaddeus looked for Esmeralda all day, could not go without saying goodbye. He should have known he'd find her here, on his rock. "What are you doing out here all by yourself?"

Esmeralda's shoulders heaved with a great sniff, and she wiped her eyes with her thumbs. "You don't have to leave. I won't talk to him anymore."

Thaddeus frowned, shaking his head. "It's not about that. I know you're just friends."

She covered her face, hiding her pain. "Then why are you going?"

Thaddeus stood well away from her and said, "You know why."

Esmeralda folded her hands and pressed them against her lips. "Why couldn't I have been born earlier? Why? Why does my age keep us apart?"

"Because it does." Thaddeus absorbed her, imprinting his mind with her curly brown hair, her delicate chin, her gorgeous big eyes. "You need time to grow up, to find out who you are going to be. You need to do that without me lurking around like some... lecherous old man."

Her lower lip trembled, but before she could protest, he cut her off. "I swim in a deep ocean of regret and self-recrimination, Esmeralda. I don't need to add despoiling little girls to my conscience."

"We have never done anything to be ashamed of. You've never done anything to be ashamed of."

"And I plan to keep it that way," he said in a strained voice.

"I don't understand," Esmeralda whispered, tears spilling over her lashes.

"I know you don't, and that's why I have to go. Esmeralda, I'm hanging on by a fibril." She rose, and he stepped back. "Don't. Don't touch me. Don't come any closer."

"Thaddeus?" She raised an arm toward him and then covered her mouth, her face contorting. "Are you coming back?"

"No." He set his jaw. "I'm not. Grow up normal, Esmeralda. Find a nice young man your age, get married, have babies. Have a good life, kid. I've enjoyed knowing you."

Her broken sob followed him out of the woods, cementing itself in his mind. It was the last time he was going to let a woman fall in love with him, because he ended up killing them all, one way or the other.

Part 2 - Esmeralda

September 2, 989 ME (Four Years into Rebellion)

The Left Side of Blue

Esmeralda did not follow Thaddeus back to town, could not bear to watch him leave. The other girls already thought she was peculiar, and she would not give them more proof. It was hard enough pretending to be normal on a regular day, so she could not manage it today, the worst day of her life.

Thaddeus was gone.

She wept into her hands, not caring that her cries carried deep into the woods. It drew her friends, and she let them come. Kit, the fox, slid into her lap, his magnificent tail tickling her arms. The big snapping turtle, Chelydra, scrambled up the rocks and regarded her with a baleful expression. Mustela, her favorite black mink, crawled up her back and settled himself around her shoulders. Barnabas and Ethel, the year old brown bear cubs, took positions on either side of her, their soft fur damp after a morning swim. But even her furry friends could not soothe the wrenching heartache, and she cried until she wore herself out.

"I heard you from my house," a familiar voice said from behind her.

Esmeralda refused to look up. "Good." She sniffed loud and thick. "I hope He heard, too."

"He did. That is why I am here."

"Well, then He should stop it," Esmeralda moaned. "He can make him stop, make him stay!" She raised her head and met the sapphire blue eyes of her companion. "Go tell Him!"

Jelena, the Gune, smiled, sad and knowing. "It is not to be, Esmeralda. Thaddeus' steps are ordered, and he is doing the Iron King's will."

Esmeralda's face contorted, and she pushed the animals away with jerky motions. "Leave me alone, then. All of you, just leave me alone. Let me cry like anybody else. I have a right to cry!"

"You do." Jelena settled beside Esmeralda and drew her close.

At length, Esmeralda scrubbed away her tears and said, "It's not fair. I've done everything He asked me to do, everything you've ever told me to do."

"You have done well, little miss, but it is not for you to question why. The Iron King knows what is best. Remember what the Scripture says, 'All things work together for good to those who love God, to those who are called according to His purpose.'" Jelena brushed a curl out of Esmeralda's eyes.

"What is my purpose, then? I always thought it was Thaddeus." Her voice broke on her beloved's name.

"Our purpose is never another person. You know this." Jelena cupped her cheek and repeated the creed, "Thy steps are ordered, thy path guarded, and thy purpose?"

Esmeralda turned toward the falls, whispering in resignation, "My purpose, to serve the King."

Jelena patted Esmeralda's knee. "That is right. It is easy to serve Him in comfort, but you were not called to a life of ease and isolation. Your purpose is higher."

"Like Ian's." Esmeralda's shoulders fell in dejection. "But even he is leaving now."

"You got to meet him. There was purpose in that." A warm wind blew Jelena's wondrous hair, which flowed like black onyx down her back.

Esmeralda nodded, knowing Jelena spoke the truth, but taking no comfort in it.

"What color do you see?" Jelena prompted.

Esmeralda covered her face. "Bluish gray, it is cold."

Jelena squeezed Esmeralda's hand. "The blues."

"But blue is not pain, not like this," Esmeralda protested. "Blue is life, and water, and sky. Blue is sweet and tastes like blueberry ice cream. It smells like limestone waterfalls and coconut; it feels like floating in a calm lake when the water tickles your body and laps over you. I know the Blue, Jelena!"

"That is the right side of blue, but there is another. The left side of blue is cold." Jelena's sapphire eyes changed from dancing beauty to frozen danger.

Esmeralda drew back. "The left side?"

With a blink, Jelena's eyes changed back. "To this point in your life, everything you have learned is the right side, the good, and the lovely. But down here, Esmeralda, there is another side."

Esmeralda's face grew solemn. "So, now you are going to teach me the left?"

"Not me, little miss, for I am Gune and no longer abide in this world, so you must learn most of it on your own." Jelena smiled ruefully. "When you do, then I will come back."

Esmeralda closed her eyes and shook her head in weary resignation. When she looked up, Jelena, too, was gone.

Tomorrow is Too Long

As darkness fell, Esmeralda knew it was time to go home. Her mother worried, and that was against the rules. There were many rules, living how she did, seeing things other people didn't, knowing things. Some rules she made up for herself, some Jelena gave her, others came from Him, those were the important ones, the ones she never ignored.

Long ago, she stopped trying to explain what she saw. She pretended not to know the things she did and never elaborated on how she understood people or situations. Esmeralda ben Claude did her best to act normal, but she was not.

She was five before she knew better, before she learned to keep her mouth shut. Her mother sent her to talk to Pastor. He listened politely as she fluttered around his office, telling him what she saw, what things meant. She did her best to show him; she tried to explain. But the more she tried, the more pained his expression grew. Though he smiled indulgently, he did not even begin to fathom what she told him.

Afterward, he discussed her like she was not even in the room, summing up their conversation by saying, "Esmeralda has quite an imagination." Then the adults laughed, uncomfortable and patronizing.

Sitting in that big chair in his office, staring at her red shoes, she vowed never to try to explain it again.

As she grew older, she realized they were not being mean, they simply did not have the capacity to understand. They lived in a world of beige and gray and did not see, not like Esmeralda. For her, the world was alive, her faith was alive, and everything, every day, was full of magic, mystery, and signs. All they had to do was look. People, places, things revealed their secrets, told their tales, and showed their power. It was all there, but people were blind. She could not explain it, and black and white thinkers could not understand. Esmeralda saw the world in living color, with all the glory, power and majesty of creation and its Creator.

Occasionally, when she poured someone a drink of water, they saw things like she did, but it never lasted. She enjoyed watching their faces when it happened. It knocked Thaddeus on his butt. The effect lasted longest on Ian, but he was more like her. He saw things, too.

It made her seem strange, like she existed on a plane others did not occupy. She was different, and she made people uncomfortable, especially when it was heavy on her. So, Esmeralda took great pains to hide it, to never divulge what she saw, what He showed her. On a certain level, everyone understood it. That was evident by common figures of speech, a green thumb, red hot, royal purple… the blues. People could get it if they tried, but most people did not want to look beyond the gossamer veil. They went to their shops or the mill and never saw what was right in front of them.

Grandma Eve understood it, at least as well as she could. At first, they made it a game. Esmeralda told her things, and Grandma Eve did not dismiss her out of hand. Grandma Eve liked to paint, so she asked Esmeralda questions without patronizing. "If I want to paint this bowl and make it warm and homey, what color should I choose?"

"Brown, of course." Esmeralda answered without missing a beat. "Brown is warm and slow, think of chocolate or coffee. It feels nice," she covered a soft giggle and whispered, "like poop."

Grandma Eve chuckled and decided a fruit bowl should not be brown after all.

A few months later, she said, "Esmeralda, I have not fixed up the house since Silas passed away, and I think it's time for an update. What if I paint the outside light blue?"

Esmeralda crinkled her nose. "That would be okay if your boarders were ladies, Grandma, because light blue is a feminine color. It is cool and a bit fussy. It holds teacups like this." She held her pinky straight out and took a delicate sip. "But men won't like it."

"Well then, what do you suggest?"

Esmeralda launched into a full discourse on what she thought men would like. "I would add some dark green inside, like the forest, paired with all your plants it will make people feel like they are in the woods, which helps them relax and sleep well. Add touches of gold, like the King's domain. It's rich and vibrant. No one worries surrounded by gold because they know the Lord will provide."

"That he does." Grandma Eve smiled.

"Go with butter cream for the walls, and pale yellow for the outside. Those colors are powerful and welcoming."

"Is that so?"

Esmeralda nodded. "It is."

She cherished the day when they finished remodeling the boarding house. Grandma Eve looked around her new surroundings with a keen eye and recognized the power. She knew then, this was not a game.

Leaving the woods, with her eyes swollen and her heart broken in a thousand pieces, clouds obscured the sun as Esmeralda cut across the square toward home. She averted her eyes away from Grandma Eve's, unable to bear the sight of it now that Thaddeus was gone.

Ian spotted her and left the front porch to walk her home. "Are you all right?".

She looked up and saw the color of pain reflected in his eyes, pale blue gray. "No, I am not, Ian."

"He had to go, for himself, and for you."

She backhanded a tear. "That's what everybody keeps telling me. I'm sorry, but it does not help."

"No, I suppose it wouldn't." He rubbed his chin thoughtfully. "I saw my brother go through this. It was brutal to watch, let alone feel."

"And how is your brother now?" Esmeralda needed to know.

"Grand. The Lord worked it out." He elbowed her. "He'll do that for you too, lass."

Esmeralda tucked a stray curl behind her ear. "I'm mad at Him right now, at both of them!"

"It won't be forever, Esmie. I promise." Contentment washed over him as he led her to the front door.

"Even tomorrow feels too long," Esmeralda said in quiet weariness. "Pray for me, Ian. Pray for Thaddeus because I don't know what is going to happen to him without me." She hung her head and walked through the blue door.

October 31, 990 ME (5 ½ Years into Rebellion)

One of Those Days

A little over a year after Thaddeus left, Esmeralda opened her eyes and knew it would be one of *those* days. Before she got out of bed, she knew.

She was ten the first time it happened, when the Black made itself known. She woke up to her parents fighting. They never fought, never had a harsh word for each other, but the day Prince Eamonn died, Claude threw a breakfast plate at Julianna. They both stormed out of the house, her mother in tears, her father in a huff. Scared, Esmeralda crept into the kitchen and found the shattered plate. The air smelled acrid, and she saw the toast, burned to black, laying by itself. But as she stared, the shadows elongated and crept toward her like venomous snakes, ominous. She fled the house in her nightgown.

The day Prince Eamonn died, Esmeralda saw the Black.

The second time it came in fire. A house burned to the ground, smoke billowing into the gray sky, putrid and foul. They said Phil had been drinking and fell asleep with his pipe, but no one knew for sure. Esmeralda walked past the smoking wreckage, gnarled like a giant beast in pain. A frigid wind blew over the destruction, reeking of sulfur and death.

The day they crowned Prince Korah ben Adam, Esmeralda smelled the Black.

To date, February 11, 986 ME proved the scariest. After spending the day in the forest, she walked across the square, alone. Shockwaves pulsed in the air, and the hair on her body stood on end. She froze, feeling something coming. She spun in a circle, searching, but saw nothing. Then, one after another, three terrifying bolts of lightning crashed into Rephidim, blinding her, the imprint of terror scorched onto her retinas. The resulting ground thunder sucked the air from her lungs and deafened her.

Blind, deaf, and breathless, Esmeralda felt the Black.

After that, a wicked presence crept around the edges of Rephidim, tested the borders, and tried to push in. She felt it lurking out there, malevolent and wicked. Thaddeus was in its grip the morning she stumbled upon him, which was why she covered him, why she left the water. She saw him dying under its power. She prayed it would not find him, that it would not take him again.

Esmeralda saved Thaddeus from the Black.

The morning of October 31, 990 ME, she felt it coming again. However, this time, she vowed to fight. Trembling, she rose from her bed, dressed in her plain clothes, but hid her special tunic and leggings in her knapsack, along with her sword. Making an excuse to her mother, she left the house. No longer a scared ten-year-old kid, Esmeralda became a warrior.

She walked the perimeter of the town, praying a hedge of protection with each step. "Protect us, Oh Lord, as you did your servant Job in the last days. I pray a hedge around our town that your shield would repel wickedness." On and on, she walked and prayed.

When the townsfolk stirred, she left the perimeter and ventured deep into the woods. On Thaddeus' rock, she changed into the White. Shadows retreated in her wake. A bevy of black crows landed in front of her. She rebuked them, and they scattered. Her heart pounded with fervent prayers; scriptures dripped from her tongue. She held the Bible in front of her, wielding the sword, covering herself and Rephidim in the word of prayer.

Throughout the day, she battled the Black.

She kept her eyes to the east, listened, and watched. Nothing penetrated the fortress of Rephidim. As night fell, she left the woods, satisfied the Lord spared them.

Esmeralda climbed into bed, exhausted. On the edge of sleep, a vision swept her away. Fire and glassy eyed animals surrounded her. The stench of death and blood assaulted her nose, gory and rancid. Her stomach contracted in a wave of nausea; she was going to be sick. Then Esmeralda saw her tormentor—a voodoo witch with her face painted like a skeleton, ghastly. She danced around a green fire, shaking bones and chanting filthy words. Esmeralda tried to scream, but she was paralyzed and realized she was seeing the horror through the eyes of someone else. A black-haired man stood beside her, but he could not move either. He was frozen like a zombie.

Esmeralda struggled in vain, trapped and terrified. The witch unsheathed a blade and with a single stroke, decapitated a rooster. Blood spurted everywhere. The cock was still crowing when she threw its severed head into a boiling pot. Then a monster moved into the firelight, his gigantic mouth salivating with anticipation, there to feed.

"Yeshua, help us!" Esmeralda prayed in the Spirit and was sucked out of the horror back in her room. She slid from her bed, onto her knees, praying long into the night for the young couple taken by the witch.

Halloween Night, 990 ME, Esmeralda had a vision of the Black.

A hundred miles away, while Esmeralda was on her knees, a weary traveler dropped his bag on the stoop of a well-appointed townhouse in New York. He contemplated the brass door knocker, then made his decision. A servant looked at his travel stained, dusty coat and scuffed boots with skeptical appraisal but greeted him. When Thaddeus stepped over the threshold, the servant's expression changed from dubiousness to surprise.

"Follow me. He is at home." A light knock on the study door was followed by an old man's call to enter. Jarrod ben Adriel announced him. "Sir, Thaddeus ben Todd to see you."

Bushy eyebrows rose in surprise as Sir Preston ben Worley grinned. "At last, the prodigal has returned."

June 22, 992 ME (Seven Years into Rebellion)

Sing, Mary, Sing

"Are you nervous?" Julianna asked as she fussed with Esmeralda's hair.

"Give me that." Esmeralda took the brush from her mother's hand. "You are making it worse. You can't brush it. Now look at me." She stared with mournful resignation into the mirror. "I look like a bell."

Julianna's mouth quivered. "Sorry."

"Don't laugh!" But her actions belied her words, as she moved her head back and forth, making bonging sounds, ringing like a bell.

Julianna did laugh then. "We could cut it."

Esmeralda's horrified expression conveyed what she thought of that idea. "Like you did to me when I was seven? I am still traumatized."

Julianna rolled her eyes. "That was ten years ago, and it was adorable."

Esmeralda shot Julianna a look every teenage girl ever born perfected just for her mother. "It looked ridiculous, square on top, tapered in the back. Awful." This was an old conversation, funny now, tragic at the time. Esmeralda spritzed her hair with water, wetting down the frizz.

Julianna perched on the edge of the bed and said, "My mother always hated her curly hair."

"With good reason." Esmeralda eyed herself critically, gave up leaving it long and began platting her customary French braid. "It's a curse."

Mother and daughter's eyes met in the mirror. "You are lovely, hair and all." Julianna raised an eyebrow, a knowing expression on her face. "And I am not the only one who thinks so."

Esmeralda grimaced. "Don't start."

"What? He's cute. I've always thought so, and he's obviously interested in you." She nodded to a vase of flowers on Esmeralda's dresser.

"Leo ben Jordan has terrible breath, and he spits when he talks, Mother."

"Well then, his brother Simon? I saw him looking at you in church last week."

"Eww, Simon? Have you ever heard him eat? He sounds like a pig." Esmeralda rose and went to her closet, flipping through her wardrobe. "What do you think about this one?" She held up a blue dress.

"It's pretty, brings out the color of your eyes." Julianna nodded her approval.

"The blue…" Esmeralda dropped her head, becoming melancholy.

"Esmie…"

Esmeralda straightened her shoulders. "I'm fine, Mom."

Julianna looked up from beneath her brown lashes but did not pursue the conversation. That touchy subject was a sure way to get her evicted from Esmeralda's room. "You never answered my question. Are you nervous?"

Esmeralda slipped the dress over her head. "No. I've been practicing. Besides, if I make a fool out of myself, by the time I get home from Aunt Jean's, everyone will have forgotten."

"That is probably true, but you won't make a fool of yourself. Your voice is lovely." Julianna helped Esmeralda button the back of the dress.

"I am only doing this because Grandma Eve insisted," Esmeralda said, studying her reflection. "She is relentless."

"I've been saying for years you should do it. I am glad she convinced you." Where maternal coaxing failed, other godly women filled the gap. "Which song are you going to sing?"

Esmeralda shrugged. "One of the three, it will all depend on how the Spirit moves."

Walking onto stage at church, Esmeralda decided the Spirit was blue. So, she chose a song about Mary, her favorite lady in the Bible who knew the Blue.

Help is on the Way

"Does she have to come?" Elizabeta ben Yoder complained, fluffing her hair, and admiring her reflection in
the mirror. She rubbed her lips together, testing the new lip
gloss. "She is odd."

"Watch thy tongue, Daughter. 'Tis no way to speak of
thy cousin," Jean ben Mathias scolded, "when she is come to
help us."

"Thou doest not know her, Mother. She makes me uneasy, always has, to be sure." Elizabeta turned to the side and
drew her shoulders back, smiling at her slender figure.

Jean braced her hand behind her spine and pushed up
from the chair. "Nonsense. Esmeralda is a kind and thoughtful soul; unlike some I might mention."

Elizabeta ignored the jab, adjusting the neckline of her
blouse. "Be that as it may, she is strange."

"Thou will appreciate her in the middle of the night after
the baby comes. I know I shall."

At thirteen, Elizabeta had no inkling what having a newborn in the house would be like but figured nothing could
be worse than spending the rest of the summer with spooky
Esmeralda. "She is constantly gazing off into space, looking
at nothing, mumbling under her breath."

Jean pursed her lips. She had noticed that too. "Esmeralda is very devout, as thou should be."

Elizabeta rolled her eyes behind her mother's back. She
had little use for Esmeralda's brand of devotion, taking a
pragmatic, modern approach to matters of faith and life. She
and her friends looked toward the New City and the wonders
coming from it, rejecting their parents' old fashioned beliefs.
"I am devout, in my own way," she protested.

Jean felt a twinge in her lower back and grimaced. "Seek
to be cordial, Elizabeta. We need her."

Elizabeta raised an obstinate chin and said, "Fine, just
please do not ask me to take her with me everywhere I go."

"I am certain the last thing thy cousin wishes is to be with thee and thy friends. She is nearly grown, thou art still a child. Doubtless, there is little to worry over," Jean soothed.

The small bell rang in her parent's room. Father had awakened. Elizabeta cast a hopeful look at her mother.

"Be a dear and attend to thy father? My back hurts."

Elizabeta huffed and went to the sick room where her father lay for the last month. He sustained a terrible beating on his way home from work and was now confined to bed. Perhaps it would not be so bad having her spooky cousin around to help. Let her attend to the sick. Elizabeta had better things to do with her time.

Thyatira Woods

Esmeralda reined the horse up at the crossroads. To the right lay the path to Bezetha and Aunt Jean's, to the left, Endor. For a month, she contemplated this decision, since the letter arrived asking Julianna or Esmeralda to come. Esmeralda readily agreed, excited at the prospect. She loved babies and at seventeen had never left the haven of her own village. But more than altruism or familiar duty prompted her acceptance. Esmeralda secretly wanted a chance to explore the ruins of Endor.

Her parents were reluctant to let her travel the ten miles to Bezetha on her own, but she knew if anyone came with her, she could not take her side visit. So, she adopted a stubborn obstinance they mistook for a declaration of independence. Many of her contemporaries were getting married, others attending this year's pilgrimage, and two more left Rephidim altogether. The debate raged for a solid week, but in the end, they relented.

Father made her memorize the map, Ernst supplied a horse, and between her mother and Grandma Eve, she had enough food and provisions to see her to the New City, let alone the two-hour ride to Bezetha. The map did not list Endor, but Esmeralda knew where it had been.

Today, sitting at the crossroads, she had a choice and a chance. With a determined flick of the reins, she turned left—to Endor.

Her fierce longing for Thaddeus drove her to the deserted village. She wanted to be reunited with him. Jelena said she would return when she learned the other side, the left side, and Esmeralda reasoned Endor was the best place to do it.

She had not ridden long before the road became overgrown. Signs warned travelers, 'Dead End, turn back.' In them, she detected Ernst's handiwork; they looked like the paint he used on his compost sign. Ducking under a low branch, she pressed onward, ignoring the warning, though her heart picked up speed.

Dark moss covered the trunks of the live oaks. The Green surrounded her, fecund and humid. She smelled fungus growing in large ears on fallen logs. A deep layer of dead leaves, disturbed by her passing, wafted up, earthy and wet. The leather tack under her thighs squeaked, and a small animal rustled in the underbrush. Otherwise, the only sounds in the forest were the horse's hoofs.

Accustomed to being alone out here, the dense Thyatira Woods were as familiar to her as the freckle on the back of her right hand. Yet as she rode, the shadows lengthened and obscured the sun. The overgrown vegetation forced her off the road in several places, and she had to coax the horse to press on when the animal seemed inclined to turn back. She battled the recalcitrant mare and spurred it forward. Thorny vines snagged her clothing and pricked her fingers as she fought to free her cloak from a briar.

An hour and a half after taking the fork in the road, she found Endor.

The old folks said fire destroyed the entire village in righteous judgment for Endor's sin against the Iron King. Esmeralda expected to find an open clearing, perhaps burned-out remnants of buildings returning to the earth, but the deserted town was nothing like she ever imagined.

Endor

Much of it was burned. Vast swaths of charred stone were covered in thorny vines. Tumbled chimneys gave evidence to houses that once stood. In others, trees grew through collapsed roofs. Yet, there remained some dwellings completely intact, and these drew Esmeralda. She wanted to see inside, wanted to see what made this place so wicked. What would she find? Were there black walls and pentagrams, or had their sin been more salacious? She caught fragments of conversation over the years that led her to believe it was a mixture of the two.

Peering in a dusty window of a partially burned house, Esmeralda experienced a moment of vague disappointment because it looked ordinary. A table was set with fine dishes, covered in dust and dirt, but otherwise waiting for the long-deserted occupants to sit down and eat. A rocking horse creaked on the wooden porch; the child who rode it long dead or fled. It had painted flowers for eyes, and a real horsehair tail which fluttered in the damp wind, tangled with leaves and spider webs.

Walking among the desolation, darkness settled around her shoulders, so she decided to mount the horse in case she needed to make a fast exit. Behind the houses, in the outer rings of the village, sat row after row of stables and paddocks. Long abandoned and given over to destruction, their once fine fences had fallen, turning gray from wind and rain.

One particular stable drew Esmeralda, half burned and dilapidated. "She escaped." The words came to her unbidden as she saw a vision of a fleeing woman carrying a bundle. Young and blonde, she sobbed as she ran into the burning building, her dress and attire from long ago, but she broke free of the burning stable, riding a white horse, bent low over the saddle. The sound of gunfire, galloping hooves, and wailing echoed in her mind. Esmeralda turned away as the woman's overwhelming fear and heartbreak seeped into her soul.

Then she froze.

Slithering out of an abandoned house across the street was the largest black snake she had ever seen. Twenty feet long, if it was an inch, its body writhed and undulated rapidly toward her. The horse reared, and Esmeralda fought for control. The massive snake coiled itself ten feet from her. Its forked tongue flickered, red against black—mortal danger.

"What are you doing here, little girl?" a malevolent voice hissed in her mind.

Esmeralda's insides turned to ice. She kicked the frightened horse into a gallop, tearing up the turf as she rode.

"I know you," the voice called. "You are not in Rephidim anymore. You are in my town."

Mist rose out of the ground, obscuring her vision. Sulfur filled her nose, and she gagged, unable to breathe as her lungs filled with the polluted stench, yellowish green, vile; the left side of Yellow.

In abject terror, she choked, "Go!" to the panicked animal. But mid-gallop, their momentum arrested, and an evil force held them suspended in midair. With dawning horror, Esmeralda recognized this phenomenon, having experienced it once before, and knew a witch was coming.

"What is your hurry?" said the voice. "I have awaited our meeting for quite some time. It is rude for you to rush off before we have chatted."

Esmeralda tried to breathe, but only little sips of foul air kept her alive as black spots danced before her eyes, and an invisible band crushed her chest.

A shimmering vibration disturbed the air, like a wavering pulse, reminiscent of the day lightning crashed in the square. Then out of the ether, the ghastly skeletal face of the witch materialized.

Every sinful thought Esmeralda ever had swamped her, shaming her with the vileness of her own mind. Jealousy, covetousness, envy, pride, anger... lust, it was all there.

"That's right," the witch crooned. "You have darkness inside you, so do not pretend otherwise."

Esmeralda saw herself through the eyes of others, haughty and strange. Then with a clarity long forgotten, Thaddeus' beloved face swept over her, laughing, smiling, teasing… leaving.

The apparition circled, taunting her. "I have him, you know. He is in my power."

Esmeralda saw Thaddeus in a dark bedroom, naked, a woman straddling him. "No!" she screamed, but no sound erupted.

The witch cackled in bawdy delight.

Then another vision fell, one of blood and hacked bodies—Thaddeus' wife and sons. She heard him screaming, experienced his desperation. She smelled the putrid gore, and worst, oh worst of all, she watched in helpless desolation as Thaddeus pulled the lifeless body of one of his sons to his chest, wailing in anguish. Esmeralda fought it off, but the witch held her, and it rolled on, wave after wave of slaughter and death.

Furious, Esmeralda pushed back, and the vision cleared.

But another took its place, unknown and sinister. A desperate man stood before the witch, sliced his wrist, and dripped blood into a chalice of black slime. "No!" Esmeralda screamed, desperate to stop him. However, the vision was old, the man lost long ago. He drank the cup of abomination, and when he turned his face was painted with the same skeletal horror as the witch's, his eyes dead, his fate sealed. He held up his hands, covered in blood that dripped down his elbows onto the floor.

"Submit to God, resist the devil, and he will flee from you." The verse flashed across Esmeralda's mind, and she latched onto it. "I resist." Was all she could manage.

The invisible bonds released, and the horse fell with a crash.

She thrust her hands forward and shouted, "I rebuke you in the name of Yeshua. By the power of the blood of the Lamb, and the testimony of the saints, begone foul witch, for thou may not lay a hand on the chosen."

The apparition wavered, but she taunted, "We'll see about that, little girl." Then she vanished.

Esmeralda did not tarry; she pushed the horse to a blinding speed. Barbs whipped at her face and tore her clothes. Her body jolted with each footfall, jarring and painful. Esmeralda ben Claude turned to the right and fled Endor.

A hundred miles away, the witch returned to her body, laughing with wicked delight. She stepped out of the pentagram, shed her black hooded robe, and reached for her phone. "Our enemy has left Rephidim. See she does not return."

Bezetha

Esmeralda tried to act normal, truly she did, but even the stoutest spirit would have quaked after Endor, and within moments of arriving at Aunt Jean's, she sealed her fate. Terrified, she did not enter the house, instead she circled the property a dozen times, whispering fervent prayers.

Elizabeta stared out the window, her face scrunched in disgust. "What is she doing?"

Jean joined her at the curtain. "I cannot fathom."

"See, I told thee," Elizabeta crowed.

Jean heaved a sigh and went to the door, certain the neighbors were spying. Esmeralda did not hear her greeting, muttering as she paced, heedless of the spectacle she was making. Her hair had come loose from its braid and tangled about her shoulders, obscuring her face. The fine cloak she wore billowed as she walked, covered in mud, great splashes up the back. Her trousers were torn, and a small branch trailed behind her, twined in the laces of her boots. The lathered horse fared no better. It ran around the yard, its sides heaving, its eyes wild.

"Esmeralda, come hither," Jean barked in her sternest maternal voice.

Esmeralda shuddered, noticing her for the first time. "Aunt Jean! Is all well within the house?"

Jean stiffened at the look in her niece's eyes; the girl appeared to have gone mad. Esmeralda clutched the sides of her head. With her hair held back, Jean noticed a nasty cut, blood running down her cheek. "It is well, and thee? Esmeralda, did calamity befall thee on thy journey?"

"Auntie, I was accosted on the road."

"My heavens, thou art hurt!" She waddled off the porch, now alarmed rather than miffed.

"I'm fine," Esmeralda shook her head convulsively, "just frightened."

"Thy cheek is bleeding."

Esmeralda dabbed at the cut, her hand coming away bloody. "Oh, I had not noticed. I rode through some briars. One must have caught me."

"Come in, we will get thee cleaned up. What occurred?"

Esmeralda stared at the blood on her hand, feeling the unease pulsing of her aunt. It warned her to remain silent about the events in Endor. Drawing upon a lifetime of practice, she glossed over the truth and said, "It was nothing, just an old woman who startled the horse with me atop it. The beast bolted, and we had a wild ride. Nothing more."

Aunt Jean's forehead creased in suspicion. "Then why wast thou pacing about the house muttering?"

Esmeralda wiped her shaking hand on her trousers and gave her aunt a tremulous smile. "I did not wish to upset you. I have come to help, not add to your burden."

Aunt Jean nodded. "I thank thee for coming. I am sorry thy journey proved difficult."

Esmeralda's voice held a faint tremor as she fought to appear normal. "Please, do not worry, Auntie." She gestured toward Elizabeta, who emerged from the house, looking peeved. "Greetings, Cousin."

"Hello." Elizabeta smoothed her red shirt and added with a sneer, "What happened to thee?"

Aunt Jean flashed an overly bright, fake smile and took Esmeralda by the elbow. "Thy cousin's horse bolted and gave her a fright, nothing more."

"She's filthy." Elizabeta wrinkled her nose. "Are you going to get that horse?"

Esmeralda snapped her head around, noticing the agitated mare. "Yes, of course." She looked down, noticed her mud-stained clothing and added sheepishly, "I am filthy, I beg your pardon."

She managed to capture the slack reins of the cantering horse and lead the animal to the small stable. Alone, she made a keening groan, trembling so violently she was forced to use the stall to stay upright. Taking several deep breaths, she let the comforting smells of wood, hay, and manure calm the fire storm coursing through her veins—the Brown. "Lord God, protect us, please protect us," she prayed. "Protect Thaddeus, please Lord."

Not Wanted

"Thou should not have sent for her," Yoder ben Joab growled, surly in his confinement and cranky at his wife. "Elizabeta has the right of it for the once."

Jean eased onto the edge of their bed, exhausted. "I would not have, but thy accident necessitated it." She squeezed her temples, seeking respite from the pounding headache behind her eyes. "Besides, 'twas nothing but a bolt from a horse, which thou knowest is unnerving."

"I will not have the odd girl nurse me, Wife!" Yoder kicked at Jean, nearly dislodging her from her perch. "Dost thou understand?"

Jean recoiled in surprise. "What has gotten into thee?"

Yoder turned away, sucking his teeth, a deep red flush staining his pallid cheeks. "Keep her away from me."

Jean gave him a sidelong glare. Since the beating, his moods and personality changed. The doctor claimed it was a side effect, a consequence of multiple blows to the head. She withdrew from their marital bed and the stranger who occupied it. "Fine, I will keepeth her away."

He rolled, presenting his back. "See to that, Jean, otherwise I shall eject her from this house. Do not doubt me. She is not welcome here."

Jean's eyes widened, and she wondered where her kind, mild-mannered husband had gone.

Upstairs, Elizabeta held up one of Esmeralda's dresses, admiring herself in the mirror. "I will say this about Rephidim, the clothing is extraordinary."

Esmeralda blinked, trying to focus on her vapid cousin, who within moments of unpacking began rifling through her belongings. "Thank you, please borrow as you like."

The corner of Elizabeta's mouth lifted. Out of earshot of her mother, she tested her plain Alanthian speech, "Do you mean it?"

Bezethians were one of the few villages in the region still using the formal speech of ancient Alanthia, adopted in part because most of the surviving books from the Last Age were King James bibles. Sermons were preached, scriptures memorized, and the speech patterns of middle age England were resurrected.

"Yes, of course, borrow what you want," Esmeralda said, trying to build a bridge between her and her cousin. They had never been close.

"This one is pretty!" Elizabeta cooed as she pulled an iridescent white tunic from the closet.

Esmeralda caught her wrist. "Except that one."

"Why not? This is the one I really want."

"No." Esmeralda forced the garment back in the closet. "That one is special."

Elizabeta relented and reached for a green top. "How about this one?"

Esmeralda grew still and said with a touch of irony, "I think the green suits you fine."

With the cut on her cheek throbbing and spent adrenaline draining her energy, Esmeralda fell back on the bed, hoping her cousin would get the hint. She did not.

"Look, this color brings out the flecks in my eyes. I know Jeremiah will think I look pretty in it."

"Who is Jeremiah?"

Elizabeta puckered her lips and practiced a pouty expression in the mirror. "My boyfriend."

Esmeralda yawned, grimacing as the action opened the cut, renewing the bleeding under the bandage. "Aren't you a little young for a boyfriend?"

"At least mine is my age. How old was your crush when you were thirteen, fifty?"

Esmeralda flinched at the insult, but replied slowly, "No, he was not." Visions of Thaddeus flashed, and she lost her patience for pretense and her cousin. "I'm tired, Elizabeta. Please leave."

"Whatever, fine." She took the green top and stomped out the door.

Esmeralda closed her eyes, desperate for the images of Thaddeus to stop. She willed away the sound of his cries as he held his dead son, tried to block the flashes of him with another. But in the unfamiliar room sadness overwhelmed her, and she wept, alone, in silence.

June 23, 992 ME

House Calls

Esmeralda disliked the doctor on sight. From his avuncular tone to his oily skin and colorless eyes, he made the hairs on the back of her neck stand on end. He represented the dark side of red. A man to cut, burn, and bleed, this doctor was no healer; he was a butcher.

"Thy aunt bade me to attend thee. Sit down," he ordered.

Esmeralda took a step backward. "Thank you, but no. I am fine."

Doctor Nephel licked his lips. "As thou wishes, but yon wound still bleeds. If it goeth unattended, it will scar."

Esmeralda touched the bandage. It still hurt, and he was likely right, but nothing could persuade her to let this man touch her. "I am confident it will be fine." She spun on her heel and fled to the kitchen.

Nephel narrowed his eyes at the girl's retreating form, coltish and striking, not classically pretty, but intriguing. In Yoder's sickroom, he commented in German, "Your niece is lovely."

Yoder made a disgusted sound in the back of his throat and extended his broken arm for inspection. "She is my wife's niece, no relation to me."

Nephel unwrapped the bandage and said, "I am gratified to hear it, brother. I do not believe she will trouble you long."

Yoder's eyes narrowed as he smiled. "Lodge?"

A slow grin spread over the doctor's face. "Indeed."

"Jean won't like it," Yoder whispered in German, then grimaced as Nephel manipulated his wrist, harder than necessary.

"You do not have a choice in the matter. Next time, you won't end up in bed."

Yoder tried to pull his arm away, the implication ringing sinister in the sick room. "I will help. I told you I would. In exchange, leave my family alone."

Nephel narrowed his eyes, light pools of deadly intent. "You are in no position to bargain."

Blinking in fear, Yoder whispered, "Whatever you ask, I will do it."

Nephel tilted his head and pursed his thick lips. "We knew you would come around to our way of thinking." He gave a bone crunching squeeze of Yoder's injured hand and said, "Rest well."

Yoder spasmed in pain but managed to choke, "Thank you, Doctor."

"No, thank you. I will return soon. Your baby will arrive any day now."

"Don't hurt them," Yoder begged. "Please."

But the door closed without a reassuring word from the doctor. He left Yoder in a chest heaving mess, cursing the very day he stepped foot in that lodge.

June 24, 992 ME

Baby Baby

Esmeralda cast nervous glances between the unfamiliar houses, dodging shadows and startling at noises of unknown origin. Spooked and unnerved, the last place she wanted to be was on a dark street in the middle of the night, seeking Doctor Nephel, but there was no other physician in Bezetha. Aunt Jean's birth pains began at 2:07 am, and within the hour she was in full blown labor, progressing fast.

In wary trepidation, Esmeralda knocked on the doctor's door. Several hard bangs later, an elderly woman wearing a ghostly white gown greeted her.

"Please ma'am, can you send the doctor? My Aunt Jean is in labor, Jean ben Mathias. Her pains are coming fast, and I fear there is not much time."

"Who art thou?" The old lady squinted, holding the candle up to Esmeralda's face.

Esmeralda drew back, smelling singed hair. "I am her niece, Esmeralda, come to help from Rephidim."

The woman turned her body, checked behind her, then whispered, "Thou art in grave danger."

Esmeralda blinked, unsure she heard correctly. "Pardon me?"

A hacking cough erupted from the old woman's chest, and before she could recover or say more the doctor loomed out of the darkness, appearing like a specter.

"Is Jean in labor, child?" he asked, oozing false concern.

Esmeralda nodded. "Yes, Doctor. I will meet you back at the house." Without waiting, she turned and sprinted down the narrow stone path.

But as Aunt Jean's house came into sight, a wave of nausea hit her, and she doubled over, retching. Shivers ran down her legs, as the world spun. She grabbed a fence post to steady herself, but jerked her hand away, the remnants of a slug wiggling on her palm. She shuddered in revulsion and stumbled toward the house.

As she entered, a panicked Elizabeta grabbed her shoulders and shrieked, "What took you so long? The baby is coming!"

"The doctor is on his way. I just left him."

"Get in here!" Yoder yelled.

"Go." Esmeralda pushed Elizabeta toward her parent's room. "I need a minute."

Opening the front door, she checked for the doctor, but the street was empty. "Lord, help me," she prayed.

A humid wind blew through the yard, bringing the scent of a lilac bush in full bloom—the Purple. Regal, strong, and powerful, in the Purple, she was capable, in control.

She closed her eyes, stretched her neck side-to-side, and with a confidence that belied reason, Esmeralda took six steps into the bedroom and delivered a baby.

The doctor arrived in time for the afterbirth and to tend the umbilical cord. Her new cousin blinked up at her with eyes the color of dawn. Aunt Jean reached for him as Uncle Yoder and Elizabeta stared in slack jawed amazement. With steady hands, Esmeralda handed the docile baby to his mother.

"A son," Yoder whispered, tears coursing down his cheeks that still bore the yellow tinge of bruises. "Wife, we have a son!"

Esmeralda stepped away and leaned against the wall, as a fierce delayed reaction hit her.

Elizabeta, sedate for once, stroked her baby brother's conical shaped head, downy with black hair and wet. "He is beautiful."

The blotchy red newborn, covered in milky cheese and blood, was anything but beautiful. However, the small Bezetha family could see nothing but the glory and wonder of birth. It pulsed and glowed around them, warm Red, full of love, hope, and heat.

Esmeralda exhaled a long, powerful breath, relieved. Her head lolled to the side, and she caught the doctor sliding the afterbirth into a jar, surreptitiously stashing it in his bag. He looked up at her and smiled, then flicked his tongue at her like a snake. Esmeralda stumbled backward, crashing into a small table. All heads turned. The baby cried. With fumbling hands, she righted the contents and stammered, "Excuse me. I need to wash up."

A wicked presence chased her up the steps. She sprinted down the hall, praying, "Oh, God." Hitting her bedroom door with both hands, Esmeralda flung herself inside and bolted the door.

June 30, 992 ME

Six Days and Six Nights

Within hours of baby Zachariah's birth, illness struck with a vengeance—dysentery. It spared only Esmeralda and the baby. Jean, Yoder, and Elizabeta were devastated. The doctor's treatment seemed to make their conditions worsen, so while she could not bar him from the house, she poured his vile concoctions down the sink as soon as he left. Day and night, Esmeralda nursed them and the baby, spooning broth, changing sheets, washing linens, diapers, bed clothes, emptying basins of vile sickness, cleaning excrement splattered commodes, even the wall. Aunt Jean, weakened and vulnerable from the birth, became the sickest. On the fourth day, Esmeralda feared for her life, yet she fought back when Esmeralda put the baby to her breast and let him nurse.

Esmeralda drove herself past the point of exhaustion, never resting. There was no day, no night. She moved from one task to the next, one patient to the next. Somewhere around the fifth day, she suspected Elizabeta had recovered. However, the girl stubbornly refused to leave her bed, afraid, no doubt, that Esmeralda would enlist her to wash filth or deal with vomit that was not her own.

The evening of the sixth day, Esmeralda collapsed, resting her head on the kitchen table. Darkness invaded the room, surrounded her, and pressed her into the chair. Trembling with fatigue, she surrendered to it, but instead of the restorative sleep her body craved, Esmeralda fell into the vortex of a nightmare.

Colors flashed, vivid and bright. Moving and changing, they grew and glowed before swirling together in a wondrous rainbow. Then they bled together, and everything turned black. Drowning in the depths, battered by great waves, she gasped for air and inhaled oily slime. It tangled in her hair, covering her eyes and face. She fought, tearing at the sinuous tar ribbons that bound her hands and strangled her neck.

Spotting a faint red light, she swam for it. As she broke the surface, she gulped sulfurous air, which caused her to gag as she struggled for breath. Terror covered her like a shroud as she found herself in a black chamber. Hooded figures surrounded a cauldron, chanting, with dark music and drums beating in the background. The witch leaned in, her face painted and ghastly, blood dripping from her tongue. "We are coming for you, little girl."

Esmeralda woke with a scream and fell out of her chair, landing with a bruising thud on the tile. Scrambling to her feet, she looked around in panic. The temperature in the room plummeted, frosting her gasping breath, and chilling her blood. A presence hovered in the doorway, the manifestation of such evil she could not even make a noise. The floor shook, and a water pitcher flew across the room. She ducked, but it grazed the top of her head before shattering against the wall. Her vocal cords loosened, and she yelled, "I rebuke thee, foul spirit, in the name of Yeshua!"

The apparition grew, filling the room with black smoke and sulfur. His voice boomed in her head, guttural and wicked, emanating from the bowels of Hell. "I have a right to be here. I was invited. You were not!"

The force of his hatred blew her backward. She slammed against the counter, bruising her back, slashing her wrist on a shard of glass. "You have no power over me, for I am sealed by the blood of the Lamb."

He laughed, wickedness beyond the age. "I killed the Lamb! You will be much easier."

"No!" Esmeralda backed into a corner. "I am called. I am chosen. You shall not touch me!"

The Black moved into the kitchen.

Esmeralda screamed. Men shouted, banging on the back-door, demanding entrance. In desperation, she grabbed a kitchen knife from the butcher block and held it before her. "No! I rebuke you, in the name of Yeshua!" But her words held less conviction than before, quavering and scared.

With a mighty crash, the door burst open, and black clad police officers rushed in. Esmeralda climbed atop the counter in full blown terror. Wielding the knife, she screamed, "Stay away from me!"

"We are here to help thee, miss. The neighbors heard a ruckus and called. It's okay, come down. No one will hurt thee."

"No!" Esmeralda shouted, wild-eyed, looking like a lunatic with her hair standing on end, bushy and tangled. The men wore armbands that bore the sign of the witch. "Leave me alone!" she shrieked.

She saw her aunt and uncle, standing beyond the kitchen door. Elizabeta held onto her father, crying. "You are in danger, run! Leave this place!"

Yoder limped forward, his face pale and sunken. "No, Niece, we are not in danger. All is well, come down now."

"You don't understand!" Esmeralda shook her head. "The Witch… she sent these men… You have to believe me!"

Uncle Yoder's shoulders drooped in resignation, and he withdrew.

"Take her!" an officer ordered. En masse, they converged, fifteen grown men against one scared, exhausted girl.

They took her.

July 4, 992 ME

Beige Pajamas

When she woke on the fourth day, it was too late. Armed with the testimony of her aunt, uncle, cousin, the police officers, and Doctor Nephel, the court had all the evidence it needed to remand Esmeralda ben Claude to the Pennsylvania Institute for the Insane. Without defense, without due process, without her parents, Esmeralda became a ward of the state, deemed a danger to herself and society. They claimed she poisoned her family, then attempted suicide with a shard of broken glass, and when law enforcement intervened, she assaulted them with a deadly weapon. A court psychiatrist, without even interviewing her, diagnosed her as a manic-depressive schizophrenic who experienced delusional episodes accompanied by hallucinations.

Wearing scratchy, ill-fitting beige pajamas, she fought them until they pumped her full of drugs, tied her hands and feet to a metal bed, and cut off all her hair.

The slam of the heavy door of her room sounded like a death toll, the click of the lock, terrifying. They imprisoned her, caged and chained, alone—in the Black.

Part 3 - The In Betweens

January 6, 997 ME (Twelve Years into Rebellion)

Just a Dream - Bethlehem, Pennsylvania - Esmeralda

Twenty-two-year-old Esmeralda ben Claude sat straight up in bed and screamed, "No!" Tangled in blankets, she punched at the air, fighting invisible hands that restrained her.

Her roommate registered her displeasure at being awakened by rolling over in a grumpy thrash of squeaking bedsprings and bulk.

"Sorry, sorry... bad dream," Esmeralda sputtered, as fragments of the nightmare shattered like broken glass. Covering her ears, she tried to silence the echoes of a man's defiant shouts as black robed figures forced him into a dungeon cell.

Untwisting the sheets, she resettled herself, rolling toward the cinderblock wall, trying to slow her breathing. As the night terror faded and rationality returned, she unclenched her fists and closed her eyes, reasoning a recent article about

Prince Peter ben Korah, celebrating his nineteenth birthday, must have prompted the night terror. That was why her brain superimposed his face over her fear of being seized and bound against his will. She shuddered and whispered into her flat pillow, "It was nothing, not real."

But tomorrow her roommate might mention it in group, so Esmeralda had to come up with something innocuous, normal. Her court hearing was in six weeks, and no nightmare was going to keep her from getting out of this place, none. Tracing the rough surface of the cinderblock, she decided to say she dreamed she showed up at her new job without her pants. The psychiatrist would interpret that as subconscious worry about life on the outside, feeling unprepared for what lay ahead.

No power on Earth could make her divulge the truth, that she dreamed of the Witch, heard her voice, saw her skeletal face, and watched her order the Prince of Alanthia chained to a wall and injected with drugs. That was crazy, and Esmeralda had to convince everyone that term no longer applied to her.

February 14, 997 ME

Cured - Allentown, Pennsylvania - Esmeralda

"Upon careful examination of the evidence and under the recommendation of her attending physician, I hereby rule that Miss Esmeralda ben Claude is no longer a danger to herself or society and order her released from the Pennsylvania Institute for the Insane. Good luck, young lady." The gavel banged.

Esmeralda was free.

Julianna shot to her feet, pulling Esmeralda into a hug, smothering her with kisses. Claude wrapped his muscular arms around mother and daughter, weeping openly. They stood together in the courtroom, rejoicing. Their long ordeal was finally over.

Finally extricating herself, Esmeralda wiped away tears and grasped Doctor Allison ben Whitaker's hands. "Thank you. Thank you for everything."

Doctor Allison smiled in genuine delight and whispered in a cracked voice, "You worked hard, Esmeralda. I've never seen someone so determined to get better. Never be ashamed of what you accomplished, there are few who leave behind a lifetime of mental illness as you have." Her chin quivered. "I am so proud of you."

"I could not have done it without you, Doctor Allison." She tapped her chin, trying not to cry but overcome with emotion. "I would still be so lost and confused if you had not come along."

Julianna and Claude stood arm in arm, beaming with pleasure. "Doctor, we have our daughter back, thanks to you." Julianna leaned her head against Claude's shoulder and gave a watery smile.

Doctor Allison nodded graciously. "It was my pleasure. Esmeralda is one of those patients who reminds us why we got into medicine." She turned in reluctant parting and directed her words to Esmeralda. "You call me if you need me. Day or night, I will always be there for you."

Esmeralda sniffed, pulling at a lock of hair. "I appreciate that, but I am sure I will be just fine." She drew back her shoulders, straightened her spine, and turned to her mother and father. "Let's go."

Get Out of My Dreams and Into My Car - New York City - Esmeralda

The car ride did it; she was certain of it. There was no other logical explanation as to why she dreamed she was riding with Prince Peter, escaping the Palace in a sleek black sports car, no other reason at all.

If she were honest, she had a crush on the Prince and followed him closely the four and a half years she spent institutionalized. Reading material at the asylum was always in short supply, and newspapers often featured stories about him. His glamorous life, good looks, and boyish charm endeared him to the entire female population of Alanthia. Esmeralda was no different, and she liked that about herself. It felt normal.

That was why she dreamed about him, did so regularly, had for years. She simply wished he was kissing her, not floating in the air and being spun around, or seized by men in black robes and drugged.

As hard as she tried, remnants of the old Esmeralda emerged occasionally, especially at night. However, she would never tell a single soul that little nugget because Esmeralda ben Claude had worn her last pair of beige pajamas.

Role Play - New York City - Thaddeus

Thaddeus ben Todd stood at the window of his forty-second-floor apartment looking out at the New York skyline with a glass of wine dangling from his hand. But he did not see the lights or glimmering monuments, he practiced blanking his mind, thinking about nothing, because if he examined what he was about to do, he might pick up the phone and call it off.

It was a joke, or at least it started out that way, by accident, or so he tried to convince himself. One lonely night in June of '92, when he could no longer bear it, he picked up a curly-haired, high-priced prostitute in a hotel bar. He'd not lain with a woman since his wife died five years before, but he was a man and had needs. However, in the throes of passion, it was not Olivia's name he called out, it was Esmeralda's.

He tried to forget her, tried to put her out of his mind. He threw himself into his work and played a lot of basketball. But about once a quarter he did it again. At first, it swamped him with shame and self-loathing, but as the years passed, it was what it was, he liked what he liked, and he stopped punishing himself for it. The irony that the east coast Director of the Criminal Investigative Unit of the FBI regularly procured prostitutes and had them role play was not lost upon him.

He steadfastly refused to investigate what had become of Esmeralda, determined when he left Rephidim that he would not return. He told her to move on with her life, and he let her. He figured she was married by now, maybe with a child or two, curly headed kids with big blue eyes and bright smiles… but they were not his.

He had a wife, had a family, but no more—not to be. Thaddeus, the rising political star, and man about town, was dead, buried with them. Yet he carved out a decent life for himself, albeit a solitary one, and he was resigned to his life as a bachelor.

Turning away from the window, he poured another glass of wine. The doorbell rang, and he took a long drink. When he opened the door, she was the type: tall, lean, blue eyes, and curly hair. "Hello, Esmeralda. It's nice to see you again."

April 12, 997 ME

Beulah - Pepperwood Ranch, California - Persa, James, and Peter

"Are you ready?" Persa asked, floating into Peter's bedroom at Pepperwood.

Peter turned away from the study of his reflection and grinned.

"Well, that's inventive," she said, smiling at his attempted disguise. Sunglasses shaded his emerald eyes, and a cowboy hat pulled over his forehead covered his long blond hair. He was still too thin, but no longer emaciated like two months ago, though the custom made jeans hung low on his hips. His well-worn boots cost as much as one of her stallions, and the diamond and gold watch on his wrist could have put a down payment on their entire ranch. "But they are still going to recognize you."

"It will not matter, Pers, even if they do."

She sighed, knowing he was right. "You'll cause a stir."

Peter shrugged. "There is nothing unusual about that."

James came in from the hall and kissed her cheek. "You smell nice, Fey." He gave her a twirl, appreciating the view of her in the mint green party dress. "And you look grand, too."

She batted her eyes and said, "You don't look too bad yourself, Jay."

He flashed her a toothy grin that creased the sun lines around his eyes. Ironed and pressed, James wore a blue and gray plaid shirt and new jeans, rancher's attire.

"If you two are done flirting with each other, I think we better go, or we will be late to the ceremony. If I know Mack, it will start promptly." Peter put his wallet in his back pocket and ushered them out the door.

James gave him the once over. "You know they are going to recognize you."

Peter threw up his hands in exasperation. "Yes, of course they will recognize me, but there is nothing untoward about me attending the wedding of the man who has guarded me for the last seven years."

James harrumphed but made no further comment as he descended the steps.

"Besides," Peter put an affectionate arm around Persa's shoulders, "all eyes will be on the bride and this lovely little lady right here. Persa, you look amazing."

She tilted her pointed chin up at him, her face shining with pleasure. "Thank you, Peter."

His dimple showed as he pulled her tight with a playful squeeze.

"James, I forgot the lemon bars. Will you run back into the kitchen and fetch them?" Persa batted her eyelashes and smiled.

"Yes, dear." James obliged and left Peter and Persa by the truck while he quick-stepped back to the house.

"We could take my car," Peter said, eyeing James' old pickup truck dubiously.

Persa snorted and jumped in, sliding to the middle of the bench seat. "Then they will recognize you for sure. How many of those vehicles have they made... four?"

The corner of Peter's mouth twitched. "I have no idea."

"Shut up, brat." She patted the seat beside her. "Get in. It won't kill you to take a ride in old Beulah."

"It is not vanity, Pers. I would just as soon not have a spring bugger me."

Persa bounced on the seat, which squeaked under her scant weight. "See, perfectly safe. No buggery."

"Ha!" Peter teased. "If a spring broke loose, it would launch you out of the windshield of this hunk of junk, all ninety-five pounds of you."

She settled herself with the imperious grace of a princess, turned her nose up, and declared, "Ninety-seven, mister." James came around the driver's side and handed her the plate of lemon bars. Persa tattled, "Prince d'Or is too snooty to ride in Beulah."

"Oh, for pity's sake." Peter jumped in the truck and pulled the passenger door shut with a bang. A piece of trim fell onto his boot. He turned a condescending, raised eyebrow on Persa. "Lovely vehicle."

"She gets the job done." James gave the dash a friendly pat and started the loud engine.

The tinny radio sprang to life. "This is Baby Elvis coming to you live from the Underground Cave. Up next, this gem is getting requests from all over, mined from our exclusive source of Last Age music, *The Fighter.*"

"Oh, I love this song!" James turned it up. "Fey, you always said this to me when we were vaulting."

Persa danced in her seat as James sang he would not let her fall. Midway through, Persa picked up the female stanzas and belted them out. Their love of performance rose out of the past, and James and Persa had a blast.

Peter watched their playful banter with a grin. James rarely showed this side of his personality, usually only with

Persa, and he felt privileged to be included in their tight knit little family.

The wedding offered a rare day away from the ranch. But after nursing him for months, their celebratory anticipation of Mack and Lavinia's wedding bordered on giddiness. They all needed this. Bouncing down the road in an ancient truck with the two people he loved most in the world, Peter vowed to enjoy himself. He had one last day in the shelter and safety of Pepperwood.

He was leaving tomorrow.

The negotiations for his return to the Palace had concluded. Mack was safe from Korah's revenge for the role he played in Peter's escape. However, Peter knew he headed back into the devil's den without his stalwart protector; but armed with a daring plan that with enough luck would send the devils back where they belonged.

Best Man - Redding, California - Thaddeus and Mack

"Are you nervous?" Thaddeus asked.

Mack snapped out of his absent pacing with a start. "Hell, yes. Weren't you when you married Olivia?"

Thaddeus' mouth quivered. "I had the runs for two days."

Mack burst out laughing. "Gah, you sounded just like him when you said that."

Thaddeus grinned. "That's why I said it."

Mack pursed his lips and closed his eyes, remembering his best friend. He swallowed thickly and murmured, "Thank you for standing in for him."

"It's my honor, Mack. You honored my brother, naming your son after him."

"Thaddeus, he was the best friend I ever had. Still, to this day, I consider Richard my best friend." Mack's gaze did not waiver. "I only regret—"

Thaddeus held up his hand. "No, Mack. Not on your wedding day, not when you are marrying that amazing creature. Not today, we don't mourn today."

Mack closed his eyes and took a fortifying inhale. "You're right."

"I know it." Thaddeus nodded resolutely. "This life is a bitch. Take these days, these rare happy days, and cherish them, so on the bad days, you can take them out, unwrap them, and remember." Thaddeus rose and went to the door. "Now, come on, let's get you a good memory."

Wine Country Shindig

Prince Peter was correct. No one had eyes for anyone save the bride the day Mack and Lavinia got married. Lavinia ben Anthony was a stunner, even in her everyday attire of long flowing gypsy skirts and off the shoulder peasant blouses, but she was exquisite in white beaded silk. The simple dress, short sleeved and slim, fell just above her knee and showcased her amazing legs and beautiful olive skin.

Mack grinned from the front of the little chapel like he won the lottery. In a blinding moment of realization, Peter understood the magnitude of the sacrifices Mack had made for him. Heretofore an abstract thing, his mind had been too full of his own trials, plans, and pain to seriously consider it. He had not known in '92 when they left Redding that Mack was in love with Lavinia. He and Mack did not have that type of relationship back then, or even now. Sitting in the last pew, with a cowboy hat pulled low over his forehead, it hit him how much Mack's service cost the bride and groom, and what their future involvement with him might cost them yet.

Persa held James' hand, her attention fixed on the preacher's words. Peter's heart twisted, watching her. Resolute determination to keep Persa and James out of The Resistance cemented in his mind. They would be safe. He would protect them and Pepperwood with his life, not simply because he loved them, but for his own sanity. There had to be somewhere he could just be Peter. To date, the only place and the only people who knew that man were right beside him, here.

He reached down and took Persa's free hand.

She brought it to her lips in a kiss, then did the same with James', pressing them both to her heart, and smiling contentedly. "My boys," she whispered.

Peter closed his eyes, absorbing the moment. He was going to need it where he was headed.

The reception proved completely foreign to Peter. Affairs in the royal household and his high-flying social strata did not involve lemon bars nor anything remotely resembling a covered dish. Not that he did not enjoy himself, he simply felt as if they had dropped him into a strange land. Semi-silent whispers confirmed what James and Persa predicted; he was discovered. When it became conspicuous to leave his sunglasses on, he took them off and confirmed what they all suspected. Prince d'Or was at the wedding.

To their credit, they did their best to pretend he was any other guest. Persa guarded him like a mother hen, and Nathan ben Henry, assuming his role as Peter's Head of Security, scowled at anyone that came too close. Peter found it a refreshing change from the glamorous set he usually ran with and did not have many chances to be among them, his people, Alanthians. One day he might rule them, and as much as he railed against it, the prospect remained a distinct possibility. He would do well to take this opportunity to get to know them, if he could, if they would let him.

When James pulled Persa to the dance floor, he ambled over to the groom, who stood with a group of neighbors, talking about wine. "Mack, will you introduce me to your friends?"

Mack gave him a knowing smile. He approved. "With pleasure, my Esteemed. Gentlemen, may I present Prince Peter ben Korah?"

Study in the Park

"I attended one of your shows last month in New York." Thaddeus sidled up to the bar beside the artist, Filippo ben Vincente.

Filippo turned in surprise, a grin spreading across his handsome Italian face. "Is that so?" An exuberant wave of his hand motioned the bartender over. "Wine, here, for my friend." His eyes sparkled at Thaddeus. "I buy you a bottle, if you bought a painting, eh?"

Thaddeus chuckled. "I cannot afford your paintings, Mr. ben Vincente. I was merely there as an admirer of your work."

Filippo bowed graciously. "Very kind of you to say. You have a favorite?"

Thaddeus pressed his lips into a flat smile. "Study in the Park."

"Ah! The curly-haired girl reading her book, such hair she had." Filippo opened his palms. "She was a beautiful, eh?"

Thaddeus made a breathless laugh. "Yes, she was."

Vindicated

"Hello, puppy." A sultry voice tickled Peter's ear.

A deep chuckle began in his chest. Only one person called him that, and he remembered her well. He tilted his head back and said with a grin, "Hello, Kayah."

"Not your usual scene, I dare say." She lifted an eyebrow at her surroundings. "You don't strike me as the barbeque type."

"The barbeque is actually quite good. Did you have some?"

She waved a hand in bored dismissal. "Perhaps I am not the barbeque type."

Peter laughed, "You are a bigger snob than I am."

"Ha! Please…" Humor danced in her hazel eyes. "It's rather charming actually, if you are into covered dishes." She sat down beside him, slinky in her thousand-shekel pantsuit. "I think there is a gelatin mold over there."

"I believe it is an aspic," Peter said drolly.

"Vile," Kayah intoned.

"Well, did you bring the caviar, Princess?" Peter teased.

"As a matter of fact, I have some in my purse. I figured you might be starving to death, and perhaps I could earn a commendation for extraordinary services to the kingdom." She patted the beaded clutch at her side.

"I venture there is more than caviar in that purse, Kayah." Prince Peter ben Korah had done a bit of checking up on Kayah ben Samuel.

She looked him up and down. "With you around? No way. I'm cautious around you royals, a brutal lot, vipers, to the last one of you." She winked then, her gaze resting on the radiant bride. "Besides, it would be exceedingly bad form to be ejected from my best friend's wedding."

Peter regarded the groom and said, "I do not believe Agent Mack would throw you out, that would dampen his wedding night."

Kayah gave him a knowing grin. "Agent Hottie over there does not look like he would have any such qualms." She sent Nathan a flirty little finger wave. "I wonder if he remembers me?"

"He better." Peter was serious. "If he does not, he has no business taking Mack's place." He reached out and toyed with her hair, a lecherous grin spreading across his face. "I must say, the blonde is becoming. Perhaps we should pick up where we left off last time now that you are no longer a redhead."

Kayah narrowed her brows and said, "Sorry, puppy, that ship has sailed."

Peter shrugged, humor dancing in his green eyes. "You cannot blame me for trying. I have been in a bit of a drought lately."

When James and Persa returned from the dance floor, Persa glanced between them, silently asking if she needed to run interference. Peter made an imperceptible shake of his head.

Kayah did not miss the interplay.

Peter rose and said, "Kayah ben Samuel, may I present my friends, Persa ben Yereq and James ben Kole, proprietors of the famed Pepperwood Stables."

They shook hands, and Kayah settled back in the chair beside Peter, with Persa and James sitting opposite them.

James repeated her name, trying to jog his memory. "I believe Peter has mentioned you before?"

Persa gave James a big-eyed stare that told him to shut up. In Peter's delirium, he called her Kayah several times, usually in conjunction with the phrase that he did not want to kiss her. "I think it was Lavinia, James," she said, trying to cover the awkward moment. Turning to Kayah, she said, "You are one of her dearest friends, are you not?"

Kayah raised a golden brow at Peter in speculation, then turned back to Persa and answered politely, "I am."

Persa studied the gorgeous woman, as out of place and conspicuous as Peter, wearing her expensive sage pant suit and five-hundred-shekel shoes. She plucked at a stray thread on her mint green dress, purchased off the discount rack two seasons ago, her strappy sandals picked up from Mil-Mart. Tucking an errant lock of hair behind her ear, she felt outclassed and self-conscious.

An uncomfortable silence descended on the foursome, worlds colliding. Peter rose and offered a hand to Kayah. "Shall we dance?"

Kayah regarded him with an amused lift of her brow. He was an incorrigible little shit, but she remembered the night they danced with fondness and accepted his invitation. The crowd parted as they made their way to the dance floor, both stunning in their blond elegance.

The lead singer of the band nodded toward Peter and asked. "Do you have a request, my Esteemed?"

With the aplomb of a lifetime spent in the spotlight, Peter flashed his famous smile, and everyone quieted as Kayah slipped to the sidelines. "Please join me in offering my sincere congratulations to the bride and groom." Applause broke out, glasses raised, and a shuffling of chairs sounded as everyone rose. "I would like to express my appreciation for the years of loyal service and sacrifice these two have made for the Kingdom of Alanthia. Many of you might not know that Mack was forced to delay joining Lavinia while fulfilling his duty as my Head of Security in the Royal Guard." Peter closed his eyes and nodded toward his trusted bodyguard. "Thank you."

With a few carefully chosen words, Peter exonerated Mack and changed his neighbors' perception, justifying his delay in joining Lavinia and Richard.

"Agent Mack ben Robert saved my life on multiple occasions, the first time when I was twelve, and most recently, about two months ago." Peter swallowed hard. "The Palace will not be the same without you, Mack, but I wish you many years of blessings and happiness."

He gestured for Mack and Lavinia to come forward. Mack's color heightened, and Lavinia blushed with pride and pleasure. They embraced, and the guests broke into thunderous applause.

Peter turned to the band. "Do you know, '*Love Me if You Can?*' It has always reminded me of Mack, and I think it is a fitting tribute."

Peter moved to stand beside Kayah as Mack and Lavinia swayed, dancing alone to the poignant song.

Kayah's expression was unreadable. Without looking at him, she cleared her throat and said, "Every time I meet you, you surprise me."

Peter grinned. "I am a selfish bastard. That was purely for show."

"Good show," she deadpanned, then added, "Thank you for doing that. She had to sell her bar over the scandal."

Peter pitched his voice low, for her ears only. "James told me last week." He nodded toward Lavinia's mother, who was wrestling with baby Richard. "He is a cute kid."

Kayah sniffed, a secret smile hovering in the corner of her full mouth. "You know they conceived him the night we all went out dancing?"

"That was a good evening all the way around, was it not?" Peter pulled her to the dance floor as the dedication ended. "Come on, Kayah. Let's show these country folks how the big city parties."

Himari and Filippo strolled out to meet them. Gus got the attention of the sound engineer and slipped him a shining CD, labeled in his exacting handwriting: Dance Music–Mack and Lavinia's Wedding. With a nod, the engineer slid the CD into the player and Mack and Lavinia's wedding turned from a wine country shindig into a full on California dance party.

Namesake

Thaddeus ben Todd was never one for dancing. He liked kids though, and when Lavinia's mother Violet looked like she had enough, he took the squirming baby off her hands. Richard stared at him with the biggest brown eyes he had ever seen. His mop of curly hair lay damp against his forehead, sweaty after the struggle he put up against his grandmother. Drool covered his chin. Thaddeus wiped a finger on his slacks and rubbed it against a swollen gum. Richard bit down enthusiastically, and Thaddeus grinned.

"Good evening," James sat down in the chair beside Thaddeus, "Nice wedding."

Thaddeus wiped Richard's chin with the elbow of his sleeve and said, "It is, and I believe this little guy is tired."

James cast an eye to see where Persa was, and finding her back turned, he leaned in and gave the baby a tickle on his chubby tummy. "He's cute."

Thaddeus beamed. "He's named after my brother."

"Is that right?" James cocked his head in interest.

"He is." A shadow crossed Thaddeus' face. "He died in a raid, going after the men who killed that young man's mother." Thaddeus nodded toward Peter, who was dancing with an amazing looking blonde woman.

James stiffened. "Indeed? I'm sorry for your loss."

Thaddeus shifted Richard to his other knee and said, "Thank you. He was the groom's best friend. I'm merely a placeholder today."

James looked up at the sky. "I've got a brother. I can't imagine life without him." The two men sat in silence for a bit, the reception in full swing around them.

Baby Richard fell against Thaddeus' chest with a grunt, sucking his left thumb.

"I'm James ben Kole, by the way. The pretty lady in green is my wife, Persa."

"The one dancing with the Prince?"

James craned his neck, looking through the crowd and said, "No, the little one with the strawberry blonde hair."

Thaddeus wrapped his left hand around Richard and offered his right. "Thaddeus ben Todd, nice to meet you, James ben Kole."

James smiled and shook his hand.

Thaddeus wrinkled his forehead, studying James. "Ben Kole? You say you have a brother? He wouldn't happen to be a tall, skinny, white-haired guy, would he?"

James lit up. "That sounds like Ian."

"I'll be damned. I've met your brother. That's one hungry son of a bitch."

Richard pulled his thumb out of his mouth and smiled lazily. "Damn, sum bitch."

Thaddeus clapped his hand over his mouth, trying to stifle a laugh.

James fought for control over his face with his shoulders shaking. "You have definitely met Ian."

"I always wondered what happened to him. Where is he now?"

James settled back in his chair, proud. "He's working with street kids in the New City and New Orleans."

"Is that so? Is he in the New City now? I've got business in town while I'm here, and I'd like to look him up. He did me a solid a few years ago."

"As far as I know, he's in the New City right now. That's where he's based, but he travels between the two centers."

Thaddeus nodded thoughtfully. He supervised a unit that specialized in missing and abducted children. It might be worth more than nostalgia to reconnect with Ian ben Kole. Looking out at the dance floor, contemplating this thought, Prince Peter swung the pretty blonde around on his arm and a jolt of recognition hit Thaddeus.

"What the hell is she doing here?" Thaddeus looked around, trying to spot Violet.

"Who?" James inquired.

Thaddeus' eyes never left Kayah. "Someone I have been trying to meet for a very long time. If you'll excuse me, Mr. ben Kole? It's been nice chatting with you."

Mutual Interests

"Hello, Kayah," Thaddeus said, lounging against the wall outside the bathroom where he cornered his quarry.

She struck a sultry pose. "Hello, Thaddeus." Kayah stalked toward him, graceful as a cat. "Or do you prefer, Director?"

"Thaddeus will do. We are at a social engagement, are we not?"

She lifted her eyebrows, considering him. "We are." He was meticulously handsome, in a strait-laced, square jawed, cop sort of way, not a hair out of place, but he had the most enticing vertical groove between his nose and upper lip that begged for kisses, and no flabby desk body hid beneath his well-tailored suit.

Thaddeus chuckled. She radiated sex appeal; dangerous and dark, juxtaposed against golden elegance.

Heat passed between them, mutual desire.

"It surprised me to find you here, not your normal environment."

Kayah shrugged noncommittally. "For one night, I can fit in just about anywhere."

"I suppose we have that in common." Thaddeus let his eyes travel the length of her in masculine appreciation. "Among other things."

Kayah moistened her lips, the gloss shimmering in the dim light. "What sort of things… Director?"

Thaddeus closed the gap between them, his body mere inches from hers. She was the prime suspect in four ongoing investigations, yet there was not a shred of evidence to justify his office even bringing her in for questioning. "I think you know, Kayah."

A long talon stroked the edge of his jaw. "I know a lot of things," she cooed and brought her finger back, licking it.

He growled as lust exploded in his loins. Her legendary reputation did not even begin to encompass the living, breathing reality of her. "I suspect you do."

The door at the end of the hallway opened, shattering the moment. Persa looked between the two, and her face flamed. "Pardon me, I need the loo."

Thaddeus and Kayah broke apart to let Persa pass, muttering apologies as she did.

The corner of Kayah's mouth lifted. "Saved by a little green fairy. Good night, Director."

Journals - New York City - Esmeralda

"It's getting late, Esmeralda. Do you want to walk out with me or are you staying?" Doctor Moreh ben Sephar, the library supervisor, asked.

Bleary eyed and distracted, Esmeralda realized Doctor Moreh had spoken but was so engrossed in her work she did not process the words. "I'm sorry, what did you say?"

He smiled with fond understanding. "I said, it is late. You should walk out with me. Go home, get some food, it will be here tomorrow."

Still lost in the Trumpet Judgments of the Last Age, she blinked at the big clock on the wall, 10:45 pm. "I didn't realize it was so late."

"The sign of a true researcher," he chuckled, then gestured for her. "Come now, I dislike leaving you here by yourself."

Esmeralda rested a gloved finger on the journal she was transcribing, considering his proposal. The letters wavered and an old rule came into her mind, 'Do not push past physical limits—eat—sleep.'

"Yes, sir. I am coming." She closed the ancient book and placed it in its protective cover. When she rose, her body protested, semi-frozen in a study position.

Moreh waited while she gathered her things. "You know, you do not have to stay in the basement. You can bring your work upstairs. There are no windows down here. Doesn't that get depressing?"

Esmeralda smiled. "I don't mind it. I like the smell."

As they topped the stairs, she gestured to the empty desks in the main library. "Besides, the people up here would distract me."

"Alas, the life of a researcher. You are very talented and have done amazing work since you joined us." He smiled, his eyes full of regret. "But don't end up like me, with nothing but books and no one to go home to."

His melancholy transmitted to her, and she confessed, "I had someone once." Making a small snort of self-recrimination, she added, "I found out last week, he lives here, but I haven't gone to see him."

Moreh locked the staff entrance door and took her elbow as they entered the side alley. Though old and frail, he served as protector in the heart of New York City. "You should get up the courage to seek him out. You are too young to spend your entire life in the basement."

Esmeralda stared at the glass high rise around the corner from the library. She walked past it every day and never failed to watch, hoping for a glimpse of his tall form. To date, she hadn't seen him, but each morning and each evening she took this route. "It was a long time ago, Professor."

He scoffed, "Pshaw! How long could it have been, you are but a child?"

"Well, sir, it might surprise you." She flashed him a toothy grin and kept walking.

June 30, 997 ME

Hellish Week

Esmeralda descended the library stairs on trembling knees, refusing to equate these steps with the dark stone passageways in her dreams. "They are not real! Not real!" Her hand shook, and she steadied it with an iron will. The comforting smell of old books greeted her, not sulfur, not copper blood—vellum!

She reasoned the anniversary of her final break from reality triggered the nightmare, five years since she descended into knife wielding madness in her aunt's kitchen, that and too many articles about Prince Peter and his betrothal to Princess Keyseelough of Egypt. The papers and celebrity gossip magazines went into frenzied back-to-back coverage during the weeklong celebration. Like the rest of Alanthia, the spectacle swept Esmeralda away. It was a fairytale story of a handsome Prince and beautiful Princess, in love and engaged to be married. For the shy, quiet researcher, it was a simple, normal fantasy, a healthy fascination with the royal couple, like everyone else. Except everyone else did not dream the things she dreamed, dark rituals and chants, hooded cloaks and blood, the Witch behind it all, dancing with delight.

Esmeralda sat at her desk, determined to end this once and for all. First, she would stop walking by Thaddeus' building every day. The crushing disappointment of never spotting him was detrimental to her recovery. She should never have looked him up, if she did not know where he lived, perhaps she could finally put him out of her mind.

Second, she vowed to stop buying those magazines, stop reading articles, and stop paying attention to the life of Prince Peter ben Korah, because if she did not, she might just find herself back in the hospital, raving like a lunatic.

She had to stop thinking about, no, she mentally corrected herself, obsessing over two men she could never have because they existed in fantasy land. She might have moved on if it weren't for those dreams, false memories, and damnable delusions with their smells, sounds, tastes, feelings, and fears. They seemed so incredibly real, but they were not. They could not be.

Pushing the troubling thoughts aside, she pulled out the fascinating journal she was transcribing. Diving in, she immersed herself in the days after the fifth Trumpet Judgment, and the brilliant mind of a computer scientist from Silicon Valley, Professor Slater. After months of study, Esmeralda simply referred to her by her given name, Erica.

September 2, 998 ME

A Favor

That was it, merely a favor, something she owed Aunt Jean. She repeated it like a mantra, just a favor, one she would grant because she felt obliged. Esmeralda looked at the letter for the dozenth time in a week. She knew the words and the pleas contained therein would not change, yet she read it again.

Dearest Esmeralda,

I hope this letter finds thee well and enjoying thy job in New York. Julianna tells me it is a good position, well suited for thy talents and skills, since research and reading have always been thy love. I know thee will prosper among the books and ancient manuscripts, though I know Julianna misses thee and wishes thee would return to Rephidim. A mother never truly lets go of her children, and her worry over thee in that vast place, alone, troubles her.

'Tis for that reason, I write today, to plead for thy help. Elizabeta and her friend, Jenny ben Rip, ran away from Bezetha four weeks past. We have searched hither and yon, without sight of them. Thy cousin has been much distressed these last nine months, since her long-time beau and his family left to emigrate to the Golden Kingdom. Elizabeta has been inconsolable over the loss of Jeremiah. I fear she and her friend have taken a wild notion to seek the wonders of the New City, against the staunch objections of her father and me.

The local authorities helped in the initial search, but we have been unable to persuade them to expand it beyond the region, and I fear for their safety. Yoder is much recovered, but the doctor says he will never be free from his blinding headaches, and thus, our ability to chase after them is severely limited. Jenny's family seems to be well rid of her, though I cannot conceive how they can so blithely dismiss the disappearance of their own in such a manner.

Which, dear Niece, brings me to the crux of the matter, to ask of thee a favor, that thou might seek thy old acquaintance, Thaddeus ben Todd and request his assistance in tracking down Elizabeta and Jenny. His position within the FBI gives him access to resources we could not hope to procure in the search. I understand it is a lot to ask of thee. Julianna tells me thou hast not had contact with him in many years, but I must weigh that against my fear for my daughter. I beg thee to put aside thy reservations and seek his help on behalf of thy foolish cousin. It may indeed be her only hope.

I have always been fond of thee, Esmeralda, and want thee to know that there was not a day that went by that I did not pray for thee and thy recovery. We are so gratified the Lord heard our prayers. I ask this small favor, that mine own daughter might be restored unto me as you have been to my sister. Thank you, I knowest thou will do what is right.

Love,
Aunt Jean

Esmeralda wanted to crumple the paper and throw it in the trash, she wanted to pretend it never made it to her mailbox. She did not want to seek the man who represented everything she knew about her childhood madness—Thaddeus.

Yet they had been friends, her mother assured her that much was true. She also brought him to Rephidim, deep in grief over the deaths of his family, she now understood the significance of her actions, how it saved him. In that regard, he owed her a favor.

She dressed in blue, defiant that it meant nothing, signified nothing. It was simply a color, and she liked the dress because it set off her eyes. She would at least look her best, not a bedraggled, red-nosed kid, wailing after him as he left her by the waterfall. She was convinced he recognized her madness, even then.

Nine years to the day since he left Rephidim, Esmeralda pushed through the glass door of the lobby of his building and presented herself to the front desk. "My name is Esmeralda, and I am here to see Thaddeus ben Todd." Her voice quivered with trepidation.

The guard looked up from his monitors with a leer. "Don't be so nervous. He's not rough."

Esmeralda blinked in confusion.

Her innocent expression amused him. He gestured to the elevators. "I'll buzz you up, 42A."

She walked on leaden limbs toward the elevators, her mind reeling at how easy it had been. She did not expect him to be home, and even if he was, she expected the guard to call him down or send her away. Instead with a fist that shook like she was about to have a seizure, she rapped on his door.

Confusion clouded his face when he opened it, then he frowned studying her, and seemed to shrug. "Hello, Esmeralda. It's nice to see you again."

Part 4- Over the Rainbow

September 2, 998 ME

Come to Poppa

When Thaddeus opened the door, he realized there had been a miscommunication over when he wanted his next date. Never one to squander good fortune, he stepped aside and let the girl in. She was a damn good facsimile, and he decided not to send her away, not after the week he just put in at work.

"Hello, Thaddeus. It's nice to see you as well," the girl said in a trembling voice.

She was obviously new to this, looking at him without the normal hard-eyed appraisal, but she played the role, and that was good. Aspiring actress, he decided, the city was full of them. He reached out and touched her cheek. A scar marred her beauty, old with a slight pucker at one end. "How did you get that?"

Her fingers fluttered, going to her face. Large slate-blue eyes stared up at him. "Um… a riding accident," she swallowed thickly, "a long time ago."

He nodded and ran a hand up the back of her neck. "Don't be nervous." He brushed his lips against hers in a light kiss. She tasted like lemonade and sunshine, very nice.

She made a small whimpering noise, her breath caught in a shallow gasp.

Thaddeus wrapped his arms around her, drawing her close, molding her body against his own. She was exquisite, a little bustier and taller than Esmeralda, but that suited him just fine. Some of them balked at kissing, but this one did not seem to mind, so he toyed with her, coaxing her to kiss him back.

"Oh, my," she said with a quick indrawn breath, then draped her arms around his neck and kissed him back.

"That's right, honey, very good." He approved of the innocent act and decided this one had a future in acting, the best fake Esmeralda ever, exactly what he fantasized about. Sometimes the role play turned raunchy. Other times it fell flat, and he merely satisfied his basest desires. This girl had the potential for the most potent one—the rare one. He gave it a shot. "You know, I have wanted to do this for a very long time."

She cupped his face, holding it close, staring into his eyes, hers blue and watery. "Me, too."

His heart thundered. Perfect! He reached behind her and loosened her braid. Freeing the locks, running his fingers through the bountiful curls, he groaned, "You haunt me, Esmeralda. Every day I think about you."

Her face screwed up with emotion, she buried it in his chest, shoulders quivering. "I thought you forgot me. I thought it wasn't real."

Thaddeus chuckled, low and deep. He was aflame and wanted this girl in his bed, now. "Does this feel real to you?" He pressed his erection against her.

She gave a little gasp, playing the innocent.

That was his undoing. He paid by the hour, so there was no need to continue dallying with her in the foyer. Thaddeus scooped her up and carried her to the bedroom. She looked around nervously, her body trembling. "Don't be scared. I won't hurt you," he soothed.

He laid her down and stretched out beside her, running a hand up her leg.

She shook her head, breathless at his touch. "I know you won't."

He caressed the silky skin of her inner thigh, and she tried to close her legs, drawing up with a gasp.

"Shh, let me."

The little whore looked terrified. What an actress.

"I want to touch you," he whispered, nuzzling her cheek, kissing the old scar.

She closed her eyes and rubbed her face against his, relaxing. "Okay."

Running his fingers through her springy mass, he found her hot and dewy. "So nice." He smothered her jolt with a kiss, driving his tongue deep into her mouth, teasing and toying with her delicate mound, arousing her.

She made a little feminine sigh of pleasure and moved her hips, seeking his touch.

He groaned and rose from the bed, shedding his clothes. "Take off your dress, Esmeralda. I want to see your body."

"Thaddeus, what are you doing?" She blinked up at him, desire and shock reflected in her big blue eyes.

"I am going to make love to you." He pulled her up and lifted the dress over her head, kissing away her fears.

She stood before him in a white bra and hip hugger panties, no sexy lace or whore's drapery. She was utter perfection, long limbed, brown skinned, stunning. "You are beautiful," he murmured.

She moistened her lips and reached out a finger to touch him. "As are you."

He unsnapped her bra, revealing her lovely young breasts, pert with rose-brown nipples, exactly how he imagined. The sight sent him spiraling backward, toward the place he kept hidden, where he banked fierce longing and quashed secret desire. "Oh, baby," he breathed, brushing his cheek against her breast. She smelled clean, like linen and paper. She arched her back when he caressed her nipple. It pebbled to a hard peak as he suckled. Pulling her deep in his mouth, he thought he might die from this sensation.

"I have to have you." He slid the panties down her long legs and lifted her onto the bed.

"You want me?"

Gripped with an absolute frenzy of lust, he transitioned in his mind, fully embracing the fantasy, as deep as he had ever gone. Positioned between her thighs, he lost all pretext that she was a whore. She became Esmeralda to him. He pushed at her entrance, slick and wet, delicate and tight. "Esmeralda," he rocked against her seeking admittance, "open your legs for me, let me inside. Let me touch you. Let me love you."

"Thaddeus, Thaddeus…" Tears rolled into her hair, and she did as he bid her.

With infinite slowness, he pressed into her. She met him, seeking. She was so tight, he thought he might explode before he even took her, but as her body adjusted to him, he lost control, coming into her with a hard thrust.

Then he froze.

His body stiffened with shock. She cried out in pain and arched; her eyes squeezed shut. He did not move. "Good God Almighty, you're a virgin."

"Of course, I am. There was never anyone else. I told you that day over eclairs, you were going to be my husband."

He instantly went flaccid, flying off her as if she burned him.

"What? What did I do? Oh no, what did I say?" She recoiled, curling into herself.

Thaddeus gripped the sides of his head and looked down on her in horror. Her blood was on his body, his filthy, vile, traitorous body. "Holy shit!"

That set her off. She scrambled from the bed, reaching frantically for her clothes, sobbing.

Reason, or a semblance of it returned, and he took her shoulders, forcing her to face him as he fell to his knees in front of her. "Stop, stop! This is my fault. You did nothing wrong."

She turned away, trying to hide her face and cover her breasts at the same time. "Then why did you quit? Why did you look at me that way?" She pushed at him, panicked. "I'm sorry I said that about the eclairs. I know it wasn't real. Sometimes I remember things that didn't happen. I'm sorry."

He blinked at her in confusion. With a gentle hand, he turned her delicate chin toward him and wiped a tear from her eye. "What are you talking about, Esmeralda? We ate eclairs the day you told me I was going to be your husband."

Her eyes popped open, her expression one of utter astonishment. "I did?"

Very slowly he nodded, sensing this was of more importance than anything he had ever done. She was no fantasy. "You did, and then you followed me around for two-and-a-half years, until I fell so hopelessly in love with you that I had to leave."

She pressed her lips together so hard they turned white. "You loved me? I didn't imagine that? I didn't make it up?"

Thaddeus cupped her face, her precious face, a wave of tenderness washing over him. He wanted to take away that horrible, bewildered look in her eyes. "No, you did not make that up." He leaned in and brushed a kiss against her trembling lips. "You did not imagine the way I felt for you." He pulled her into the bed beside him, cradling her, kissing away the tears. "The way I… the way I… feel." It was the truth. No matter how hard he fought, he had never gotten over her.

"Thaddeus," she breathed his name and spoke to his heart, "make love to me. Make me real."

"Real?" He stroked a delicate finger over her hip, astounded that he was touching her. "You are real. Heaven help me, you are truly here."

She nodded, looking grave. "My Aunt Jean asked me to come."

The corner of his mouth lifted. "We'll talk about Aunt Jean later. You and I have a very long-awaited assignation in this bed."

The ghost of a smile lit her eyes, the first true spark of the imp he had seen since she walked through his door. Had she looked at him that way at any point before he laid her down, he would have known, would have recognized her, would have known the truth. Yet something had robbed her of that light, that fundamental fire in her eyes, and he wanted to bring it back. Brushing his lips over hers, he murmured, "How old are you now?"

She grabbed the back of his head and smiled. "Twenty-three and a half."

"Oh, that's good." He let her pull him in for a deep kiss, cupping her breast, as lust swamped him anew. "It took you long enough."

Arching her back, she moaned, "It took forever."

He ran his hand down her flat belly, resting it over her womanhood, growling, "No, baby, I've wanted to do this forever." With tender care, he touched her. Soft and slick, her virgin's blood stained the inside of her thighs, precious and pure. A fierce desire seized him, gripping him by his loins. He wanted to possess her, to take her; not some cheap imitation, some perfumed whore playing the role—her!

He drove her mad, teasing and toying with her body. She kicked at the sheets, struggling to take what he gave. "Please," she whimpered. "Please, Thaddeus, make it real."

Braced above her, quaking with desire, he entered her with tender slowness, letting her surround him with her life, her passion. "Real," he breathed and threw back his head in ecstasy.

Carefully, he began to move. He did not close his eyes, neither did she. They held each other's gazes, afraid it might become a dream, a fantasy, a delusion, desperate that it was not.

Her little feminine cries drove him to the brink. She was so tight, and he was so deep inside her that he could not hold back any longer. The orgasm seized him, fierce and primal, right. It swept away any semblance of reason. Shuddering surrender, he pumped a decade's worth of lust, love, and longing into her.

She accepted it, took it, reveled in it, every ounce. Lying beneath him, she offered what always belonged to him, that he never dared take, her heart. Esmeralda, his at last. It was the most fundamental moment of his life.

Covered

She dozed in his arms, trusting and innocent. Thaddeus wrapped a corkscrew curl around his finger and brought it to his nose inhaling her warm, earthy scent. He felt like an ass, ashamed to the core over what he had just done but too sated to care.

No longer blinded by lust, he studied her. Her woman's face was different. The smattering of freckles across the bridge of her nose faded into oblivion. Her cheekbones were high and beautiful, but that scar? He traced its length, touching it. She had been hurt, and no one attended her injury. It had not healed well. How could that have happened? She was supposed to be safe, sheltered in the perfection of Rephidim. But he knew with bone deep certainty that scar was not from Rephidim.

"Who hurt you?" he whispered, stroking her lean arm. He traced his finger over the tendons just below the skin, rip cord and hard, where she should be soft. In the faint city lights streaming through the crack in the bedroom curtains, he saw her ribs. She was thin, as if she did not eat well, did not nourish herself as she should. No one looked like this in Rephidim. They all had a glow of health and vigor. Esmeralda did not. She was lovely, to be sure, but underneath, he could see... something was wrong.

Driven by impulse, he eased out of the bed and went to the top drawer of his dresser. He returned and settled the blanket she had given him over her. Then joining her underneath, its soft length covered them, shielding them from the outside world.

Esmeralda gave a sigh of contentment and snuggled into him. Her eyes fluttered open, and she said dreamily, "Hi."

He kissed the tip of her nose. "Hi, to you."

"You're real." She smoothed the delicate skin under his eye with her thumb.

"I am." He lazed on the pillow, staring into her eyes. "So are you."

She made a breathless snort. "Am I? There are some who might take issue with you over that."

His forehead wrinkled. "Tell me who. I will set them straight."

"Perhaps later." She moistened her lips. "I simply want to lay here and look at you. I want to touch you. I have always wanted to touch you, to run my finger over this widow's peak."

He closed his eyes and smiled.

"I want to smooth your brow that curves down, just at the end, right here." She drew a light circle with the tip of her finger. "I want to know why there are faint blue circles under your eyes." She kissed his cheek gently. "I want to make them go away."

His voice was husky and low. "I've had those blue circles since the day I left you."

"The blues," she whispered on a note of wistful sadness

She looked so forlorn, he wanted to weep. "Esmeralda, what's happened to you, baby?" He shook his head on the pillow and ran his finger around the soft shell of her ear. "Something's hurt you."

She withdrew, the blanket fell away, and a shield went up. "Nothing, I'm fine."

Thaddeus ben Todd, the investigator, knew she was lying, but he also knew when to push and when to back off. He backed off. There would be time enough to discover the source of the pain behind her eyes. Right now, she was naked in his bed. He brought the blanket back over her shoulders and adopted a lazy smile. "You are fine." He wrapped his arms around her waist and pulled tight.

Desire, yet unsatisfied for her, erupted anew, and she wiggled with delight.

He laughed, enjoying her pleasure at his touch. "You know what I am happy about?"

Esmeralda moved her hips against his. "What?" The spark was definitely back.

With a long finger, he traced the cleft of her buttocks. "That I can do this and not go to jail for it."

She slid her leg over his waist, opening to his touch. "I would have let you."

He growled. Fire shot through his body, and he pressed his finger deeper, drawing her close.

She arched into him with a faint mew of pleasure. "I wanted you to touch me. I wanted you to take me."

He shook his head, denying her words. "It was wrong. I couldn't. Oh, Esmeralda, I couldn't. You were just a girl."

With feather light fingers she traced the length of his desire. "No, I was never just a girl. I have always been… yours."

"Mine?" he panted and thrust into her hand.

"And you… have always been mine."

His moan sparked something inside her. Old power surged in her veins, sure and true. For the first time in years, she did not tamp it down, did not deny it, but relished it, embraced it, and let it flow. A lightning storm began to brew. Thunder crashed in the deepest part of her soul. Emboldened, she rolled atop him and braced her hands against his shoulders. Blue fire blazed in her eyes. Her hair fell around her face, wild and glorious, unbound.

He licked his lips, staring up at her.

She saw him, to the depths of his soul, the way she used to. She knew him. He needed her. He had always needed her. "You do not hold back from me any longer, Thaddeus ben Todd." She slid herself along the length of him, teasing, pressing, fanning the flames.

"Vixen!" He grasped her hips and rocked with her.

She leaned forward and bit his neck like a she animal. Primal power and desire rocked her. She took the tip of him, just inside, and withdrew. Pure instinct controlled her movements, and she felt his body grow rigid as she teased him. He made a guttural noise in the back of his throat as she pleasured them both.

He fell under her spell and gave her control. Her nose flared, basking in the power. She took him fully, relishing the stinging pain, the overwhelming need. She rose above him, riding in a rhythm as old as time. He licked his thumb and stroked her delicate place, circling with gentle pressure. She threw back her head and gasped as the intensity built. He matched her rhythm, and guided her with his hands, never stopping that amazing touch of his thumb. The world changed. His thrusts grew faster, deeper, as he tried to reach the very center of her soul.

And then, he did.

It built with wave upon wave of intensity, spasms washing over her, then exploding in a deafening crescendo. As he pumped his seed into her, colors flashed and converged. They swirled into a maelstrom that solidified into a single brilliant source, blinding beauty and power. "Yes!" she cried out and let it crash.

There it was, at last—the left side of White!

Across the kingdom, sitting at a fine table, surrounded by linen and bone china, the Witch fell out of her chair in front of twenty guests. Servants ran to assist, but she shooed them away, accepting the hand of her most trusted underling. As he lifted her to her feet, she grabbed his tie, pulled his ear to her mouth, and hissed, "The White bitch, find her."

Above the forty-second-floor New York apartment, Uriel, the archangel, unsheathed his sword. He sensed them coming, astral projections. Evil people split their spirits from their souls and bodies, flying into the ether to kill and destroy. Wielding malevolent power, they swarmed him, screeching in the spirit, intent on destruction. However, this night, nothing was getting past him. No one, except Thaddeus ben Todd, would touch Esmeralda ben Claude.

September 3, 998 ME

A Good Start to a Relationship

Esmeralda slept... and slept... and slept. At noon, she rolled over, disoriented by her unfamiliar surroundings. She experienced a momentary jolt of panic because the last time she awoke in a strange bed after a sleep like that, she was in a mental institution. But instead of stark gray walls and a thin cot, the warm brown tones of Thaddeus' bedroom enveloped her.

She let out a shuddering gasp and willed her heart to stop pounding. As the fear subsided, she pressed her fingers over her eyes and breathed. A great yawn stilled her movements, and she stretched her body into the sensation. She felt a faint, burning soreness between her legs. Blood rushed to her face as she remembered. She buried her head in the pillow, stifling a groan and a giggle. Had she not found herself in his room, felt the evidence on her body, she might be inclined to think she experienced another powerful delusional episode, this one infinitely more pleasant than the last.

The White.

The thought came to her unbidden. Emotional overload cracked her open last night, and the old Esmeralda leaked out. But in the daylight, she took back her hard-earned control. With practiced determination she squashed the notion, pushed it away. "No… you will not go into that, not now. He is in the next room, and you have a shot. Do not blow it."

Throwing off the blankets, she tiptoed to the bathroom, scanning the floor for her discarded clothing, which was curiously missing. A stack of clean towels sat on the counter, so she wrapped a bath sheet around her body and bathed her face and other parts with an oversized washcloth. Running water over her hands, she tried to tame her wild tangle of curls, wondering where her hairband had disappeared to. Using the bottle of mouthwash under his sink, she gargled and rubbed her finger over her teeth. The alcohol stung her swollen lips, but at least she would not have the breath of a dragon.

His bedroom was pleasantly dark, brown curtains blocked the morning light. He had chosen masculine furnishings, warm and solid. His watch laid on the dresser, his Rephidim blanket over the suede duvet. Resting her hand on the bedpost, she looked down at the king-size bed where they made love last night. There were three drops of blood on the tan sheet where he had taken her virginity. Her face flamed, reliving that insane moment.

"Why did he react that way?" She pulled the blankets over the stain, shaking her head.

She had no choice but to sneak into his closet for something to wear. Masculine cologne hit her as she stepped into his wardrobe. She breathed deeply, a clean fresh scent, but beneath it, him. After a game, he smelled like the outdoors and sweat. That was here. Other times, he smelled like water and fishing—the outdoorsman—that was missing. There was a new smell, wool and paper, the office. She buried her face in one of his suit jackets and in a flash of blinding clarity, the Silver hit her. But it was tarnished silver, hidden, covered.

A shudder ran up her spine, and she jumped back.

She had to get out of this closet. She selected a soft moss green t-shirt from the top of a neat stack and slipped it over her head. The sleeves hung past her elbows and the length hit her mid-thigh. She bolted out of the closet.

Reentering the room, she caught her reflection in the mirror and stopped. Green was a good color on her, though she rarely wore it. It reminded her too vividly of Thyatira, but today that memory did not hurt. She spun around, looking at her legs over her shoulder. They were pale, and the t-shirt looked like a mini-skirt. Light happiness, long forgotten, bloomed in her heart. Her feet sank into his thick, luxurious carpet, and she smiled into the mirror.

"Okay, Esmie. You can do this."

She crept to the door and peeked out. Her heart stopped at the sight of him lounging on the couch, reading the morning paper. He wore loose shorts and an athletic shirt, his old basketball clothes. Her eyes burned with unshed tears and remembrance. She stepped through the door and whispered, "Good morning."

He lowered the paper and sat up, his eyes sweeping her in his shirt. "Good morning, sleepy head."

She bit her lip and looked down, pulling the shirt lower in self-conscious modesty. "I couldn't find my clothes."

He waggled his eyebrows. "I hid them."

Her head snapped up. "You did what?"

He rose and walked toward her, lanky grace and power. "I didn't want you sneaking out while I went to get breakfast." He gestured to a white pastry bag and coffee on the kitchen counter.

"Oh." She moistened her lips, staring up at him. "Not much chance of me going out dressed like this." Not unless she wanted to end up back in beige pajamas, but she did not say that.

He lifted her chin and gazed down at her with hooded eyes. His voice sounded like warm honey. "Exactly my diabolical plan, now that I have you in my clutches." He leaned in for a kiss.

He tasted like coffee and orange juice, brown and orange. Delightful. She stood on tiptoe and met him. Innocent wonder bloomed like a morning glory.

Thaddeus laced his fingers behind her back and smiled in sweet affection. "I still cannot believe you are here."

"I am. Though you didn't seem surprised last night, at least at first."

He wiped at his mouth and cleared his throat, embarrassed. "Yeah, um, about that…" He rubbed the back of his neck. "I'm just glad to see you. How about we leave it at that?"

He was hiding something, but there were things she did not want him to know, things she never wanted him to know, so she dropped it. Esmeralda understood secrets. "I think I can do that, if you can?"

His shoulders relaxed. "I can." He nodded and a slow smile built across his face. "Are you hungry?"

"Food!" Suddenly ravenous, she sashayed into the kitchen. "What did you buy?"

The corner of his lip quivered. "Eclairs."

Her hand stilled halfway to the bag, and she turned slowly. "That's a good start." It hung in the air. She waited to see if he remembered, hoping she had not made it up.

He looked her up and down, then threw back his head and laughed. "Because I've already seen you naked."

She clapped her hand over her mouth and giggled. Relief and mirth washed over her. "Your expression when I said that!"

His chest shook. "It was indeed an interesting way to begin a relationship, Esmeralda."

A tremor of excitement ran up her leg, and her eyes filled with happy tears. "You cannot know, cannot understand, what this means to me."

He dug in the bag and pulled out a sticky eclair, holding it out for her to take a bite. "I think I can."

She took a tentative bite, giggling as the chocolate coated her upper lip. With a flick of her pink tongue, she licked it away.

He groaned, "Vixen."

With a little shake of her shoulders, she did it again and kept her eyes glued to his face. It was like the spark of a match. He dropped the eclair and pulled her to him for a deep kiss of chocolate pastry and creme. Lifting her onto the counter, he stepped between her legs, running rough beard stubble over her sensitive neck. Her hair tangled in his beard, and he pulled away, laughing and sputtering. "This hair!" He dug long fingers in it, massaging her scalp. "It is glorious!"

"It is wretched," she countered.

He fluffed it out, doubling it in size. "No, it is amazing."

"Ah!" She swatted at his hands. "Quit, you'll make it crazy!"

"I like you crazy, Esmeralda. It's part of your charm, always has been."

She startled and drew back. "Don't say that." A faint shudder hit her, and all banter evaporated.

"I was just teasing you."

"Don't!"

I Remember When

Pieces, clues, hints – he gathered and organized them. Running his thumb over her scar, he said, "Okay, I won't."

She turned away and covered the scar with her fingers, refusing to meet his eyes. "Sorry, I can be... I can be a little sensitive."

Tread carefully, his brain screamed into the silence. He did not move, treating her like a frightened animal that would flee at the merest movement. "I see that."

She squeezed her eyes tight. "Darn. I'm sorry."

"Hey, don't." Very gently he drew her chin back toward him.

She kept her eyes closed, her nose flared, and he watched her try to regain her center. "Esmie," he called her by the pet name her mother used, "what happened? How are you here and not at home?"

She tucked her chin, drawing into herself. "Please don't ask me."

If he had not been inches from her, he would not have heard the heartbreak behind her words. He gathered her in his arms, as if she were made of spun sugar. Alarms blared in his mind, and he thought, 'You were supposed to be safe. What the hell have I done by not finding you, and what turned you into this trembling version of yourself?' But he did not speak the words, instinctively knowing she would shut down. Instead, he soothed, "It's all right, Esmeralda. I've got you now."

Her head fell back like a rag doll, and she went limp in his arms, her eyes becoming glassy and unfocused. He saw her slipping away, falling into some dark place, giving over to its power. He wanted to shake her, to snap her out of it, but something warned him against taking that tactic. "Hey, come back to me. It's all right."

She jerked as if she had just grabbed a live wire. Her eyes focused, and she blinked, looking around as if she was not quite sure where she was.

"It's all right," he soothed, watching her, alert.

"Is it?" Her voice sounded tiny and scared. She grasped his shirt and covered her face, hiding again.

Thaddeus recognized her bewilderment, remembered the emotion behind that expression. He knew the pain of being cut in a thousand pieces, bleeding everywhere. She was in-explicably broken, shattered by something, the jagged edges of her pain protruding everywhere. His throat tightened in empathy.

After Olivia and the boys, sometimes he would reach down and try to pick up a piece of himself, but he would pull away when the memories sliced him open. He had known it had to be done, however, knowing and doing were two separate things. In Rephidim, she forced him to do it and been there to bandage him up. He would have bled to death without her.

"Esmeralda, it's all right. You don't have to tell me." He ran a hand over her curls, letting it travel down her back, rubbing in soothing long strokes. "Think about it. How many times did you ask me to tell you about Olivia and the boys?"

She shook her head, still hiding. "I don't know."

"Dozens of times, but I was not ready, not for a long time. I can wait."

Esmeralda sniffed and wrapped her arms around his chest, holding tight.

"I would get so mad at you." He continued stroking and said, "I would yell, and you would just look up at me with those big blue eyes, say something profound, and leave me with a smile."

She gave a breathless laugh. "That sort of sounds like me."

"It *was* you, amazing, smart, beautiful girl who captured my heart."

All the strength seemed to go out of her body as she lolled in his arms, like she was drugged. He had to hold her up. In a voice barely audible, she slurred, "No. Don't say that. You are confusing me. They told me it was not true. I imagined it."

Adrenaline roared up his spine, he wanted to tear whoever did this limb from limb, but he controlled his tone, kept it soothing and calm. "What did they say you imagined?"

"Everything." She leaned into him, letting him support her.

He felt like he was making a break for the hoop against an entire defense with no clear path to the goal. So, he faked to the right and drove into enemy territory, "How about this, we'll play a game, like one of Grandma Eve's, hmm?"

Through hooded eyes, she looked up, considering. "As long as I don't have to cluck like a chicken."

Despite the gravity of the situation, he laughed. "Deal." He lifted her off the counter and guided her to the sofa, keeping her against his side.

"Okay, let's call it, Remember When? You tell me something you remember, and I'll tell you whether you imagined it or not."

She looked up at him with a dubious expression, her eyes veiled and sleepy. "That's a dangerous game, Thaddeus."

He raised a sardonic eyebrow. "I fell in love with a four-teen-year-old girl when I was twenty-nine. I wrote the book on living dangerously."

She laughed and settled against him, deciding to stick to the parts they already covered. "Remember when I found you passed out in the woods?" she began.

"Not one of my finer moments, but yes, I do."

"You still have the blanket, so that part is true." She laid her open palm against his chest. The constancy transmitted through her fingers, stilling the palpitations in hers. "Remember when I saw you naked by the waterfall?"

"Again, another fine moment. Jupiter's Moon, you were twelve, but at the time I thought you were about eight."

"Remember when I told you I would grow?" His warmth transmitted itself to her and color returned to her face.

"Remember when you did?" he asked with wry amusement.

She made a low chuckle, full of female power. "Remember when your eyes popped out of your head when I turned around in the stable?"

He groaned and lifted her breast, because he could. "Yes."

She wiggled deeper into his embrace brimming with feline satisfaction. "Remember when I told you that you were too tall? You got really mad and left. So, I ate your eclair, and Mother could not figure out why I wasn't hungry for supper."

His chest shook. "I don't know about the supper part or if you ate my eclair, but I was mad, and not because you said I was too tall."

"Oh, yeah, that." She wiggled away from him and scampered into the kitchen, coming back with the eclairs. "I'm hungry now."

She sat cross legged on the end of the couch. "So, I am pretty clear on most of that day." She took a bite of the eclair and closed her eyes in beatific pleasure.

"Good." He smiled and leaned forward with his mouth open, seeking a bite of the eclair.

She fed him and licked the chocolate from her finger. Watching him carefully, she furrowed her brow and narrowed her eyes. "This is a hard question, and I want you to answer me honestly."

"Okay." He swallowed the eclair and adopted a relaxed pose, but inside he coiled tight as a spring. "Shoot."

"Did I leave you a jug of water?" Esmeralda's eyes did not waiver as she watched his face for clues.

He stilled. They had never spoken about this. He had never told another living soul about that day in the woods or at her lunch table. "Yes, you did."

Palpable energy pulsed around her, she almost shimmered with it as she breathed, "What happened after you drank it, Thaddeus?"

He narrowed his eyes, met her gaze, and handed her the key to a prison cell that held her for five years. "It knocked me on my ass, and then I could see."

"What?" She leaned forward, her face alight, eager and demanding. "What did you see?"

"Colors."

Esmeralda threw her arms in the air, lifted her face to Heaven, and cried, "Thank you!" She held the position for several heartbeats, then dropped her arms and gave him the first truly happy smile he had seen since she arrived. "What else? What else happened?"

"I could see. I could hear, there were animals… everywhere." Thaddeus blinked, remembering.

She scrambled across the sofa, pouncing on him. "Do you remember which ones?"

"A black ferret?"

"Mustela!" she exploded. She kissed him hard and fierce. "He was a mink, but whatever. What else?"

"I didn't want the whiskey anymore," he whispered.

She covered her mouth, her eyes shimmering with un-shed tears. "That really happened? You remember?"

He still was not clear about what happened to her, but he saw her pick up a piece of herself and smooth it back in place, like a tourniquet to stop the arterial bleeding. He settled her more comfortably on his chest and smiled. "Of course, I remember, Esmeralda. I remember everything about you, about our lives in Rephidim. I could never forget."

She covered her face and sobbed. But they were not tears of sadness, it was like watching the rain wash away the muck. She dropped her hands and stared at him, with wet tracks down her cheeks.

He smiled and said, "Grandma Eve always came up with the best games." Then he brought her lips down to his for a very long leisurely kiss, and she warmed under his touch, clearly intent on a much more enjoyable game.

Your Place and Mine

After a quick romp, Thaddeus lay panting and out of breath with Esmeralda collapsed on top of him. "Come on. Let's go get you some clothes before you kill me." Thaddeus ran his hand up Esmeralda's naked back.

She lifted her head from his shoulder, her breath still coming in shallow pants. "I need a bath."

The corner of his mouth lifted in a lecherous grin. "We can do that, too."

She buried her face in the crook of his neck and nipped. With their bodies still joined, she murmured, "Making up for lost time."

"Oh, I've done it now," he chuckled. "I can already see the headlines, 'Young girl kills old man… he died with a smile on his face.'"

She ran her tongue around the shell of his ear. "You don't feel old to me."

He groaned in surrender and let her take him again on the sofa, certain he was going to die.

"You have lived three blocks from me for a year and a half?" Thaddeus smacked her butt as she ran up the steps to her one-bedroom brownstone apartment. She yelped and sped up, but she was no match for his long legs. He swept her up in a spinning hug, kissing her as she giggled.

The neighbor in 3B cracked open his door and glared.

"Sorry." Esmeralda's face flamed. "Put me down," she hissed without moving her lips.

Thaddeus ignored her request, turned, and met the censorious glare of the old man. "Good afternoon, don't mind us." He took the keys from Esmeralda's hand, ducked through the door, and kicked it closed.

The massive tapestry that once hung in her parent's living room dominated one wall of her single room efficiency. The vivid colors and textures took his breath away. Time dulled remembrance swept over him as he beheld the stunning artisan workmanship. "Tabitha," he whispered in awe. He lowered her to the ground and walked toward it, tracing a reverent finger over the delicate yarn. He turned slowly and said, "You saved my life the day you brought me to the place that produced this."

She gave him a tremulous smile. "It is indeed a marvelous place."

"Why aren't you there?" he asked, his voice low, deep with emotion.

Esmeralda looked away. "It was time for me to move on." She made a dismissive shrug. "I never really fit in any way."

Thaddeus scrunched his face in a doubtful expression. "That is ridiculous! You were Rephidim, Esmeralda, with all its joy and peace."

She rubbed an eye, pressing hard. "Joy and peace? I think you took those with you the day you left." She sighed and moved to a stack of mail, absently straightening, and muttered, "The left..."

"You know I had to go."

She looked up, holding herself very still. "I was never the same."

He blinked and looked down. "I'm sorry, that was never my intent."

She waited. Waited for him to say the words she longed to hear. In the silence, she heard his cold departing words. 'I am not coming back. Have a good life, kid.' They had taunted her, played in her mind for years until she wanted to scream in her silent cell for them to stop. Surrounded by darkness, she took them as proof that he never loved her, that he fled her obsession, her insanity. She took a step toward him and demanded he tell her. "Did you forget me? Did you walk away and never look back?"

"Forget you?" He covered his eyes and groaned. "I tried, but I could not. No, I did not walk away from you and never look back. I do not think a day has gone by that I did not look back."

"All these years, I thought—" She turned away with a gulping sob. "I believed the worst. The worst about you, about us. You hurt me, but I forgive you."

His head snapped up, his expression aggrieved, full of regret. He knew the pain he caused her, had always caused her. To his reckoning, he owed her... everything. "Precious girl, what have I ever done to deserve you?"

She twirled a corkscrew curl around her finger and bit her bottom lip. A flash of her old impish spark twinkled in her eyes as she said, "I think perhaps you are the only one who has ever been able to put up with me." She let go of the curl, it sprung back, dancing over her lashes. "I'm a bit unusual."

"Extraordinary," he breathed.

She rubbed her upper arms, hugging herself. "I've tried to be normal."

He brushed the curl from her eye. "Normal is boring. The entire world is normal, but there is only one Esmeralda." He laughed with a scornful edge in his words. "Trust me, I know."

"And there is only one Thaddeus. Trust me, I know." She leaned her head into his hand, her face soft with affection.

"Esmie, I love you."

She blinked rapidly, her lower lip trembling. "I love you, too."

He saw her press another piece of her soul back in place, and he took the final step toward healing. Stroking her cheek with his thumb, destiny and his innate sense of honor demanded he do right by her. "Will you marry me, Esmeralda ben Claude, be my wife?" As he spoke, he realized that while unplanned and spontaneous, the words felt right, and the notion took root.

Subconsciously, he waited for her, believed her all those years ago. 'When we get married…' The echoes of her childish voice rang in his heart. He held onto that promise like a spider silk filament of hope that one day she would come back to him. Now that she had, he was not going to let her go, ever.

Her breath caught, and she closed her eyes. A jolt shot through her body, then she stiffened and looked up at him, desolation and panic written all over her face.

"Thaddeus, what if you don't know me anymore? What if there are things about me now that you won't like? What if I am not the person you think I am?"

He shook his head. "I know you, the real you, Esmeralda."

The real Esmeralda? His words caused a crack to run down the walls of her defenses. "I don't even know who that is."

"I do. I'll help you find her again, just as you did for me."

"I don't need a therapist, Thaddeus." Esmeralda's voice shook.

"Husbands are infinitely better than therapists." He brushed his lips against hers. "Say yes."

She wanted to, with everything inside her she wanted to. But she was terrified, afraid she would wake up and discover this was just a dream, a happy delusion, not real. It crashed in on her last night, and she did not trust herself to maintain the pretext. "I can't, not yet."

He could feel her fear, pulsing in great waves. The scar on her face turned pink across the canvas of her face, white and bloodless. With a great exertion of self-control, he suppressed his disappointment, sacrificed his own will, and pretended her words did not cut him to the quick. "Oh, I see how it's going to be," he teased. "You are going to make me work for it, like I did you?"

She grabbed the lifeline with both hands. "Certainly." She swallowed and adopted a flirty expression. "I have always been entirely too easy for you."

He threw back his head and laughed. "Easy? Good Heavens, girl, you are the hardest thing I have ever done in my life."

The color returned to her cheeks, and she traced a delicate finger down the front of his shorts. "I think I shall enjoy making it hard on you."

All laughter faded as his eyes grew stormy. "Vixen."

The Truth, Again

"I think they heard that all the way in Endor," Esmeralda giggled.

Thaddeus could not move, he could not speak, he could barely breathe. He simply lay on her little bed, exhausted. At length he laughed. "Holy shit, you are going to kill me."

Her chest vibrated. "I really like doing that."

Breathless, he stared up at her with hooded eyes. "I can tell."

She snuggled by his side, granting mercy, and toying with the light brown hair on his chest. When he touched her, she let herself go and found clarity. In his arms, she felt sure of her place and herself, gone for so long, it roared back. Power, old and true, surged through her whole being, and she gloried in it, in him. She held it in her heart, this sure knowledge, precious and new. It felt like dew on an Argiope web, fragile and delicate, but poised on silken steel, which in the right hands, spun into power, and Thaddeus was a spinner.

His breathing became sonorous, regular. The tense lines around his eyes softened. His hair stuck up in an adorable tumble. It always looked like it needed to be combed when he was in Rephidim but was meticulously in place when he came to the door last night. He looked much like he did the day she found him at the falls, relaxed and naked. She smiled in wonder. He was real. He was actually real! He loved her... She had not imagined it. Sighing, she let the truth wash over her.

She fought the doctors for the first year, stubbornly refusing to accept what they told her. So, they drugged and restrained her, until she quit fighting and started listening. It was a long hard battle, coming to grips with the fact that she was nothing special, not chosen, not different. She was simply a young, confused, girl who fancied herself more important than she really was. The isolation of her village and the doting of her parents spawned it. Outside of Rephidim, Esmeralda was just like everyone else.

In less than twenty-four hours, the man lying beside her cast doubts on everything she believed to be true... again.

Options

"What do you mean, you could not get to her?" the Witch hissed from behind her enormous desk.

The besuited messenger took an involuntary step backward. "Beg mercy, Ba'alat Ob!" he cried and called her by one of her illustrious titles, Mistress who speaks to the dead. "Pray, do not strike your faithful servant down in anger! A great enemy prevailed against us, through the night and day."

She slammed the flats of her palms down on the desk and rose, leaning forward in fury. "What great enemy?" she snarled.

The man fell to his knees, prostrate in submission. "I do not know, beloved High Priestess, but he was an impenetrable foe, the likes of which we have not ever seen. His face was that of a falcon, his sword flashed as lightning, a mighty warrior of our sworn enemy."

Foul curses fell upon his bowed head, papers flew around the room as the Witch's anger erupted in a whirlwind. "Fools! Incompetent imbeciles! Must I do everything?" she screeched. "If you cannot get to her, then bedevil her!"

She hurled a granite paperweight, it struck with a sickening thunk, but the blood spatter temporarily assuaged her anger. "Depart from me."

On hands and knees, dribbling blood across her Persian rug, he murmured apologies, and fled like a beaten dog.

The Witch collapsed into her chair, shaken. She could feel the little bitch's power breaking loose, but even worse, she was protected again.

Options. She had options. Absently drumming her talons on the ebony desk, she reviewed them from the most heinous to the least, in terms of cost to herself. A quarter-hour later, she chartered a jet to Greece.

Dreams

Asleep in Esmeralda's narrow bed, with his feet hanging off the end, Thaddeus walked streets of gold, marveling at the glorious Temple of the Iron King. His mortal eyes could not absorb its true splendor, but his body basked in the golden light, pulsing, warm, and healing.

Magnificent New Jerusalem hovered above it, home of the Gune and the angels. Heaven. Brilliant, sparkling gemstones the size of mountains adorned its surface. In his heart, he understood the reason for the mandate; the pilgrimage was not for the Iron King, it was for the man. Only personal experience could impress the majesty and power of the Iron King on a man's heart. Then, they would revere who they served. All the books and paintings in the world could not convey the power of the Golden City. It touched him to the very depths of his spirit, connected him to the Creator, which would have been impossible from the comfortable recliner at Eve's Boarding House. The insignificance of his own life overwhelmed him, as if his troubles disappeared in the presence of such awesome majesty.

"Thaddeus ben Todd."

In reverent fear and dread, Thaddeus fell to his knees. "My Lord."

"Arise, my son." Yeshua rested a nail scarred hand on Thaddeus' head.

"I am unworthy to raise my head, Lord. I am a sinful and vile man." Thaddeus trembled under the touch.

"As far as the east is from the west, so far have I removed your transgressions from you. Just as a father loves his children, so I, the Lord, love those who fear and worship me. For I know your bones, Thaddeus, that you are made of mere dust."

Peace washed over Thaddeus, but he did not rise, he could not. His shame was too deep.

"If it were Jacob or Matthew kneeling before you, seeking forgiveness, would you smite them?"

"No," Thaddeus cried from his soul, "I would not smite my boys. I loved them."

"How much more then, do I love you?" Yeshua dropped to his knee and opened his arms.

Broken before grace, Thaddeus fell into the Savior's embrace and wept.

"Come, let us walk." Yeshua helped Thaddeus to his feet.

The Golden City changed, becoming the familiar Thyatira Woods. His boulder and waterfall lay ahead down the path. "This place, you brought me here."

Yeshua nodded. "I did. I have always ordered your steps, Thaddeus. You have done well."

Thaddeus began to protest.

Yeshua held up a hand. "Man is not perfect, not in the flesh. Now that you have taken Esmeralda as your wife, sin no more."

Thaddeus' shoulders slumped. "But Lord, she will not yet have me."

Yeshua smiled, with unfathomable knowledge. "Esmeralda took you as her husband long ago, Thaddeus."

The truth of Yeshua's words washed over him, sweeping away the trouble in his heart. "She is greatly injured, Lord. What would you have me do?"

Yeshua nodded, pleased with the question. "Keep her by your side, for the enemy seeks her destruction. In the darkness, help her find the light. She will speak the truth."

Thaddeus turned to ask what Yeshua meant, but he was gone. Out of the corner of his eye he saw a flash of color and turned toward his boulder. Shining bright as the sun, perfect and whole, stood his family: Olivia, Matthew, and Jacob. His sons appeared as they had been, not as they were with the Lord, a gift beyond measure, to replace the last vision of them with this new one.

Olivia's lovely face shone with glory. She leaned down and spoke to the boys, who took off, running on sturdy legs toward their father. "Daddy!"

Thaddeus loped toward them, arms outstretched, tears streaming down his face. He scooped up his sons, one in each arm, crushing them to his chest. Rejoicing and weeping happy tears, he surrounded them with his love. Then Olivia was in their midst, hugging him around the waist, resting her face against his chest, warm and substantial. He smelled her hair, yellow sunshine and morning gardenias. He held them all, murmuring unintelligible words of love and longing. "I did not forget you," he promised. "I did not!"

Olivia cupped his face, and he stared into her familiar green eyes. "I know. You mourned us for a long time. But I grieve for how lonely you have been, Thad." She raised up on her tiptoes and kissed him gently. "You do not betray us, by loving Esmeralda. You never have." She smiled in glorious splendor, glowing in pure light. "Be happy but keep her safe. The same evil that took us from you, seeks to destroy her."

His face contorted with denial, but before he could protest. Olivia pressed a finger over his lips. "We love you, and
we will see you again."

"Wait!" he cried, but a strong wind blew, and they faded
away in his arms.

Thunder crashed overhead. The sky turned black, great
clouds rolling in. Darkness pressed him into the dirt, a wickedness that had substance and presence.

"Thaddeus!" Esmeralda cried.

He turned and saw her standing alone on his boulder.
Black smoke swirled around her like a funnel cloud, cutting
her off from everything and everyone.

He sat straight up in bed with a cry of panic.

Esmeralda startled, the book she was reading flew out of
her hands and fell to the floor. She covered her heart and gave
a shaky laugh. "You scared me!"

"Pack your stuff!" His hair stood on end. "We're getting
out of here—now!"

"Thaddeus, slow down!" Esmeralda panted after him,
afraid he might wrench her arm from its socket as he pulled
her down the busy New York sidewalk. He used her large
suitcase as a battering ram, clearing a path.

"Come on!" His pupils dilated, making him wild eyed.
His skin looked ashen, his fear palpable. In an instant, she
knew. She stopped dead, frozen. He whirled on her, and she
read it all in his face. "What did you see?" she yelled over the
city noise, honking horns, and construction clatter.

He scowled and looked around, sucking in air. "Something is coming for you."

Esmeralda's eyes bulged and horror struck her like a blow,
sending her stumbling backward. He caught her around the
waist, and in a single motion turned and ran, clutching her
to his side.

They almost made it.

Bedeviled

In the history of New York City, being accosted by a lunatic in broad daylight was barely noteworthy, but Thaddeus and Esmeralda's encounter was anything but ordinary.

A harridan rose out of the street, appearing out of thin air, or so it seemed to Thaddeus. "You got a smoke, little girl?" the woman asked.

Esmeralda recoiled with a violent jerk, the phrase… the name… little girl. "No, sorry."

Rotten teeth smiled out of the cavern of a black mouth. "Are you sure?" Her head tilted at an absurd angle.

"Come on." Thaddeus pulled Esmeralda forward.

The woman, dressed in black rags, cut off their path, moving in front of them. "I asked her a question." Her body undulated like a snake. "Do you have a smoke?"

Esmeralda withdrew, desperate to keep her voice steady. "I don't smoke."

"Hmm, shame. I do." Evil eyes narrowed, she opened her mouth and blew.

Esmeralda whimpered, as the stench of rotten eggs hit her full in the face. She covered her nose and mouth. Sulfur!

Thaddeus grimaced and pushed past her, continuing their headlong rush down the street.

Esmeralda fought for control, *It was nothing, you just imagined it, the woman's breath was just bad. It was nothing!*

The guard at the front desk rose as they entered the lobby. "You've decided to keep this one around, huh?"

Esmeralda gasped and moved behind Thaddeus, recognizing the malevolent leer in the guard's eyes.

Thaddeus glared. "Joe, this is my fiancée."

"Fiancée?" he scoffed. "Sure, Director, whatever you say."

Thaddeus stood, flabbergasted at the behavior of the weekend guard, totally out of character. He would have a word with the man, but not here, not in front of Esmeralda.

He guided her toward the elevators as Joe's laughter followed them across the lobby. "Enjoy your honeymoon, Director. When you're done, send her back down. She's a pretty one."

Esmeralda whimpered.

Thaddeus whirled and dropped Esmeralda's hand, storming back to the desk. He had taken two steps, when all three elevator doors opened at once, disgorging their occupants in a mad rush of humanity. They caught Esmeralda in the stampede. Separated from Thaddeus in the sudden crush, she stumbled backward, propelled by the mass, and fell, landing hard. A black shoe kicked her in the ear. She writhed, crying out in pain.

A gaudily dressed woman reached for her with long red fingernails that came toward her face like bloody claws.

Esmeralda screamed and rolled away.

"What's wrong with her?" the woman asked in a thick New York accent.

Thaddeus broke through as the crowd disbursed.

The red nailed woman looked at Thaddeus with a dubious expression and tapped her temple. "Is she all right?"

Thaddeus scooped Esmeralda up, ignoring the woman who made the hairs on the back of his neck stand up. "Hold the elevator!" he shouted. Without a backward glance, he snagged Esmeralda's suitcase and rushed the elevator.

An elderly couple took two steps, as if to board, and Thaddeus barked, "Take the next one!" The doors closed on their shocked faces.

Esmeralda leaned against the back of the lift, holding her ear, blood running through her fingers. "Ouch."

"Come here." Thaddeus tilted her head, examining the wound. "Oh, that looks bad. Otherwise, are you okay?"

She closed her eyes and took several deep breaths. When she emerged, her face was serene, her voice distant. "Yes, I'm fine. It was just an accident. I fell."

He shook his head to clear it. That was one of the oddest experiences of his life, and she stood there, gushing blood and acting as if everything was normal.

The elevator doors opened onto a dark hallway. Someone must have turned off the overhead lights. Esmeralda smothered a small noise but raised her chin and marched past him. Thaddeus held her back. When the elevator doors closed, the sudden change from light to dark was disorienting, the air felt ominous.

"Hold on." He illuminated the hall with his cell phone.

Shadows shifted and stretched, coming alive as they walked. A large vase of artificial flowers toppled over, clattering in the silence. Esmeralda jumped. Thaddeus cursed.

"Sorry, I must have bumped it," she murmured.

He shot her a look. She was at least a yard from the table. He picked up the pace, running with her to his apartment. His hand shook as he fumbled with the lock. He barreled through the door and pulled her inside. Triple locking the bolts, he dropped her suitcase in the foyer, and said, "Holy shit! What was that?"

"Nothing." She moved like she was in a fog. Blood from her ear dripped onto her shoulder, unheeded.

"Come on, let's clean your ear."

She tilted her head, looking sideways in the hallway mirror, her expression eerily similar to the faraway trance she lapsed into on his kitchen counter. "It's fine."

"You are bleeding." He enunciated each word deliberately.

Esmeralda looked down at her fingers and then back at him. "Oh, I suppose I am." Unperturbed, she walked to the bathroom.

He stared at her in open mouthed astonishment, then went after her.

She was studying her ear with distracted interest.

"Sit down. Let me see." Thaddeus pulled a first aid kit from beneath the sink. Her only reaction was a sharp hiss and an involuntary stiffening when he applied the disinfectant. Otherwise, she remained detached. "I think this needs a stitch or two, baby."

She sprang to life then. "No. I am sure it will be fine."

"No, it won't," he protested. "Your earlobe is pulled away from your head. It needs a couple of stitches otherwise it won't heal right."

She blinked rapidly, taking shallow breaths through her nose. "No doctors, just put a bandage on it."

His lips pressed into a thin line. "Like you did this?" He traced his thumb over her cheek.

Esmeralda covered her mouth, and from behind her fingers she whispered, "I have to go."

"No."

"Just put a bandage on it," she begged, "and let me go. I can't stay here with you."

She wasn't going anywhere, and he planned to sort this out, right now. "Why? Why can't you stay here with me?"

"Because I have to go home," she shouted. "I don't belong here. This was a mistake."

It was a jab right to the heart, but he had delivered a thousand such rebukes to her during his years of mourning. He figured he owed her about nine hundred and ninety-five more before they were even, so he changed tactics and asked, "Why are you afraid to have this tended, Esmeralda? Are you scared of doctors?"

She sprang up from the edge of the tub. "I'm not afraid of doctors! Who in their right mind is afraid of doctors?"

"Only someone who has been hurt by them," Thaddeus countered, showing no mercy.

"Don't be ridiculous. Doctors don't hurt people. Doctors," she faltered, "are supposed to help people."

"But they don't always, do they?"

She cupped her ear and turned away from him. "No, they don't."

He pulled her into his arms. "I won't let them hurt you."

"You won't be able to stop them. No one could stop them." She began to cry. "If they are coming for me again... no one can stop them."

Resources

Esmeralda flatly refused to go to the hospital, and after the afternoon they had, he did not blame her.

"He was a medic, and he works for you? He's not a doctor?" She repeated his proposed compromise back to him.

Thaddeus nodded. "I've known him for years. He's a veteran. It will be okay. Let me call him."

She fought the instinct to flee, but experience taught her to behave rationally, to be normal like everyone else. "Go ahead."

He had his phone out before she could change her mind, leaving the room to make the call.

Esmeralda stared at the mirror, her cheek and jaw swelling, faint bruising already visible under the skin. However, she focused on her eyes. Were they crazy? It was hard to think over the throbbing, but she forced herself. They narrowed in pain, but she expected that was normal. Several curls broke loose, but otherwise her braid held, and for that she was grateful. Recently electrocuted, on the verge of a nervous breakdown, was never a good look.

She almost cracked—three times today. Once on the counter in the kitchen, once when he asked her to marry him, and just now as he held her while she cried. At this rate, she would spill her guts by tomorrow morning, and then everything would all fall apart. He wouldn't want her if he knew the truth, if he knew she was so crazy that they put her in a mental hospital for years. He would leave her, and she would spend the rest of her life reliving the one glorious moment when she had him back. She imagined herself holding tight to those few hours before everything crashed in, when they were just Thaddeus and Esmeralda.

"He's on his way. Come on, baby. You need to lie down." He gestured to the bedroom.

She nodded in wordless acquiescence and followed him. He'd pulled the curtains, making the room dark and warm. "I don't want to bleed on your bed."

"I'll get a towel, hold on." He returned with a fluffy brown towel.

"Don't you have an old one? Blood stains."

Thaddeus shot her an impatient look. "I know about blood stains, Esmeralda. I am a Director at the FBI." He shrugged and put the towel down. "Hydrogen peroxide gets it out."

"Really? I did not know that." She filed that nugget away in her large repertoire of interesting facts. "Just something else I've had to learn in the outside world. Arachnid cloth doesn't hold stains, does it?"

The corner of his mouth lifted. "No, it doesn't. It doesn't wear out either. I still have everything I owned."

She gave him a sleepy smile. "Show me. Put on that brown shirt you used to wear all the time."

He laughed, "That's the first time you told me to put something on."

"If my ear didn't hurt so bad, trust me, it would be a different story."

His expression became vaguely pained. Since she walked through his door less than twenty-four hours ago, they made love five times, and that wasn't counting the bathtub which had been all her. "You little vixen." He climbed into bed with her. "How about we do a fashion show another time?" He lifted the loose bandage and checked her ear. "It's still bleeding. That was a nasty fall."

She closed her eyes lest he see the truth. Someone kicked her on purpose. She saw the man's face as he did it, a black-eyed devil. Pushing that out of her mind, she said, "Tell me about your life."

Thaddeus stretched beside her, keeping his voice deliberately mild. "You don't want to talk about what just happened?"

"Not particularly." She snuggled into him, finding his warmth a comfort. "I'm trying to take my mind off the pain."

Thaddeus figured she did that a lot but held his words. "Well, like I snapped at you a minute ago, I'm a Director at the FBI."

The corner of her mouth lifted. She knew that already. "What does a Director do?"

"I direct."

She made a sleepy giggle. "Direct what? Because there are a lot of different kinds of directors, motion pictures, orchestras… trains."

"All of those would be infinitely less hazardous than what I actually do, which is oversee organized crime and missing persons units. Though, I am not in the field much anymore. I think these days I direct paperwork."

"I love paperwork. That's what I do."

"Good, you can come do my paperwork. You're hired." He rubbed her shoulder affectionately. "You're much better looking than my current assistant."

She sighed. "I'm sure I look particularly fetching at the moment."

"Fetching?" He smiled and whispered, "I've missed your words."

"Just my words?" she asked, dozing.

"Among other things."

Stitched Back Together

A disheveled stranger answered Director Thaddeus ben Todd's door. "Paul, thanks for coming."

"You betcha, Director. What's amiss?" Agent Paul ben Casper asked in his native Minnesota accent, studying Thaddeus for the injury he had been summoned to attend.

"It's not me." Thaddeus ran his fingers through his hair, mussing it further, totally out of character to the groomed professional Paul worked with every day.

"All right," said Paul, taking in the scene.

"This is confidential and off the record. I can count on your discretion?" Thaddeus asked, rubbing his stubbled chin.

Paul gave a nod of assent. "Fer sure."

"Sit down, please," Thaddeus said, motioning toward the living room. When they settled, Thaddeus cleared his throat, looking grave. "My fiancée is in the next room, and she's been injured."

"Fiancée?" Paul asked, stunned. The Director, as far as he knew, had zero personal life. He was a good man to work under, but nobody put in more hours. Paul knew he kept several changes of clothes in his office because it was not unusual for Thaddeus to shower in the gym and return to work, often not leaving the building for days.

Thaddeus smiled, looking chagrined. "It's a long story, but we've only just been reunited." He cleared his throat again, uncomfortable. "I need you to keep this confidential."

"Yes, of course," Paul said.

"Her name is Esmeralda. She is shaken up, and she is hurt, so put on the kid gloves."

"Understood, Director."

"Okay then, I'll bring her out." Thaddeus left the room.

Paul rose and took a casual glance around the apartment, enjoying the spectacular view as twilight fell over the city. An oil painting over the mantel dominated the room. Done in vibrant, rich colors, it depicted a girl reading a book. Wandering to the bookshelf, Paul perused the titles. The books were arranged by subject and alphabetized. Dozens of law books intermingled with text on investigative techniques, and true crime novels. The bottom shelf held four books on textile manufacturing and a small volume titled, 'A History of Thyatira' written by Ernst ben Otto. As far as Paul knew, the Director was a native New Yorker, so the slim volume intrigued him, incongruent among the other titles.

When the bedroom door opened, Paul expected a tall skinny blonde, the Director seemed the type. The shaken girl was nothing of the sort. Her dark curly hair defied her braid and broke free while she slept, tendrils and locks framing her striking face, not classically beautiful, but arresting, with a wide mouth and large blue eyes. On the tall side of average, she was lean with a nice shape. Her olive skin was already turning blue under the bruising, swelling from the injury puffing the right side of her neck and face. Thaddeus steadied her as she took painful steps into the living room, his arm draped around her shoulders. The bandage she held over her ear showed signs of copious bleeding.

"Thank you for coming," she said and attempted a smile but grimaced when it hurt. "I'm Esmeralda."

"Paul ben Casper, ma'am. It's nice to meet you." They shook hands as she sized him up. "Let's have a look at that injury. We'll have you fixed up in no time."

She sat down gingerly, taking a kitchen chair, and clearly dreading the exam. "Thaddeus, should you go get that towel?"

"No need, I've got a sterile drape in my kit," Paul assured her, laying out the instruments. "How did this happen?"

She pressed the bandage to the side of her head and said, "I fell."

"Did you lose consciousness or become dizzy?"

"No."

"Do you have a headache?" he asked, checking her pupils.

She winced. "I think so, but it's hard to tell if it's just my ear or my head."

"Have you taken anything?"

"I don't take drugs," she said, closing her eyes. "In general, they don't agree with me."

"Well, you will probably want to take some mild pain killer. This will hurt tomorrow." Paul lifted away the bloody bandage and made a clicking sound with his tongue. "Fer sure it probably doesn't feel too nice now."

"I'll live," she said stoically.

"I thought it would need a stitch or two, what do you think?" Thaddeus asked, growing pale.

Paul shined the flashlight on the wound. "It looks like about four to me. I'm no plastic surgeon. Are you sure you want me to do this? The doctors over at the hospital would do a better job of it."

Esmeralda put a trembling hand over his. "Please go ahead. I know you'll do a fine job." Her eyes drooped in pain but there was a faint sparkle in their blue depths. "You always wanted to be a doctor. You should have. You would be a good one."

Paul blinked in surprise, almost no one knew that.

Thaddeus quirked an eyebrow at Paul and gave him a knowing smile, looking absurdly gratified by her observation.

Paul glimpsed what the Director saw in this young woman and wanted to ask her how she could possibly know that about him. However, her ear needed attention, and he returned to the task. She surrendered to his ministrations with no fuss. He'd patched up soldiers who made more of a scene than this shaking young woman. She merely winced when he numbed the area. "I think we should get you on your side. You'll be more comfortable and relaxed."

Esmeralda agreed and rose to walk back to the bedroom. Paul cleared his throat. "I think the kitchen counter is a better venue. We've got the sink right there and the height is perfect."

Esmeralda paused, looking at the counter with profound resignation as if bad things happened on kitchen counters.

"Come on. I'll help you up." Thaddeus helped her settle. "You all right?"

"Yeah, let's just get this over with."

Paul took his time, aware if he botched the sutures she would be scarred for life. Using a technique he learned from a plastic surgeon, he repaired the wound behind her ear and used adhesive glue and a butterfly bandage on the front. As he finished, he smiled down at her, pleased with the job. "You will need to have those removed in about a week, but I don't think it will scar."

She seemed to deflate as she nodded.

Thaddeus settled her back into bed, after much debate over whether she should take the analgesic Paul suggested. In the end, Thaddeus prevailed, and she took a dose.

Paul was packing up when Thaddeus returned. The law enforcement officer in Paul had to ask, "Director, how did the injury occur?"

Thaddeus raised an eyebrow, recognizing the tone and the question for what it was. "We were waiting on the elevator. When the passengers disembarked, Esmeralda got caught in a stampede. She fell in the crowd."

Paul closed his case with two loud clicks. "That wound was not caused by a fall, sir. The scratches are consistent with a shoe. Someone kicked her, and from the looks of it, it was not an accident. A normal gait would not create the amount of force necessary to separate the earlobe from the cranium."

Thaddeus' nose flared as his fist balled at his sides.

"Sir, I have to ask. Was her injury sustained in a domestic altercation?"

Thaddeus' snapped up. "What? No!"

Paul's gaze never wavered. "Then why is she claiming she fell, and why didn't you take her to the hospital?" He shook his head, looking every inch the superb investigator he was. "You've got to admit, this doesn't smell right."

"There were a dozen witnesses to the incident, Agent. I assure you it happened just as I described, though I did not see who kicked her."

"Do you want me to look into it?" Paul asked.

Thaddeus seemed to run over the question, then shook his head. "Not at this time, no."

"All right, you let me know if you change your mind." Paul lifted his case, intending to have a word with the guard at the front desk on his way out. The whole thing seemed fishy to him, fishy indeed.

September 4, 998 ME

Run Over By a Truck

"Oh, my Heavens!" Esmeralda gasped at her reflection the next morning. "I look like I've been run over by a truck!"

Thaddeus grimaced. "Perhaps a moped."

"At least an SUV."

"You are still beautiful to me." He kissed the uninjured side of her neck.

Esmeralda rubbed her cheek against the top of his head, settling into his embrace, strong and sturdy. She sighed, letting his presence surround her. "Thank you for saying that and taking care of me. Not exactly the reunion I envisioned."

He rested his chin on the top of her head, watching her face in the mirror. "How did you envision it?"

She closed her eyes, and smiled wistfully, resting her arms over his. "Over the years there were dozens. I think my favorite was pretty simple, actually."

"Tell me." He kissed her hair.

"I would be sitting on your boulder, watching the waterfall, thinking about you, missing you. Then I would hear a sound behind me, I'd turn, and you would be there." She swallowed thickly. "You would tell me it was a mistake, that you never should have left. You came back because you couldn't live without me, and you loved me."

"I never let myself think that. I'd have gone mad if I did."

She made a breathless snort. "I can understand that. How did you envision it?"

He buried his face in the side of her neck and nipped her. "Pretty much exactly the way it happened."

September 5, 998 ME

Bits and Pieces

Monday morning, Thaddeus leaned over and kissed Esmeralda goodbye. "I don't think I will be gone long; much will depend on where we are in several key briefings I have today. Otherwise, I would take a page out of your book and call in sick." She looked adorable, snuggling, and sleepy in his bed.

Esmeralda covered a yawn, wincing in pain. "I've never taken a day off since I joined the staff. Professor Moreh was very understanding."

Thaddeus, who regularly lost unused vacation, considered taking it all, just so he could spend it with her doing absolutely nothing. The novelty of sleeping beside a woman, having her in his house, her toothbrush beside his, was as much, or more, appealing than the sex. He could not remember the last lazy Sunday he spent, and yesterday was amazing. Mundane tasks, like making breakfast, took on a deeper meaning when there was someone to share it with.

He discovered Esmeralda was gentler than she used to be, quieter. Where the child had been whimsical, the woman was thoughtful. She still laughed, but there was a tentative uncertainty to it, not the carefree laughter he remembered. Her mind and love of books had not changed, so he knew her job as a researcher suited her well. Sitting cross legged on his couch, eating an enormous slice, she gave him a discourse on why New York pizza tasted so good and why it couldn't be recreated elsewhere. Her mannerisms were much the same, the way she twirled her hair or pulled at a stray lock and watched it bounce back. The tilt of her head when she was about to say something funny, or the way she pressed her thumb against her chin when she was deep in thought were quintessential Esmeralda. But other than the insight she dropped on Paul about his desire to become a doctor, that part of her seemed missing. Most glaring of all was her complete disconnection from the Iron King. In all their hours together, she had not quoted a single Scripture.

He did not tell her about the dream, and she didn't ask further questions about what he saw. Neither did she seem disturbed by the bizarre events on the walk from her apartment to his. Her reaction, and the bits he'd pieced together, alarmed him. The dream terrified him.

Walking into his office, he decided to see if he could find out what happened to her. With the resources of the FBI at his fingertips, he expected it wouldn't take long.

It didn't.

Esmeralda settled on the couch with a remote control, studying the buttons and wondering what they all did. She should have asked but was loath to tell him she had never watched TV. If she confessed that, it might make her seem strange to him. Of course, they did not have modern technology in Rephidim, but her apartment was more modern than her parent's house and had a landline phone, though she never used it, and it never rang. They did not have television in the hospital.

A vague pounding headache precluded reading, so she decided to watch a movie from Thaddeus' extensive collection. From the modern to the ancient, he owned hundreds of them. After pizza yesterday, they snuggled on the couch, and he treated her to her first movie, a new release, action packed cop thriller. She loved it.

That morning, it took her a half hour to select a title. She picked an ancient one that looked promising. The colors on the front jacket intrigued her, and the wistful expression of the girl reminded her of herself: a magical city, rainbows, and a yellow brick road.

Twenty minutes later, she finally coaxed the machine to play. When it started, she groaned in exasperated disappointment to discover the film had been made in black and white. She considered selecting another, but the story and the girl captured her imagination, so she watched. When the screen changed to color, Esmeralda gasped, thoroughly charmed by the spectacle, letting the magic and the music dazzle her. But as she watched, tears began leaking from her eyes. It felt like the story of her life, captured more than a thousand years ago. When the credits rolled, she wept, profoundly affected by the film, a journey in technicolor, over the rainbow.

On shaking limbs, she dragged herself into the bathroom. She cried in the shower and while she packed her suitcase. She held Thaddeus' blanket to her face and sobbed into it.

Over the rainbow…

She didn't sneak out, didn't slip away without a word. That was not her style, and he deserved better. Once, he had the courage to tell her goodbye; she owed him nothing less.

At 2:00 pm, he came home and found her suitcase by the door. She perched on the edge of the sofa, her battered face less swollen, but her jaw set in a firm line of determination. He gestured to the suitcase and asked, "What's that all about?"

"Come and sit down, please." Her smile quavered. "I need to tell you something."

He drew his brows down, wrinkling his forehead, not caring for the tone of her voice or her prim posture.

She stared at her folded hands and said, "I wasn't going to tell you. I did not plan to say anything because… I was scared and ashamed." A tear ran down her face unheeded. "But I realize that is wrong. I would be lying to you and myself if I pretended."

"Stop." Thaddeus shook his head. "You don't have to say anything."

Little ticks of emotion dotted her face. "I do, and you have to let me."

He wanted to stop her, wanted to take her in his arms and kiss away the words she seemed so determined to say.

She rose from the couch and handed him a movie. "Have you watched this?"

He took it from her trembling fingers and swallowed. His boys loved this movie, had watched it dozens of times. Matthew called it 'The Biz o' Boz', and he and Olivia adopted the name. At one point, Thaddeus could recite large portions of the dialogue by rote, but he had not watched it since they died. He held it over his heart and nodded. "Yes, I've seen it."

"I'm Dorothy, Thaddeus," she sniffed. "That was my life, every part of it, real. Except, when I woke up, I wasn't in my bed surrounded by my friends and family. I was in the hospital, and they kept me there for a very long time." She covered her mouth, stifling a small cry. "I wasn't going to tell you, couldn't bear to see your face. But I realized that I can't keep it from you. I can't wonder every day if today will be the day you find out."

"It doesn't matter," Thaddeus asserted. "It changes nothing."

She squared her shoulders. "No, it does. Ever since I walked through your door, I am back in it, back into Oz, but it's not real." Her chest heaved. "Over the rainbow... it's a euphemism for insanity, nothing but beautiful, wondrous, delusions full of magic, and colors, and witches!"

"It's just a movie, Esmeralda." Thaddeus stood up. "Don't let it do this to you."

She shook her head in emphatic denial. "That's the point. To you and everyone else, it's just a movie, but I lived it." She pointed at the disc. "That was the girl you knew. That was how I saw the world, in Oz before the witch showed up. I even had my own Glenda. But I didn't drop a house on the witch. She dropped one on me."

He did not know what to say, denials died on his tongue, so he simply gathered her in his arms and held on.

"I fought for a very long time to get better. I can't tell you how hard that was. Thaddeus, they cut my hair." She sobbed into his chest.

He rocked with her. "I'm so sorry, baby. I'm sorry they did that to you."

"I have to go home. I think it's starting again, and I can't let it." She withdrew and walked to the window.

"You think what is starting again?" Thaddeus demanded, his words holding the edge of anger that dogged him since he read her case file.

She refused to look at him. "The madness."

"You are not mad!" He stalked over and turned her to face him. "You have never been mad. I don't know what they told you, or what they made you think, but I knew that girl and you were not mad! Neither is the woman standing before me now."

Esmeralda cupped his cheek. "You don't know. You don't know the things I see, what I struggle with."

"Don't I?" He shook his head ruefully. "You of all people know what I struggled with, what I overcame. You forget. I know what it is like to be haunted."

"But you were not crazy," she said, and her voice broke.

"Wasn't I? When you found me, I was out of my mind with grief, drinking myself to death. I daresay, they would have put me in the hospital, too."

"It's different." She pressed her lips together in a sad smile. "What happened to you was real."

His face clouded. "Whatever happened to you was just as real."

She choked out a laugh. "Oh, I doubt that."

"Like Saturday wasn't real?" He pushed; this had gone far enough.

Her big blue eyes widened. "Nothing happened on Saturday."

"Really? A crazy woman did not appear out of nowhere?"

She inhaled sharply and pulled away. "Just a homeless woman, the city is full of them."

"Huh, didn't seem that way to me," Thaddeus said, emphatic. "You wouldn't know, but Joe's behavior downstairs was totally out of character."

She clenched her jaw. "Men stare. It's normal."

Thaddeus considered himself somewhat of an expert on lust. "No, it wasn't. There was something in his eyes that shouldn't have been there."

"Nonsense." She crossed her arms. "You just imagined that."

He ran a finger along her bruised jaw line. "We didn't imagine this, that you were hurt, that someone kicked you... on purpose."

Her face faltered for an instant, but she resolutely declared, "It was an accident. I fell."

"I've lived in this building for three years. They time those elevators to never be on the same floor at the same time. Minutes after I receive a message that you are in danger, you are bleeding," his voice cracked, "on the ground, and I let it happen."

"It was an accident," she begged him to agree with her, didn't dare delve into what sort of message he received. It was madness, and she was sucking him into the vortex.

"No. You are in danger," he ground out, "and you cannot imagine how much that terrifies me."

The intensity of his fear hit her like a pulse. It jolted her back in time, and she heard the echoes of his screams, saw the slaughter. "Stop!"

"Stop what? Telling you the truth?" He took her shoulders, squeezing harder than he intended.

"Ow!" she protested in pain.

He loosened his grip but did not release her. "Listen to me. You are not now, nor have you ever been, mad. I see what you do. In Rephidim, I saw what you saw. I lived that life with you, the one they twisted up and made you believe wasn't real. That I wasn't real." He kissed her fiercely, smothering her protests. "That this, isn't real."

She wanted to fight and pull away. She wanted to scream, but her body reacted, overriding everything. She surrendered for a glorious second, then pushed him away. "I can't do this. I can't think straight when you do that."

He bore down on her. "I think the only time you are thinking straight is when I do that." He pulled her against him, hard. "Because you can't pretend then, can you? You can't pretend I'm not real when I am touching you." He kissed the side of her neck. "When I'm inside you... loving you."

Fire erupted between them.

He led her to the bedroom, full of intent, because she was not leaving him. Laying her on his bed, he undressed her and saw the battle raging behind her stormy eyes, so he fanned the flames of desire until they burned away her resolve to flee, to hide. He forced her to feel, just as she had once forced him.

Kissing his way down her naked belly, he settled between her thighs, breathing life into her, reveling in the scent of her, clean and pure. He buried his face in her curls, and she let out a maidenly cry, trying to close her legs. "Oh no, Esmeralda, you don't get to hide, not anymore and not from me."

Then he taught her the truth, relentlessly, persistently, and methodically he drove her to the only madness that was real.

As her body spasmed with pleasure, and the waves crashed over her, he taunted, "Do you feel this?" He toyed with his tongue.

"How about this?" He stroked her with his thumb.

"Is this real, Esmeralda?" He came along beside her as she shattered under his touch. "Say it isn't real."

"No!" she whimpered.

He chuckled in diabolic pleasure. "You can't, can you?" He moved on top of her, pressing and teasing her. "Tell me, Esmeralda, are you imagining this?" He entered her slowly and withdrew, controlling his own passion, watching her face. "Open your eyes and look at me. Tell me to my face that I am not real."

Her eyes fluttered open, lost and confused, but overcome with need. "You are real."

His grin was lecherous as he pressed into her. "You're damn right."

All gentleness evaporated as he took her, pounding into her until she could not deny the truth. Every thrust cracked the hard shell, every stroke took a sledgehammer to the wall, until he reached her center, the hidden part of her she protected, was afraid of, and he freed her. "They lied to you!" His body began to wrack. "Say it!" he demanded.

She arched her back and cried, "They lied!"

He brought his mouth to hers, kissing her. "Come with me," he panted, "my precious girl."

All reason evaporated, only sensation and emotion remained, driving need and climax—truth.

Afterward, gasping for air, him still buried deep inside her, shuddering, she whispered, "I guess if you are joining me over the rainbow, I won't be so lonely this time."

He laughed, his chest vibrating against hers. "Just call me the wizard."

She stroked his back, staring deep into his eyes. "No… you're the Tin Man."

His lips hovered above hers. "Who finally found his heart."

Unexpected Guest - Athens

"Pardon me, my Esteemed, but you have a visitor," Captain Orion ben Drachmas announced from the doorway.

Monarch Antiochus of Greece looked up from his desk, annoyed. "Who is it? I was not expecting anyone." He narrowed his eyes and added, "My son, is he in residence?"

Orion bowed low. "He is, my Esteemed."

Antiochus motioned for Orion to depart. "Then whoever it is, send them away."

Orion drew his heels together, his posture stiff. "It is the Mistress, my Esteemed."

Antiochus flew out of his chair. "The hag?"

"The Mistress, my Esteemed, shall I admit her?" Orion refused to meet Antiochus' glare, lest he fall victim to the tumult brewing around the mercurial monarch. He shifted, uncomfortable. The situation could become volatile if Antiochus refused her entrance because Orion would have to deliver the message, and that woman terrified him.

"Yes, of course, show her in," Antiochus growled and began pacing. He hated that woman, hated all women, but especially her.

A few moments later, she swept into the room, bringing with her that odious scent, female, and he wanted to gag when she hugged him. Instead, he smiled, and for all the world they appeared to be long-lost friends.

After exchanging inane pleasantries, she gestured out the window. "I must say, it is exceedingly desolate outside. How long has it been since you've had rain?" she asked, her voice dripping with false solicitation.

"You did not come to talk about the weather," he replied. "Have a seat."

She ignored the invitation, strolling around his study, running her finger over his treasures because she knew he hated it. "My, aren't we touchy? You were more fun when we were young, Antiochus. Better looking, too."

He glared at her, then sighed. "What do you want, Ba'alat Ob? Don't you have a cauldron brewing somewhere?"

She laughed, "You are ill tempered. I flew halfway across the world to visit, and this is the reception I receive?"

"Far be it from you to obtrude," he said with a sneer.

She pointed a finger at him and warned, "You would do well not to cross me, Antiochus. Perhaps I shall conjure your sister, then leave before sending her back."

The hair on the back of his neck stood on end. "You are a vicious bitch."

She narrowed a kohl-lined eye at him. "It's part of my charm, wouldn't you agree?"

Charm indeed, like a rattlesnake was charming. He smiled, sarcastic and sick. "You are delightful."

She lifted her breasts. "Aren't I, though?"

Antiochus grimaced and controlled his revulsion. "Save that, you know it doesn't work on me."

She made a dismissive flick of her wrist. "It works on him, though doesn't it? Take me to see him."

Despite his loathing, he warned, "That is perhaps unwise. He has become increasingly unpredictable."

"Taken to wandering the countryside, has he not?" she said in a banal tone. "It's creating quite a storm, all those dead pilgrims."

"Peasants," Antiochus spat. "No one cares."

The Mistress laughed, low and menacing. "Yet, how many patrols do you have inside Greece, five, six?"

There were actually eight, but he was not going to tell her that. The invasion of the Iron King's troops within the boundaries of his kingdom was a sore spot. "Come, I think it's dinnertime. Perhaps he is hungry."

She caught the implication. "Perhaps, Monarch is on the menu?"

"Or better yet, Bitch." Antiochus offered his arm.

"Philomela…" she called in a sing song voice.

Antiochus made a disgusted sound in the back of his throat. "Fine," he relented. "I am sure Zuzite will be pleased to see you."

She smiled in malevolent anticipation. "Of course he will. He has been completely wasted with you."

"Oh, I wouldn't say he has been wasted." Antiochus opened the door and led her out to the grounds. They walked across soft, green grass, watered at great expense to the kingdom. "I suspect you will be interested in his latest prophecy." The words hung in the air, and his eyes glowed with vicious satisfaction. "Does Rephidim mean anything to you?"

He felt a jolt go through her arm, then dropped it, and left her standing on the lawn, furious.

Treat - Deep in the Louisiana Bayou

"Emite," Mademoiselle Charlotte warned, a bull whip hanging from her fingers, "what are the rules?"

He swallowed thickly and looked away, sulking. "Not without asking."

The tip of the whip trailed behind her as she glided toward him. "You should not have done that, *petit cochon!*" She called him a pig and leaned in, her face a mask of fury. "It draws attention."

He held onto his prize defiantly, but as the whip cracked, he protested, "No one will notice."

"*Imbécile!*" she snarled. "They already have. They have launched an investigation, and you do this, without my permission?" She raised her arm.

"Ba'alat Ob is in Greece," he said hastily.

Her arm froze, as he hoped it would. "Greece?"

He gestured to the glass orb on the table. "Look, *Maman.* I expect she has gone to see my brother again."

Charlotte screeched, "What is she doing?"

"If you put down the whip, I will tell you," Emite coaxed. "Then can I enjoy my treat?"

"Tell me first, and then we will discuss your treat."

He rose on ponderous feet, the floor vibrating under his enormous weight. With infinite care, he laid the dead child on the floor beside him, and said, "Yes, *Maman.*"

When Opportunity Knocks

Sir Preston ben Worley studied the report on his desk, then looked up with a chuckle. "She fell out of her chair at a formal dinner? I would have liked to have seen that."

"Yes, Sir. You'll note also her staff heard her fly into a rage the following day. It is rumored she attacked her personal secretary."

Enormous eyebrows drew down in concentration. "Unhinged, is she? She normally keeps that side of her personality out of the office."

"The account is uncorroborated, but our source has been reliable."

Sir Preston drummed his arthritic fingers on his thigh. "Then she flew off to Greece." He reread the report. "Find out what she is about."

The messenger cleared his throat. "Our source inside Athens… you'll transfer the money? He does not come cheap."

"Yes, of course. The good Captain is always exceedingly helpful. Find out what he knows."

The messenger nodded and departed.

Sir Preston narrowed his eyes, studying the report again, then buzzed his secretary. "The Whitaker case, file the motion today, and get before a judge. The Bitch is out of the country."

Back Channels

"Even for you, this is over the top," King Korah ben Adam growled into the phone.

"I have no idea what you are talking about, Korah. It's the middle of the night, why are you calling me?"

Korah felt a spike of anger at her cool dismissal. "Do not play coy with me."

She let out a long sigh. "Merely a side trip, the Aegean is lovely this time of year."

Fire shot up his spine. "Your presence in Greece has leaked to the press. We've spent the better part of the day quashing the story."

"If you cannot quash it, then spin it," she said, utterly unconcerned at the uproar she created by taking an unauthorized, unsanctioned trip to Greece.

"You have the diplomats in an uproar. What were you thinking?"

"Ugh, diplomats?" she scoffed. "They work for you, make it go away. Besides, I've gathered some interesting tidbits."

"Indeed, what pray tell, did Antiochus have to impart?"

"His son is more interesting than yours, though yours is prettier," she cackled.

"I control mine. Antiochus has no such skills," Korah countered.

"Do you think?" she taunted. "Speaking of Peter, I'm flying to Egypt later this week. Your future daughter-in-law shows promise. I may bring her back with me."

"I am certain Peter will be thrilled," Korah intoned drolly.

"Doubtless. I will concede, he has been exceedingly pliable since we brought him to heel."

"Like I said, I control mine." Korah tired of the conversation.

She yawned. "I daresay, you learned from the best. I'll see you on Mabon. Give my regards to the Dark Master and have my chamber ready, will you, pet?"

Korah's lip lifted in scorn as he disconnected the line. "Bitch!"

Marks and Numbers

"You bit me!" Esmeralda complained.

Thaddeus craned his neck toward the spot she indicated, the inside of her thigh. "Sorry, I got a little enthusiastic down there."

"Is that what you call it, enthusiastic?"

He laced his fingers behind his head, gratified. "You cannot blame me; you are entirely too delicious."

"I am entirely too sore. Friday morning, I was a virgin."

Thaddeus chuckled, "Not anymore."

Esmeralda kissed his cheek. "Had I known we were going to have this much fun, I would have shown up a long time ago."

"Why didn't you?"

She shook her head. "It's like I've been under the wicked witch's spell."

He kissed her gently. "I think I'll buy you some magic slippers, in case you get lost, and need to find your way back."

The Red, she thought she knew it. She hadn't a clue.

"If you do, I shall wear them all the time. It could become my signature." She giggled at the thought of wearing them with her sedate librarian attire. "I did always adore sparkly things."

"Everything in Rephidim sparkles, you were just the brightest."

"Huh, I seem to recall you did your best to chase me off." She rolled to her back and crossed her arms over her chest.

"Until you made me jealous."

She drew back in confusion. "How did I do that?"

"With Ian," he said, narrowing his eyes and remembering their intense confrontation.

"Who?"

"Vixen, you know what you did."

Esmeralda's eyes clouded, and she stiffened. "No... I don't."

"Ian ben Kole, white hair, tall, skinny guy, remember?"

She blinked in confusion, her face going pale. "No, I don't remember him. Should I?"

Warning bells blared in Thaddeus' mind because Esmeralda and Ian were inseparable during his brief sojourn in Rephidim. She should remember him but clearly did not, so he tread lightly. "He was only in town a few weeks, and it was a long time ago."

She rubbed her temple, as if the thought was there and she could jar it loose. "It's a hole. I think there are a few of those."

"Don't worry. I am sure they will come back."

"I'm not sure I want them to."

"I'll be right here when they do." He brushed her fingers away from her temple and took up a gentle massage. "In the interim, we need to get you a phone so you can call me if you need me."

She made a deep groan of pleasure as his fingers soothed the headache plaguing her since Saturday. "I don't know your number."

"Hmm, we must remedy that, especially since you insist on going back to work tomorrow." The idea of her leaving the safety of his apartment made him uneasy, but he knew he could not hold her prisoner, as appealing as the idea may be. "If anything strange happens, call me. I'll come right away."

"The only strange thing happening in the research library is this journal I've been transcribing. I believe," she met his gaze, "and not just because of my history, that I am reading the writings of a woman going mad."

Thaddeus ceased his methodical head rubbing. "That could be dangerous, don't you think?"

Esmeralda shrugged. "I don't see how. The woman lived over a thousand years ago. She became very ill after being bitten by one of the armored locusts in the Great Judgment."

Thaddeus shivered. "Abaddon's locusts? Those things were nasty."

"Tell me about it. She describes it in detail, face like a man, teeth like a lion, and a scorpion's stinger. The whole experience was brutal. I stopped reading the other night, just as she came up with a plan to escape the torment."

Thaddeus pulled a blanket over them. "I thought there was no escape from the torment. It lasted five months, right?"

Esmeralda snuggled into him. "That's just it, she is in the middle of the third month, and the pain is driving her insane."

His investigator's mind engaged. "What did she decide to do?"

"I don't understand all the technical jargon. I'm just supposed to be transcribing it." Esmeralda's eyes glimmered with the light of discovery. "But from what I can decipher, she plans to upload her mind into a computer."

Thaddeus grimaced. "That sounds fatal."

"At this point, I don't think Erica cares."

September 8, 998 ME

Scrapes and Bruises

Esmeralda considered telling Thaddeus about the odd things happening to her, but she convinced herself they were unnerving rather than dangerous. After a lifetime of keeping her own counsel in such matters, she was loath to mention it. He was already on hyper-alert, and it was just little things like laying down a pen and seconds later finding it across the table. Her papers and journals went missing or were misfiled, even though she took great care never to misplace anything. A bit more ominous were the flickering lights and shimmering shadows, so she moved upstairs, and Dr. Moreh seemed pleased, but everywhere she went books fell off the shelves when no one was around. And then, there were the men. They leered and made vulgar comments when she walked past. It seemed as if New York's lunatic fringe came out of the woodwork to taunt her.

Yesterday was the worst, she felt as if she'd run a gauntlet on her walk home to Thaddeus' apartment. She sprinted the last hundred feet into his lobby, sighing with relief when the elevator showed up empty. Just as the door closed, the man who kicked her stepped inside. Instead of maintaining a socially acceptable distance, he crowded her, wordless and menacing, which sparked a mild panic attack, and that scared her the most.

On Thursday, a rag man and his dog chased her. She arrived at work winded, her hair disheveled, her knees bloody from a fall. Esmeralda refused to meet her coworker's eyes, retreating to her basement haven.

At 8:15 am, Moreh summoned her to his office.

"Esmeralda, is everything all right? Lucas informs me you were in quite a state when you arrived this morning." Moreh studied her. She perched on the edge of her chair, her spine ramrod straight, appearing composed, but beneath her bruised exterior, he saw her shaking.

"I'm sorry about that, Professor. I, um," she hesitated, "I seem to have attracted the attention of a particularly aggressive vagrant living in the neighborhood. He's been harassing me on my way to work."

Moreh's gray eyebrows shot up. "Oh my, that is quite disconcerting. Are you injured? Shall I call the police?"

Esmeralda's breath caught. "No, Professor. I assure you, I am fine."

She clearly wasn't and hadn't been all week since she returned from her accident. She crossed her legs in nervous agitation.

Moreh pointed at the lacerated skin on her right knee. "Esmeralda, you are bleeding."

Her face turned crimson. "Oh, I did not realize. I stumbled and fell, trying to get away from the man. It doesn't hurt."

Moreh came around the desk. "Regardless, you cannot work among the ancient text while bleeding." He flipped over her palms. They were scratched and abraded.

She withdrew her hands and brought them close to her face, as if just noticing the injuries. Her large blue eyes regarded him beneath thick black lashes, looking scared and contrite.

"I understand academic zeal, young lady, but you must go home and take care of these injuries. Three times this week, you have misplaced items, and you have been distracted. I think perhaps that bump to the head was more serious than you led me to believe. Now you have been hurt again. I think more rest is in order." He patted her shoulder. "Do not worry, those texts will be here next week. Take it from me, your health is more important. Go get your things. I will walk you home."

Twenty uneventful minutes later, Moreh left her in front of her brownstone. The comfort of her little apartment seemed exactly what she needed.

She stepped into the shower, hissing as the water revealed undiscovered cuts and scratches. Toweling off, she slipped on an old tunic and leggings, the Rephidim cloth felt soft against her injuries, a comfort.

Fatigued and still a bit shaky, she sat on the edge of her bed and called Thaddeus. His voice mail picked up. Still unaccustomed to using the phone, she stammered out a message. "Hi, it's Esmeralda. I'm fine, but I had a little accident on the way to work. Dr. Moreh offered to walk me home, and I was too embarrassed to tell him I was staying with you. But I am a little tired, so I'm just going to lay down in my apartment. Tonight, let's get takeout. Vietnamese. Pho' sounds nice. Oh, I have to go, someone's at my door. I love you."

She cracked the door, peeked out, then exclaimed, "Dr. Allison, what are you doing here?"

Voice Mail

Thaddeus felt the phone vibrate in his jacket pocket, but he was in the middle of an intense briefing about a string of disappearances of young kids off the streets in New Orleans and the New City, so he let it go to voicemail. The statistics were grim, the leads slim. Dozens of kids were gone.

At the end of the meeting, Thaddeus passed out sketches. "Please circulate these among the field offices. These two, Elizabeta ben Yoder and Jenny ben Rip, were reported missing six weeks ago from Bezetha, Pennsylvania. Their parents believe they are runaways, making their way to the New City. I am acquainted with Elizabeta ben Yoder's family and promised I would distribute their pictures."

He paused, staring down at the pair. Sudden inspiration hit and he stunned them by announcing, "Gentlemen, given the update we've had today, I believe a trip to the New City is in order. I have a contact who works with these kids in both locations, so I plan to pay him a visit."

"Tired of sitting behind that desk, hey Director?" Agent Vaughn ben Daniel called out.

Agent Paul ben Casper regarded Thaddeus with interest. The book on Thyatira, the young woman with an accent from the region, and now two missing girls from Bezetha? He knew instantly whose family had sought the Director's help.

"It keeps me from getting rusty, Agent Vaughn. I was a damn good field agent, and I didn't get this job on my good looks alone." The room erupted in chuckles. "I might even take a few days vacation while I'm out there."

That surprised every person at the table, except Paul, who suspected the Director might not be making this particular trip solo. The room cleared, and Paul stayed behind. "How is Esmeralda healing?"

Thaddeus smiled. "Quite well, Agent. Thank you again for your assistance."

"My pleasure, Director. Have a good trip." He winked and left the room.

Thaddeus smoothed his eyebrow, lost in thought. He did not relish his agents knowing about his personal life but given the circumstances he had no choice. His phone buzzed again, reminding him of his missed call. Esmeralda. He grinned and accessed the voice mail, hoping she'd left him something salacious. His blood ran cold when he heard the message.

Who Are You?

Traffic snarled, and Thaddeus cursed, feeling alternately anxious and ridiculous for driving across midtown to Esmeralda's apartment. He had thrown his travel bag in the trunk of the car he procured for his New City trip, which seemed even more ludicrous than leaving work in the middle of the day to check on his girlfriend. However, he trusted his gut, and it told him to get over there now and not on foot.

The ambulance parked in front of her building chased away all doubts. He came to a screeching halt, blocking the vehicle on the narrow street. "Hey!" he bellowed at the woman in the white coat helping Esmeralda down the flight of steps. "What's going on?"

The woman wrapped a protective arm around Esmeralda and said, "Step aside, sir. I have a very sick patient here."

Esmeralda whimpered, her eyes glassy and unfocused.

He took her limp hands. "Esmeralda, what's wrong?"

Esmeralda blinked at him and slurred, "Who are you?"

The blood drained from his face, then he turned to the woman and snarled, "What have you done to her?"

"This is a medical emergency, and you are interfering with my patient's care."

"Your patient?" he asked, shooting venom at the woman. "She is not your patient. She is my fiancée, and you are not taking her anywhere!"

The woman adopted a patronizing expression and said, "I'm sorry, sir, but Esmeralda has suffered a severe psychological break and needs immediate medical attention."

"Psychological break? I just saw her this morning, she was fine." He squeezed Esmeralda's hands, trying to gain her attention.

Esmeralda flinched. "Ow! Dr. Allison, what's happening?"

"It's okay, dear. This man won't hurt you. I've got you now."

Esmeralda's head lolled as her knees buckled.

Instinct, honed during hundreds of investigations, kicked in, and before the doctor or ambulance attendees could react, Thaddeus moved. He grabbed Esmeralda around the waist, hefting her over his shoulder. The action snapped her out of her trance, and she fought like a wildcat. He nearly dropped her but righted himself and made a break for the car.

The driver's door stood open, the car's engine still running. He heaved Esmeralda inside and jumped in behind her. She scrambled across the seat, reaching for the handle, but he had the presence of mind to lock the door and set the child safety button. He pulled away to the protesting shouts and fruitless foot pursuit of the ambulance attendees.

Esmeralda whirled on him. "No! Let me out! You can't do this! Let me go!"

"Stop it!" he yelled, his voice booming inside the car.

She huddled against the door, as far away from him as she could get. "I need my doctor. I have to see my doctor. Doctor Allison was there to help me."

Thaddeus skirted traffic, tearing through midtown like a maniac. "That woman was there to do something, but it was not to help you, Esmeralda!"

Her eyes widened. "How do you know my name?"

Thaddeus jolted. "What?"

"Let me out!"

"Yeshua, help me," he breathed. He was going to need it because Thaddeus ben Todd, eighteen-year veteran, and Director of the FBI, had for all intents and purposes just kidnapped Esmeralda ben Claude and was about to transport her across state lines.

Riding on the roof of their car, great sword unsheathed, stood Uriel, the archangel. His giant wings obscured the vehicle, no camera captured it, no police officer received a report, and not a single astral being prevailed against him. Thaddeus and Esmeralda disappeared from man's view under the protective cover of the angel.

Catatonic

Thaddeus' mind raced, "Where am I going to take her? Where will we be safe? What the hell did that ghoul do to her, and how am I going to break the spell?"

He first thought to take her to Rephidim but discarded that idea. Her parents might not approve of his actions, and the people after her would surely search there. No... he had to get her somewhere else, and he needed to get her the hell away from New York and Pennsylvania where the pursuit would be the most intense.

She at least stopped fighting and screaming, but the cata-tonic state she lapsed into was even more concerning. There was nothing to do about that at the moment, so he used the silence to think. An idea was born, the vague notion floating around in his brain for the last hour, but the more he consid-ered it, the more he decided it was his best course of action.

With his destination set, he relaxed a degree. Esmeralda ben Claude, who had never left the confines of the northeast, was about to embark on a journey across the kingdom, with a man she did not recognize, to see an old friend she did not remember.

Thaddeus decided to take her to Ian.

September 10, 998 ME

In the Belly of the Fish

She ate, she slept, and attended her body's needs, but oth-erwise Esmeralda remained in a dissociative state. Sometimes he filled the silence with their story, and he always started at the beginning. Other times he blasted music. He rolled down the windows and let the sound of the rushing wind fill the empty miles. She never moved, just stared at the dash-board in unblinking monotony. If he shouted, she flinched. When he spoke softly, she would occasionally sigh, but that was her sole reaction. He did not think she heard a single thing he said.

The evening of the third day, in a small motel outside Cheyenne, he got an idea. If he was not so freaked out by the situation, it might have occurred to him sooner. She lay on the shabby comforter, stiff and staring. Gingerly, he took her hand and said, "Esmeralda, I want you to listen to this." He put the phone up to her ear and played her voicemail.

It did not register, so he played it again, fighting frustra-tion and fear, praying fervently the voice message would not be the only evidence he ever had of their amazing six-day reunion, and terrified she was lost to him forever. The third time it played, he buried his face in his hands and made a muffled cry of pain.

"Thaddeus, what's wrong?" she asked in a voice cracked from disuse.

He raised his head, thumbing the tears from his eyes. "Esmie?"

She touched his cheek. "Don't cry."

"Thank you," he breathed a prayer, "thank you for bringing her back."

"Where have I been?" She knitted her brows, her eyes darting around the unfamiliar room. "Where are we?"

He moistened his lips, regathering himself. "Currently, we are in the Open Arms Motel in Cheyenne, Wyoming."

"Wyoming? What in the world are we doing in Wyoming?" Her voice climbed with each word.

"Come here, just come here for a minute," he said, pulling her into a fierce hug.

"Thaddeus, what's happened?" she asked, clinging to him.

"It's okay. I've got you now." He wanted to howl at the moon when she went limp in his arms. "Esmeralda," he shook her, "come back to me!"

She jumped and pushed him away. "Why are you yelling at me?"

He grabbed the sides of his head, panting. "Oh God… that's it! That's a trigger." He blinked as understanding crashed. "Those bastards!"

Esmeralda covered her mouth, dissolving in tears. "Thaddeus, tell me. What is happening?"

He paced, his long legs crossing the small motel room in three strides. "Tell me the last thing you remember."

She wanted to shriek, but she did her best to calm herself, to find her center. She closed her eyes, and at length said, "I don't know."

"Try!" he demanded, fury pulsing off him as the implications of a trigger registered. "Thursday, Thursday morning? Do you remember anything?"

"You… you made me a bagel."

He stopped, relieved their reunion had not been wiped from her brain. "Then what?"

"We got dressed for work." A ghost of a smile quivered at the corner of her mouth. "Then we got undressed, really quick."

His legs gave out, and he slid to the floor, laughing. "Yes, we did."

"Then I walked to work." She looked away, hugging herself. "Someone attacked me on my way in. He was so creepy, and he had a dog. I feared it was going to bite me. It was really mean."

Thaddeus climbed up the bed and hugged her. "It's all right, he did not get you."

"No, he didn't. I ran. That's when I fell. I think I hit my head again. I didn't even notice I was bleeding."

He let out an angry sigh. "That's happened to you twice, where you've been hurt and did not feel it."

She rubbed the scar on her cheek. "I think it's happened more than twice."

"Could very well be. But go on, after the dog chased you where did you go?"

"Yes, okay. I remember. Doctor Moreh called me to his office and told me I was too hurt to be there, so he walked me home." She pinched the bridge of her nose, concentrating. "I took a shower, and I got dressed, then I called you. Is that the message you played for me?"

"It was." Thaddeus rolled over and took his phone from the nightstand. "Here, listen to it again." He played it, her shaky voice echoing in the silence. "Who was at the door?"

Esmeralda bit her bottom lip. "I can't remember."

"Please try, this is important." Thaddeus encouraged, "You can do it."

"Someone's at the door… Dr. Allison ben Whitaker!"

"Yes, it was. Go on."

"She was in town for a conference. She said she stopped by the library to see me. Doctor Moreh told her I'd been hurt and was at home, so she came to check on me." Her face ticked with confusion. "I don't remember anything after that, just waking up here. What happened?"

Jaw muscles flexing, Thaddeus gritted his teeth and said, "I don't know exactly, but that fucking broad did something to you that turned you into a zombie."

She covered her face with both hands. "I had a mental break?"

Thaddeus pulled her hands away, staring into her eyes. "You did not. She triggered something that caused it. I saw it happen. I've seen it happen to you several times."

A shudder wracked Esmeralda's frame. "A trigger, she triggered me? I didn't go over the rainbow on my own?"

"No, you did not," he said, a menacing edge to his voice.

Esmeralda began to weep. "I thought she was a good one. There were so many mean ones. When she took over my treatment, I thought I could trust her."

"I'm sorry."

"Thaddeus, what's happened to me? What did they do? Who does that to a person? Who steals their life and their memories? Who makes somebody think they are crazy?" She rocked in his arms, repeating the word. "Crazy… crazy… crazy…"

He held on until her tears turned into sniffles, then he tilted her chin up and said, "You are not now, nor have you ever been, crazy. As for who did this to you, I promise I am going to find out."

Esmeralda pursed her lips, looking fierce. "Good."

September 11, 998 ME

Dirty Secret

Thaddeus woke the next morning to find Esmeralda staring at him. Without preamble, she said, "Let's just assume I'm not crazy."

He blinked, shaking himself awake. "Okay." His voice sounded like gravel.

"And that is a heck of an assumption, because for the better part of the last five years, I believed I was." As she spoke, her fury built. "But from what you've told me I'm not, nor have I ever been, crazy. Do I have this right?" she asked rhetorically. "Because if I do, then it's not an assumption, it's a fact!"

"There is ample evidence to support it," Thaddeus, the attorney, answered and climbed out of bed to pour a cup of coffee.

"Well, there is also plenty of evidence to support the other side," Esmeralda countered.

Thaddeus conceded with a quick nod but shrugged. "I could take the other side apart piece by piece. In the end, we build the case that you are not."

Esmeralda furrowed her forehead. "I need an attorney."

Thaddeus grinned and raised his coffee in salute. "You've got one."

"You can't be my attorney. From what you told me last night, you're in as much trouble as I am, maybe more. Kidnapping…" She made a disgusted noise in the back of her throat.

"I wasn't talking about myself, Esmeralda. Monday afternoon, I called my attorney, who is now also your attorney."

"You did? Who?"

"Sir Preston ben Worley, of Worley, Blake, and Standish, Attorneys at Law, who on Friday morning presented a petition to the court for a restraining order against Dr. Allison ben Whitaker, her associates, and anyone from the Pennsylvania Department of Health and Human Services, which is likely why she was in town and came after you." He held her gaze, "Worley is also preparing documents to sue the commonwealth of Pennsylvania for false imprisonment and mental anguish. In a dual motion, they are petitioning to have your record expunged."

Her mouth fell.

"He's a crafty old bastard. Trust me, you are in good hands. Even a first-year law student could see the potential in your case. You were denied due process and proper counsel, baby. I had a look at a few of the court records, you got shafted. The whole case stinks to high heaven." Days worth of frustration and anger broke free, as he added, "And if anyone from your family would have contacted me, I would have advised them as such! Dammit, Esmeralda why didn't you? Why didn't Eve, or Ernst, or your parents, why didn't somebody tell me what the hell was going on?"

Esmeralda covered her eyes and squeezed her temples. "I told them not to."

Thaddeus put his hand on his hip, leaning forward in disbelief. "You did what?"

"I thought I was—" She arrested the word before she spoke it, amending, "I imagined I might find you someday, and you would never have to know."

She stood up and pointed a finger at him. "It's not like being sick, like if you get a disease or something, there is shame in mental illness. It's a dirty little secret. And do you know why? Because once people know, they don't see you the same. They don't treat you the same. They are always watching to see if you are losing it again. I read it in Doctor Moreh's eyes the day he sent me home. I did not want to live my life, with you, like that! I didn't want you to look at me that way! If I acted silly or had a dream," her voice caught in an angry sob, "I did not want you to wonder."

There was truth in her words, since he found out, since she went catatonic, he was afraid for her.

"The thing is, I did have an episode! I don't remember much about it, but I ended up standing on a kitchen counter brandishing a knife, bleeding, and screaming." Her voice broke. "So, forgive me if I didn't ever want you to know that!"

"It would not have mattered," Thaddeus whispered.

With her fury spent, she sagged in defeat. "It did to me."

What Color is That Car?

They rode the first two hundred miles in relative quiet, exchanging pleasantries, pretending normalcy, each lost in the tumult that erupted between them and the ramifications of the trigger.

"What color is that car?" Esmeralda pointed ahead of them.

He looked at her dubiously. "Yellow, why?"

"What if I told you it was green?" Esmeralda's words held a dark edge.

"I'd tell you that you were mistaken. That car is yellow." Thaddeus wondered where she was going with this and fought down exactly what she accused him of, suspecting she was going over the edge.

"All right. What if there were four other people in the car, and they all said it was green?"

"Then all of you would be mistaken." he declared emphatically.

"Would we? How can you be so sure?"

"Because the freaking car is yellow, Esmeralda."

She nodded. "What if ten more people said it was green? Would you believe them? Would you rub your eyes and look again?"

"I see where you are headed with this."

"No, I don't think you do. Do you know why? Because your mind is trustworthy. It hasn't lied to you." She pressed her thumb against her chin, deep in thought. "For five years, I was told that the car was green by everyone. Then last week, I walked through your door, and you told me the car is yellow. In my mind, I've always thought it was yellow, but I pretended to see green, because normal people see a green car. So when I look at it now, I think it's yellow, but it might be green."

Trust

Mile after mile they drove, through sparsely populated towns and landscape reverting to desert. New City technology, that kept the edges of California in water, did not extend out here. Most of the residents had migrated, east to the Golden Kingdom or west to the New City, leaving behind once thriving farms and communities. The barren landscape matched the mood in the car.

"I've been thinking about what you said earlier." Thaddeus broke the silence. "I understand. But you were right all along. You knew the truth. Using the car example, you knew it was yellow." He reached across the arm rest and took her hand, "They just hurt you bad enough to make you say what they wanted, but it didn't change the truth."

She squeezed his hand. "No, it did not change the truth, but it made me doubt, and I think that is what they wanted."

"Then the bigger question is motive. Why did they do it?" Thaddeus brought her fingers to his lips and pressed a kiss. "We figure out motive, and that will lead to who."

"I was seventeen, Thaddeus. I'd never even left Rephidim. How would anyone on the outside know anything about me to even make me a target?"

He shook his head. "You must have seen or heard something they wanted kept silent."

"What? It does not make sense."

"That's what we need to figure out. Somebody pretty well connected went to a lot of trouble to make sure you never told and even if you did, nobody would believe you."

She withdrew her hand, turning away from him. "The thing is Thaddeus, I never stopped seeing the yellow cars. I just stopped telling people when I was five, and after the hospital, I told myself I just imagined them."

"What do you see?" he asked, keeping his voice steady.

She made a rueful laugh. "These days, it's not so much what I see, though I expect I could again, if I tried. It comes in flashes, but it crashed in on me the other night, hard." Her smile held a secret, and she looked at him with hooded eyes. "Tin Man."

He grinned and waggled his eyebrows at her. "Vixen."

Some of the tension evaporated. She turned sideways in her seat and brought her feet to the armrest. "So, let's just assume, the car is yellow. I can see it, and you can see it. But what if I told you there is an angel riding on the roof?"

He turned slowly. "You see angels?"

"Among other things." She dared him to look at her and not have his face cloud.

"I might be... um... a bit interested. I'd like to know more about that angel," he replied carefully.

She chuckled, "But you can't see him. I can. So, then it becomes a choice. Do you believe me, or am I mad? Because now, I've asked you to step over the rainbow." She gave his shoulder a little kick. "It was easy to sit over there and tell me the car was yellow and ask me to trust you. It's a different story if there's an angel on the roof."

Thaddeus concentrated on the empty road. Esmeralda ben Claude had never been an easy girl, and now he knew why. The words of Yeshua came to mind, *Help her find the light, she will tell you the truth.* He measured his words, saying, "You have always been extraordinary. Even as a little kid, you saw things, and said things, that left me wondering all the time how you knew what you did. You did it the other night, with Paul."

She touched her ear tentatively. "I was hurt, and my guard was down."

"I love that about you. It's one of my favorite things." He smiled with a raise of his eyebrows. "You're right though, it does come down to trust. Not about the way we feel about one another, I think we've pretty well established that." He stroked her ankle. "You trust me when I tell you the car is yellow, and I'll trust you when you tell me there is an angel on top of it."

She nodded and added with a sarcastic glint in her eye, "All right, Thaddeus, take me to see the wizard."

Part 5 - The Grand Adventure

September 12, 998 ME

Not in New York Anymore

Esmeralda pressed her face to the car window and said, "This looks nothing like New York."

Thaddeus, the consummate New Yorker, snorted. "Of course not, it's California, home of the fruits and nuts."

"Well then, I ought to fit right in," Esmeralda replied drolly.

Thaddeus rolled his eyes. But if she could joke, her trauma was losing its power. She reminded him of a butterfly emerging from a cocoon, peeking her head out, and taking stock of a new world. Last night, she insisted he remove the stitches from her ear. The bruising disappeared, as did the downward cast of her eyes. And with each hour, he watched her heal.

"I'm ready to be out of this car, even if it is the New City," he grumbled.

"The ride didn't seem so bad to me."

Thaddeus turned to her, incredulous, but the teasing glint in her eyes made him laugh. "I suppose it wouldn't, sleepyhead."

She blew him a kiss. He leaned in, tapping his cheek, and she obliged with a loud smooch.

"I wonder why I cannot remember Ian ben Kole."

"I don't know, but you should. He seems to be the only person you've forgotten, which could be significant, taken with the other holes in your memory. I hope seeing him jogs something."

Esmeralda made a quick shrug. "I'll try."

"It's all you can do." He cleared his throat. "They did a number on you in there. It might just take time."

She crossed her arms and said, "Part of me wants to remember everything, but there is another part that does not. There might be good reasons I can't remember."

He knew what that felt like, though he had sought oblivion in booze. "When you are strong enough and the time is right, it will come. It took me two years to tell you about my family."

Her words were soft as she looked up at him. "You had a beautiful family."

A new vision came to his mind, and he was profoundly grateful. "They still are."

She tilted her head, studying him. "You've seen them."

It was a statement, rather than a question, her old insight returning. "I did. I had a dream."

"You did?" she asked with enthusiasm. "Tell me about it."

As they negotiated the New City traffic, Thaddeus relayed his dream, leaving out the part about his guilt over the prostitutes and glossing over the intense danger she was in. She asked him several excited questions, and when he finished, a contemplative silence settled around her.

"The Lord uses dreams. He has since the beginning of the Age of Man, though not in the Millennium, not until the end. You know that's a prophecy, right?"

He raised an eyebrow and waited.

"It's in Joel, and in Acts, 'In the last days, God says, I will pour out My Spirit on all people; your sons and daughters will prophesy, your young men will see visions, your old men will dream dreams.'"

"Are you saying I'm old?"

Esmeralda cracked up. "You are a bit long in the tooth."

"Hey!" he protested. "That's not very nice. I'm a sensitive old geezer with a hot young chick."

She pointed to herself. "That would be me."

"Heaven help me, don't I know it?"

She ran a hand up his thigh. "We could turn around and go back to the hotel. That bed looked comfy."

"Tempting, but then we'd miss dinner, and I told Ian I was paying. Though, I should have stopped at the bank and got more cash. I never saw a guy eat like that."

"So, he's a big man?"

Thaddeus snorted and pulled into the Center for Street Kids of Alanthia. "You'll see."

Esmeralda looked around, craning her head as they drove up. "What an interesting place. It was a winery?"

"I don't know, was it?" Thaddeus put the car in park and studied the buildings. When he'd come last year, he had not given the place a second glance.

"I think so. Look around. The offices there, I'll bet that is where they stored the machinery. That building over there, I'd say that's where they aged the wine, and that sports field looks like it was once part of the old vineyard."

"Ask Ian about it, or Joanna, she founded the place." He held the door for her, and they stepped inside.

A rather large woman with a severe hairstyle and feet swollen to the size of watermelons met them. She was leaving for the day and looked miserable. "Good evening. How can

I help you?" Her put out tone of voice belied her friendly words.

"Hi, Thaddeus and Esmeralda to see Ian."

Her smile did not meet her red-rimmed green eyes. "Sure, around the corner to your right." She moved past them without a backward glance.

Esmeralda gave her a wide berth and whispered to Thaddeus as the door closed. "She is disturbed."

"I ran into her last year. You might be right," he whispered back.

"I am." Esmeralda nodded with solemn assurance. "Trust me, I've been around enough of them to know."

Thaddeus laughed, "Come on, let's go find Ian."

Long-Lost Friends

Ian rose from his desk when Thaddeus ducked through the door and said, "Good to see you, man."

"You as well, my friend."

Ian flashed a toothy grin.

Esmeralda hung back, lacing her fingers demurely. Her first impression of Ian ben Kole was stark white hair, startling on a face so young. Her second was he was not fat and nearly as tall as Thaddeus.

Basketball... he played basketball; her heart pounded.

Thaddeus stepped aside and motioned her forward.

Ian took her in. If possible, his smile widened. "Look at you, all grown up."

Esmeralda felt her face glowing pink. "Hi."

"Hi, yourself! Come here." He opened his arms.

She glanced at Thaddeus, then took a step forward. Ian enveloped her in a powerful hug, as the presence surrounding him flowed into her. It felt like running under a gentle waterfall, full of life, truth, Spirit.

Esmeralda gave a startled cry and clung to him. "Ian." She pulled back, cupping his face in her hands. "My friend, I remember!" Then she fell back in his arms, happy tears leaking from her eyes.

Thaddeus wanted to shout with joy, then he looked between them and wasn't sure how pleased he was about the hugging. "All right, still trying to steal my girl."

Esmeralda rested her wet cheek against Ian's chest and smiled up at Thaddeus.

Ian threw his hands up, protesting his innocence, and stepped out of Esmeralda's embrace. "I see some things haven't changed." He looked at her fondly. "Though you haven't, just as pretty as ever." He did not remark upon the scar on her cheek. Evil had touched her.

Esmeralda preened under the compliment, her smile wide and bright. "Thank you, though I think you are bigger than you used to be."

Ian patted his flat stomach. "It's the dreaded middle age paunch you are seeing."

Thaddeus scoffed, "You should weigh four hundred pounds."

"Speaking of food… let me go grab Joanna and we'll go."

"Is that your wife?" Esmeralda asked.

Ian faltered. "No, my partner. We run this place together."

Table for Four

Esmeralda suspected Joanna ben Luke was the most intimidating woman she ever met. Intensity pulsed off her in coral-colored waves, vibrant pink, orange, and red; everything about Joanna burned hot. Her brown eyes missed nothing, and Esmeralda would have given her eye teeth for a fraction of her confidence and poise, not to mention her razor cut straight hair. Joanna was also the fastest walker Esmeralda ever saw. Her three-inch black pumps beat a rapid staccato toward their table in the fashionable restaurant she chose near the Center. She paused at two tables, exchanging pleasantries with the diners, and called the waiter by name before he introduced himself. After a cursory glance at the menu, she set it aside, declared she was ordering the grilled salmon salad, and turned her attention to Esmeralda.

"You are a librarian?" Joanna asked, and Esmeralda determined she was not rude, simply direct, and more interested in discussing matters of substance rather than making small talk.

"Well, I work at the Metropolitan Library in New York as a research associate."

"Research? What sort?"

"Currently, I am transcribing ancient texts, primarily journals and diaries written during the Great Judgment."

"How interesting. Tell me about it."

With that, Esmeralda launched into the safe ground of research and books. Without realizing it, she relaxed into the conversation. Joanna smiled where appropriate, asked pertinent and thoughtful questions, and engaged in a way that few outside of academia could do. At length, Esmeralda blushed. "Please forgive me. I get a little carried away."

"Not at all. Doing the work you love, of any type, is a worthy pursuit." She turned to Thaddeus and added, "I understand from Ian that you and he worked at the most interesting manufacturing facilities I have ever heard of. Though, I did not believe him when he first told me about it. So, please tell me the truth. Did you really turn spiderwebs into fabric?"

Thaddeus, Esmeralda, and Ian enthused about the wonders of Arachnid Weaving. During the conversation, Esmeralda experienced an intense longing for Rephidim, akin to physical pain. She had not returned since that fateful day she left for her aunt's house. Sitting at the dinner table, surrounded by friends and strangers, she remembered riding away, remembered the feel of the horse, the color of the grass... and a crossroads. She reached for a glass of wine and her hand trembled.

Thaddeus squeezed her knee under the table. "Are you okay?" he asked under his breath.

She nodded, though her pale countenance telegraphed something was amiss.

Ian took a bite of salmon from Joanna's plate, so she passed him her half-finished salad along with the breadbasket. He smiled in thanks and between bites said, "Thaddeus tells me he has to spend the day at the office tomorrow. Joanna and I are taking a group of kids out to Golden Gate Park. You should join us."

"Oh, you should. Have you ever seen the redwoods?" Joanna asked.

"As much as I hate it, I will have a full day tomorrow. You should go," Thaddeus said.

This morning they were relieved to hear there were no charges pending against him in New York, which validated his suspicions about Dr. Allison ben Whitaker. A legitimate physician would have certainly reported his abduction of Esmeralda to the authorities, yet Sir Preston's office confirmed no such report had been filed.

Esmeralda met Ian's gentle eyes. "Are you sure it won't be a bother? I do like kids."

Ian nodded. "Ah, no bother, at all. It's been a long time since you and I took a walk in the woods. It will be grand."

A waiter dropped a tray of dishes, startling Esmeralda right out of her chair. Thaddeus turned to her with a sardonic grin and quipped, "I think they heard that all the way over in Endor."

Esmeralda paled.

September 13, 998 ME

A Path Through the Woods

Pictures and drawings could not do them justice. The giants, sentinels from the Last Age, thousands of years old, loomed above them like guardians of the past. "These are the coastal Redwoods. The enormous ones are up north and over in Sequoia," Ian informed her. "My brother and sister-in-law's place backs up to some of the most amazing specimens you will ever see."

"Bigger than this?" Esmeralda breathed in awe, resting her hand on a trunk thirty feet wide. "It's hard to imagine. My mind cannot even grasp that this is a tree!"

"This is an amazing place, isn't it?" Ian gestured to the group of kids running ahead. "That's why we bring them out here, so they can see something other than the concrete of the New City."

Esmeralda stared after the exuberant kids. "Some of them are so young. Where are their families? How do they come to you?"

Ian smiled, amused to find rapid-fire questions were still part of her personality. "Each story is different, but in some ways all the same." He shook his head. "When Joanna first started, the kids were mainly orphans from the Civil War. Since then, we get a lot of runaways, kids who take off, lured by the promise of the New City."

"We've got one of those in my family, my cousin, Elizabeta, and her friend Jenny. Remind me to give you the flyer Thaddeus made up. His office is helping, but their disappearance worries my aunt."

"She's got good reason to worry. It's dangerous for the runaways. They get it in their heads that the New City is going to be paradise, but when they get here, they find naught but drugs, gangs, and all too often, life in a brothel. Paige, the wee lass in the pink, Joanna pulled her out of an S&M brothel two years ago. She's from Georgia. Her family decided to emigrate to the Golden City, and she ran off."

Esmeralda stared after the little brunette with the black-rimmed glasses. "She looks about fifteen."

"She is, and she spent nine months chained to a bed."

Esmeralda faltered.

Ian steadied her. "Are you okay?"

Visions of bondage, strait jackets, and ties flashed through

Esmeralda's mind. She rubbed her wrists, remembering the pain and frustration of being unable to move, and the desolate hopelessness those bonds brought. "Yeah, I'm okay."

"Thaddeus didn't go into detail, but he said you've had a rough time."

Esmeralda sighed. "You could say that, but in comparison, I think Paige had it rougher."

Ian's face remained neutral. "You know, we can always find somebody who's had it worse, but that does not negate the struggles we all go through. The Lord gives each of us a path He wants us to walk, for our good, and His purpose. It's not a contest, Esmeralda."

She absently rubbed her ear, soothing the itchy healing. "I used to be so sure of the path I was on, never questioned it. I've lost that."

Ahead, the boys roughhoused, the girls congregated in groups, talking and laughing. Joanna knelt, soothing a little one, brushing dirt off her blue jeans.

"Do you remember the day Thaddeus left?" Ian asked in a companionable voice.

Esmeralda's blue eyes flashed in disbelief. "Yes, it was a bit of a pivotal moment."

He snorted. "What did I tell you? God has his timing."

"And my answer was, 'Tomorrow is too long.' I didn't have a clue how long it would actually be."

"Yet here you find yourself, with Thaddeus."

Esmeralda looped her arm through his. "It's amazing. I cannot even convey to you how happy I am, despite everything. I have him back."

Ian hugged her arm. "Then enjoy it, Esmeralda. It's a gift… being with the one you love."

Esmeralda tilted her head, looking deep into his eyes. "You love Joanna, don't you?"

A jolt ran through him, and his face fell as he said, "I'm not free to."

"You're already married?" Esmeralda asked, incredulous.

Ian grimaced. "No. It's not that. I simply haven't been given a sign or permission to pursue any relationship."

Esmeralda leaned her head against his shoulder, full of compassion. "I know what that's like, to love someone and the timing not be right. You get up every day and want to be with them and know that you can't, not yet."

Ian hung his head. "I suppose you do."

"But the Lord has His timing." She repeated his words back to him.

Ian stared at Joanna, watching her direct the kids across a wooden bridge onto the hiking trail. "And tomorrow is too long."

"You and I, we're not like everyone else." Esmeralda followed his gaze. "We see things other people don't. We know things. Be patient, Ian, don't lose heart. Your time will come."

"As has yours, little miss."

Ian and Esmeralda froze. Esmeralda tightened her grip on Ian's arm and answered without turning, "Jelena."

"Hello, Esmeralda, Ian."

They turned in unified awe, greeted with the ethereal beauty of the Gune, who never failed to take their breaths away. Today, she stood before them glowing white, her black hair shimmering blue onyx, her skin opalescence and flawless, statuesque and stunning.

Esmeralda swallowed audibly. "You are even more beautiful than I remembered."

Ian flashed his Kole brother's toothy smile and said, "Nigh on a decade since we last met. It's good to see you."

Jelena winked at him. "Of course it is. I am Gune, thus, fabulous. But it is not you I am here to see, not this time. Though I love you." She blew him a kiss and held her graceful hand out to Esmeralda, who moved forward without conscious effort.

"Oh, you're still bossy, I see," Ian teased.

Jelena raised an elegant shoulder in a shrug. "For eternity, it is how I was made. Now, you come." She took Esmeralda by the hand. "We have much to discuss."

"I'll see you at the end of the trail." Ian waved and left, joining Joanna and the kids.

Esmeralda and Jelena veered into the depths of the dense forest, away from the crowd and off the trail. They walked through the thick vegetation, stirring up decades of fallen leaves and damp moss, filling the air with the comforting smell of autumn.

Colors came into vivid focus and the old calm, once so familiar, settled over Esmeralda like slipping on a favorite t-shirt. "You have been gone so long that I thought I imagined you." Esmeralda's words echoed the awe she felt.

"Was that truth?" Jelena asked cryptically.

Esmeralda gave her a sidelong glance. "Obviously not."

"You say that now because I am here, but if I were not, would you be so sure?"

Esmeralda decided to be honest. "Perhaps in time."

Jelena nodded. "Which is why I am here; you have no time. They come after you again. This time, you fight."

Fear shot down Esmeralda's spine. "I lost last time."

"No, you went into the furnace. It is different." Jelena's sapphire eyes flashed. "What color did you see in there?"

"Black," Esmeralda answered without hesitation.

"Only black?" Jelena challenged.

Esmeralda looked away, then unbidden anger erupted. "No! They were all there, the left side, and I learned them all, alone! So I suppose that's why you're back?"

Esmeralda whirled, her voice rising. "Where were you when they were brainwashing me? Where were you when they tied me up? Where were you when they cut my hair?" She stomped her foot and pointed an accusing finger. "I called upon Him, and He abandoned me! I lost, and they took me! Where was He?"

"I was there."

Esmeralda fell to her knees; Jelena departed.

"Be strong and courageous. Do not fear or be in dread of them, for it is the Lord your God who goes with you. I will not leave you or forsake you."

Esmeralda hid her face in shame, mortified to be confronted in a moment of anger and disbelief. "I'm sorry!" she cried. "Please forgive me. I did not mean it."

"Ah, but you did," Yeshua countered.

She could not deny it.

He had compassion on her, for on the cross the Father turned away from Him, and Blackness had a single moment of triumph over the Son of Man. He said, *"Eli, Eli, lema sabachthani?"*

Supernatural understanding flowed through her, and she raised her eyes, staring at the one who had uttered the most plaintive cry in history, 'My God, my God, why have you forsaken me?' On the cross, the Son had borne the last moments—alone.

When she stared into his eyes, she saw that He knew her suffering, but she also read the difficulty ahead, not unto death, not equal to the suffering of the Son of God, but for His glory. Her trials had been ordered. He had not turned away, even if she had not known, even when she felt abandoned. Her voice shook with the vow she had not uttered in five years, "My steps are ordered, my path is guarded, and my purpose, to serve The King."

Yeshua smiled and lifted her into his arms, holding her tight. He whispered, "Fight the good fight, finish the race, keep the faith."

Then He was gone.

Esmeralda collapsed to the forest floor, weeping in joy, relief, and wonder. Passersby heard, but could not see, for the Rephidim garment she wore hid her from all eyes, human and otherwise.

That Was Some Walk

Joanna paced by the van. "Do you think we should go back and look for her?"

Ian leaned against the driver's door and crossed his ankles. "No, she'll be along."

"I can't believe you left her. She's bright, but she doesn't know these woods, and she's scared as a rabbit." Joanna put her hand on her hip, perturbed at the delay.

"That grant application will still be there when we get back," Ian said, having surmised the real reason for her impatience.

"Pfftt," she snorted at him, "I'm going to make you do it."

He grinned at her. "No you won't. Every time I try, you take it back and tell me I'm not doing it right."

The corner of her mouth quivered. "Well, you don't."

He chuckled, "I just don't do it the same way you do. There's a difference."

She turned her nose up in the air. "I can't help it, it's just the way I'm made."

"That's twice today I've heard that, both times from bossy women."

"I'm not bossy!" Joanna protested.

Ian threw back his head and laughed. "Maybe not inside, but outside…"

"Oh, you be quiet, Ian ben Kole. What do you know?" Her brown eyes sparkled with familiar affection because he was the only person who truly knew her.

"After three years? Just about everything, Princess."

She looked away, hiding her pleasure at his words. "Don't let the kids hear you call me that. They get ideas."

Ian grabbed the back of his neck, thinking he had a few ideas of his own. *"When, Lord? When?"* he prayed, but he received no reply and was ripped from his revery by Joanna's gasp. He turned to see what caused Joanna to make such a noise, and his jaw dropped.

Esmeralda emerged from the deep woods with a streak in her hair as white as his.

Mayday!

Twenty minutes after their scheduled departure time, the Mistress loomed in the cockpit door and said, "I do not care what your flight plan says. I've paid good money for this aircraft, and you will deliver me on time. Do you understand me, Pilot?"

"Madam, there is considerable congestion over the continent tonight, and air traffic control sets our flight plan," the pilot replied, trying to reason with her.

She lifted her lip in scorn, then pressed a blood-red fingernail between his eyes and ordered, "Then fly above them!"

The pilot gagged as a wracking shudder convulsed his body, and his eyes rolled back in his head.

The copilot rose from his seat. "See here, madam!"

She turned her wrath on the protestor. "Yes? You have something to say?"

The copilot's innards turned to liquid fear as he experienced a vision of his wife and children murdered. He recoiled in horror.

"I thought not," she spat and turned to the navigator. "And you, do you have anything to say?"

The young woman shook her head in mute terror as the air in the cockpit turned icy, revealing the frost of her terrified gasps.

"Good," the Mistress said, flashing a look of malevolent satisfaction before pushing past the steward and retaking her seat.

"A lesson, Princess," she said, settling beside Keyseelough, "never let them tell you how it will be. You control the destination and the method for getting there."

Keyseelough wiggled, aroused by the power emanating from her traveling companion. She slid her hand into the woman's lap, watching her eyes. "Yes, Mistress."

The older woman moistened her lips and looked at Keyseelough with hungry eyes. "Perhaps we will continue our lesson in the back?"

Keyseelough touched her chest and cooed, "It would be my honor."

"Indeed."

The flight attendant watched in fascinated horror as the Chief Justice of the Alanthian Supreme Court disappeared into the private jet's bedroom with Prince Peter ben Korah's betrothed.

An hour later, a distress call blasted over the speakers in the air traffic control tower in Houston. "Mayday, Mayday flight A-13. Our aircraft has lost pressure... severe hypoxia affecting passengers and crew."

The stewardess stumbled through the cabin, her limbs as heavy as granite, her body screaming for oxygen. She fell against the door with a thud, gasping, "Madam. Prepare. For. Emergency. Landing."

Lying naked and entwined with a girl thirty years her junior, the Mistress Angelica ben Omri, Ba'alat Ob, High Priestess, and Chief Justice of the Alanthian Supreme Court, never stirred. Atop the plunging aircraft, the angel Gabriel kicked back and flashed twenty percent of his fingers at Marduk, who appeared like a comet out of the sky.

Two thousand miles away, emerging from the redwood forest, Esmeralda ben Claude laughed.

Another Day at the Office

Thaddeus left the New City FBI office with a vague sense of nausea, plunging into the snarl of rush hour traffic, reviewing what he learned that day. Official reports rarely contained the instincts of the investigators on the ground, nor could a phone call elicit the candor an in-person meeting might uncover. Thaddeus had been a Field Agent, they respected him, so they told him the truth, and the news was worse than anyone in New York imagined.

The statistics were startling: thirty-five kids missing in the last two years, most of them from the old section of the New City. He suspected the story from New Orleans would be much the same and determined after a quick visit to Mack in Redding, a trip to the Big Easy was in order. He planned to meet several of his team members in Louisiana. They needed to get a handle on this before more kids came up missing.

He pulled up to the business offices of the Center and spotted Ian on the basketball court with several residents. He looked down at his suit and tie with a grimace but remembered he had a gym bag in the trunk. A good sweat and a little hoop were exactly what the doctor ordered, as long as the doctor wasn't named Whitaker.

He called to Ian that he was going to change, then emerged from the business office bathrooms ready to play.

"Oh, it looks like Mr. Ian goin' have some competition. I 'member him from lass year," called a lanky black youth. "Mr. Ian, he wiped the court wiff you!"

"By my count, we're 1 and 1, Ishmael. Take yourself and your house off the court. Let the old men show you young folk how it's done."

"Oooo!" Elijah ben William called, poking Ishmael with a pointy elbow.

What Thaddeus lost in youthful energy, he made up for with experience and skill. But since Rephidim, Ian played regularly. They pushed each other to their physical limits, and it felt good.

Wringing wet, Thaddeus dropped to a bench, accepting a drink of water and a towel. "Not bad for a California boy."

Ian passed the ball to Elijah and collapsed beside him. "Not bad for an old New Yorker."

"Don't I know it." He looked around. "Where is Esmie, anyway?"

Ian chuckled, "She's inside. I believe the library was her destination. She organized a story time and had the kids following her around all afternoon."

Thaddeus laughed. "Shocking. Esmeralda among books."

"Well now, speaking of shocking." Ian ran a hand through his sweaty hair.

Thaddeus snapped his head around, alert. "What?"

"She's fine, don't worry," Ian reassured him. "Just a slight change in hair color." Thaddeus wrinkled his forehead in confusion, and Ian shrugged. "On the bright side, your age difference will not be as noticeable."

Thaddeus narrowed his eyebrows, his face a mask of incomprehension.

Ian pointed to his white hair. "It happens."

Thaddeus stood up. "What happened?"

"She had an encounter in the woods, but I'll let her tell you."

"Unreal," Thaddeus rolled his eyes and followed Ian into the main building.

He realized as he walked into the library, the scent of books always surrounded her, vellum, paper, leather. If he hadn't been witless with lust that first night, he would have recognized it, instead of incorporating it into the fantasy. He inhaled, absorbing it, preparing for whatever new shock was to come. "Esmie?"

"Back here. Did you talk to Ian?" she asked from behind a tall shelf.

"I did. Come out and let me see." He prepared for the worst, but when she peeked around the books, he sighed with relief. About an inch wide, framing her face on the right side, her front lock was white as snow. The corner of his mouth lifted. She looked adorable. "So you ran into a mad hairdresser on your walk in the woods?"

She pulled the white curl straight then watched it recoil, her eyes dancing. "A pair of them."

"I like it, makes you look more exotic." He closed the distance between them.

Esmeralda's smile grew slowly. "I am exotic."

He ran his fingers over the curl, the texture soft as velvet. "Erotic."

Heat passed between them. He smelled of clean male sweat and the basketball court, his forehead glistening, his t-shirt damp. She moistened her lips.

"Not in the library, if you please?" Ian's voice cut through the interplay.

Esmeralda covered an embarrassed giggle with her fingers. Thaddeus took her by the hand and pulled her past Ian. "We'll see you all for dinner… at eight."

As they departed, Ian heard the distinctive sound of a masculine hand meeting a soft female rump, followed by a squeal of delight. He covered his eyes and groaned with envy.

On the drive to the hotel, Esmeralda relayed the events of the day to Thaddeus with a confidence missing from her voice heretofore. "I called Doctor Moreh when we got back to the Center."

"You did?"

"I resigned."

His eyebrows shot up in surprise. "Why?"

Measuring her words, she said, "I don't trust him. He may or may not be involved with Doctor Allison, but she helped arrange the job, and he told her where I was. I can't work there after that."

She nestled in her seat and continued, "I enjoyed working with the kids at the Center today. I think I have something to offer, something to help them because I know what it is like to get in trouble. I don't know, I just seemed to connect with them, and I think it is time for me to stop hiding in the basement and do something meaningful." She glanced over at him, relaxed and at peace. "I spoke with Joanna about volunteering. It turns out, they are opening a center in New York. She asked me if I'd be interested in coming on board, and I told her yes."

Thaddeus gave her a half smile and took her hand. "Well, you had a rather eventful day."

Her sultry eyes held a promise as she murmured, "The day is not over yet."

His half smile grew into a full one.

Wrapped in an oversized hotel robe, her hair still damp from the shower, Esmeralda sipped a glass of wine, enjoying the indigo and yellow sky as the sun set behind the mountains. A breeze blew in from the Bay, ruffling the bougainvillea that looked as if it should smell heavenly, but bore only the subtle fragrance of dusty honeysuckle. Thaddeus joined her on the balcony, a towel slung low around his waist. He kissed the side of her neck, and she leaned into him with a leisurely sigh. "It's beautiful here, different though. There is a frenetic energy that New York doesn't have."

Thaddeus rested his chin on the top of her head, enjoying the view and the woman. The sonorous sound of the waves ebbing and flowing against the shore pleased him. "Different from Rephidim as well."

Esmeralda placed her wine glass on the table and turned in his arms. "That's where I'd like to get married."

"Rephidim?" He closed his eyes and rested his forehead against hers. "You'll marry me?"

She breathed a featherlight kiss. "Yes."

He opened his mouth against hers. "My precious girl."

A Bit of Advice

Esmeralda and Thaddeus arrived twenty minutes late to dinner.

They met Ian and Joanna in a busy city square several blocks from their hotel, an eclectic, funky section of the New City that teemed with tourists and residents. A talented busker played for tips in front of Zuzah's Chocolates and Confections, and a young girl about eighteen looked bored, sitting on a stool beside a cart selling t-shirts and sunglasses. The open-air square was full of young families letting their children run off the day's energy, and college kids sitting on blankets, flirting or studying, sometimes both. Shopkeepers lingered in open doorways as the bars began coming to life.

"You've got a ton of choices around here." Joanna gestured to a large row of restaurants grouped together across the square. "There's Greek, Italian, Hungarian, they have the most amazing chicken paprikash, Chinese of course, and down the way, my favorite ramen house."

Ian's eyes widened. "Oh, that place is grand, even if the owner is a grump."

"Ken?" Joanna shrugged. "He's just dedicated."

"Said one workaholic about another." Ian rolled his eyes and said to Esmeralda, "You should think twice before going to work for Joanna. She's a slave driver."

Joanna gave him a playful slap. "No, I am not." She turned an innocent smile on Esmeralda. "Ignore him. He would just rather play basketball or hike in the woods than actually work."

"Any normal human would rather do those things than work, Princess."

Thaddeus stomach growled.

Esmeralda patted him and said, "It sounds like we need to get this man some food."

Joanna nodded and showing her signature decisiveness said, "Ramen it is." Then she took off at breakneck speed down a narrow alley.

Ian took a moment to appreciate the view, then raised an eyebrow at Esmeralda. "I was not exaggerating. Get ready to work."

Over steaming bowls of the most delicious soup any of them ever tasted, Joanna reviewed the basic plans for the new Center.

Thaddeus listened with distracted interest, preoccupied by the missing kids investigation. At a lull in the conversation, he broached the subject. "Remember last year when I came to see you? I told you we were investigating several disappearances." At their nods, he continued, "The investigation is ongoing. We all know these kids run away, being transient by nature. I don't have to tell you that."

Joanna leaned back in her chair with a haunted expression. "No, you don't."

"Regardless, I know you report runaways to your local precinct. Can you do me a favor and keep me informed also?"

Ian narrowed his eyes. "What did you find out?"

"Nothing substantial. There is just a higher concentration of missing kids here and in New Orleans than elsewhere in the kingdom. I've decided to detour down to Louisiana before heading back to New York." He waggled his eyebrows at Esmeralda and added, "With a stopover in Rephidim."

Ian looked between them. "Is there something you two care to share?"

Esmeralda rested her head against Thaddeus' shoulder, beaming. "We're getting married."

Ian and Joanna both smiled, though Esmeralda detected their sadness as they offered their congratulations.

"Ian, would you care to stand up with me?" Thaddeus asked.

Ian's blue eyes warmed. "I would be honored."

"You were there when it started." Thaddeus lifted his glass of water in a toast.

"I was indeed." Ian clinked his glass against Thaddeus' and winked at Esmeralda.

"Well," Joanna began, looking down at her folded hands, "not to be opportunistic, but, Ian, if you are going to the East Coast for the wedding, you can detour over to New York and look at the properties the real estate agent sent me."

"That's not a detour, Princess. I'll have to fly into New York to get to Rephidim." He raised an eyebrow at her because she knew that.

"Well, along those lines, Esmeralda, not that I am trying to ruin your holiday or overshadow your joyous news," she shot a warning look at Ian, "but since you are already going to Redding and New Orleans, perhaps you would like to meet the people you will work with? Ian's brother and sister-in-law run a summer camp in Redding, and we have a center in New Orleans."

Esmeralda and Thaddeus exchanged a look. "What do you think?"

Thaddeus shrugged. "I don't have a problem with it."

Esmeralda smiled and said, "Sure."

Joanna pushed her barely eaten bowl of ramen in front of Ian, who accepted it with a wordless nod of appreciation. "It would give you a feel for the things we are doing, and it could be a valuable learning experience. I'll put you on the payroll."

Between bites, Ian added. "I'll make some calls and let them know you are coming. I'm sure the Landry's will roll out the red carpet. They like any excuse for a *fais do-do.*"

"A what?" Esmeralda laughed.

"A party." Joanna shook her head. "It is a different world down there."

Saying goodbye, Joanna hugged Esmeralda and whispered, "Be prepared. Beau Landry is beautiful." She pulled back and chuckled. "I thought you would like to know. No one warned me."

Esmeralda covered a giggle and said, "Okay."

"I am quite serious. He is unbelievably handsome." Joanna's brown eyes flashed as she pretended to fan herself.

Esmeralda laughed, "I've only ever had eyes for one man."

"He is not a man. He is a French Cajun god."

"Oh, my." Esmeralda snorted a laugh.

"He is also obscenely charming and quite a flirt." Joanna looked up at the overhead light, thinking. "Harmless, though, madly in love with someone else."

"He's married?"

"That is a long, long story, but no, he's not."

While Joanna and Esmeralda chatted, Ian said under his breath, "If you get a chance, talk to Beau Landry." He cast a surreptitious look toward Joanna, who was hugging Esmeralda, and continued, "Lenox funded the New Orleans Center because they noticed how many kids were going missing down there."

"Lenox?"

Ian nodded. "Yes. They are the primary donors for both centers, though funds for New York came through an anonymous endowment."

Thaddeus narrowed his brows at that bit of info. "No idea where the money came from?"

Ian shook his head. "None, but it came specifically earmarked." He shrugged. "Probably some wealthy financier who is tired of being harassed on his way home."

"Do you want me to dig around?" Thaddeus asked, slightly uneasy that Esmeralda would be working for an unknown benefactor.

"Not at this point. The funds came through a well-known law firm."

"Well, as long as they are not sending you big bundles of cash, I guess that's okay."

Ian laughed. "No, it's all above the board, but I suppose you would know all about that, doing what you do."

Thaddeus shrugged. "Organized crime is not known for their altruism, but I would not put it past them."

All teasing went out of Ian's eyes. "So the rumors are true, they have come over from Italy and set up shop in Alanthia?"

Thaddeus smiled enigmatically.

"Well, I'll leave that to you then." Ian clapped Thaddeus on the back as Joanna joined him. "We have a good friend on the local police force here. I'll tell Elias and the boys over at Precinct 11 to stay alert and let you know if I hear anything."

The Match

The divisive Chief Justice Angelica ben Omri had very few friends in the state of Texas, even fewer in law enforcement. She regularly ruled against the police, and in the last five years helped overturn hard fought convictions in four high-profile cases, writing scathing opinions that likened law enforcement to thugs. She was antagonistic, in public and in private, toward all who donned a uniform in service and defense of Alanthia.

Thus, when rescue crews at Lonestar International Airport in Houston boarded flight A-13 and found the unpopular Chief Justice *in flagrante delicto*, they were not inclined to hush it up. When they discovered her companion was none other than Princess Keyseelough, the betrothed of the wildly popular Prince Peter ben Korah, the story exploded. Even King Korah's stranglehold on the media could not control the firestorm, and it all started with a single match.

Alaina ben Thomas was the match.

With her face scrubbed clean of makeup, weary after an all-day photo shoot for a new men's cologne, she opened her computer and received the first image from a member of The Resistance working in the Houston Fire and Rescue Department. Alaina nearly fell out of her chair.

Within minutes, she uploaded it to a half a dozen Resistance controlled websites. An hour later, she posted an anonymous video overlaid with a dubbed computer simulated voice and made a call. Loud dance music blasted in the background when he answered. "Falcon, we might have found a key to your snare. Pick me up at the Coffee Beanery in thirty minutes."

September 14, 998 ME

Peccioli

Thaddeus stepped out of the car in Mack's driveway and stretched his arms over his head. Sick of driving, his body felt permanently cramped, and the two-hour trip up to Mack's thoroughly tested his patience. Esmeralda did not drive, and he could not justify spending another ten days cooped up in a car, so despite how much he dreaded flying, he bought plane tickets for the rest of their trip.

"Now, this feels a lot like Rephidim," Esmeralda declared, looking around the Peccioli Vineyard and Winery. "Redding seems nice."

"Mack likes it here, says it reminds him of Virginia before the war and the drought." Thaddeus waved at Mack coming toward them from across the vineyard.

"He's southern?" Esmeralda asked. "It's terrible what has happened down there. I read there's hardly anyone left."

"Mack will tell you that. He left nine or ten years ago, and it was desolate then."

Esmeralda glanced up at the sky, deep in thought. "That entire part of the kingdom migrated. Almost all of them are in the Golden Kingdom now."

Thaddeus came around the car, resting a hand around Esmeralda's waist. "Mack's whole family left, his mom and dad, all his cousins, everyone. They are all there."

"Why didn't he go?"

Thaddeus shook his head. "Duty and loyalty, his work kept him here. He's aces, Esmeralda. You will like him."

Esmeralda studied the sunbaked man ambling toward them. He was ruddy, a man of the soil, tough, steady and calm, like the Brown. Blended in, she saw glimmers of fire red, passionate and fierce. She had never met anyone bathed in those colors, to Esmeralda's eye Mack ben Robert was Umber.

"Thad!" Mack smiled in greeting; his accent obvious in a single word. "Good to see ya. Glad you came up." He turned warm brown eyes toward Esmeralda and said, "You told me you were bringing a surprise, but you didn't tell me it was a pretty lady. How do you do, ma'am? I'm Mack ben Robert."

Esmeralda smiled and offered her hand. "Hi, I'm Esmeralda."

Mack took her slender fingers in his and raised them in a courtly kiss.

Esmeralda's breath caught, a vision flashed: Mack jumping in front of Prince Peter, his face set and determined, men scattering and shouting.

"It's nice to meet you. Welcome to Peccioli, Esmeralda."

Esmeralda tried to control her expression as the vision changed. She saw Mack bursting into a room, finding young Prince Peter contorted in pain, suspended above his bed. Mack bellowed a Scripture, and the black smoke departed, but the stench of sulfur lingered.

Her eyes grew huge as she whispered, "The black smoke... you fought it...you saved the Prince from it."

Mack jerked his hand away.

The vision cleared and Esmeralda looked at him in horror. "I'm so sorry. I should not have said that."

Mack, turning to Thaddeus, drawled, "Well, she is a surprise. You brought me a seer?" He raised an eyebrow at Esmeralda, recovering his composure. "Come on in and we'll crack open a bottle of wine. If y'all drove up here to talk about that wicked bastard, we're gonna need it."

Thaddeus stood there in shock, unsure of what just happened. "Perhaps we should say hello to Lavinia and the baby first?"

The corner of Mack's lip twitched. "She'd probably appreciate that, though if she's in the middle of an equation, she don't even notice if you run through the house naked. Trust me, I've done it."

Esmeralda giggled.

Mack turned to her. "You ain't seeing that are ya?"

Esmeralda fell into Thaddeus, roaring with laughter. "No." She held up a hand. "It doesn't work that way."

"Well, praise God for small blessings." Catching her hilarity, he added, "Not... not that it's small."

They all laughed at that.

Lavinia came out to greet them, a picture of lithe Italian elegance in her customary off the shoulder peasant shirt and flowing skirt. Her golden-brown hair was pulled up in a messy twist; sun kissed strands escaped and framed her delicate features. She wore gold hoop earrings and a pair of gold bangles on her left wrist that chimed as she waved hello. Esmeralda instantly relaxed, discerning Lavinia's aura, lovely, inside and out.

When she spoke, her voice matched her appearance, low and husky, with a breathy quality to it. "Thaddeus, we are so glad you've come to visit, and who have you brought with you?"

Mack folded his arms over his chest, a slight smile hovering in the corner of his mouth.

Thaddeus rested his hand on Esmeralda's back and brought her forward. "Lavinia, this is Esmeralda."

"Hi, I'm Esmeralda ben Claude."

Lavinia extended her hand. "Very nice to meet you, Esmeralda."

When they touched, Esmeralda entered a world she had never seen before, full of numbers, letters, symbols, symmetry, order, beauty… and loneliness. It was a world not so different from her own. Strange and wondrous, a place others did not understand but real, nonetheless.

Esmeralda's eyes brightened, and she said, "Thaddeus has told me about your son. I am excited to meet him."

Lavinia smiled in maternal pleasure. "Please come in. He was waking from his nap when you drove up."

As the two ladies disappeared into the house, Mack caught Thaddeus' eye, gesturing toward Esmeralda. "That was rather tame. I expected her to come off with some interesting algorithm or equation. She about pulled a demon out of me."

Thaddeus grimaced. "Sorry about that. Esmeralda sometimes marches to her own beat."

Mack chuckled. "Have you met my wife? I'm somewhat familiar with that." He tilted his head and the good-ole-boy disappeared. "Who is she, Thad?"

"Shit, the introductions didn't go quite the way I planned." Thaddeus rubbed his forehead and said, "She's my fiancée, Mack."

Mack pressed his lips in a firm line. He knew, perhaps better than anyone, the grief Thaddeus suffered after losing his family. "That's mighty fine." He pulled him into a back slapping hug. "Congratulations."

A sudden knot of emotion lodged in Thaddeus' throat. "Thanks. I'd like for you to stand up with me, be my Best Man."

As Thaddeus had done for Mack, standing in for his brother Richard, Mack considered it a privilege to return the favor. "It would be an honor. When's the wedding?"

Thaddeus looked out over the vineyard. "We haven't firmed up a date. I suspect we will need to wait until you get this harvest in."

"I'd say that's my one caveat. Last year, we finished November 14th. This year, it will likely be earlier." He shook his head, farmer's worry etched on his tanned face. "It's hot and dry. They are crushing the white already. I'll hold out as long as I can for the cabernet, but it's impossible to tell. A day or two can make the difference between wine and raisins." The corner of his mouth lifted in a smile. "I think we put up an excellent vintage last year. I'm barrel sampling today. Are you interested in being my first tester? Lavinia's been doing it for years, but the '97 is my first. I'm curious to see if I pulled it off."

"I'll bet it will be the finest wine I've ever tasted, Mack."

"From your lips to the Iron King's ears, Thad." Mack clapped him on the back and said, "Let's go get your stuff and get you settled in. How long you known that girl, anyway? You didn't mention her at the wedding."

Thaddeus made a clicking noise with his teeth and said, "About twelve years."

"Wow." Mack shook his head in wonder. "I was planning on picking at you for robbing the cradle. I had her pegged early twenties, even with that hair."

Thaddeus popped the trunk, his face flaming. "Well, she is in her early twenties, twenty-three to be exact."

Mack wrinkled his forehead. "I'm no math wizard like my wife, but if you've known her twelve years, and she's twenty-three... What are you, forty now?"

Thaddeus lifted both suitcases, demonstrating his vigor. "Thirty-eight," he answered, a bit touchy.

Mack was running the numbers, then exclaimed, "Great balls of fire."

"I assure you they were, which is why I left." Thaddeus set the suitcases down and tried to explain. "We just got together, at perfectly acceptable ages, in case you haven't worked it out."

Mack gave him a pained look. "Ew."

"Shut up, Mack. It wasn't like that."

"Did her father run you out of town with a shotgun?"

"No." Thaddeus shuffled his feet, kicking at the dirt. "She was just a kid, and I never touched her, not back then. Remember when I spent a few years in Pennsylvania before going on pilgrimage? She's from that village. We got to be good friends, only friends. You'll understand when you get to know her. She's an extraordinary person, Mack."

"I reckon I got a glimpse of that." Mack nodded in acknowledgment. "I also know a thing or two about bad timing when it comes to love." Mack picked up the suitcases and added over his shoulder. "Though mine wasn't twelve."

Thaddeus sighed with resignation. "You are going to bust my chops about this the whole time I'm here, aren't you?"

"You're damn skippy." Mack grinned. "Now come on, Richard's got a new toy in there that your bride might like."

Thaddeus trudged after him. "Why did I drive all the way up here to see you?"

"Because I'm one of the few people in this world that has known you long enough not to kiss your ass, Mr. High and Mighty Director."

"I just left the other one, and I've changed my mind. I think I will ask him to be my best man," Thaddeus said as he walked through the door.

Richard ran up the hall on his two-year-old sturdy legs. "My Daddy is the best man!" He threw himself into his father's outstretched arms.

All irritation evaporated at the sight of Mack hugging his brother's namesake. The boy was the same age as Jacob and Matthew when they died. Thaddeus tousled Richard's brown curls. "That he is, Richard. That he is."

Bread

Esmeralda became enthralled with Lavinia, from the timbre of her voice and her effortless grace, to the hospitable way she welcomed them into her home. By mid-afternoon, Esmeralda was helping in the kitchen, changing diapers, and picking up toys like a member of the family. Mack and Richard took Thaddeus for a tour of the property, while she and Lavinia made bread for supper.

"My bread is not as good as my mother's, though I follow her recipe precisely. There is something about dough that eludes me." Lavinia studied it critically. "Sometimes it turns out perfect and other times it doesn't, like now." She pulled her hand away, covered in a sticky mess. "I think there should be a recipe that considers variations in temperature, barometric pressure, and relative humidity. Plus, the input, I mean the ingredients, are inconsistent. I suspect the weight by volume and protein content of flour fluctuates in every bag. I can measure the weight but not the proteins, not in my kitchen. When you factor in the unknown quantity of active cultures in the yeast, it is no wonder bread never turns out the same. There are too many variables."

Esmeralda poked a tentative finger into the gloppy mass and said, "I think it needs more flour."

"That's just it, I made this recipe three days ago, and it

turned out perfectly, which is why I attempted it again for dinner tonight." Lavinia shrugged. "Mack raved about it."

"Grandma Eve, back home, used to make pie crust almost every day. I would watch her. She never used a recipe, and she measured nothing. She just did it by feel."

Lavinia narrowed her eyes, staring at the bread like it was a complex problem to be solved. "My friend Filippo says cooking is an art, baking is a science. Using that logic, I should be a great baker, but I am not."

"How funny, Grandma Eve was an amazing baker but just an average cook. I think she took the opposite view."

Lavinia sighed. "If I follow a recipe for soup, it turns out the same every time. Humans and bread never behave the way they are supposed to."

Esmeralda laughed. "Wouldn't that be nice if every person came with a recipe? Like a set of instructions on how to interact with them."

"That would be the most complex algorithm ever created." Lavinia gazed off into space. "Though, I think for men it would be simpler, fewer variables."

"Are there?" Esmeralda dipped a scooper in the flour bag and tossed it in the bowl, working it into the dough.

"Yes, I think so." Lavinia glanced over Esmeralda's shoulder, pleased to see the dough coming together. "I run them all the time. X = 5:30 pm, then start dinner. Y represents the number of words spoken after work, if Y < 25, then leave him alone, if Y > 25, then ask how his day was."

Esmeralda looked at her in fascination. "That's extraordinary. So, our brains run complex algorithms, but we don't know it."

Lavinia's eyes lit up. "Exactly! You would not believe how many people do not understand that."

"Oh, yes I would." Esmeralda turned the dough onto the floured board and said, "I think in colors."

"Ooh, interesting," Lavinia said, picking up the glass bread bowl and examining it, calculating the wavelength and the refraction of light waves that created the hue, saturation, and luminosity of it. "Color has physical and mathematical properties, but I've never considered thinking in color. Though, I can see how you would."

Esmeralda stopped kneading and breathed, "You do?"

"Sure, of course. I'll bet you run algorithms in your head about it all the time. Tell me one."

In one of the most extraordinary conversations Esmeralda ever had, she said, "Well, take this dough for example, it's pale yellow. On the surface everyone can see it, and that's where they stop. I go deeper. In my mind, I wonder, what is pale yellow?" She shrugged and stepped aside. "Here, touch it."

Lavinia dug her palm into the dough. "It's warm."

"Exactly, but it's more. It's soft, and it's tough. The more you work it, the stronger it gets. It stretches but doesn't break. It feels cozy." She pinched off a piece and held it up to the light. "There is so much going on under the surface. Yeast is working, flour and water are interacting, and the kneading produces gluten." She pressed the small piece back and worked it in. "Yellow is hot and can be chaotic, but add enough white," she sprinkled more flour on the board, "and it changes. Under pressure and heat, the yellow and white do amazing things. Add time, and it grows."

"How intriguing. Perhaps then the answer to my bread dilemma is color," Lavinia said, tapping her thigh.

Esmeralda smiled. "Could be."

"If you think in color, do you see people in color? Because if you can solve my bread and my people problems, I want to know." Lavinia took up the kneading.

"Like you said, people are more complicated. Their hues, shades, and tints vary, but in general they usually have a color," Esmeralda confided.

Lavinia smiled, conspiratorial. "What color is Thaddeus?"

"Silver," Esmeralda answered without missing a beat. "Created under intense pressure, strong and precious, shiny.

He can be cold and hard and go gray without the light. Put him in the fire, and he turns to liquid, running molten and fast, beautiful."

Lavinia's amazing brain whirled. "And Mack, what color is he?"

Esmeralda chuckled. "Umber, a mix of earth and fire, a balance between steady and hot."

Lavinia hooted. "Exactly. What about me?"

Esmeralda picked up a loaf and set it on the pan, suddenly shy. "I think you are pale yellow, Lavinia."

Lavinia tilted her delicately clefted chin to the side, considering. "Hmm, you might be right." She looked around. "I've been contemplating what color to paint this kitchen. I think buttery yellow is the perfect choice."

Esmeralda smiled with profound relief. Grandma Eve was the only person she ever shared this with, but unlike Eve, Lavinia truly understood. When she answered, her voice was as breathy as Lavinia's. "That would be lovely."

Lavinia covered the loaves with a tea towel and asked, "What color are you?"

Esmeralda lifted her hands in a helpless gesture. "I have no idea."

They retired to the living room, and Esmeralda suddenly wished it was raining so she could curl up on the sofa with a soft blanket and simply visit. Thaddeus told her Lavinia was a genius but knowing it and experiencing it were two distinct things. Always inquisitive, Esmeralda wanted to bask in Lavinia's amazing brain.

Lavinia, who lived outside most human connection, engaged with Esmeralda in a rare and poignant manner. The world thought Lavinia odd, Esmeralda did not. She found a few people with whom she could communicate, but mathematicians were notorious outliers. She had lifelong friends, but it was a precious thing to discover a new one.

That afternoon at Peccioli was a gift for them both.

Two hours later, a wail shattered the tranquility. Mack rushed through the door, a red faced and screaming Richard in his arms. At the sight of his mother, the crying grew frantic. Lavinia flew off the sofa, taking her distraught child, and cooing gently.

"He got stung by a wasp," Mack explained.

"It's... a... boo-boo! It's a hurt!" Richard held out his little arm, sporting two angry welts.

"Oh, Bino! I'm so sorry. That does hurt. Come on. Mommy will make it better."

"The wasp... he's a mean damn thing." Richard buried his face in his mother's shoulder and cried.

Every adult in the room tried not to laugh. Mack's face reddened, and Lavinia shot him a glare. She knew where Richard picked that up. Mother and father went to doctor their little one.

"Poor little guy. What happened?" Esmeralda asked.

"He ran over to show me a cluster of grapes and got stung." Thaddeus shook his head ruefully. "That was one thing I did not miss when I was in Rephidim, no biting bugs."

"So true." Esmeralda walked into the open kitchen and pulled the loaves out of the oven.

"What are you cooking?"

"Bread."

"Let me have a piece." Thaddeus eyed it.

"It's for supper." Esmeralda looked around. "You'll have to ask Lavinia."

"Did you make it?"

Esmeralda inhaled the heavenly smell and smiled proudly. "I'd say it was a joint effort."

"My Uncle Bailey used to make bread. Aunt Susan got sick one fall, and he had to take over the cooking. Bread became his specialty. Even when my aunt got better, he kept baking bread. I ate a whole loaf one time when I was thirteen."

Esmeralda looked at him through hooded eyes and said, "I'll bake you bread."

Thaddeus grinned. "I'd like that."

Esmeralda returned his smile, running an algorithm:

Z = food preference, then pay attention.

If Z + fond memory, then make food.

Wine and Secrets

After supper, Lavinia excused herself to get Richard ready for bed. Mack gestured for Thaddeus and Esmeralda to join him on the back terrace, a bottle of wine under his arm. He poured, giving a brief discourse about what they were drinking, and after a time said, "This conversation is confidential. If I'd ever filed an official report, it would be highly classified. It's for damn sure explosive. So I'll have your word you'll treat it as such?"

Thaddeus and Esmeralda nodded.

Mack studied the wine with a critical eye. "You asked me about the black smoke. What did you see?"

Esmeralda noted he did not question whether she had seen something. She gave Thaddeus a smile and plunged ahead. "I've seen several things over the years, sometimes in person, occasionally in visions, more often in dreams. When you kissed my hand, I saw you protecting Prince Peter."

Mack took a sip of wine. "I did that for several years."

Esmeralda conceded anyone could find that out, but she shattered any doubts he might have with her next statement. "I've seen Prince Peter floating above his bed, spinning, writhing, and contorted in agony. An evil presence floods the room, and it stinks."

Mack massaged the back of his neck, closing his eyes. "The Prince calls it a monster, but there's an evil spirit living in the Palace."

Thaddeus rose from his chair and looked out over the vineyard, keeping quiet about his complex feelings toward the royal family.

Esmeralda swallowed hard. "It doesn't always stay there."

Mack frowned. "I reckon it doesn't. He's a nasty son of a bitch."

"I think I've met him, or one like him." Esmeralda absently traced the line of her scar.

Thaddeus' head snapped around. "What?"

Esmeralda paused before answering. Night sounds seemed to grow louder in the silence. A black rail called in the falling darkness. The crickets sang in sonorous constancy, juxtaposed to the pounding hearts of the humans. Esmeralda pressed her thumb against her chin, thinking. "My memories are returning, but they are not fully formed. So, for now, I need to know how Mack fought it."

Mack was unsure what memories she was talking about but willing to share what he knew. "Scripture, darlin', plain and simple. He couldn't abide it. Blood of the Lamb and sword of the Spirit, I put on that Ephesians six armor every day I worked in the Palace."

Esmeralda twisted the white curl around her finger, contemplating. "I know how to do that. It used to be second nature for me."

Mack answered with confidence born of experience. "When you are in the thick of it, it's essential."

"I have terrible dreams about that thing, more often than not, Prince Peter is in them," Esmeralda confessed.

Mack drained his glass and poured another. "That stands to reason, because it hates him. Don't let the public persona fool you, that's one tough kid."

Esmeralda covered her mouth, to have the horrors validated, even in small part felt earth shattering. "How has he survived?"

Mack offered the bottle to Thaddeus who gladly accepted it. "If you can believe it, I think he's somewhat accustomed to it. It's lived in the Palace a long time. That's not to say he doesn't bear scars." Mack motioned with his chin inside, Lavinia was in the kitchen with Richard, and he did not want either of them to hear this conversation.

"Thank you for telling me, Mack." Esmeralda whispered, "But now that you are gone, who protects him? The dreams are bad now, often very confused, like he's spinning."

Mack stared through the French doors at his wife and son, going through their nightly bedtime ritual: bath time, two stories, and a glass of water. The kitchen light illuminated Richard's little arm, plastered in multi-colored bandages, which he insisted made the hurt go away. Mack never doubted his decision to leave the Palace, but Esmeralda's question hung in the air. "That's the hell of it, I don't think anybody truly protects the Prince now."

Esmeralda closed her eyes and murmured, "Lord, have mercy."

September 15, 998 ME

Sanctuary

"You've got the directions? I'd drive you over if I weren't so busy." Mack apologized as he hefted a case of wine into the trunk. "Take this, if you would. We have a mutually beneficial business arrangement with Pepperwood."

Thaddeus looked perplexed. "Wine and horses?"

Mack shrugged. "The same people who buy horses, buy wine. When they sell a horse, they seal the deal with a glass of wine. Their customers like it, and James gives them directions to Peccioli. Nine times out of ten, they make a side trip over here and buy my wine. James and Persa finish the bottle." Mack shut the trunk and smiled. "It's a win-win for everybody. Besides, it keeps it friendly between neighbors."

Esmeralda did not comment. She simply got in the car and shut the door. Uneasy since their conversation on the patio, she felt like she had fallen asleep reading a scary novel. Terror stalked her, creeping into her dreams, and the eerie feeling still lingered this morning, except this was no fantasy, no delusion. Last night confirmed it, her nightmares were real. She buried her face in her hands, breathing a desperate prayer. "Give me discernment, Lord."

When Thaddeus got behind the wheel, he detected her distress. "What's wrong?"

Esmeralda straightened in her seat. "I don't know, something's niggling at me."

"You didn't sleep well."

Esmeralda thumbed her chin, deep in thought and prayer. The closer they got to Pepperwood the more burdened she felt. "Stop for a minute." She brought her folded hands to the bridge of her nose and earnestly sought the Lord with her heart thundering.

At length, she received her answer: *While you are at Pepperwood, do not speak of the things I will show you, the time is not now.*

She blinked her eyes open. "It's all right."

"You sure? We could go back to Peccioli. I'm confident Mack would appreciate the extra hand. He's doing something called racking today that sounds interesting," Thaddeus said, giving her a way out.

"No, I'm fine. They are expecting us, and I'm curious to see how they run the camp. I had an idea that once we get the new center running, perhaps we could use Rephidim as a retreat for the kids. Ian says they love going to Pepperwood."

"I think that is a good idea. The only challenge I see is the logistics of getting them there." Thaddeus pulled back onto the road.

"True." Esmeralda nodded. "That could prove challenging. I suspect they drive them up here in a bus or something."

"Can you imagine the ruckus that would cause in Rephidim?"

Esmeralda snorted. "You couldn't get a bus into Rephidim."

Thaddeus shook his head, thinking of the dense Thyatira Woods. "Nope."

"Oh, well. It was just a thought." Esmeralda shrugged.

"It's a good one. Rephidim is good for the soul." He reached out and squeezed her hand.

"I am looking forward to seeing it again." She rubbed the top of his knuckles.

Thaddeus winked and said, "I am, too." He squinted looking for the driveway that should be right around the corner. "Here it is."

As they turned off the main road, Esmeralda gasped. Sparkling dust and diamonds as far as the eye could see hovered over the property in a golden dome. "Do you see that?" she whispered in awe.

Thaddeus looked around in confusion. "See what?"

Esmeralda blinked and rubbed her eyes. "Never mind," she said, absorbing the moment, planning to tell him later. The car penetrated the shield without the merest sign, and golden light flooded the cab. Esmeralda took a deep breath and relaxed for the first time since last night. "What an amazing place."

The metal gate stood open, welcoming visitors. A sloping driveway led to an enchanted valley of pastures and paddocks in brilliant green, the likes of which Esmeralda had not seen since leaving Rephidim. A horse run circled the perimeter, though there were no time trials or races happening at the moment. The horses cantering in their paddocks were magnificent. Esmeralda was no equestrian, but even she could tell they were spectacular. A white farmhouse with a wide front porch and a green roof sat in the center of the valley. A covered portico from the side of the house connected the stable, and behind it sat the permanent dormitory for the summer camp kids.

Sanctuary.

Thaddeus parked and turned to Esmeralda. "You all right now?"

She flashed him a toothy grin. "All is well. I am excited to meet Ian's brother."

"I met him at Mack's wedding, he seemed like a stand-up guy."

"You can tell by this place," Esmeralda said to herself as Thaddeus moved around to the passenger side to open her door.

A breeze blew through the valley, ruffling the strawberry blonde ponytail of the proprietress moving to greet them. Kelly green, Esmeralda thought as she watched the tiny woman. As she drew closer, Esmeralda discerned a streak of darkness, as if someone had splashed her with black paint. Persa ben Yereq was marked. Esmeralda reflexively touched her own cheek, running her finger over the scar, feeling a kinship with the woman. Setting her face in a smile, she said, "You must be Persa? I'm Esmeralda ben Claude. Thank you for having us."

"It's my pleasure." Persa's hazel eyes squinted against the sun as she looked up at Esmeralda and Thaddeus. At 4'10", she had to crane her neck to meet his eyes as they shook hands. "We met briefly at the wedding; it is nice to see you again. I won't comment on your height, if you don't comment on mine. Deal?"

He laughed. "I think that is a deal."

"Fair enough." She winked and turned to Esmeralda. "Welcome to Pepperwood."

When their hands touched, a vision flashed, Persa suspended at a dizzying height, the determined face of a young man holding her up. Then she flew through the air in a free fall, rebounding onto the back of a horse into a curtsy. Esmeralda startled at the unfamiliar sensation.

"Thank you for having us," she stammered inanely, repeating herself, locked in the memory of the acrobatic feat. Blinking, she tried to calm the rush of adrenaline and added, "Ian has told me a lot about you two."

Persa's chin pointed when she pressed her lips into a dubious line. "Hopefully it was good. He gives me a hard time these days." She did not elaborate or wait for an answer, instead waved them toward the stables. "Come on, let's go find James."

The Pepperwood stables were cleaner than most houses and definitely cleaner than Mack's equipment barn, which Lavinia complained he was turning into his own personal pigsty. Rich dark wood stalls ran the length of the long stable with ten enclosures on each side. At the far end sat a large tack room, opposite it, a living quarters.

"Our manager is delivering a horse up in Portland," Persa said, gesturing to an empty stall. "He's our only full-time employee."

"You have a beautiful place here," Thaddeus said and waved to James, who had come in from the paddock to greet them.

Each stall held a plaque with the horse's name etched in gold letters, except one. The first stall in the building had a hand painted white sign decorated with flowers, 'Lightning' written in a young girl's elaborate hand. The sign drew Esmeralda, and she reached out, touching the well-worn paint. A young blonde girl came to mind, sitting on a porch, surrounded by toy horses. Esmeralda peered into the stall, while James and Thaddeus greeted each other at the end of the stable. Persa held back, waiting with Esmeralda.

"She's a sweet old mare." Persa leaned on the half door, scratching Lightning just below her ear. The horse nuzzled her with a contented whinny.

"May I?" Esmeralda held out a tentative hand.

"By all means. She's gentle. But be wary around the others. The racehorses are high strung," Persa cautioned.

Lightning turned a soulful eye to study Esmeralda before consenting to be rubbed. Esmeralda touched the horse's wiry hair, and something akin to an atomic bomb exploded in her brain. Magnificent glory surrounded them, blinding, pure, and powerful. She saw a rider blazing like the sun, clothed in white, the hem of his robe crimson. She jerked her hand back as if she had just touched a flame, her eyes wide, but not in fear. "Lightning… you are no ordinary horse."

"Faithful and true, my lifelong companion." Persa smiled with great affection.

"You ride her?" Esmeralda whispered in awe.

Persa looked away, pensive. "Some."

Esmeralda did not need second sight to detect the unease pulsing off Persa. Laying a gentle hand on the small woman's shoulder, she said, "I think she is amazing." But the touch sparked another vision, as fear telegraphed through Persa's body, panic, the need to flee, to run for her life. Esmeralda's memory jogged as the mad flight from Endor crashed in on her.

Thaddeus and James joined them.

Inundated as she had not been since she was a child, Esmeralda struggled to maintain an amiable expression. But tapping into a lifetime of discipline, she managed to smile, focusing on James, and putting everything aside, planning to examine it later, in private.

Thaddeus detected her bewilderment and continued his discussion with James, giving her a moment before making the introduction. The family resemblance between the two Kole brothers was not immediately apparent. James was not as tall as Ian, broader through the chest and arms. Where Ian's eyes were winter blue, James' were golden brown. His hair was dark with an auburn cast, his temples showing the first signs of white. However, when he smiled their kinship was undeniable.

He shook her hand with his calloused palm, and she felt the power of a surging horse between her thighs, becoming one with the animal, soaring above the earth. Midnight blue flashed, deep and mysterious, private and quiet. An innate dignity surrounded him, steadfast, and something else. Esmeralda tilted her head, trying to come up with the word… noble… that was it.

James invited them on a tour of the facilities and the camp dormitory. Persa enthused about the kids, and Esmeralda could tell she enjoyed having the campers as much as they enjoyed coming. With a golden dome covering the property, she understood why they were drawn to this place and the charming couple who owned it.

Persa did most of the talking, and James let her. They had the unique chemistry of a couple together for a lifetime, functioning as a unit, singular in manner, synergies normally only observed in elderly couples. But beneath the surface, Esmeralda detected something out of kilter. Several times she observed James watching Persa with profound concern. Persa had trouble articulating the activities the campers did off the ranch, ending most sentences with, "James takes the kids for that one."

Persa insisted they stay for lunch. Afterward, Thaddeus excused himself for a pre-scheduled conference call. James attended a customer, and Persa shooed Esmeralda out of the kitchen while she tidied up. Despite Esmeralda's protests, Persa would not hear of letting her guest help, so Esmeralda retired to the living room.

She wandered to the mantle and touched a large silver trophy that read, 'Pas de deux Vaulting, World Champions 985 ME.' She felt the sweat, strained muscles, and grueling years of practice the cup represented. She saw a sumptuous banquet. Persa in fairy green, swirling on the arm of James, whose face did not bear the lines of sun and strain, both animated and happy.

They decorated the living room in beige and sage, bare of clutter and knickknacks, except a lovely glass vase on one end table. Piles of horse magazines overflowed from a basket, and mismatched soft blankets of indeterminate origin draped over the backs of the comfortable overstuffed furniture. Esmeralda took a magazine off the top of the stack and plopped down on the sofa.

She should not have done that.

A violent shudder rocked her, and she writhed in agony. Broken... hurt. "My hand, they broke my finger, and the puncture wounds on my arms are infected. Starved... beyond hunger now, I could not eat even if you gave me something. Where am I, Pers? How did I get here? Do not let them find me. They will find me, and then they will kill me for sure. Worse, I need it… give me another shot. It is a monster, clawing at me. Craving, beyond hunger or thirst… need. Strange, all consuming. Desperate. I am going to die, but I wanted to be here when I did it."

Esmeralda leapt from the sofa, revolted and gasping.

She heard an echo of Persa's voice. "No, you aren't going to die. He does not have the power of life and death. He's not going to get you. We're not going to let him."

Esmeralda fought the urge to flee.

As inconceivable as it seemed, she had just fallen through a wormhole into a nightmare, with Prince Peter cast in the starring role. It clung to her, sucked her down into desolation and terror. On that couch… he had lain on that sofa and nearly died not that long ago. The memory was recent.

She moistened her lips, her mouth dry, her body crying out for something, and Esmeralda ben Claude gave it a name—heroin. That explained her recent dreams of him. He was spinning out of control. A monster had him in its grip and held him in something worse than her nightmares. She closed her eyes, praying. "Lord, help him. Please Lord help him. He is in trouble."

Realization struck like a lightning bolt.

The Lord was showing her others who encountered the thing that haunted her, who prowled the perimeter of Rephidim, and threw the glass pitcher the night they took her. That monster left the Black on everyone he touched… on Persa… James… Peter. Even Mack bore battle scars.

As if He was standing in the room, the Lord's voice came clear, *"Now you understand, but do not speak of it."*

Esmeralda nodded convulsively. Alone in the living room of the Pepperwood sanctuary, she understood the hedge of protection. Wickedness beyond the age stalked the edges, waiting for another chance to seize those who took shelter and found a haven under the golden dome.

Persa ben Yereq was afraid… with good reason.

Skirmish

Thaddeus drove up the winding drive, away from the Pepperwood Ranch, his expression grave, reviewing the call he'd just had with his office. New Orleans uncovered three more missing kids, and there was an urgency to get there. In his preoccupation, he did not spare a thought for Esmeralda sitting beside him.

"Thaddeus, stop!" she shrieked, slapping a palm against his chest with a hollow thud. The car skidded on loose gravel, and Esmeralda flew forward in her seat. "Look!" She pointed a shaking finger at the main road ahead.

Thaddeus looked between her and the road. "What? I don't see anything!"

"Oh, heavenly Father, Yeshua, protect us!" she breathed, her arms stiff and braced at her sides. Beyond the golden hedge loomed a fallen angel and a phalanx of black spirits. In her life, she had sensed them, now she saw.

The angel was massive, thirty feet tall, black clad in leathery gilded armor. He wore a crown of many spires, and his hair appeared as live eels. A face of reptilian horror stared at her with black and gold dragon eyes that did not blink. He sensed her vision of him and smiled, malicious and evil. Flicking his forked tongue, he tasted her fear, then bared his fangs and roared.

Esmeralda screamed and jumped to the backseat.

Thaddeus whipped around. "What is it?"

Esmeralda shook, her breath coming in ragged gasps. "He's.... he's ahead, and he's not alone."

"Who?" Thaddeus craned his neck, straining to see what she saw. It was futile, though the hairs on his body stood on end.

"A black angel," Esmeralda cried, then choked out, "and the Witch!" A shimmering figure emerged from the crowd; her face painted in skeletal terror. Bones hung around her neck, and she wielded a wand, black smoke spewing from its end. "Yeshua, please help us."

"Give me your hands!" Thaddeus ordered as the Holy Spirit fell upon him. Esmeralda huddled in the backseat, curled into the fetal position. Thaddeus threw the car into park. Using his long arms, he pulled her forward, surrounding her and called in a loud voice, "The Lord rebuke you!"

Esmeralda closed her eyes against the vision, but the peace of the Spirit and the touch of his body filled her, and she calmed. In the stillness, she murmured Scriptures buried deep in her brain, ones she knew from years past, embedded in her mind, and recited as she patrolled the perimeter of Rephidim, fighting the unseen.

A soft knock shattered the silence.

Esmeralda opened her eyes and saw Persa leading Lightning, a pensive expression across her pretty face. "Is everything okay?"

Esmeralda turned to the road. The wicked beings were gone. With a lifetime of experience, pretending things were fine when they were not, she swallowed and nodded.

Thaddeus ran his fingers through his hair, which was disheveled and sticking up in wild angles all over his head. "Yeah, you know how it is. We just stopped for a brief smooch."

Persa narrowed her eyes, registering intense skepticism. "All right then, safe travels."

Subdued

Esmeralda climbed into the front seat, drained and exhausted. She leaned into Thaddeus across the armrest and hugged herself.

"Is it safe to proceed?" he asked gravely.

She sniffed and wiped her eye with the back of her thumb. "They're gone."

"Esmie, are you okay?" He pulled her tight to his side and kissed the top of her head, blinking with surprise at a second stark white curl, a mirror image of the first, intertwined in her braid.

She nodded, wordless and weary.

They drove in silence, but he never stopped stroking her arm, soothing and steady. He fought the instinct to interrogate, to understand what she saw. He had seen nothing, but he felt it, overwhelming evil. Whatever it was, he needed to find out. But she was shaking, and he knew she was fragile. As they drove, he held his tongue, giving her a brief respite after the ordeal. However, he would have to question her, to push her.

He did not return to Peccioli, pulling instead into Redding Township Park. They passed it on their way into town yesterday, and the secluded picnic tables and rolling open spaces seemed an ideal place to talk. He parked, and she looked around dazed. "Come on, we'll take a break before we go back to Mack and Lavinia's."

Her eyes darted, wary and troubled. Seeing no menacing spirits, she moistened her lips and assented. While he was walking around the side of the car to open her door, she prayed, *"What can I tell him?"* When he opened the door, the slight creak of the hinges seemed to whisper, *"All."*

He helped her out with infinite care. Settling a large hand on her back, he guided her to a remote picnic table in the shade of an immense redwood. She stopped at a water fountain and drank deeply, washing away the taste of bile and fear.

"Is that spot okay to talk?" he asked, laying his hand on the rough wood table where someone had carved SR - RM.

Esmeralda nodded and sat down, hugging her knees to her chest, resting her chin. She peered out at him with eyes as stormy as a hurricane.

"Tell me what happened and start at the beginning." His tone was clipped and professional.

In a halting voice, she poured it all out. In the telling, her Rephidim speech pattern and cadence became pronounced, evidence of her weariness. He asked very few questions as she spoke.

"I have always been able to sense things, but since Wyoming, and especially since my encounter in the Redwoods, I can see them." With her middle finger, she rubbed her forehead above the bridge of her nose. "It used to only be in dreams, but I am awake now. I know things that have happened and are happening."

"Future things?" he inquired, the investigator contemplating the power of that particular skill, especially considering the escalating disappearances of the children.

She watched the swings, a little girl laughing with her father. Her exuberant cries floated on the air. "Push me higher, Daddy!"

"I don't think so. Though it is hard to gauge whether what I am seeing is the future or the past. It's not something I can simply ask. Like today, I could not say to Persa, 'Tell me what happened to Prince Peter on this couch.'" Her voice was full of self-mocking. "For one, the Lord barred me from speaking of it. For another, if it had happened, how would I explain what I knew?" She trailed off; her face contorted with imagination. "And if it hadn't happened yet?

"Thaddeus, you know there are no prophets in this age. Among the faithful, I would be shunned or cast out. In the world, they would either think I was a lunatic or turn me into some sort of freak show." With profound resignation, she added, "Either way, I've made myself a target for the wicked."

Thaddeus pressed his folded hands to his lips, then rubbed his palms together, contemplating. "I don't believe you did anything to cause this, but you are likely right. That is why they are after you because you see what they are about." A hypothesis formed, and he continued, "I expect when we go home to Rephidim, a similar golden hedge, like the one you witnessed around Pepperwood, will be present."

Esmeralda stretched her neck, stiff from all the stress. "Which is why they could not get to me while I remained at home." She made a disgusted sound in the back of her throat. "I was a fool for not seeing it sooner. I rode right into their hands."

"You mentioned last night that your memories were returning. Are you up for the telling?" he asked, mindful of her pale countenance, keenly aware she had been comatose less than a week ago.

"Not yet. It's still bits and pieces like flashes in the dark."

He scooted forward on the bench, cupped her face, and leaned in for a soft kiss. "You are extraordinary, my love."

She met his tender kiss, breathing, "Thank you."

He rubbed his nose against hers. "Esmie, you have a new beautiful white streak."

Esmeralda reared back, blinking in surprise, and undoing her tight braid. "Where?" She pulled out the band, undoing the curly mass.

He gave her a crooked smile. She had very little personal vanity, often lamenting her mouth was too wide, her hair too curly, the charming bridge of her nose too pronounced. Taken together, she was compelling, not classically pretty. He surmised people would describe her as attractive, but to Thaddeus, she was precious.

She fluffed out her hair and took the new white corkscrew between her fingers, pulling it in front of her eyes, then looking up at him with a comical expression. Esmeralda twisted them both around her index fingers. "I have a pair now!"

He chuckled at the unusual strands. "That you do."

She stretched them above her head in a V. "My antenna for detecting evil."

Thaddeus grabbed her around the waist and laughed. "One of your many talents, Vixen."

September 17, 998 ME

New Orleans Brings It Out in All of Us

In all the years Esmeralda knew Thaddeus ben Todd, she had never seen him frightened. Angry, reticent, surly, sulking, grieving, recently passionate, often sarcastic, staid and serious, but even in the face of a spectral army of evil beings, she had never seen him afraid. Boarding the plane at Korah International Airport, she realized he was terrified. His terse answers and rapid clenching and unclenching of his jaw gave him away. Esmeralda, by contrast, was thrilled. The uncharacteristic change in their roles, amused her to no end, though Thaddeus was in no state to appreciate her casual banter and refused to be teased out of his terror.

Being as tall as he was, he upgraded their tickets to first class. Despite the additional space, he resembled a grandaddy long-legged spider crammed into a tiny seat. Clenching the arm rests in a death grip, his nose flared, and the tendons in his neck grew taut.

When the engines fired up, Esmeralda felt him jolt, and for an instant, she thought he might make a break for the exit. Patting his hand, she soothed, "It will be fine."

"Do not talk to me." He grimaced, his lips a bluish gray.

"Breathe," Esmeralda coaxed.

He grunted, fighting down panic as he relived the crash of Alanthian Airlines flight 374. It haunted him for months after the investigation, and the gruesome images of twisted wreckage and burned corpses rose from the depths of his brain, swallowing him whole. The airplanes ponderous progress toward the runway felt like a walk to the gallows.

"Are you sure you are okay?"

He shot her a look.

"Fine."

He closed his eyes, knowing he could get through it if she would not talk, if he could just be still. *Four hours saves four days, four hours saves four days...* he repeated his personal mantra.

Esmeralda recognized the stubborn side of Thaddeus, had witnessed it frequently, especially when he first came to Rephidim. She knew how to deal with him when he was like this, leave him alone, so she pulled a book from her bag and lost herself in a novel.

The normally sober Thaddeus ben Todd got roaring drunk on the plane. So, when they disembarked, he was ready to take on the Big Easy, and he fit right in. The rental car had to wait, since Esmeralda had not learned to drive, and there was no way he was getting behind the wheel.

She discovered he was a magnanimous drunk, giving the taxi driver an extravagant tip before stumbling out of the vehicle into the thriving French Quarter. She had to remind him to get their luggage and winked at the driver with a helpless shrug. The driver grinned and pocketed the cash, unfazed.

Across the street, a jazz quartet played, an overflowing tip bucket in front of them. The melodic notes of a soulful clarinet floated across the bayou spiced air, causing Esmeralda to sway a seductive rhythm, falling under the spell it wove. Thaddeus growled and abandoned their luggage, pulling her close and dancing on the sidewalk. "I think I am going to like it here, Vixen." Heat passed between them like liquid fire. "Let's check in... I need you."

She shimmied against him suggestively. "Capital idea." She turned and strutted inside, purposely swaying her hips, enticing, teasing him.

Seizing the luggage, he barreled after her, a man on a mission. At the front desk, he registered them as Mr. and Mrs. ben Todd because he felt like it. Their trip to Peccioli had not engendered amorous feelings in either of them, but Thaddeus planned to put an end to their two-day abstinence—right now. For a man who closely governed his passions, twelve years of pent-up sexual energy roared to life like a tiger.

Upstairs, they could still hear the street musicians soulful song. Esmeralda opened the balcony door, enjoying the view from their third story suite. Taking in the crimson and purple evening sky, she relaxed against Thaddeus who took up the slow sensuous dance they began on the sidewalk below.

"*Mon amour.*" He kissed the delicate skin below her ear.

"Ooh, French." She ground her hips into his, feeling his raging arousal.

"Six years of it." His eyes grew hooded, hazy with desire. "*Venez à moi, ma belle.*" He danced her back in the room, leaving the door cracked. The sultry music provided a soundtrack for a night he envisioned lasting until dawn.

"Take down your hair," he murmured, then kicked off his shoes and laid on the bed, banking his desire as he watched her.

Esmeralda leaned against the dresser, meeting his eyes. Moistening her lips, she raised her arms and took up the beat of the music below.

He rewarded her with a smolder.

Turning her back to him, she loosened her hair and swayed a seductive rhythm. He growled, and she looked over her shoulder, sweeping his body with an ardent gaze.

"Take off your shirt," Thaddeus breathed, more turned on than he had ever been in his life, and she was fully clothed.

She ran the flat of her palms over her breasts, continuing her sexy little dance. With deliberate slowness, she lifted her knit top, giving him a tantalizing view of the soft, flexing muscles of her stomach.

He wanted to bite her. "Tease," he ground out, enjoying the show.

She kicked off her tennis shoes and socks, then bent in half, giving him an amazing view of her firm derriere. The music changed, low and bluesy. She slid her jeans low on her hips, giving him a glimpse of lace panties. Thaddeus made a ragged inhale.

"You like it?" Esmeralda taunted, caressing her body.

He leered. "Immensely. But your clothes? Take them off."

She lifted the shirt over her head with delicious slowness. Her olive skin glowed smooth and flawless in the dying light. She traced a finger along the lace of her shimmering, lavender bra. A blues guitar wailed, soulful and sweet, through the crack in the door. Keeping the rhythm, she inched her jeans down her body, revealing matching lavender panties.

"Holy shit," he breathed and tried not to stagger as he got up, intoxicated with alcohol and lust. "Do you know how many times I fantasized about you in my bed?" He ran his fingers through her curly mass of hair and pulled her into a fierce kiss. Then with a desperate groan loosened his trousers and dragged her onto his lap, positioning her knees on either side of his thighs.

She unbuttoned his shirt, running her hands up his body, inflaming him further. She tasted like Lavinia's red licorice and moved against him with moist heat. He raised against her, demanding entrance, lifting her. "Come to Poppa."

She moved the tiny scrap of lace to the side and slid along the length of his arousal. He threw back his head, his chest rising and falling, guiding her in a seductive cadence. Esmeralda opened for him, taking him in slow degrees, teasing withdrawing, tempting, until the shudders began deep in his belly, his limbs quaking like a thoroughbred racehorse. As she rode him across the finish line, release annihilated him, and he cried out, "I love you, oh I love you... Vixen!"

September 18, 998 ME

Water of Love

The next morning, a low, plaintive moan emerged from a tangle of sheets and pillows. "Ugh, my head hurts." Thaddeus covered his eyes with a pillow. "Esmie... I need a glass of water, please."

Dressed in her comfy old Rephidim tunic and leggings, she looked up from her novel with an amused gleam in her eyes. "What's wrong?"

Thaddeus smacked his parched lips. "Not funny."

"Oh, you were plenty of fun last night…. Poppa," Esmeralda giggled.

He slung an elbow over the pillow and groaned, "I did not say that, did I?"

"Oh, yeah. Several times." Esmeralda poured a glass of water and moved to the bed on silent feet. "I liked it."

Embarrassed color crept up his neck. "What else did I say?"

Esmeralda pressed the water into his hand. "Plenty. We acted out several of your lude fantasies. Behind that serious demeanor, you are quite depraved."

Thaddeus raised up on an elbow, looking sick, avoiding her eyes. "Hangover…" He smacked his lips and drained the glass.

It hit him like a snowball to the face: sudden, startling, cold. He felt the water coat his throat, descend his esophagus, extinguish the blaze in his roiling stomach, then blossom into his cells. "Ugh, thank you," he sighed in relief. Cracking a crusty eye, he looked around and gasped. "That water… you did it again!"

Esmeralda straddled him, excited. "It happened? It's been years! Do you see?"

He knuckled the sleep out of his eyes and blinked, his vision clear. Relaxing into the pillow, he grinned. Pink light haloed her, sparkling and intense. The white streaks in her hair glowed, iridescent and pure. Ghost freckles, normally invisible, danced across the bridge of her nose, recalling her eager, girlish face. Colors shifted into focus, and he perceived depth and nuance in everything. His hearing fine-tuned, and he detected the swish of a broom as a hotel porter sang a low, bluesy song as he swept the sidewalk. He smelled beignets and powdered sugar, chicory coffee, and spilled rum punch drifting on the breeze. And he felt Esmeralda's fine young body, pressed against his naked one, strong and healthy.

"It's more than sight. It's touch, hearing, taste." In blissful wonder, he murmured, "Is this how you experience the world?"

She planted her palms on either side of his ears, absolutely radiant. "That's the right side."

Thaddeus became enchanted by her long brown eyelashes. "I like the right side."

"I do, too," she murmured and lowered her lips to his.

The next twenty minutes were the most surreal of his life, as he bonded with her on a molecular level, fusing his body with hers, pouring out his soul. Thaddeus drank the heavenly gift of Esmeralda. When it was over, surrounded by pale silver light, he held her tightly to his chest, with no concept of where she began and he ended; they were simply one.

Blue on Black

Beau Landry fell asleep at dawn. The darkness that stalked his mind fed on the power of night, and during those times, if he slept at all, it happened after sunrise. He was in the throes of a bad episode, battling the mind monster that seized his reason and consumed him whole. The ringing phone on his nightstand brought him to bleary consciousness. He rubbed the sticky gunk out of his black lashes and tried to keep the grogginess out of his voice when he answered, "*Maman*, morning. Where y'at?"

"It's not morning, Beau. You're sleeping in the day again."

He groaned, "*Je vais bien.*" I'm all right.

"You do not sound it." Sarah Landry did not coddle, and unlike the rest of his family, she did not dance around the truth. "Do I need to come?"

He sat up, plucking the sleep from his azure eyes. "No. I'm not fit company."

"Which is exactly why I'd come. Have you forgotten we have guests coming tonight? It's Sarah Beth's birthday, and Ian and Joanna sent that couple down to visit. You are supposed to be their host, Beau. If you are not in fit shape to do it, you need to let me know. I'll step in." Her clipped New England accent revealed the intensity of her worry.

He scrubbed his hands over his face and felt his beard, matted and dry. The phone fell in his lap because he *had* forgotten guests were coming and hated facing people when the madness stalked him. His mother's tinny voice came through the line. She would be in the car if he did not answer, but if he capitulated and let her come over, the next six weeks would find her up his rear like a cattle prod.

He picked up and said, "I'm fine, *Maman*. I'll be there. You go tell everybody how to run the birthday party. Give Sarah Beth a hug, tell her I said happy birthday. I'll see y'all tonight." He disconnected the line before she could protest and flung the phone onto the bed.

Glancing at the clock, 10:00 am. He'd fallen asleep just after dawn. On sluggish feet, he stumbled into the kitchen and turned on the coffee maker, the pot prepared the evening before. Out of long habit, he occupied himself during the long nights with mundane chores, reasoning routine and ritual kept the demons at bay. His house was pristine, clean and orderly, compulsively so, when he was fighting. He arranged the coffee cups in perfect rows, their handles turned to precise angles, organized by size, color, and height. In the darkness, it became imperative to control the tempest by organizing the objects around him precisely. In the early days, any disruption sent him into a rage, now it was about control.

He opened the refrigerator, everything similarly classified by color, size, and food group. When it was heavy on him, he transferred all the food into matching containers. Beau sighed because he had poured three bottles of juice from their store jugs into identical pitchers that created a spectral arrangement: red, orange, yellow. He took the orange juice out and drank straight from the pitcher. In the light of day, he put the orange juice in front of the red fruit juice. He slammed the refrigerator door and turned away, then with a vicious curse repositioned the pitcher, putting them in proper color-wheel order. Glaring at the now different levels of liquid, he forced himself not to add water to the orange juice or drink the fruit juice and lemonade to identical volume. He spied the half and half, also in a glass pitcher, and retrieved it from its assigned spot, behind the whole milk and in front of the coconut water, loathing himself for the insanity in his own refrigerator. If his mother saw this....

He had to keep her away, all of them, had to keep them out of his house. If a single member of his family saw how he was living, they'd be there with the white coats and the damn doctors, and he'd had enough of those voodoo head shrinks. He was fine. There was nothing wrong with being organized.

His hand shook as he poured the coffee. He was tired, that was all. He wasn't sleeping, and when that happened, he became vulnerable, and forty-seven nosy family members climbing up his ass all the time made it worse.

They made it worse!

His mind raged... their fault... they made him ashamed. He was, what he was, damn them all to hell! Looking at him the way they did, watching him... waiting for him to break, or say something odd. They were like panthers stalking, hunting in the darkness. It was them.

He should go, should leave this forsaken place with their tiresome meddling. He would be better if he could go, but he couldn't. He couldn't leave. That counter, he'd backed her against it and kissed her, felt her sexy denim mini skirt and long beautiful legs. She was here. He could still feel her... here. The office where she dreamed of doing her computer work, the wall she painted, the drip of paint on the molding in the kitchen from her brush, she was here! If he left, he feared he would lose the rest of his mind, and with it, Alaina.

He took his coffee and unlocked the door to her study. Her pictures covered the walls, arranged in precise chronological order, identically framed, and mounted, perfectly symmetrical and spaced. The office served as both a haven and a testimony to his obsessive madness. Beau began the ritual, three sips of coffee, two steps, set down the mug in the center of his desk, and say, "Good Morning, Alaina."

It started with the photographs of them together, the precious ones. They sat on his desk, overlooking the lake she loved that had ultimately taken her away. The first photo was of him and Alaina the week after they met. She wore fishing gear and held a pink rod. He was looking at her with a teasing grin on his face.

The next, of she and *Grand'Mere* Isabelle, had become hard to look at. His heart broke, as he swallowed a lump of grief. *Grand'Mere's* death last month started this current slide. His lively, wonderful *Grand'Mere* was gone. He held the picture. They were both gone. Two of the three women he loved most in the world were gone. He had taken this picture in the little yellow cottage, Alaina's hands were covered in flour, as *Grand'Mere* taught her to make biscuits.

The next picture was always the hardest, but he loved it most. It reminded him of the truth. She was real, they were real. There were many pictures taken of them that night, but this was his favorite. Alaina, dewy with perspiration and dance, with one arm resting on his shoulder, had turned to the camera when someone called their attention. She raised her leg behind her and flashed her new engagement ring with a joyous smile. He stood with her, proud and whole on the happiest day of his life.

The last picture on his desk, taken the week before, he mentally corrected himself, their last week together, was the one that bound him to this house, to this place. Alaina, her hair covered in a kerchief splattered in paint, held a paintbrush like it was a torch, and she was the Statue of Liberty. She was celebrating her victory in wall color. He had wanted gray. His walls, to this day, were rose beige.

He left the photos, going to Serendipity, the original. It was gorgeous, not only for the subject, but as a stunning piece of art. Beau moved to his habitual place in the room, across from it, so she was looking at him. A tear escaped his eye. "I'm not better, Jolie Catin." His voice sounded ragged in the shrine's silence. "I try. I fight, but I'm not better, Bébé."

Then he fell to his knees and wept.

A Right Mess of It!

Korah exploded out of the chair behind his desk. "You leave me with no choice, Angelica!" he shouted, his pupils turning black with rage. "Look outside and see for yourself. The press is in a frenzy. We got Keyseelough out of the country, and all but the fringe outlets have accepted that part of the story, but you," he pointed a finger at her, "are done! You are finished. There is no way to salvage this. It was your plane, flying under your orders, and they found you naked with Peter's fiancée! This is your responsibility, and you are not taking my kingdom down with you."

Angelica lifted an imperious chin. "Do not speak to me in that tone, you maggot."

"Or you will do, what?" Korah narrowed his eyes. He and the Dark Master agreed, she had become a liability, old, reckless and doomed. Before she could retort he cut her off. "Nothing, precisely nothing." He bared his teeth at her. "I will have your resignation—now."

"I made you!" she hissed.

"At what cost?" Korah bellowed. "It cost me my wife! It cost me everything! And I have repaid you a thousand times over. Now get out of my sight."

Angelica ben Omri rose from her chair with slow menace. "We made a pact. You cannot just dismiss me."

"It was the worst decision I ever made." A storm of emotions crossed his handsome face before he shielded them and adopted his customary expression of bored cynicism. With a flick of his hand, he dismissed her, as if she were nothing.

"You have no power here, not while the Dark Master rules, and we both know where his favor lies. It's not with you, Angelica, especially after your debacles this week."

The only reaction she showed was a tightening of her mouth. Her eyes blazed hatred. They promised revenge. Without a word, she turned to leave. When she reached the door, he added one parting shot. "The White Woman, the third prophecy has been made, you are doomed."

Angelica turned with a snarl, "Your confidence in your own knowledge has always been your greatest weakness, Korah." She raised a razor-sharp, diabolic eyebrow. "I know who she is. I also know what actually happened to your wife."

With a flash of pink suit, Angelica ben Omri left Korah ben Adam speechless.

Weaver's Daughter

Thaddeus insisted on taking Esmeralda shopping. The few pieces they picked up for her in Wyoming and the New City were not enough to carry her through the rest of the trip, and he was certainly not taking her to a party at one of the richest families in Alanthia dressed in Mil-Mart, even if Sarah Landry once owned the chain. He had to give credit to Mil-Mart though, those lavender panties were memorable.

Thaddeus was not a wealthy man, but he was single, frugal, and invested wisely. He collected a substantial life insurance policy when Olivia died and never touched a shekel of the money. It had grown over the years. He never took vacations, had no expensive hobbies, well, at least not anymore. Being a city dweller, he did not own a car, using official vehicles if he required one. He wore nice clothes, and the apartment in New York had not come cheap, but he lived modestly and retained control of most of his earnings.

With someone to spend money on, he delighted in showering Esmeralda with gifts. Once he started, spending fervor took over. He morphed into Thaddeus, the Director, thrusting garments at her to try on, consulting, approving, and discarding those he did not like. The clothing she wore the first week of their reunion in New York, save the blue dress, were all beiges, grays, and muted pastels—librarian's clothes. She shimmered like a star in jewel tones, and he heaped them on her in mass profusion.

"What am I going to do with all these gowns?" she protested, collapsing in the chair beside him at their fifth clothing store.

Thaddeus raised his eyebrows at her. "You don't think they will find the money to run the NY Center for Street Kids under a cabbage leaf, do you? Ian and Joanna spend half their time at fundraisers."

Esmeralda looked aghast. "But they don't expect me to do that, do they?"

"What do you think tonight is about?" Thaddeus asked slowly, amused at her naivete. "If you were just going to be reading stories to kids at the Center, they would not have arranged for us to meet the Landry family in a social setting before your visit to the facilities on Monday."

Esmeralda paled. "I'm a researcher, a librarian… a bookworm! I'm not a socialite fundraiser. People think I am weird! I am absolutely the last person who should be put in that position."

He scrunched his face and threw up his hands in a markedly New York expression. "What are you talking about? People love you. Besides, I've moved in that crowd, they will find your uniqueness intriguing, trust me."

Esmeralda looked like he had just sentenced her to hard labor. "You'll go with me? If they make me, you'll go? You'll help me?"

He refused to play into her insecurities. "If you think for a single second that I would let you out of my sight wearing one of these slinky gowns, you have another thing coming. Husbands go with their wives to things like that, Esmie. That's how marriage works."

She released the breath she had been holding and visibly relaxed. "I expect Joanna will do most of the big events. I'll probably just have to attend as a staff member. Don't you think?"

Thaddeus nodded. "I'd say that is a fair assessment. They might ask you to go to smaller functions when she's not in town, perhaps a few like we are going to tonight, casual affairs, meet and greet, that sort of thing."

Esmeralda shook her head. "I'm an idiot. I thought we were going down there tonight to meet Ian's best friend, who happens to be involved in the New Orleans Center."

Thaddeus moistened his lips and asked cautiously, "Esmie, do you know who the Landrys are?"

Her eyes widened. Her expression conveyed that she did not.

The corner of his mouth quivered. "Are you familiar with the Lenox Company?"

Her eyebrows narrowed in thought, then shot up in wonder. "*The* Lenox Company? Oil, gas, automobiles, electricity, banking, investment firms… the gigantic blue building that I walked by every day on my way to work, Lenox Company?"

"Yeah, that would be the one." He took her hand. "Sarah Landry is Andrew ben Lenox's only child. She also founded," he plucked at the pair of jeans she was wearing, "Mil-Mart."

Esmeralda held her palm up to his face. "Stop! We are going to a fai-dookey, or whatever the heck they call it down here, with *them?*" She jumped up and turned on him. "And all Joanna warned me about was that Beau Landry was beautiful? I am going to kill her!"

Thaddeus scowled at that piece of information but addressed her concerns first. "I'd expect because Joanna ben Luke is an aristocrat, it never occurred to her to mention it."

"What?" Esmeralda cried. "An aristocrat? I thought she just ran a couple of Centers for Street Kids."

Thaddeus rubbed his jaw, trying not to laugh. "Why do you think Ian calls her Princess? Though, I am pretty sure

Ian comes from money. He attended the RMA after all, but Joanna?" He chuckled. "Her blood is as blue as it gets, babe. Her grandfather was, and still might officially be, the Alanthian Ambassador to the Golden Kingdom. Her father was a member of Prince Eamonn's inner circle, and I believe her mother is some sort of cousin to Prince Edward of Europe. She is Lady Joanna ben Luke."

Esmeralda looked like she was going to throw up.

Thaddeus continued, "Though, Ian told me last year that most of the family money was frozen after the Civil War, even so, Joanna ben Luke is a bit more than an administrator for a charity."

Esmeralda swallowed audibly. "Oh, my word. I'm a weaver's daughter from rural Pennsylvania who grew up in a house with one bathroom! I also spent four years... well you know where! I don't belong with these people." She whirled on him. "Next thing you are going to tell me is that you are related to King Korah!"

Thaddeus slouched in the comfortable chair. "No. I'm a working-class kid just like you. I went to college on a basketball scholarship and took out loans and worked an internship to earn my law degree."

"But you are comfortable around them! I remember you telling me about being their Golden Boy. They wanted you to run for office, and I read books!" Several customers in the store turned to stare, and Esmeralda blushed.

Thaddeus picked up their shopping bags, her two current purchases, and motioned to the checkout counter. On impulse, he added earrings, a necklace, and two bracelets to their purchase. He would not see her shamed, not when this small thing was in his control.

They emerged onto the busy street, it was time to head back to their hotel and get ready. "The thing about rich people, Esmeralda, is they are just people. You had two dinners with Joanna and never knew a thing."

Esmeralda waved a finger at him. "That's where you're wrong, she scared the pee out of me. I just didn't know why."

"Well, if I'm honest, she scares me a little, too."

Esmeralda giggled. Nobody intimidated Thaddeus. His sheer height helped. She gave him a punch in the arm and said, "You were not."

He smiled, glad he teased her out of her panic. "No, I wasn't, but that assistant of hers, now, she scares me."

"Judith?" Esmeralda grimaced. "With good reason, I've been around plenty of disturbed people. I can spot the real ones a mile away. I am planning on steering well away from that woman."

Thaddeus imitated Richard's little voice. "That Judith, she's a mean damn one!"

Esmeralda cracked up.

An X or a Check?

Beau Landry stared at his reflection, smoothing his closely cropped beard, checking the lines to ensure they were straight. He considered shaving the damn thing off, but it provided good camouflage. Some days, his inability to make it perfect drove him mad, and he ended up with a goatee because he messed with it too much. But keeping a perfect goatee proved even more exasperating than a beard. He ought to quit shaving altogether, but that made him look like a swamper, a wild man, and he didn't need more help in that regard, so he hid behind the beard, resigned to facial hair grooming for more hours than he would ever admit to a living soul.

For eight years, he wrestled with this madness. He was shell-shocked when he returned from the Civil War, but he had come out of that, and by the time he met Alaina he was ready to put the past behind him. He reckoned he wasn't the first man to struggle in the aftermath of battle. There were plenty of soldiers out there who did. But the Bayou? Something broke in him that night, and try as he might, he could not put himself back together.

Some days were worse than others; some days he was fine. There were seven calendars stacked neatly in his closet, the current one hung inside the door. A red check mark showed all the good days, a black X, the bad. In '95, he'd put together one hundred forty straight red check marks, the magic number, where he would call Alaina was one sixty-eight. He was running at ninety, then *Grand'Mere* died, maybe tomorrow would be a red check mark day, today already had a black X, every September 18th in the stack of calendars did.

It was Sarah Beth's birthday, and he promised Ian he would meet and entertain his friends from New York. Ian didn't send people to Beau, so the significance and the confidence his old friend had in him drove him out of the house on a black X day. He just hoped he would not regret it.

The *fais-do-do* was underway when he pulled up. Had it been an afternoon affair, he'd have driven the boat. But the festivities would run well into the evening, and Beau Landry did not go on the water in the dark, ever. So, he drove.

His mother met him before he could stow his sunglasses and turn off the truck. She stood outside his driver's door with her arms crossed, highly perturbed. Her expression did not engender confidence that he had a pleasant evening in store.

She said without preamble, "Your guests are already here. They arrived thirty minutes ago. Where have you been?"

He glared at her. "I was shaving."

She rolled her eyes. "Is it an X day or a check day? Just tell me now."

Beau moved past her with languid grace. "The day's not over yet, *Maman*."

"Beau," she growled in a warning tone, *"dis-moi la vérité."*

He was sick of that tone, but more exhausted by what was behind it. He did not turn. "I'm fine. I'll get through it. It's Sarah Beth's birthday. You don't need to worry about me howling at the damn moon."

Sarah covered one eye with the tips of her fingers, and she could tell by the look in his eyes it was an X day, even if he wouldn't admit it. "Well, that's good." She took his arm and allowed him to escort her inside. "I'll introduce you to Thaddeus and Esmeralda. They seem to be a nice couple, though he is older than her."

Beau chuckled. "You never change, *Maman,* and I love you. Don't worry about me tonight. I'll be fine."

Sarah Landry was a realist, but more than anyone, she'd been by her son's side during his long illness and knew the power of positive affirmation. "I know you will. Come on. Let's get in there before Uncle Boudreaux scares the crap out of that girl with one of his bayou boogie man stories."

"Uncle Boudreaux's stories scare me sometimes." His riverboat pirate grin did not travel to his eyes.

"Then you should not listen to them." Sarah's smile did not meet her eyes either.

Harbingers, the Landry house band, led by Beau's nephew Justin, played a lively zydeco tune as they entered the reception hall. The song was a crowd favorite. The music contrasted with the black mood that covered him. Dread rested like a weight on his chest. He gritted his teeth and tried to keep his expression pleasant, nodding greetings and following his mother to meet their guests. When he saw the curly-haired woman, he felt the monster take a huge bite.

Playing With Your Food

Clothed in rose colored silk, Mademoiselle Charlotte Durant ascended her throne in the Grand Ballroom at Loa Hall. Behind the throne hung a red velvet curtain embroidered with ancient symbols of power. It also hid Emite the Nephilim, her son and greatest weapon. One by one, in reverential fear, the elite invited to this special ceremony came forward. bearing gifts. They offered bouquets of roses, sweet beverages of various flavors, young chickens, and confections dipped in syrup, tokens of their love and esteem. Those she accepted were placed at her feet. Those she rejected burned in the fire. The congregants were also sorted, accepted moved to the left, rejected to the right. Tonight, the rejected outnumbered the accepted twelve to one.

With no discernable rhyme or reason to Charlotte's preferences, the congregants approached not knowing if they would be blessed or cursed. What earned her favor one week, did not the next. They never ascertained what made her happy, which was by design. The only constant with Charlotte was protocol. The slightest misstep, the smallest breach, real or perceived, elicited her wrath. Flippancy or deliberate irreverence could prove fatal, for them and their families.

They sought her power, and by extension, their own. In doing so, they sacrificed their free will, their lives, and ultimately their souls. In exchange, they vied for her favor, a capricious endeavor, but once gained she cursed their enemies, bless their finances, and taught them the forbidden ancient power lost for a Millennium. They cast spells, threw hexes, committed crimes with impunity, and flew through the night air free of body and bone to bedevil all who dared cross them. Mademoiselle Charlotte's coven ran the gamut from whores operating in sleazy hotels, to the rich and powerful. Her tentacles invaded every part of New Orleans society, except one, Landry's.

Tonight, she planned to change that.

Angelica ben Omri's fall from grace positioned Charlotte to assume the highest rank in their order, if she proved herself worthy. Today, they summoned her to the Palace, ending her thirteen-year exile. Her time had come. Charlotte dismissed her rivals vying for the position, including that bitch, Princess Keyseelough. She wielded a power their paltry potions could not touch. She had the Dark Master's son.

When the offering ceremony concluded, Charlotte levitated out of her throne and flew above them. Flames from hundreds of candles cast moving shadows up the walls, incense burned thick and sweet. Those out of favor groveled with their faces on the ground. Those in favor bowed their heads. Charlotte and Emite kept a silent running dialogue, speaking in each other's minds. He held her afloat; she controlled them all.

"Only twelve pleased me this night." She spoke in French in a voice low and deadly. "As a sign of my favor, each of you will receive a token of my esteem as you depart. Go!"

By rank and order, they filed out, eager for their prize. Mademoiselle often bestowed love potions, hexes, and the most coveted of all, spells. No one spoke, lest they lose their treasure and face her wrath. The favored left the hall, oozing haughty arrogance and pride. Whispering with slanderous tongues, their feet raced to do evil.

Charlotte turned her colorless eyes on those out of favor, all seventy-eight of them. "Come forth, and you will answer for your failure." Emite threw an electric curse over the crowd. They jerked in unison, much to Charlotte's sadistic delight. She resumed her throne and called them by their secret names. They crawled forth, on hands and knees, begging for mercy. Some Emite cursed with sickness, some convulsed, others spun in the air like gyroscopes, a few escaped with nothing but a severe rebuke. Each retreated from Loa Hall, glad to be alive and determined to do better next time.

The final twelve remained, a mixed group of witches and warlocks, selected for their special talents, and whose inclusion in this group Charlotte predetermined. "I am particularly displeased with the lot of you. You may escape with your lives if you prove yourselves worthy. Follow me. We are going to war!"

Confident in her victory, she swept from the room with a swish of rose silk skirts. She chose her warriors well. The ceremony had been painstakingly prepared, and Emite stood at the ready. They were flying tonight, deep into the heart of the last enemy stronghold. Her diabolical battle plan was a reenactment of her greatest defeat, and this time, Beau Landry would not survive.

Touch of Love

Dressed in a new slate blue pantsuit, Esmeralda clung to Thaddeus' arm like a barnacle. Despite his reassurance, she hid behind him, withdrawn and nervous. The Landry's net worth and prominent social status proved insurmountable stumbling blocks, so she could not relax and enjoy herself. Overwhelmed with shyness, she watched the party from behind lowered lashes and pink blushes. Growing up sheltered in Rephidim and hospitalized for years, she never learned the art of small talk and had never been easy in the company of strangers. She felt conspicuous, like she occupied one of her nightmares where she showed up naked.

The Landrys were generous, accommodating hosts. Plying them with Cajun food, they engaged she and Thaddeus in conversations and regaled them with tales from the region. She liked Uncle Boudreaux's outlandish stories and flashing blue eyes. Ian's friend Beau was as beautiful as Joanna warned, though tonight he did not feel well. He was pale beneath his cropped beard, and a sheen of perspiration dampened his forehead. But to his credit, he stood by them, introducing them to dozens of family members, even serving Esmeralda a glass of sparkling wine that Sara Beth adored and flowed in abundance. Toward the end of the evening, Esmeralda saw the party was taking a toll on him. Looking ill, Beau excused himself.

Esmeralda shifted uncomfortably and whispered, "Um. where is the lady's room?"

"Oh, it's back this way. Come on, chèr, I'll take you." Beau touched her elbow just as the band began a lively little song, *Sweet Touch of Love.*

Pain shot down her spine, his pain. Esmeralda controlled a gasp as he walked her across the dance floor. His aura came into sharp focus, Prussian blue, and she saw clearly that he was a lonely, heartbroken man, trying to hold it together.

When he loosened his grip, the intense emotion faded, and she followed him down a narrow hallway on the side of the building where the restrooms and kitchen service entry were, away from the crowd. Ducking into the ladies room, she let out a shaky breath. Far from being enjoyable, the party was taxing, and Beau Landry's pain drained the last of her fortitude.

Determined to convince Thaddeus to leave, Esmeralda exited the bathroom in a rush and stumbled into Beau Landry.

"Whoa!" he said, trying to balance her. "Hold on. I've got you now."

Triggered.

Esmeralda's vision wavered. Something broke in her mind, fell out of place, and she spiraled into the vortex of her first real nightmare—The Bayou.

"There you two are. Come on, it's time to cut the cake." Sarah Landry stepped out of the kitchen, holding a silver cake knife.

In Esmeralda's mind, the hall shifted and transformed into the swamp. Fires blazed around them, and the stench of dead animals fouled the air. She turned in Beau's arms with a strangled cry. The Witch came forth, brandishing her knife, and out of the shadows the giant loomed. Esmeralda tried to scream, but her vocal cords froze, and she only managed a strangled sob. Beau's arms tighten around her waist, and she looked up, recognizing him as the blue-eyed, black-haired man who haunted her dreams. He grimaced in panic, their eyes locking in mutual fear and dread. Beau and Esmeralda slipped beyond the veil into an alternate reality where Sarah Landry became the witch, Thaddeus, the giant.

"In Yeshua's Name!" Beau cried. Without letting Esmeralda go, and moving faster than any human ought, he disarmed the witch and bore Esmeralda backward, protecting her from the rapidly approaching giant. "You're not taking her, you ugly *feet pue tan!* She's mine, and you won't touch her." he bellowed with rage, wielding the witch's knife. "I'll kill you!"

"Beau!" Esmeralda cried, but it wasn't her voice, it was a stranger's. "Get me out of here!"

His arm tightened as he backed out the door. "Run, Jolie Catin! The boat is this way!" He pushed her toward the docks, escaping the horror, death, and stench—their current shared reality.

Running as fast as she could in her new high heels, Esmeralda cried, "We're not going to make it!"

Behind them they heard pounding feet, yelling, and wailing.

"Allons, chèr!" Beau pulled her faster, running like the wind. He jumped into the boat, leaping like a gazelle. "Get the rope!" he ordered, unlashing the rear one and diving for the wheel. "They ain't gonna get you, I promise."

The roar of the engine sounded like sweet salvation to Esmeralda as she pushed hard against a piling. Beau gunned the engine, and they flew away from hell, into the dark waters of the Louisiana bayou.

Thaddeus' shout reverberated across the black water and penetrated her brain. "Esmeralda!!! Come back!"

She jerked back into reality. Beau Landry did not.

Black Water

Esmeralda retched over the side, coughing and sputtering as the boat raced away from Landry's. Collapsing onto the seat, she wiped her runny nose and dabbed at her eyes. "Oh, my word, what just happened?"

"It's okay. I've got you now."

Triggered again, Esmeralda swooned and fell backward.

Beau scooped her up before she hit the deck and pulled her into his lap. Murmuring French, he wrapped an arm around her waist to keep her from sliding. She relaxed onto him, taking comfort in his strength. A pale half-moon provided

their only source of light on the water. She squinted, studying him. He looked determined, but angry and scared. She
rested her fingers against his bicep and slurred, "What was
that?"

He shook his head, his chest heaving. "Bad loa, *chèr.*"

"What's a loa?" she asked, her voice sounding strange to
her own ears, huskier and deeper than normal.

"An evil spirit." He rested his cheek against her head, seeing Alaina's blonde hair, immersed in the bayou nightmare.
"*Mon Dieu,* it ain't the first time I fought one. There was one
in the war. It tried to kill me then, too. I had a thousand
wounds all over my body. The doctors, they never knew how
I got them, or how they healed. But I woke up in a shroud,
like I was already in the tomb. When they unwrapped me,
the wounds were gone… but I could still feel them, where
they pierced me." As he spoke, his tongue thickened, drifting
away. "I think the worst was here." He pressed her limp hand
to his temple. "I keep seeing it. I keep feeling it."

Esmeralda sobbed as his terror and pain bled into her soul.
Riding on that black water, she experienced the confusion
and chaos of battle. She smelled brimstone, and whimpered
in horror when a beast, astride a black horse, materialized. It
roared and cursed in a foul tongue. Bodies exploded, heads
fell in the dirt, then she felt her body ripping apart. "Oh
Beau, I'm so sorry! So sorry!" she sobbed.

Pulling her hard against his body, he straightened in the
captain's chair, hoping he was taking them to safety, not
deeper into darkness. "It's all right, Jolie Catin, I'm going to
get us out of this. I'll take care of you."

Esmeralda turned in his arms and cried tears, both familiar and unfamiliar, in a voice not her own.

Stand Down

Three thousand feet above La Petit Pishon, Gabriel, the
Messenger of God, turned to the Prince of Hosts, Michael. "I
despise standing down, watching the enemy attack."

Michael folded his great arms and said, "It is the will of the Most High, for His purposes."

"She is naught but a babe," Gabriel growled, "and they have tormented that man beyond enduring."

"The Lord knows the end from the beginning, brother." Michael moved his hand, and the boat below corrected course.

Gabriel turned to the west and shook his head, resigned. "They will be overwhelmed down there."

"They must learn to stand, both of them." Michael touched his sheathed sword and added, "In the meantime, we wait."

Gabriel watched the horde of astral spirits bearing down on Esmeralda and Beau. "There is no prayer cover."

Michael set his jaw. "We do not engage tonight without it."

Frustration boiled up in Gabriel. "We can usually count on the mother. Where are her prayers?"

"I do not know." Michael watched the scene below with growing concern.

Conflicting Priorities

Alone at the end of the Landry dock, Sarah fell into a heap, heedless of the rough boards picking the fabric of her four-hundred-shekel trousers. Thaddeus stared after the disappearing boat in astonishment, then looked around, ready to take one of the moored boats and go after them. There were several to choose from, but he was a city boy, unfamiliar with the area, and knew he had no chance of catching them in the dark. "What the fuck just happened here?" he demanded.

Sarah rocked on her knees, her hands covering her face, sobbing. "My son, my son!"

"Your crazy ass son just took off with my fiancée, woman!" Thaddeus bellowed. "And he had a knife!"

In the darkness, her weeping grew so intense it went silent. He listened as the distant whine of the boat faded away, leaving a surreal quiet in the marina. In the hall, the band continued playing, the guests kept dancing, and no one stepped outside. No one saw the drama unfold, except the two bewildered people on the dock.

Thaddeus pulled out his phone and said, "This is Director Thaddeus ben Todd, calling in an abducted female, location twenty miles south of New Orleans in a settlement on the outskirts of Delacroix referred to as Landry's. The abductor is armed and dangerous, suffering a probable psychotic break. Requesting hostage negotiator and all available field agents. Suspect is Beau Landry of Delacroix, and the victim," Thaddeus swallowed hard and ground out, "is Esmeralda ben Claude of New York City. She is also my fiancée."

Thaddeus paced, as the dispatcher confirmed the report. "I am requesting Agent Paul ben Casper as lead. He is on assignment in New Orleans." He paused, listening to the party on the other end. "That is correct. I will respect protocol." His control shattered and his temper flared. "Which is why I am calling this in and going through official channels. Now do it!"

When Thaddeus turned, Sarah Landry had risen from the deck, her face morphing into a mask of suppressed rage. "You did not just call in the FBI!" she demanded.

"You are damned right I did!"

Sarah's fists balled at her sides. "He needs medical attention. He does not need to be arrested."

Thaddeus drew himself up to his full height, meeting her lethal look with one of his own. "Madam, my concern right now is not for the abductor but the abductee who you seem to have little regard for and have failed to mention." He stalked past her. "Now if you will excuse me. I am going to put an end to this party."

"Wait!" Sarah's desperate plea reverberated across the water.

Thaddeus stopped but kept his back to her.

"I'm sorry. She'll be all right. He won't hurt her. I can promise you that."

"Considering he threatened to kill me with a knife, forgive me if I do not put much stock in your words."

"It was a cake server!" Sarah exclaimed. "And he will not hurt her. He thinks she's Alaina, and he would never hurt Alaina. He loves her."

Thaddeus' interest in who Alaina was extended no further than that it might be useful to the negotiator. "Who is Alaina, and why do you think he believes Esmeralda is her?"

Sarah Landry moved in front of Thaddeus, forcing him to look at her. "He called her Jolie Catin. That is his nickname for Alaina ben Thomas."

Thaddeus' lip curled in an ugly snarl. "The supermodel? Your son is obsessed with a supermodel? That's reassuring, lady."

"You listen to me for one minute. You do not know the first thing about my son or his life. Now, we can do this the easy way or the hard way, and I can promise you, Director, the outcome of this will be a hell of a lot better, for everyone, if you choose the easy way."

Thaddeus stared her down. He did not give a shit about her power, or her money, or her influence.

Sarah Landry, mamma grizzly, seemed to grow. No one messed with her son. "Stop sneering at me and listen because I can help you. I can get Esmeralda back, safely, with no complications or injury to either of them. That is the goal here, is it not?"

Inside Thaddeus raged, ready to tear Beau Landry limb from limb. He wanted no part of some rich woman's machinations to cover up her dangerous son's crimes. But she was right, Esmeralda's safety was paramount. Reluctantly, he said, "I'm listening."

Cleaving

The lights from Beau's lake house on La Petit Pishon shone like a beacon, promising safety, a refuge from the storm brewing around them. Beau gunned the engine, flying across the open water, and docking the boat with practiced skill. Killing the loud motor, he called, "Tie it up, Jolie Catin."

Esmeralda picked up the rope with shaking hands and looked down at it in helpless befuddlement. "I don't know how."

He took the line from her and with a quick motion secured the boat. "Go on," he said, boosting her up the ladder onto the dock. "Get inside."

He surveyed the lake. Nothing moved save an abnormally chilly wind through the cypress trees, but he felt something bearing down on them, something wicked.

"Come on!" Esmeralda pleaded. "I'm not leaving you out here alone."

With a final scan, he nodded and rushed her toward the house.

When they crossed the threshold, an electric jolt hit Esmeralda. She shuddered and grabbed the sides of her head, her system going haywire. Beau slammed and locked the door, then moving quickly he pulled the heavy curtains on the floor to ceiling windows. She watched in detached fascination as he shut them inside, blocking out the night.

"This is your house?" Esmeralda asked, dazed, and staring at the workout equipment and assorted sporting gear. Beau ignored her and ran from the room, locking everything down as he went. Unsure what to do, or how she had even got here, Esmeralda peeked upstairs, then decided to follow him.

He emerged from a bedroom with his face set in a mask of black fury. "You okay?"

Esmeralda pressed the pads of her fingers against her temples. "No. My head hurts, and… what's happening?"

Beau took her in his arms. "It's okay, Bébé. I've got you now."

Esmeralda experienced it again, a snap in her brain, but this time she fought it, retaining a part of herself and her own consciousness as she swirled down the rabbit hole. The room did not change, it appeared exactly as it had, but she felt different.

A strange image in the living room mirror caught her attention, and she moved with wild-eyed wonder toward her reflection. She brought her hands to her face. A beautiful woman stared back at her with aquamarine eyes, strong cheekbones, and full lips. Straight, blonde hair tousled around her shoulders, Esmeralda's fantasy hair. With a squeaky cry, she looked down. Long, elegant limbs wore unfamiliar clothes, and feet much larger than her own sported pink ankle boots.

"Is this a dream?" she breathed in a voice not her own.

Beau made a strangled groan.

In the mirror, she saw an evil spirit hovering over him, its hands around his throat. Esmeralda whirled as another hit him, this one, going through his body. He bent in half, blowing out a gush of air like someone punched him in the gut.

"No!" she cried, plastering herself against the wall.

"Get out, Jolie Catin, they are coming!" Beau fell to his knees gasping, then convulsed and disappeared under their assault.

Esmeralda froze in abject terror as black shadows swarmed the room. She screamed as something huge detached itself from the hoard and turned its attention on her.

The Witch's Flu

The flu hit Alaina ben Thomas like a freight train. One moment she sat in her computer room, the next waves of nausea and violent chills overwhelmed her. She experienced the disconcerting sensation of spiraling down a dark tunnel into the terror of her worst nightmare—the Bayou.

Everything went black.

She woke up on the floor, disoriented and terrified, knowing if she passed out again behind the secret door, no one would find her. Using every ounce of strength she could muster, she crawled to the bathroom, trying not to vomit as waves of nausea buffeted her.

After the violent sickness passed, she stumbled into her room, collapsing onto her four-poster bed, breathing heavy. Feeling blindly for her purse on the nightstand, she fumbled for her phone and dialed. "Hey, can you come over? Something's wrong, I've gotten sick all of a sudden."

"What's happening? Do I need to call a doctor?" Ellen ben Quincy, Alaina's business partner and long-time assistant, asked.

Alaina heard Ellen's car keys jingling. "I don't think so, but this hit me hard and fast."

"All right, I'm on my way. Do you want me to stop and pick up anything?"

"Ice cream," Alaina murmured, "my throat hurts and I have a terrible taste in my mouth."

"I'll bring sorbet."

Alaina groaned, "I hate you."

"No, you don't. See you in a bit." Ellen disconnected the line.

Clawing at the comforter, she pulled the blanket up to her chin, her teeth chattering. The phone rang. So close to her ear, it startled her. She answered without looking at the screen, assuming it was Ellen calling back. It wasn't.

"Alaina?" The bayou voice was smooth and deep.

Her breath caught. "Beau?"

"Alaina, it's Jorge Landry."

A sudden coughing fit seized her, as she mentally rejected whatever made him sound that way, fearing the worst. *No, Lord please, no!*

"You okay, honey?"

The coughing fit passed, and Alaina croaked, "Sorry. I'm okay, what's wrong?"

"I'm sorry you're not feeling well, honey." He paused. "I need you to do me a favor, please pray for Beau. He's had an episode tonight, *chèr*."

Alaina whimpered, and the cold tremors got worse. "Oh, no. Is he okay?"

"I'm sure he will be. Normally, I wouldn't call, but it's a bad one," he said, weariness and worry travelling across the line.

"Jorge, what's happening?" Alaina asked, trying to suppress another wave of sickness.

Background noise made it difficult to hear what he said. "I can't go into detail right now, but I'll call you later."

"Do you know what day it is?" Alaina choked, tears flooding her eyes. "It's the day we got engaged."

Jorge made a hoarse sound in the back of his throat. "I'm sorry, Alaina."

Alaina felt an oppressive weight settle on her chest, making it hard to breathe. She brought her ring to her lips and whispered, "I'm praying."

"I know you are, honey. Pray hard." Jorge disconnected the line.

Ian ben Kole's favorite basketball team was playing as he settled onto the couch with a bag of potato chips, four hot dogs, and a giant soda. Such was life as a bachelor, alone in his small apartment on a Saturday night with the game for company. He was vaguely annoyed when the call came in and considered letting it ring. Usually a call at this hour meant trouble at the Center, which meant no game tonight. With profound resignation, he muted the TV, and answered the phone.

"Ian, it's Jorge Landry, I don't have much time. Beau's having an episode, and it's as bad a one as he's ever had. He's in trouble."

"What's happened, Jorge?"

"I didn't see it, but Sarah did. Beau pulled a knife on his *maman* and ran off with that curly-haired girl you sent down here to visit. Her fiancé is fit to be tied, and he's called in the FBI. I'm afraid of what's going to happen this time. It ain't good."

"Lord, Jesus," Ian breathed.

"I believe that's who you need to be talking to, which is why I called. I'll let you know how it goes." Jorge hung up.

Ian covered his face as the words of his best friend's father sank in. He turned off the television, got down on his knees, and prayed the most fervent intercessory prayers of his life because he felt deep in his spirit that Beau and Esmeralda's lives depended on it.

Sarah Landry was making her own phone calls, first to the family attorney, who was on his way. The second, and most painful, to Beau's doctor, who was also coming. Icy control governed her every word, every action. She blocked all emotions, stifled her fear, and did what had to be done. Taking Thaddeus ben Todd by the arm, she informed him, "I'm driving out there. I cannot get a call through to either his house or his mobile. The phone at the house doesn't even ring, and the mobile goes straight to voicemail."

Esmeralda's phone was in her purse, which Thaddeus had picked up from outside the bathroom and stowed in their rental car. Official protocol dictated he wait, give his report, and stand down. He found, just then, that he did not give a shit about protocol. Esmeralda's life was on the line and every second counted. Further complicating any hope of him maintaining his rationality, old horrors swamped him, bringing uncontrollable visions of knives and blood. Madmen had slaughtered his family, and tonight, he faced that terror again. "I'm going with you."

Sarah nodded curtly. "I'll have your word, you will let me deal with him."

"We'll see how it plays out. You can't even be certain that is where he's taken her."

Sarah smiled grimly. "I know my son, Director. That is where he went. I'll tell Jorge where we are going. He'll wait here for the cavalry." She spat the last word, furious the situation had spiraled out of her control.

Jorge took the stage at Landry's. All the children were gone, taken home and put to bed by their mommas. He looked out on the grave faces of his family and said, "It is a dark night here in the bayou, and each one of you knows this ain't the first." He held their eyes steadily, intent that they understand the gravity of the situation. "Beau don't need your condemnation tonight. He needs your prayers, and so does that girl with him." Jorge bowed his head and through a catch in his voice said, "I'd have your word that y'all ain't going to go home and gossip about this. Take that energy before the Lord. Thank you."

Jorge stepped down with a heavy thud and left the subdued hall. He walked on leaden feet outside, to join the men who were about to arrest his son, and likely, put him away for a long time.

The Swamp

Esmeralda heard gurgling sounds coming from Beau, but she could no longer see him. She stumbled and fell backward, crashing into a table and cracking her head on the granite top. The blow caused her vision to waiver as black spots blossomed in front of her eyes, and her blood pressure plummeted.

A gigantic shadow fell on her, pressing her to the floor. Her body and soul revolted, and the flesh of her cheek scorched as a fiery tongue licked her. "You are tasty. Perhaps you have been worth the wait." His voice echoed, hollow and evil. "I'm going to punish you for hurting my *maman*."

Fighting nausea and panic, Esmeralda pushed with all her strength, but with no form or substance, her hands went through him. However, she got a sense of her assailant, wicked beyond human imagination, insane, driven by an insatiable desire to hurt, kill, and devour. Esmeralda sensed his victims and the unspeakable violence and terror of their last moments. They were children.

He smothered her, and it felt as if he covered her in black filth. With her body pressed to the floor, she sensed the perverse pleasure he derived from her terror and pain. "You are pretty," he growled.

"Help," she cried weakly. "Yeshua." She felt the dark shadow loosen and depart.

With a convulsive roll, Beau broke free, shouting, "*Bébé, attendez,* hold on!" He kept rolling with his arms tight to his chest until he reached her. He covered her body with his own, shielding her.

A dark spirit flew through the floor and invaded her mind. "You're insane!" It taunted. "Crazy… crazy… crazy!" Esmeralda's eyes rolled back in her head, and she felt her brain shatter under the assault.

Beau grabbed her face, nose to nose. "No! Come back to me."

His words triggered another bomb in her brain, she convulsed.

Beau had his face buried in her shoulder with his arms covering her head. He gasped, "Please, please, please…"

It was Esmeralda's own voice who whispered in his ear, "We have to fight, or we'll die."

"I'm not going to let you die." He squeezed with all his strength. *"Je promets."* I promise.

Chaotic screaming erupted, cutting off their words, and deafening them with vile curses and taunts—blasphemy. Tables turned over, glass shattered, and objects flew out of cabinets and around the room, pummeling Beau.

"Pray with me," Esmeralda cried as Beau grunted in pain.

Her words enraged the evil spirits, who escalated their attack with vengeful fury. And under their frenzied assault, the Black consumed Esmeralda and Beau.

The Longest Ride

"He's not dangerous. He's tormented," Sarah said, navigating the winding road like a race car driver.

Thaddeus braced his feet against the floorboard as she took a blind turn at eighty miles an hour. "He's delusional!"

Sarah's mouth hardened. "Is he? Or has he just seen things he can't explain or forget?"

Thaddeus crossed his arms, Esmeralda's words echoing in his mind. *"I see them now."* He refused to look at her but ground out, "What does he see?"

"He encountered something during the last battle of the Civil War. Ian ben Kole saw it too, though he won't speak of it. Beau can't remember, but I've heard his dreams. He sees it then." Tires squealed, and the car drifted across the double yellow line as she took another hairpin turn. "And about eight years ago, he and his fiancée, Alaina ben Thomas, were abducted."

Thaddeus glanced at her, keeping his face impassive.

Sarah sniffed and the corner of her lip quivered for an instant. "I never got the complete story. Alaina was too traumatized to speak of it, and Beau?" Her voice cracked. "He didn't talk for five months."

"I'm sorry." Thaddeus managed to say, but his mind reeled over the news that Esmeralda was in the hands of a madman.

"He was never the same after that. When he came out of it, I was so happy to have him back, I didn't push. He has no conscious memory of either event, but his subconscious won't let him forget." Sarah swiped at a tear as she turned onto a dirt road.

The headlights illuminated the thick Louisiana woods, moss hanging in fingers from low branches. Canals ran alongside each side of the road as they drove deep into the swamp.

"What do you think caused the break tonight?" Thaddeus' heart thundered as Sarah navigated more slowly.

"I think it was the knife. All Alaina would tell me was that Beau saved her, saved them both. What he yelled at you; I've heard him call that out in his nightmares. He thought he was saving her, Thaddeus. He didn't kidnap her. I was closer than you were. I saw her face, and she was seeing whatever he was seeing." Sarah Landry shot him a look that dared him to contradict her. "Esmeralda ran *with* him. He did not force her into that boat. He did not hold the knife on her. She left with him willingly... and you know it."

Thaddeus pressed a palm to the side of his head, reviewing the tape in his mind. He settled on one undeniable fact, Esmeralda saw things that no one else did. "Sarah, we need to pray."

"That's just now occurring to you?" She took another sharp turn and the dirt road smoothed to cement. "I haven't stopped."

When You Have Done All

"It's over! You are finished, Beau Landry," Charlotte cried in the spirit. "No more, I've won this time."

The spirits in the room gave a collective whoop, assured of their victory now.

Beau still covered Esmeralda, they lay in a pile, barely breathing. He rose above her, blood running out of his nose and eyes. "Your hair, it's so beautiful. Those white streaks are... like Ian's."

"Ian," Esmeralda murmured.

She saw his face, and heard his voice, "Pray, Esmeralda, fight it."

The young woman underneath him no longer looked like Alaina, but he heard his beloved clearly in his mind: "I love you, Beau. Fight this. Don't give up! Come back to me!"

"Son, you take the girl." Charlotte and Emite bore down on them. "The Landry is mine."

Esmeralda's mouth filled with blood. Her eyes swelled to tiny slits, and the breath pressed from her lungs by the dead weight of Beau Landry. With a surge of power that came from outside herself, she shouted, "No weapon formed against me shall prosper, for I am more than a conqueror through Christ Jesus who strengthens me!"

Charlotte screeched, Emite roared, and a collective cry issued from the swarm.

Beau rolled off Esmeralda and with a rush of words declared, "In Yeshua's name, I rebuke you."

Two of the dark shadows disappeared.

Esmeralda sat up. "By the blood of the Lamb and the testimony of the saints, we are not afraid to die, but woe to you servants of the devil, the Lake of Fire is your destiny."

Three astral spirits screamed in agony and evaporated.

Beau clawed at the overturned table, pushing to his hands and knees, blood running off his beard onto the floor. The man who charged enemy lines a dozen times against overwhelming odds determined he would not die groveling on the floor. "And when you have done all, at last, to stand." He struggled to his feet. "Girding your loins with the belt of truth."

Esmeralda felt a band of light appear around her waist, saw an identical one on Beau, glowing white. He pulled her upright, supporting her as they stood side-by-side. The belt of truth washed away the lies, delusions, and the insanity the evil spirits implanted in their brains. The room filled with a sweet smell, banishing the sulfurous nightmare.

A blasphemous curse echoed off the walls, and another astral spirit fled.

Esmeralda raised her chin and shouted, "Covered with the breastplate of righteousness!" Jeweled breastplates covered their chests, their hearts stopped thundering, and their lungs stopped gasping for air.

Beau grabbed Esmeralda's hand. "We walk on feet shone with the Gospel of Peace."

Esmeralda looked down in wonder and had the absurd thought of ruby slippers.

"No!" Charlotte screamed and backed away. Another spirit wavered then disappeared in a puff of smoke.

In unison, Beau and Esmeralda stepped forward and cried, "With the shield of faith!" Two shimmering shields, gilded with gold, emblazoned with the Cross appeared in their hands.

This enraged Emite who charged, but the power of the shield repelled him, as if he had run into a wall. Screaming in pain, he cursed and retreated to the far end of the room.

Beau gave Esmeralda a crooked grin. "You've got to let me do this next one."

Esmeralda held up her shield and actually laughed.

"With the helmet of Yeshua, our salvation."

A malevolent spirit threw a curse at their heads in a desperate attempt to prevent the last piece of armor. The spell ricocheted off their magnificent golden helmets, returning to the evil spirit who cast it, exploding him into a million pieces.

"That was unwise, wasn't it, *chèr?*" Beau winked. "We'll do the last one together."

Covered in brilliant, holy armor, Beau and Esmeralda called together, "Wielding the sword of the Spirit, which is the Word of God."

Blinding light and fire swept through the room, and with the sound of a rushing wind black shadows disappeared into a vortex that plowed through Beau's living room like a white tornado. The astrals fled, but outside Beau Landry's house on La Petit Pishon, they encountered Gabriel and Michael who were no longer standing down.

Esmeralda held her arm straight out, her eyes locked on a jeweled sword of pure light.

Beau turned to Esmeralda with his mouth slack.

They held each other's eyes as the armor faded away.

"*Mon Dieu,* that was one powerful delusion, *chèr.*" And with that, he collapsed to the floor in a dead faint.

Lights on, Nobody Home

A loud pounding jolted Esmeralda out of her stupefied stare at Beau's limp battered body. She backed away in renewed terror until she heard Thaddeus calling her name. She stumbled to the door, fumbling with the unfamiliar locks.

He swept her into his arms, picked her up, and ran away from the house.

"Wait!" she cried. "He's hurt. We can't leave him!"

"Get in!" Thaddeus ordered and pulled the car door open. "Stay there."

He charged back inside, intending to beat Beau Landry to death. Black fury engulfed him at the sight of Esmeralda covered in blood. Enraged, he stormed into a house that looked like a bomb exploded, broken glass, overturned furniture, and blood splatter everywhere. Sarah was on her knees, cooing softly, stroking Beau's unconscious face. He wanted to fling the woman aside and kill the man, but something did not ring true, something caught his attention, and he stopped.

Cataloging Beau's condition, he expected to see bloody knuckles. They were unmarred, save for a cut on the back of his hand. Blood covered his face, but it was not swollen and there were no lacerations. Blood trails ran out of his eyes, nose, and mouth, but there was no bruising.

Esmeralda flew back into the room. "Is he okay?" she cried, but turned away, unable to bear the sight of Beau laying on the floor, beaten, and bloody.

She felt Thaddeus wrap his powerful arms around her, holding her close. "It's all right now," he soothed. "He will not hurt you anymore."

"It wasn't Beau who hurt me!"

Thaddeus narrowed his eyes, studying her in the light. She had similar injuries, inconsistent with an assault, but her left cheek looked burned.

Sarah looked up at Esmeralda, shattered. "Are you okay?"

Esmeralda nodded convulsively. Delayed reaction set in, and she trembled violently. "He saved me."

Alaina's words from long ago slammed into Sarah's heart. 'He saved me, he saved us both.' She buried her face in the crook of her elbow and laid her palm on Beau's chest and let out a plaintive cry. "Oh, baby."

"He saved you?" Thaddeus asked with skepticism.

Sarah dropped her arm and looked up at Esmeralda, pleading, "What happened?"

Esmeralda shook her head, wild-eyed with fear. "I don't know."

Sarah covered her face, refusing to believe this was happening again. She clapped her palms together twice, rocking. Then gathering her strength, she begged, "Please tell me. I won't be able to help him if you don't tell me."

Esmeralda looked up at Thaddeus. Tears mixed with blood ran in rivulets down her fiery red cheek. "I can't explain it. It was terrible, like Pepperwood or Bezetha, but much, much worse." A wave of dizziness hit her, and she slurred, "Oh, I don't feel well." Then she, too, fainted.

Thaddeus caught her and carried her to the sofa, shouting her name. "Wake up, wake up!"

Her eyes fluttered. "I hit my head."

He grabbed an overturned waste basket as she gagged, then held her hair back while she vomited.

"I'm okay. Just let me rest."

"You need to stay awake if you hit your head."

"I can't," she said with a small sob.

He wiped blood from her forehead, startled at how cold and clammy her skin felt. Murmuring softly, he urged her to open her eyes.

"What is Pepperwood and Bezetha?" Sarah asked, gripping Thaddeus' arm. "She said she encountered something like what happened here in those places. What did she see? Tell me!"

Thaddeus looked down at her hand, then met her pleading eyes and growled, "Evil, beyond this world."

White Coats

Esmeralda stirred when they lifted her onto the stretcher. When she realized what was happening, she panicked, fighting like a maniac. Thaddeus swooped in, elbowing the ambulance workers out of the way. "It's okay, we need to get you to a hospital. You're hurt."

Esmeralda kicked her feet and struggled in blind terror. "Let me go! Let me go!"

"It's all right. You're safe. I won't let anyone hurt you." Thaddeus pressed her down, trying to hold her still.

"You can't stop them! They will take me!" She thrashed, still fighting, and cried, "White coats!"

From across the room, a hoarse voice broke through her terror. *"Chèr!"*

Esmeralda whipped her head around and saw Beau Landry strapped to a similar gurney. "Beau!" She met his dull eyes, full of the inevitable, resigned.

"Don't cry. It's over now," he said, and they wheeled him away.

"Where are they taking him?" Esmeralda begged Thaddeus.

"He's going to get the help he needs."

Esmeralda contorted with pain. "No, he's not crazy. Thaddeus, don't let them take him away, please?"

Thaddeus shook his head. "I'm sorry, Esmeralda. It's out of my control."

"Then you can't stop them from taking me," she shrieked. "Oh, God. I don't want to go back. They did terrible things to me in there. I wasn't crazy, either. He's not crazy!"

"Shh," Thaddeus brought his mouth to her ear, "be quiet. They are taking you to a regular hospital, but if you keep carrying on those doctors might get other ideas."

Her chest convulsed in a suppressed sob. She knew the thin line she walked and stopped struggling. Still and quiet, she whispered, "Okay. I can do this. Don't leave me. Don't let them take me."

Thaddeus nodded, willing her to stay calm. "You've had a hell of an ordeal. I'll be right by your side. I promise." He rose and lifted her limp hand to his lips.

"Mrs. Landry?" Esmeralda called, summoning more courage than she knew she possessed.

Sarah Landry extricated herself from her husband's embrace, wearing every day of her sixty-six years on her pale face. "Yes?"

Esmeralda brushed a white curl out of her eyes and said, "He was brave and strong, heroic. I would have died tonight if he hadn't saved me. He's not crazy. He's bedeviled. Stand in the gap, you and your family, fight for him. Don't give up. Don't believe the lies."

Part 6 - Roots

September 21, 998 ME

First Day on the Job - New Orleans

"Are you sure you are up for this?" Thaddeus asked for the third time that morning. "Eighteen days ago, you knocked on my door in New York. After everything you've been through, no one will begrudge you an extra day to rest."

Esmeralda shrugged. "I'm feeling better. Besides, I rested Sunday in the hospital and all day yesterday in our hotel room. You have work to do down here, and so do I." She moistened her lips and added, "I think it will be good for me to get out of my head and stop worrying about Beau. If I stay at the hotel, that's all I'll do." She unfastened her seatbelt and turned to him. "Besides, they were expecting me yesterday. It doesn't look good to take a new job and call in sick."

Thaddeus' mouth hung open, baffled at her rationale. "First of all, Ian and Joanna are not going to say shit about you being out sick, considering they're the ones who sent you down here to begin with. Second, half the damn staff in there are those freaking Landrys and the other half are beholden to them. Anybody says a word about you being out yesterday, I will kill them. They are lucky I didn't kill Beau Landry Saturday night."

Esmeralda gave him a sidelong glare. "I will not keep arguing with you about this. He did not hurt me."

"Fine. I still don't want you around him. I'll have your word that you won't call a cab or convince one of them to take you over to the hospital."

Esmeralda scoffed, "They don't allow visitors for a new intake for the first seventy-two hours, then only family the first week. I couldn't see him, even if I went."

Thaddeus threw up a hand in frustration. "Forgive me, apparently I lack your extensive knowledge of visiting protocols in mental institutions."

Esmeralda drew in a quick breath as the zinger found its mark.

"Damn, I shouldn't have said that." He cursed his inner smartass.

Esmeralda slapped her thighs, peeved. "But you did."

Thaddeus tried to catch her eye; she refused to look at him. "This hasn't been easy for me either, Esmeralda."

"No, I suppose it hasn't," she said dully. "Not the reunion I envisioned."

"Esmie, I'm sorry." Thaddeus took her hand.

She gave it a faint squeeze. "It's not your fault, and you're right, there has been a lot to deal with."

"You're a hell of a fighter, and I don't say that lightly. I'm just worried you are pushing yourself too hard."

"I'll be fine, and there is no pressure today because I'm only getting a feel for the place. They'll probably plant me in the library. I won't overdo it."

Thaddeus exhaled in profound resignation. "All right. Call me if you need me."

"I will," she said, gathering her things. "In your meeting today, tell your agents they are looking for a very large man. He's insane, and he lives with his mother. That's who is taking the kids. That's your killer." She turned and gave him a penetrating stare. "He's the one who hurt me, Thaddeus. It wasn't Beau." She pushed open the door and began her career at the Center for Street Kids of Alanthia.

Evidence

Thaddeus watched the gentle sway of Esmeralda's hips as she strolled up the sidewalk, wondering how in the hell he might put that bit of information forward without ending up as Beau Landry's roommate in the looney bin? He was still having a hard time wrapping his head around the events of Saturday night.

On the surface, it looked like an easy case. However, just beneath huge anomalies presented themselves with no logical explanations. No one could explain what caused the destruction or Beau and Esmeralda's injuries. The forensics team found no hair or blood other than Esmeralda and Beau's. Neither had skin cells or blood under their nails that wasn't their own. Beau had no abrasions or wounds on his hands, and other than the lump on the back of Esmeralda's head, their injuries were inconsistent with a physical assault. There were no fingerprints on the broken objects, not even Beau's. Thaddeus saw photos from the undisturbed part of the house. The man was a neat freak and trashing his own house did not fit the profile.

Esmeralda poured out the story, for his ears only on Sunday evening. The truth left Thaddeus, a man of science, logic, and reason in a particularly uncomfortable situation, personally and professionally. For the second time in less than a month, Agent Paul ben Casper was called to an unusual scene involving the two of them. Thaddeus breathed a sigh of relief that Dr. Whitaker had not filed a police report in

New York. If she had, he would be under intense pressure to explain what exactly was going on with his bride-to-be.

No one would believe the truth, and the physical evidence did not add up.

He and Esmeralda argued Sunday night when he insisted she press charges. She remained adamant, flatly refusing. In the end, Thaddeus convinced her that if she wanted to stay out of a mental hospital, she had to go along with the only plausible story Thaddeus could concoct.

So, she told Paul she recognized the warning signs of a pending psychotic break in Beau Landry and willfully participated in his escape, to keep him from harming himself or anyone else. When they arrived at his house, they found it vandalized. The vandals must have still been in the house because she sustained a blow to the back of her head and was knocked unconscious. She awoke when Thaddeus and Sarah arrived to find Beau also unconscious and knew nothing other than that.

When pressed about how she knew the signs of a psychotic break, she shrugged and said it would have been apparent to anyone. Throughout, she maintained her story, defending Beau, and insisting he should be released from custody. She withstood Paul's intense questioning for over an hour before Thaddeus intervened and called an end to the interview.

In the hall, outside Esmeralda's hospital room, Paul asked for a private word with Thaddeus. "This is off-the-record, Director."

Thaddeus nodded, scanning the corridor to ensure they were alone. "Go ahead, Paul."

"Nothing adds up about this, her story, the physical evidence, motive. All of it stinks to high heaven. Beau Landry has a history of mental illness, but to date there have been no violent episodes. The only evidence we have that he is bat-shit crazy is the compulsive neatness of his house, but that is not enough to deem him a danger to society. Dust bunnies yes, society, no.

"As far as a random break in, that happened to coincide with him pulling a knife, threatening to kill you, and abducting Esmeralda? That does not add up either. Who would drive all the way out there to trash a house and not take anything? There was no theft, millions in property left untouched. The art alone is worth a king's ransom, and I'm pretty sure that's the original Serendipity hanging in his office. He has pictures of Alaina ben Thomas everywhere."

"She was his fiancée," Thaddeus grumbled.

"Lucky dog!"

Lucky was not an adjective Thaddeus would use to describe Beau Landry, but he kept his mouth shut.

"You were tight-lipped the night I came to stitch Esmeralda up, and less than two weeks later she is back in the hospital. I don't believe in coincidences. What's really going on, Director?"

Thaddeus knew there was no such thing as an off-the-record conversation in an ongoing investigation. "Exactly what she told you. I will add, and this is for your edification only, Esmeralda is insightful. She sees things in others that most people can't. She did it with you the night you met her, did she not?" Paul nodded, his face coloring at the memory. "I suspect she used that talent on Beau Landry. She saw something and acted in a selfless manner to help him. That's the gist of it."

Paul met Thaddeus' eyes, searching for deception, looking for holes and ways he could turn the conversation, but saw nothing. With profound frustration, he shook his head. "You let me know when she's ready to tell the truth. I'll listen. In the meantime, I'll write up her statement in my official report. You have a nice evening, Director."

Thaddeus shook Paul's hand. "I'll see you at the office on Tuesday, we've got more important things on our plate than some rich man's psychological problems and a simple case of vandalism gone bad."

Out of the Mouths of Babes

As they had done in the New City, the staff at the New Orleans Center organized their residents by houses, each with six children. Where possible, the kids stayed together with the hope they would form lifelong bonds. They took on the name of the house, if they chose, and referred to each other as brother and sister. Each family had two full time guardians, a male and a female referred to as 'Maman' or 'Papa'. Only the children lived at the Center, which was by design and policy. Joanna believed it prevented burn-out and curbed the potential for abuse. The New Orleans Center, open for two years, was modeled after the success Joanna and Ian had at the original Center.

Ian was technically the Director of the New Orleans facility, but an exotic looking black woman of indeterminate age and imposing bulk ran the day-to-day operations. Malandra ben Pierson, festooned in a flowing, jewel-colored caftan and turban, ushered Esmeralda around. Her big, gold hoop earrings wobbled back and forth as she spoke, and her matching gold sandals clapped against the soles of her feet when she walked. The polar opposite of Joanna ben Luke, Esmeralda liked her immediately.

The staff greeted her warmly. Esmeralda recognized the Landrys on sight. Flashing eyes, the devil's own charm, and a wry sense of humor that sprinkled the right amount of sarcasm without becoming wearisome. Malandra's speech and cadence differed from the blue-eyed Landry's and differed further from two of the family managers.

"You are from New York?" Esmeralda asked, directing her question to the middle-aged man who attended the Debone Family.

He made a clicking sound with his cheek and laughed. "Born and raised in New Orleans, ma'am."

Esmeralda narrowed her eyebrows and studied him in confusion. "I live in New York, I know what they sound like, and you sound like them." She looked at Malandra for confirmation.

"New Orleans is a melting pot, child." Malandra smiled with good natured humor. "There are about a dozen accents here, all from the same city. Large parts of the South migrated in the last decade, at least them that didn't leave for the Golden Kingdom. Many of the faithful from the New City region came down to Louisiana, too. More than likely because we still got rain, everywhere else is drying up like a worm on a sidewalk."

Esmeralda nodded. "We saw that on our ride over. It is a shame what is happening."

"That it is," Malandra commented gravely. "We a divided city, half faithful, half not. The voodoo is rising, but those who still hold the faith, who still worship and pledge their honor to the Iron King, they just as strong. He has mercy on us for reasons I cannot fathom, but He does."

"Voodoo?" Esmeralda shivered as she said the word, a cold chill running up her spine.

Malandra pushed open the library door and made a sound of disgust deep in her ample chest. "It was buried in the bones of this place. When they pulled New Orleans outta the bayou a hundred years ago, they uncovered more than the Quarter. They resurrected the voodoo."

Esmeralda's eyes widened. "What is it?"

Malandra drew back in surprise. "You never heard of voodoo? Child, where are you from that you never heard of it?"

Esmeralda blushed. "I'm from a small community in Pennsylvania called Rephidim."

"Where Moses got the water?" Malandra raised a dark brow.

Esmeralda beamed. "Yes ma'am, that is why the community was christened as such. There is a lovely river that runs by it," she said with a wistful note to her voice.

"Well, no wonder you don't know nothing about the voodoo. I expect they don't have such in Pennsylvania, but you aren't here to have me fill you up with scary stories about haunts." Malandra gestured around the library with her pudgy hand. "Here it is."

Esmeralda smiled. Cast adrift in a sea of strangeness, this felt familiar. Though small, the library was well stocked with good light, comfortable furnishings, and several tables and chairs for homework.

In a sunny corner, a small sandy-haired boy curled in an overstuffed chair, his face buried in a book. "Lars," Malandra drawled, "you feeling better, to be down here reading?"

The young boy blinked, coming out of the imaginary world of his book. "Yes, ma'am, but I threw up in the night and Papa Fontenot said it was better for me to rest today than be spreading whatever bug I caught to the rest of the school."

Malandra acquiesced to the wisdom of the house master. "Fair enough. This here is Miss Esmeralda. She's come for a visit and is going to be working in the new Center when they get it up and running."

Lars said nothing, regarding her with eyes too wise for a child his age. Esmeralda smiled and moved to greet the small boy. He tucked his hands under his armpits, telegraphing his reluctance to be touched. "It is nice to meet you, Lars. I'll try not to disturb your reading while I work."

"What kind of work is there to do in the library?" he asked suspiciously.

Spoken like someone who never considered what went into assembling, organizing, and maintaining a library. "Oh, there is always plenty to do among the books."

Lars clearly resented the intrusion, and Esmeralda suspected that time alone in a place like the Center was a rare and precious commodity. He returned his attention to his book and ignored her.

Malandra made another grand sweeping gesture. "I will leave you to it, Miss Esmeralda." Then added in a solicitous tone that told Esmeralda she knew all about Saturday night, "If you need anything or get tired, you come find me."

Esmeralda looked away, embarrassed. "Thank you, I am certain I will be fine." With that, she pulled her notebook from her bag and got to work. For a half hour, she lost herself in the shelves, reviewing, making notes, and sorting the books with unconscious efficiency.

When he spoke, Lars' question startled her. "What happened to your hair? Did you do that on purpose?"

Esmeralda smoothed her tight French braid, checking for escapees. "The curls or the color?"

Lars rested the book on his chest. "Both."

Esmeralda gave him an ironic smile and pointed to her head. "No one would do this on purpose."

"I didn't think so, but I was curious." He returned to his book, ending the conversation.

Esmeralda figured she better get used to that particular question. Children lacked the filter adults had, and after Saturday night, she was the proud owner of two more white streaks. She complained to Thaddeus that her braid looked like a zebra's pelt, if a zebra also resembled a sheep. The mental image of a zebra with a sheep's coat made her smile.

Twenty minutes later, Lars interrupted her again. "Pennsylvania doesn't have voodoo?"

This time, Esmeralda put down her shelving and sat in the companion chair beside Lars. "I am not exactly certain what voodoo is, so it is hard to say whether we have it. Perhaps we call it something different where I am from?"

Lars rubbed his smooth chin. The gesture, odd on a hairless boy, lent him a gravity incongruent with his age. He had that awkward large-toothed look of about seven or eight. His accent was a strange patois of mixed New Orleans accents. "I never considered that. Voodoo is dark magic. Though to hear them tell it, it's all goodness and light, but we kids from the street know different."

Another cold chill ran down Esmeralda's spine, remembering the victims she sensed when the evil spirit touched her. "I suppose you would."

Lars ran his tongue over his teeth, calculating. The child pulsed bright yellow, not just his hair but the blazing regard by which he studied her, taking her measure, suspicious. "It's a matter of survival around here. You want to stay alive, you stay away from the voodoo. I reckon you learned that lesson Saturday night, didn't you?"

It did not surprise her to realize the kids from the Center knew what happened. They listened by instinct and self-preservation. It was imperative they know the way things stood in a world that would swallow them whole without a second thought. Esmeralda probed the depths of his old eyes and said, "Perhaps it was, but it didn't win."

"Over you maybe, but Mr. Beau Landry's in the hospital." Lars seemed to take that as a personal affront. "He and Mr. Ian, they found me and brought me here."

Esmeralda folded her hands, recalling Ian's stories about pulling kids out of desperate situations. "Mr. Ian is a good friend of mine. I've known him for a long time."

Lars picked up his book but watched her over the top of it. "The voodoo doesn't like it when Mr. Ian's here, but I do. If you are opening a new Center, make sure you have him around. I expect the voodoo likes children from everywhere, not just New Orleans."

Lunch Date

"Esmeralda," a clipped voice called from the doorway, "would you honor me with your company for luncheon?"

Esmeralda rose from her cross-legged position on the floor, books and papers surrounding her, and met the expectant face of Sarah Landry. She dressed casually, but the cut of her clothes, the drape of the fabric and impeccable style bore the undeniable stamp of wealth. Her posture and expression conveyed the invitation was a formality.

Esmeralda glanced at the organized chaos in mute appeal.

"It will be here when you return, I assure you. Come, it is

the least I can do." Behind the intimidating manner, wealth, and poise, stood a mother. The lines of fatigue under her eyes had not been there Saturday night.

"Yes, ma'am." Esmeralda stepped over the books and followed Sarah outside.

Instead of a car, they strolled. Without visible effort, pedestrians parted in her wake. Esmeralda had never met anyone like Sarah Landry. She had a deep purple aura that blended royal blue and scarlet. She moved with regal grace among her subjects, street songs and horns seemed to herald her coming. As they walked, Sarah spoke a word, nodded a greeting, and had a ready donation for the musicians on every corner. Sarah winked at the band leader and gave a jaunty little shake of her shoulders to the beat of their lively tune. They gave her a respectful nod. One of them bowed and continued to play.

At a sidewalk cafe', three formally attired attendees awaited their arrival. Esmeralda felt conspicuous being the object of such fawning attention, but she took her cues from Sarah Landry, who accepted the service as her due.

When the waitstaff departed with their orders, Sarah asked without preamble, "You are recovered?"

Esmeralda stared at her folded hands in her lap and answered, "By and large, yes ma'am."

"I am pleased to hear it. I suppose I owe you a debt of gratitude. Our lawyers informed me you refused to press charges. They would have kittens if they knew we were having lunch, but they work for me not the other way around." Sarah's smile reached her eyes. "I am too old to be bullied by my own barristers."

Esmeralda pressed two fingers to her lips, stifling a small giggle. The woman was a force, but strangely not scary. Esmeralda supposed if she was pressing charges, that might not be the case, neither would her welcome at the Center been as warm, if they let her in at all. The Lenox Foundation was the primary donor for both Centers, though Joanna divulged that the funding for the New York Center came from an anonymous source, coincidentally via the law offices of Esmeralda's new attorney, Worley, Blake, and Standish. "I will have to keep that in mind when dealing with my own lawyers," Esmeralda remarked dryly.

The corner of Sarah's mouth quirked in a smile. "I recommend it as a strategy. They become entirely too overbearing otherwise."

Esmeralda had to agree. Thaddeus certainly had the propensity. A breeze ruffled their tablecloth, and with a quick hand Esmeralda kept her napkin from blowing away. The waiters brought salads and refilled their water glasses. Hungry for the first time in days, Esmeralda tore a piece from the fresh baguette and offered it to Sarah, who declined. Esmeralda wanted to weep with pleasure. She and Lavinia's attempt at bread paled by comparison. Fortified with a bit of food, Esmeralda ventured, "Have you seen Beau?"

Sarah met Esmeralda's question directly, gauging her reaction. "I have. He slept most of Sunday but seemed a semblance of himself yesterday."

"I did as well," Esmeralda confided.

"He claims he does not remember what occurred, but I don't believe him, not this time." Sarah dabbed at the corner of her mouth. "He lacks the bewildered look that usually accompanies a memory loss. I suspect he simply does not wish to discuss it, which is why I am here."

The fortuitous arrival of the waiter saved Esmeralda from an immediate reply. While the waiter cleared their salad plates, she closed her eyes and pled for wisdom, certain mere words could not communicate the events, afraid of sounding like a lunatic. "It is difficult to explain, ma'am."

"Humor me." Sarah's tone brooked no disobedience.

Esmeralda looked away and caught sight of a huge man rushing toward them, his expression thunderous, eyes colorless, and his body vibrating fury. Esmeralda held up her hand, praying a fervent rebuke in her spirit. The man stumbled and turned away. Esmeralda watched him go, experiencing a surge of power.

Sarah narrowed her eyes, intent.

From the opposite end of the street, a woman shouted, then raised her hands above her head. Gyrating and swirling to the music, she muttered curses and glared at Sarah and Esmeralda. Esmeralda snapped around toward the spectacle, sensed malevolent energy directed toward them, and lost her temper. She reached the limits of how many times people were going to accost her. This had gone far enough. She closed her eyes, and the Holy Spirit fell upon her. Without an audible word and barely a movement, she rebuked the witch. When Esmeralda opened her eyes, the witch was gone.

But Sarah Landry's expression made Esmeralda want to confess everything, just to make her stop staring at her that way. She hid her discomfort by taking a sip of water.

"I suppose that *is* difficult to explain," Sarah said, raising a perfectly shaped eyebrow. "But I shall endeavor to listen."

Esmeralda smoothed a ragged cuticle, not meeting her eyes. "I'm not sure I understand what you mean, ma'am."

Sarah folded her arms and inhaled deeply. Esmeralda looked up, squirming under the scrutiny. At length, Sarah exhaled, conveying that her patience with evasions had run out.

"I think I owe Joanna ben Luke an apology." Esmeralda took another sip of water. "I thought she was the most intimidating woman on the planet, clearly she could take lessons from you."

Sarah smiled with genuine appreciation, a compliment of the highest order. "I learned from the best, my father. I've also had more practice and six children. One of which, you can help me with." She paused as the waiter brought their lunch, gumbo for Esmeralda, broiled fish and steamed broccoli for Sarah.

"Shall I be frank?" Sarah asked, not waiting for a reply. "Beau is my father's sole male heir. As you might imagine,

Beau's... difficulties over the years have been a concern. The estate will pass to Beau upon my father's death, if and only if, he makes a full recovery." Her face remained composed, as she spoke in earnest. "But it is not the money that concerns me, for no matter what happens he will be provided for. It is that Beau will be robbed of what truly belongs to him, his legacy, and he will fail to fulfill his place in the world. You cannot know what a tragedy that would be."

Sarah held Esmeralda's eyes. "Thousands of people rely directly and indirectly on the Lenox company. Their livelihoods depend on the wise and prudent management of the company's interests. From an early age, it became apparent that Beau was talented enough to take the helm. Others would not be. He is brilliant."

Her mouth tightened. "Please do not limit your consideration of this to drachmas and shekels, for it is not merely a question of finances. Lenox has been a force for good, should it cease to be, the ripple effects would be far reaching." Sarah unfolded her napkin and placed it primly in her lap, allowing her words to sink in. "This is not simply a meddling mother trying to help her son, Esmeralda. There is more at stake here."

Esmeralda blew the hot gumbo and took a bite, letting the heat chase away the dread brought on by the charging man and the witch. As she considered Sarah Landry's words, she realized they were true.

Thus, over spicy gumbo and another baguette, Esmeralda relayed the truth of what occurred Saturday night. To Sarah's credit she remained silent during the telling, did not ask intrusive or disbelieving questions, she merely let the story unfold. When Esmeralda described the swarm and how it enveloped Beau, Sarah grew visibly shaken.

As the tale concluded, Esmeralda's voice rang with certainty, "Mrs. Landry, they were familiar with him, the things they said, the taunts? They did not know me. At the very end, one of them cracked me open, but they held no such reticence when they attacked Beau. They know him. And they bedevil him."

Sarah's eyes flashed. "Which is what you meant when you told me to stand in the gap."

"Only if he is protected against their attacks will his mind heal. Seconds after the Lord gave us the victory, he cataloged and labeled the experience a delusion. It will take time and prayer for that damage to heal. Once that occurs, then only the truth will set him free."

Purple light came into intense focus, calm, determined power that reminded Esmeralda of the night she delivered her baby cousin. Nothing was going to stop Sarah Landry. "Thank you, Esmeralda. May I count on you to stand with me and my family, for Beau?"

"Of course, and when you find the witch and her son, let me know."

The woman who created an empire, the daughter of a man who built a dynasty smiled slowly and said, "With pleasure."

Plan B

The Maban high holiday began at dusk, and for the first time since Korah ascended the throne, Angelica ben Omri would not be officiating the opening ceremonies in her sanctum beneath the Palace. The injustice of it gnawed at her entrails. Korah was a dead man as far as Angelica was concerned. He and the Dark Master would rue the day they dismissed her.

And while they held sovereignty tonight, their reign was temporary. As the thousand years drew to a close, a power greater than Marduk was about to break free, and the Mistress, Ba'alat Ob, Angelica ben Omri planned to be ready. So tonight, she embarked on a daring first step, that would catapult her to victory and crush those who dared cross her. There were new alliances to forge, arrangements to be made.

She drove herself to the outskirts of the New City. She had never driven before but reasoned if her moron chauffeur could do it, then so could she. Twilight fell as she eased up to an imposing estate, hidden behind a glittering black dome. The iron gate barred entrance, but with a flick of her wand it swung open, and she drove onto the grounds.

Very little shocked her, nothing actually, but a wary alertness raised the hair on her arms as she eased down the cobblestone drive. The walls around the property were the first thing that struck her. They stood twenty feet tall, constructed with stones the size of boulders, irregularly hewn, balanced with precision, and lacking any visible mortar. The second thing she noted were the elaborate gardens, their hedgerows twice the height of a man. They meandered in mazes, encompassing the vast estate. She knew who, or more aptly what, created these massive structures.

The Dark Master kept this place and its occupant secret, but when she saw that woman at Pepperwood, something clicked in her memory. She remembered Secretary Tristan's little wife… and a long-ago offhand comment that they had a son. She still did not quite understand how she had forgotten, but she had.

Angelica always believed there were only two, but there were three; and Angelica was eager to make his acquaintance, to forge an alliance.

She was most familiar with Zuzite, Antiochus' nephew. Blood thirsty and raw, his appetites made him predictable, yet still exceedingly dangerous. Orion ben Drachmas, the captain of the guard at Antiochus' palace, lost four men in the last decade, all victims of Zuzite's insatiable hunger. His mind, when he chose to apply it, was deliciously wicked, though she was still furious at him over his latest prophecy. Unfortunately, his mother had been a vapid, vain, little wench. She was flighty and impulsive, and the human side of Zuzite took after Philomela. As such he was an extreme disappointment, to Antiochus as well as Angelica.

Marduk's other son, Emite, was certifiably insane. Twisted and voracious, he had the appetites of his half-brother. But Angelica admitted to a begrudging admiration of her rival Charlotte Durant. The traitorous bitch molded Emite and wielded his power with undeniable, ruthless skill. Trained in the ancient art of voodoo since the moment he was born, Emite became an accomplished sorcerer and a talented mind manipulator. His curses were creative, brilliant, and lethal. But Emite's biggest weaknesses were his rebellious forays into the city to procure 'his treats', and his complete dependence on his domineering mother. He was incapable of functioning without her. Angelica planned to step into the power vacuum when she eliminated Charlotte.

But even Korah did not know about this one. Angelica planned to use him to eliminate every one of her enemies. With a nephilim on her side, nothing could stop her. Approaching the House of Amah, she expected to encounter a creature similar to his half-brothers.

She could not have been more wrong, and Angelica ben Omri would regret the day she blithely strolled into Rapha ben Marduk's den.

September 26, 998 ME

Nine and Six

Nine and six, the respective number of years since Thaddeus and Esmeralda left Rephidim. They rode through the Thyatira Woods on a Sunday afternoon, weary and dusty, both eager for the succor and safety of Rephidim. Bezetha was the logical choice to exchange their car for mounts, but neither suggested it.

Leery of Esmeralda's enemies they traveled incognito, using false names. She concealed her distinctive hair under a large-brimmed hat and donned her Rephidim attire. His height made Thaddeus more difficult to disguise, which precluded him from undercover work, though he was a good mimic and channeled Mack ben Robert, adopting an 'aw shucks' manner. His southern drawl was so different from his distinctive New York accent, that she had to turn away every time he spoke, so she would not burst out laughing.

With each fall of the horse's hooves, Esmeralda shed pieces of the outside world. She expected on their return journey she could pick back up the worry and trouble, it would all be waiting. But as they got closer, she vowed not to carry anything unnecessary or unpleasant with her. She was going home, finally.

Thaddeus wondered what sort of welcome he would receive, specifically from Claude and Julianna. He resigned himself to sleeping in his old room at Eve's and forgoing the pleasures of Esmeralda's bed, which caused him to question the wisdom of waiting until November to wed her.

In their hearts, they were already man and wife. The legal part of his brain screamed that he should have taken her down to the courthouse the moment she said yes. As her husband, he would have legal standing in the event they tried to take her again. But Thaddeus, the suitor, overruled the lawyer. He was cognizant of the fact that Esmeralda was a young woman. Her enemies robbed her of years of her life, and she deserved something special to mark her return to the land of the living. He knew it was important. All girls dreamed of their wedding day, and he would not deprive her of that. Though his libido, so recently out of retirement, rebelled.

"Esmie," he slowed his horse and waited for her to come alongside, "if anything untoward happens, or you get the least inkling that you are in danger, come get me, and we'll go. I don't care if it's 3:00 am, you say the word, and we're out of here. I know we both hope that Rephidim is still safe, but there are no guarantees."

A month ago, she would have argued with him, but for the last ten minutes she contemplated the same thing. "I've never seen it, and it's possible that it was never there, but I'll let you know if I see a hedge of protection. If I do, then we can rest a bit easier. If I don't, it doesn't mean anything, but I'll be on my guard." She rolled her eyes and added, "Though nothing could be as bad as New Orleans, that was unbelievable. Voodoo."

Thaddeus growled. She was right. The week they were there, they could not stroll down the sidewalk without people coming after her, making every outing akin to running a spiritual gauntlet. To her credit, she stopped cowering and began taking it in stride. No one laid a finger on her, physically or spiritually. She fought, and they fell. However, there was a cost. She was exhausted, and a third of her hair was now stark white.

Approaching Rephidim, excitement coursed through her veins. She wanted to kick the horse and gallop into town.

Thaddeus sensed her impatience and murmured, "It has been a long time since I was in these woods. I never thought I'd come back, then again, I never thought you'd leave." He reached out a hand, and she angled her mare closer to take it. "Is your father going to run me off with a shotgun?"

Esmeralda smiled and answered, only half teasing. "I think it's Mother you have to worry about."

He nodded. "Good to know."

"You know how she can be. She was determined to fix me up." She turned with a smile and batted her eyelashes at him. "But I never had eyes for anyone other than you."

Thaddeus brought her fingers to his lips. "Nor I, Vixen."

His words, still new, brought a flutter to her heart. Riding among the familiar trees, she remembered all the taunts she endured. "I can't wait to ride into town with you by my side, so I can rub it in Rosemary ben Cooper's fat face." Esmeralda whipped the huge hat from her head and began unbraiding her hair. "Let her say something about my hair, I will tell her that at least I am not marrying a man who sounds like a pig when he eats."

Thaddeus gave her a mock look of horror. "She married Simon?"

Esmeralda burst out laughing. "That particular aversion came from you, thank you very much. I never noticed anyone smacking until I started hanging around you."

"I may have pointed it out, but you have to admit, it is disgusting."

Esmeralda smacked her lips. Thaddeus' glare delighted her, and she said, "You are noise sensitive. You always have been."

"I am not." Thaddeus drew himself up with offended dignity.

"Oh, please." She snorted through her sinuses, breathing heavy to prove her point.

Thaddeus gave her a veiled look and kicked his horse faster, leaving a whistling Esmeralda in his wake.

Esmeralda reined her horse up at the edge of the familiar path, her eyes bright with happy tears.

"So it is here?" Thaddeus squinted to no avail.

She nodded.

The Rephidim hedge of protection followed a path she traversed a hundred times. She was eight the first time she prayer walked this route with Jelena. Afterward, she continued, hoping the Gune would visit again. Golden light lingered over a rock she used to step around. It descended a familiar dip in the forest floor and traveled over the fallen tree she always jumped. She realized in a blinding moment that Jelena showed her the hedge, and each time she prayer walked the path, it reinforced and strengthened the protective dome around Rephidim. Her breath caught, overwhelmed by the moment. She never truly understood why, she simply did it in obedience. But she had actually done something here, the Lord used her—to do something, and she saw the tangible proof. "It's here, Thaddeus."

"Hallelujah. Between the hedge and not having you as a temptation in my bed, I might actually get some sleep on this vacation," Thaddeus said with droll humor.

Esmeralda stared at the gold dust and diamond veil in awestruck wonder. "I don't think I've truly rested since I left."

Knowing what he did, he suspected that might be true. He also knew that however safe Rephidim was, it was only a brief respite. They could not stay forever, their work was in New York. But for now, they could relax. "Let's get you home."

She hesitated and said, "My home is wherever you are, Thaddeus. Rephidim ceased being my home the day you left."

Thaddeus dismounted, reached up, and pulled her in for a passionate kiss. He loved this improbable, impractical, impish girl. She had haunted his dreams, starred in his fantasies, but they paled in the warm reality of her.

They walked hand-in-hand, across the threshold and through the hedge of protection. Thaddeus wiped his eyes, it was fleeting, but the world focused, bursting in vivid color. He breathed in the sweet scent of the woods and cemented the moment in his mind. If he could hold on to this vision, he could use it as a charm to quell the part of his brain that still railed against what it could not see, taste, or touch. "Do you always see like this?" He gestured at the vivid green.

Esmeralda thought for a moment, then said, "I used to. I did not know any difference for a long time. But it's changed. I see more, and I see less, if that makes any sense."

"A bit, but perhaps you could elaborate?" Thaddeus asked conversationally, relaxed and content.

"It is hard to say because I don't know what you see. Perhaps I have just become inured to the vibrancy, so it's normal. But I think the Lord allows it to come into focus when I need it, so I become aware if it heightens." Esmeralda looked up and said, "I can't see the dome anymore, which doesn't mean it is gone, it simply means my focus should be elsewhere."

Thaddeus understood. "So that you might have your life and live it in abundance, while being mindful of your calling." He grinned as the temporary euphoria faded. "We serve an awesome God."

Esmeralda's eyes shone with pleasure. "My steps are ordered, my path is protected, and my purpose, to serve the King."

Thaddeus raised a brow at her. "That is the oath of the Iron King's Army."

"Is it?" Esmeralda shrugged. "He taught it to me when I was ten."

Thaddeus cleared his throat. "When I was ten, I could hang a spoon off the end of my nose."

Esmeralda giggled. "I don't know how to do that."

"Well, I will show you." He winked at her.

She lowered her chin and smiled. "You've shown me a lot of things."

"Oh, and there is so much more," he murmured, breathing a kiss to the back of her hand.

"I think that is going to have to wait. Matthew ben Henry is coming to greet us."

Thaddeus looked up, scanning the woods. It was a full minute before his friend Matthew, who had gone on pilgrimage with him, appeared out of the trees.

By the time they reached Claude and Julianna's, an impromptu celebration started. One of Rephidim's daughters had come home, along with one of their favorite adopted sons. News poured in from all sides, births, deaths, and of course, current team rankings. Thaddeus shook off several good-natured attempts to spirit him directly to the courts. They wanted to show him all the improvements they made in the intervening years. Basketball fever was alive and well in Rephidim.

"Ah! *Ist* a good day," Ernst ben Otto declared, coming up from his stable, arms open wide. "Thaddeus ben Todd, it is good for *mein* own heart to see you again."

The two men embraced. "Ernst, it is good to see you, my friend!" Thaddeus was surprised by the catch in his voice. He had been so intent to get Esmeralda home and speak to her parents that he failed to consider what his own return would mean. Wise Ernst ben Otto helped to heal a broken man by being there and abiding in silence while they fished. Ernst played a role in his life that he did not appreciate until that moment. Hot tears stung his eyes, and he said, "We will be here a week. You will take me fishing?"

"Of course, we will fish. Your ugly face scares them off as always, but you are decent company." Ernst's bright eyes flashed with a sudden moisture of their own. "And Esmeralda," he elbowed Thaddeus and grinned, "time finally let you catch her, yah?"

Thaddeus raised his eyebrows at the wily old man. They never discussed Esmeralda, or his reason for leaving, yet he was not surprised he discerned the truth. "My friend, yes it did."

Ernst smiled with approval. "You will make her a good husband which is fortunate because she would have no other." He stopped at the walkway to Claude and Julianna's. "I will leave you to speak to them. It is Julianna you need to convince."

Thaddeus cast a sidelong glance at his friend. "So I have been told."

Ernst slapped him on the back. *"Viel Glück."* Good luck.

The excited crowd left them but promised to return soon. They were dying to have Thaddeus back on the basketball court. Ernst took charge of their mounts, freeing Esmeralda and Thaddeus to enjoy their reunion.

"Why am I suddenly nervous?" Esmeralda stared at the house, familiar and unfamiliar. The door was red instead of blue, and she was not certain how she felt about that. The shrubbery had been dug up and replaced with a neat row of mums and asters which bloomed in bright autumn colors of red, umber, yellow, and orange. They were hot colors, where her house had always been cool.

Thaddeus draped an arm around her shoulders and said, "I used to feel the same when I would go see my parents. You were a child in that house, and now you are wondering how it will be to walk inside as an adult."

The front door opened, and her mother burst out. Julianna's apple cheeks flamed, as she threw her arms wide. "Esmie, what a wonderful surprise!" Claude's shout of welcome followed his wife's, and Esmeralda was swept up in their arms.

Thaddeus watched, hanging back, and realized he wasn't the only one enjoying the reunion. Friends and neighbors wiped their eyes and smiled, many hoping one day their own prodigals would return.

Claude broke away and noticed him standing there. There was a wry, knowing look in his eyes as he remarked, "Thaddeus ben Todd, have you finally come to speak to me about my little girl?"

Julianna looked him up and down, frowning. "Thaddeus."

Thaddeus stepped forward, extending his hand. "Claude, it's good to see you." When Claude took his hand, shaking it vigorously, Thaddeus realized that Claude, like Ernst, played a pivotal role in his life by taking him to the mill. The had been friendly while he lived here, not friends per se, Esmeralda's crush prevented that, but they were cordial and got along, even if the Spinners always kicked the Weaver's asses on the basketball court.

"It is good to see you, too." Claude nodded and they both turned to Julianna, who regarded Thaddeus with her arms crossed.

"Julianna, you are as lovely as ever. I have always known where Esmeralda came by her beauty."

"Flatterer." A slight smile played at the corner of Julianna's lips. "Come in, we were just sitting down to dinner. I expect you are hungry."

"That would be fitting. You fed me my first day here. I don't think I ever told you how much that meant to me." Thaddeus took Julianna by the elbow, walking with her inside. "For I was hungry, and you gave me something to eat. I was thirsty and you gave me something to drink. I was a stranger, and you invited me in."

Julianna's breath caught at his recitation of her favorite Scripture. For his ears only, she said, "My daughter cried a million tears over you. I felt every one of them."

"I never meant for it to be that way," he murmured, "and if I could have changed it, I would have. I promise, I will not cause her more."

Julianna looked up at him through her sparse lashes. "I doubt that, Thaddeus, for you are a man of the world, and the world is full of tears." She bore a mother's dread, knowing the pain her daughter would encounter away from her protection. For years she clung to the hope that Esmeralda would return, marry a Rephidim boy, and settle down here. However, standing in the foyer, that dream died. "She would have no other but you. Guard her heart, Thaddeus ben Todd, for it is a precious gift you have all too often disregarded."

"Until now, I was not at liberty to accept that gift." Thaddeus met her eyes. "I give you my word. I will guard not only her heart, but her mind, and her body, to my last breath."

Julianna gripped his elbow and brought him into her kitchen. "I plan to hold you to that promise."

Thaddeus' Family

Eve waited, sitting on her front porch. She rose when Thaddeus came around the corner, clapping her hands with glee. When he was halfway up the path, she ran to meet him, showering him with hugs, kisses, and exclamations of welcome. He scooped her up in a bear hug, and she shrieked with girlish delight.

"Too long since your feet have crossed my threshold. Come in, come in! Everyone is here. Hans, Olaf, Barton, and Krish, we are all here." Eve laid a hand on his chest, her eyes shimmering. "Thaddeus."

"Eve," he said, his voice cracking. He covered her hand with his own, pressing it to his heart. He felt closer to her than his own family.

His relationship with his mother and father had been damaged beyond repair. They all loved Richard, and his younger brother proved to be the glue that bonded them, and without him everything fell apart. Thaddeus barely knew his workaholic father, who travelled most of the time, and rarely uttered a word when he was home. Disinterested and cold, Thaddeus could not recall a single meaningful father-son exchange. His mother was one of those odd people who had the emotional capacity to love a single person, and her person had been Richard. They were never close, and Thaddeus knew if she had to lose a son, she wished it was him.

At Olivia, Jacob, and Matthew's funeral, she made a callus, offhand remark. "At least now you know how I feel."

Her words cut him at a moment when he could not withstand another blow, and her thoughtless comment cemented the wall between them. He had not seen or heard from either parent since leaving the cemetery that fateful February day.

Eve ushered him inside where his housemates waited to greet him with handshakes and good-natured ribbing about the prodigal's return. He fielded questions about what he had been doing, what his life was like, and whether he planned to play while he was here. But most of all, they were curious about him and Esmeralda.

Eve beamed. "We heard the news straight away, but I wanted to give you the opportunity to sit with Claude and Julianna. Did you win her over?"

"Who, Esmeralda or Julianna?" Thaddeus teased.

"Both!" Eve put her hands on her slender hips in mock exasperation.

Thaddeus' brown eyes sparkled, and he winked at her. "We're planning a wedding."

Eve clapped in delight. "That is splendid! When?"

He could see her calculating and suspected more than basketball fever was about to sweep Rephidim. She confirmed his suspicions when she did not wait for an answer and started listing everything that needed to be done. "We'll have Heidi bake the cake, of course. Jake will provide the spirits, and the reverend will perform the ceremony. Who do you think would be better for the food? Some say the Rhineland House, but I swear since Hubert retired it just isn't as good." She pulled him into the kitchen, blabbering about wedding plans, discussing the merits of particular catering establishments, musing about which flowers would be in season. Did he want music? How many groomsmen? What ring did he buy her? At the sick and startled expression on his face, she stopped. "Well, surely you have thought of all this. You've been married before."

Thaddeus shifted, uncomfortable, loath to mention he and Olivia married in a courthouse a week after her pregnancy test came back positive. They were both still in college. The night his basketball team won the Eastern Championship, Thaddeus ended up in bed with the head cheerleader. He never told a soul, but she lost their first baby three weeks later. But he had loved Olivia, bright and funny, smart as a whip. Despite how they began, they built a good marriage, but never had a wedding, and as Eve chatted, Thaddeus realized these were two entirely different things.

September 27, 998 ME

Mid-Morning Sugar

Ernst ben Otto liked mid-morning, his favorite time of day. Most of Rephidim was at work, the children, whose loud voices bothered him and the horses, were in school, and no one interrupted him while he piddled in the stables. Several years ago, he hired a boy who came after school to muck out the stalls and do the heavy work. Ernst never admitted to himself, or the boy, that he no longer had the strength to lift the hundred-pound bags of feed or the stamina to stack endless bales of bedding. By tacit agreement, neither mentioned it. He considered retirement but wasn't sure he could occupy all his time fishing, besides he enjoyed the horses, so he still worked, except Sunday, when he fished.

Thus, when Esmeralda called on him at 10:00 am, he was a bit perturbed at the intrusion. If she hadn't recently returned home, he would have shooed her off like when she was a kid and came poking around, yammering a thousand questions an hour. He'd never seen a person, man, woman, or child who asked as many questions as Esmeralda.

"Guten morgen," Ernst sighed with resignation as she walked through the stable door.

"Good morning, Ernst," Esmeralda said, barely meeting his eyes and moving to the stall that housed her rented mare. Offering it a sugar cube, she scratched it behind the ear. The horse gave her arm an affectionate bump, sniffing her for more treats. Esmeralda wiped her hand on her tunic and whispered to the horse.

Ernst waited, rubbing oil into a pair of saddlebags.

Esmeralda walked the stable, offering each horse a sugar cube and a little scratch. At the last stall, she seemed to deflate, rested her cheek on her hand, and gazed in baleful contemplation at the ancient gelding, Whiplash.

Still, he waited. Ernst had known Esmeralda since she was a baby and even back then she was a talker. It surprised no one when she and Eve became good friends. Those two women could talk the ears off a jack rabbit. So he almost fell over, when Esmeralda gave him a sad smile and left the barn with a mere, "Thanks, have a good day."

Something was wrong. Ernst did not like it when people did not act like they were supposed to. Esmeralda talked. She asked questions. She bothered him. Esmeralda did not come in his barn and leave with nary a word!

"Hey!" he called after her. She turned with a mild

expression on her face, not impish, not inquisitive, not that odd knowing look she sometimes wore. "Have I ever told you about Whiplash's sire? He was a stallion of old, one like you have never seen."

Esmeralda raised an eyebrow at him in speculation. "No, I don't believe you have."

Ernst grunted, playing the role they established in a hundred of these conversations. "Well, maybe I will sometime."

Distracted, Esmeralda nodded. "Okay, Ernst. That would be nice. I'll see you later."

Ernst scowled at her retreating form. Something other than her hair had changed, and he did not like it, not one bit.

Nephilim's Garden

"Honestly, you have proven to be a great disappointment," Rapha said, leaning back in his great chair in the center of his palatial gardens.

Angelica ben Omri's hands shook from age, terror, and six days of hell. She regretted the impetuousness that drove her headlong into the clutches of the giant. "I am sorry you feel that way. I still think we might form a mutually beneficial alliance."

He scoffed, and with a flick of his hand dismissed her feeble attempt to placate him. A zap of electricity convulsed her body, and she fell to her knees. "You are human, old hag. What could you possibly offer me?" He rose and loomed over her prostrate form. "You are too ugly to fuck, too old to feast upon, and your powers are puny. I fail to comprehend exactly what advantage you think you might bring to me."

It was the last night of Maban, and she knew why he brought her to this place. Being well acquainted with the final ritual, she knew within the hour she would be dead, so she made a final plea, "There are things I know, secrets I can share, and alliances I hold. I command an army of witches and warlocks. They follow me. I offer it all to you."

"I have done well enough, alone." Rapha spread his great arms gesturing to the sumptuous estate. "Why now, should I seek an alliance," he raised her chin and came within inches of her face, his head the size of an ox, his breath fetid, "with a human?"

"There is one who is coming that is not human. He will rule again. I can help prepare you to be at his side, to please him, and to take your place as the ruler of this world! You will be a mighty man of renown!" Angelica's pale eyes bore into his demon burnt orange ones.

An invisible blow slammed against her head, and she cried out in pain. He invaded her mind, searching. "The book! I have the sacred text, passed down from generation to generation. That is where I learned it all, where my power came from. I freed your father!"

He kept probing, going deeper.

He saw the ritual she spoke of, smelled the torches, felt the beat of the drums, and heard the music. Blood poured from the altar over her hands, he tasted the delicious warmth, felt it roll over his tongue. He watched her pass the chalice to a blond man who drank deeply. Rumbling shook the underground cavern, a shaking of walls and ceiling. He felt that shower of rock and dirt, heard the roar of triumph as his father manifested in a billow of black smoke. Rapha smiled at the sight of him, beloved, wicked, but absent!

He released Angelica, and she rolled to her side, gasping and clutching her head. Rapha lifted her off the ground with the power of his mind, animating her like a puppet. "Perhaps there is some worth in you, after all."

He settled back in his throne, contemplating. "This book…"

Released from suspended animation, Angelica's legs buckled, but she managed to stay upright. Starved, mind raped repeatedly, and tortured, she knew collapsing now would seal her fate. "I will bring it to you. I will teach you, and together, we will await the one who is coming."

Rapha studied her, saw the beautiful woman she had once been, felt the old knowledge hidden in her mind, and coveted the book she spoke of. "Bring it to me. Go!" He dismissed her with a flick of his hand.

The unseen gut shot sucked the breath from her lungs, and she bowed before him. Exerting more will than she ever had in her life, she stayed on her feet. Fighting the black spots that danced in her vision, she quelled the nausea and looming unconsciousness. Pressing a hand over her diaphragm, she willed it to function. It unlocked, and with a glorious inhale she straightened, facing him.

"May it be as you have commanded," she croaked. On legs quivering in sciatic agony, she moved into the maze and escaped the labyrinth with her life, barely.

Unholy Competition

The final night of Maban, the followers of the New Way, marked the last night with a competition to see who would assume the highest position in the kingdom. Mademoiselle Charlotte Durant of Loa Hall, clothed in scarlet, stood beside her rival, Princess Keyseelough of Egypt. Those already vanquished took their places among the rank and file, looking on with envy and anticipation, wondering who would emerge victorious tonight.

Korah ben Adam, dressed in black silk, sat on his throne in the underground cavern with the spirit of the Dark Master hovering behind him. With human eyes, on this plane, they could not see him, but their spirits felt his pulsating power. Korah and Marduk spoke with one voice, grinding and hollow, it echoed off the chamber walls and filled the space. "Before this holy assembly stands the final two who vie for the great honor of becoming High Priestess." Thunderous applause and shouting erupted from the coven. "Our worthy contestants have proven themselves skilled in the ancient arts of divination, pharmakeia, charms, spells, and curses." Another shout rose from the crowd. "Tonight, they face their

most difficult ordeal yet, to descend into darkness and receive
a word of wisdom from our faithful brethren trapped in torment, and thus earn their right to become Ba'alat Ob!"

Beside Charlotte, Keyseelough shuddered.

"Many have tried, most never return." A hush fell over
the cavern. Descending into Hell was a fearsome endeavor.

"Come forth and receive your instruction," Marduk
commanded through Korah.

Charlotte stood, haughty and proud, she knew the final
test would command every wile and skill she acquired in her
decades of practice. To do so alone, without Emite, would
prove to the world, and herself, that she was indeed worthy. When her name was called, she ascended the steps with
confidence.

Korah met her pale eyes, his showing reptilian pupils
and unholy intelligence. "Mademoiselle Charlotte," he said
in French, perfectly accented and smooth, "you have proven
yourself a sorceress of the highest caliber. I chose well that
night long ago. Of the three maids, you alone wield the
power I bestowed upon you."

Charlotte curtsied, humbling herself before her dark
lover.

"Yet there remains a power that eludes you, one your pre-
decessor held for decades. If you wish to assume her throne,"
Korah gestured to the dainty throne beside his, "you must
seek the source and bind it to yourself, take it from her."

Charlotte squared her shoulders, ready.

"Step forth to receive your spirit guide, who you will find
in the netherworld. You must return with an answer if you
wish to ascend." Scarlet robes hid her face as she leaned forward to hear the whispered command. "You are to seek the
highest of your order, to glean the source of her wisdom, so
that you might take it for yourself. To prove you have accomplished this task, return with the name of Ahab's first-born
son, known only to his mother, the one who sacrificed him,
proving herself worthy and acceptable to me by burning her
child on my altar, Queen Jezebel."

September 28, 998 ME

In the Light of Day

Esmeralda sought solace in the woods, walking her path, praying. She had not slept the night before, horrible visions swamped her from the moment she retired until dawn. She was thankful to be alone when they came upon her. She could not imagine trying to explain them to Thaddeus.

It began in the past, in Endor. Esmeralda had full recall of her visit to that cursed place. She watched from above, wanting to call out to her younger self to turn back. The foolish trip set her on the path to destruction, but no matter how desperately she urged, at one point forcibly taking the reins and turning the mare back, teenage Esmeralda pressed onward. In the spirit, she saw the witch, but even more horrifying than her human enemy, she came face to face, once again, with the fallen angel. Angelica ben Omri and Marduk, this morning Esmeralda knew the names of her enemies.

From the past, her vision moved to the present. She witnessed the unholy dramas taking place at the House of Amah and in the dungeon below the Palace. She was hidden from the evil wreaking havoc amongst their ranks, shielded and protected from their perception. Like a fly on the wall, she observed, undetected.

The final destination of her dark tour returned her to Endor, yet this time she was alone among the ruins. She walked in the spirit, between burned-out houses and leaning structures, until she came to a mansion, hidden until now. It stood stately and old, a black glittering dome protected it from human eyes, the converse of the golden hedge of protection. Esmeralda trembled in fear and knew she was called to enter that cursed place.

She heard His voice, distinct and calming: "Upon this rock, I will build my church and the gates of hell shall not prevail against it. And I will give unto thee the keys of the kingdom and of heaven. And whatsoever thou shalt bind on earth shall be bound in heaven; and whatsoever thou shalt loose on earth shall be loosed in heaven."

Esmeralda set her jaw and went forth, guided toward a library, the irony of her destination not lost upon her. A great, ancient book rested on a podium. Black power pulsed from it, fluttering the pages as if it were alive. She entered the library on trembling knees, sensing drugs and death, curses and spells. To her enhanced vision, the pages dripped the blood of secret, dark magic. Shuddering, she did not approach it, for it was an abomination in the eyes of the Lord. This book wrought utter destruction on those who sought to wield its power. Its presence caused the downfall of Endor. It gave birth to great evil and destroyed the innocent and the guilty with callous indifference. The souls it damned echoed in the empty halls of the Black Mansion.

Esmeralda raised a quivering hand and prayed, "In the name of the Father, the Son, and the Holy Ghost, I bind this book here on earth and in heaven, that no one shall be able to remove it, touch it, or learn its dark wisdom ever after. Amen."

Esmeralda awoke, safe in her bed.

October 1, 998 ME

History Buff

The fifth morning Esmeralda left his barn after giving a sugar cube to each horse and not asking a single question, Ernst could stand it no more. "What is wrong with you?"

Esmeralda gave him a patronizing look. "I have no idea what you are talking about."

He grunted, "You never cared about the horses before. Why all of a sudden, huh?"

Esmeralda shuffled her feet, drawing a circle in the dirt with her toe. "I met an interesting one recently. I've been testing a theory, to see if it was the horse I met or all horses."

Ernst smiled inwardly, relieved to discover there was a purpose to her inquiries. "What was interesting about the horse you met?"

Esmeralda drew a line through the circle on the ground. "What do you know about the horses from Endor?" she asked, not looking up.

Ernst invisible eyebrows drew to a point over his wide flat nose, suddenly wary of her research project. "I know as much as any man living."

Esmeralda tilted her chin and seemed to carefully consider her next words. "There were plenty who knew, but they died."

"What are you interested in that old story for?" Ernst asked with growing suspicion, nothing profitable would come from digging up the remains of Endor.

Esmeralda rubbed her fingers together, sticky from the sugar cubes. "I went there."

"Donnerwetter!" Ernst exclaimed. "Why did you do that?"

Esmeralda had just enough German slang to understand he reprimanded her like a child. Undaunted, she said, "I was curious."

He pointed a gnarled finger. "There is the Esmeralda I know. That was a foolish thing to do. When did you go there?"

Esmeralda absently rubbed the scar on her cheek. "The day I left."

"Ich glaub mich knutscht ein elch!"

Esmeralda translated roughly in her head. "What's an elk kissing you got to do with anything?"

"You do not know your German, it is smooching, and it means I cannot believe you!" Ernst exclaimed. "Why, Esmeralda? Why would you go to that forsaken place?"

Esmeralda looked at him, world-weary and tired. "I was foolish, and it was a long time ago; but I need your help and I'd appreciate it if you would stop scolding me."

Ernst caught himself short and looked at her, truly looked at her for the first time since she returned home. He saw a serious woman, not the impish child who used to pester him. Faint bruising around her jaw, gone yellow, was not a shadow as he'd first thought. The scar on her cheek stood out against her heightened color, and he considered for a moment, perhaps she had not dyed her hair on purpose. Gruff and a bit contrite, he offered, "It is time for my tea. You will join me, yah?"

Esmeralda's eyes softened, and she pressed her lips into a sad smile, her voice breathy. "That would be nice."

"You know your history. I taught you," Ernst grumbled as he prepared the tea. "You know the three villages of Thyatira. What I never told you was that I was born in Endor."

Esmeralda accepted the tea with a nod of thanks. "No, you did not. I always wondered why your accent was different."

Ernst, the history buff, warmed to the topic. "The three villages were distinct in speech. I grew up speaking German, though we all spoke English for business purposes, and the Guardians spoke many languages. Our horses were renowned. People from across the globe sought Endor, but they had to find us, which was not an easy task, most never did.

"The Bezethians, still use the plain speech with thees and thous, though the young people now sound more like Rephidimites, like yourself, modern Alanthian English with a German accent."

While interesting, Esmeralda's focus was not on the distinct speech patterns in the region. "When did you leave?"

"Before the judgment," Ernst said over the clatter of his spoon against the side of his mug.

There were no dainty delicate tea sets in Ernst's home. The heavy mug warmed her hands, which had been cold for a week. She took a sip and said, "It was a judgment by fire, most of the place is burned to the ground."

Ernst looked away. "That was destruction waged by man. The Iron King's wrath was far more severe. Your generation has no concept of the righteousness of the one who rules with an Iron Scepter. If you even stop to consider Him, he is a tyrant or a benevolent grandfather. But He is holy, and He is perfect. He did not tolerate disobedience or devilish practices in my day. I cannot fathom why He does today, but I believe it is because He wearies of mankind and is allowing one last rebellion." Ernst made a loud slurping noise with his hot tea.

Esmeralda surmised he and Thaddeus must have never taken tea. "Why did He judge Endor?"

Ernst tilted his head, as his eyes bore into hers. "Because they embraced and followed a witch."

Esmeralda sucked in her breath. She knew, but having confirmation made it all the more terrifying.

He stared out the window. "It was a terrible thing to behold. Like Satan incarnate, she was wily and beautiful. She presented herself as a prophet, speaking for the Most High. She seduced the people, and they followed her into sexual immorality and dark occult practices, which had been buried for a millennium.

"Through honeyed words, she deceived the people of Endor who panted after her like dogs in heat. Once she had them, she solidified her grip on the entire village and set herself up as supreme authority. Anyone who spoke against her, suffered dire, devastating consequences."

Ernst sighed heavily. "I was not always a bachelor, Esmeralda. I had a wife and a daughter." His face contorted. "I stood against her, and within a week, they were dead from a fever. That was how she worked."

"I'm sorry." Esmeralda reached across the table. laying a hand on his gnarled knuckles.

"You may not remember, but there was no sickness then."

She nodded. "The first sickness I ever saw was in Bezetha. It was terrible."

"Her influence spread and infected Bezetha, also. Though she did not reside there, they took up her filthy practices. I believe they still do." Ernst shook his head in disgust.

Esmeralda flinched, remembering the wickedness of Bezetha. With vivid clarity, she recalled the vision of the dark ritual, the men in black who seized her, and the bloody doctor. She kept her own counsel, loath to relive the experience with Ernst. "And the horses? I think I saw one, or something," Esmeralda's voice trailed off.

"You may have, though it would have been a rare sighting. That was the tragedy of Endor's disobedience. When the Iron King rendered judgment, the horses and their owners died in huge numbers. The night of the final fire, many were already gone, but a few escaped into our woods. The men who sacked the town, though wicked in their own right, were intent on their own purposes. But the Most High used them to destroy what was left."

"What was so special about the Endor horses, Ernst?"

"According to legend, the first horses of Endor were ridden by the Saints at the battle of Megiddo."

"Armageddon?" Esmeralda's eyes grew large.

"Aye, the first. There will be another, Esmeralda. Scripture is very clear on that point, but we need the eyes to see. We are blind to what the Word tells us. We have stopped truly reading our Bibles. Any scripture that speaks of judgment is automatically deemed to have already occurred, but that is not truth."

Esmeralda's shoulders sagged. "The time is short." She set down her mug and rose. "Thank you, Ernst."

For the fifth time since she arrived home, Ernst watched Esmeralda depart and wondered where all her questions had gone.

Boulders

Esmeralda stood on the boulder, watching the waterfall, thinking about nothing and everything. Even wrapped in her mother's long coat she felt cold. The smell of vanilla and cinnamon clung to the fabric, so Esmeralda buried her face in the soft folds and hugged herself. She heard footsteps and let out a quiet whimper when Thaddeus wrapped his arms around her waist, pulling her against his body.

"Wedding plans getting you down? Did you have to run out here to escape?"

She hung her head and shook it, laughing softly. "No, it's not that."

"Well, they ran me out. I went over to find you and spent half an hour discussing petit fours. Honestly, before today, I was not entirely certain what they were, nor was I privy to the fact that their selection was so crucial. Your mother set me straight. Trust me, I am now a petit four expert. I was not in the least bit hungry, but that did not stop them. They corralled me into the kitchen, sat me down, and force fed me until I was about to burst. I swear they had about thirty kinds." He felt her shoulders quake.

"By the way, in case you are interested, we are serving spinach quiche, stuffed mushrooms, and some sort of pumpkin sorbet thing that I thought was vile, but the ladies declared was fresh, palate cleansing, and an absolute must." He grinned. "I put my foot down, though, and got the ham and cream cheese roll-ups on the menu. I liked them, even though they said they were 'basic', whatever the hell that means."

"A sorbet thing?" Esmeralda chuckled, adding that to their repertoire of wedding fever jokes.

"It was awful." Thaddeus's voice cracked as he started laughing. "And there was a lot of lip smacking going on. I had to get out of there."

They dissolved in giddy hysterics.

Through spurts of giggles, Esmeralda asked, "Do you want me to talk to them about the sorbet thing?"

Renewed laughter shook them.

"No, it's okay," he assured her. "I don't care."

She grabbed his lapels. "But Thaddeus, what if everybody smacks when they eat it?"

He threw back his head and laughed. "Then you and I will run out to this boulder and leave our guests to their smacking."

Esmeralda absently pushed a curl out of her eyes. "No smacking on Esmeralda and Thaddeus' boulder!"

"Unless it's this kind." He smacked her rump with a satisfying pop.

She made a high-pitched squeal of delight and wiggled against him. "Do you realize this is the first week of peace we've had since we got back together, and I'm sleeping in my childhood bed… alone."

"Maybe it's a sign, Vixen." Thaddeus raised a reluctant eyebrow. "It's easy to forget out in the world, the way things are supposed to be done. Coming back here has reminded me."

She met his resigned eyes. "You, too? That's half the reason I've been so morose." She pressed her hips against his. "I like what we do."

He pulled her closer. "So do I."

"November 10th seems like a very long time to wait."

Thaddeus wound his finger around the original white curl. "We waited a lot longer, and it's my fault that we didn't do things right. You deserve a proper wedding, but you also deserve a proper wedding night, Esmeralda. I can't take back what I've already done, but we should abstain until the wedding. I want to make it special for you."

She leaned her forehead against his chest, appreciating the sentiment. "My apartment… I don't think I would be safe living there alone."

"Who said anything about you going back to your apartment?"

Esmeralda looked up at him. "I thought you said you wanted to be apart until we got married."

"I didn't say that. I said I was going to stay out of your bed until we got married, there's a difference." Thaddeus' New York accent came through heavily. "Geez, I'm resigned to six weeks of perma-boner, but I haven't lost my mind. You've got dangerous enemies, sweetheart. I'm not letting you out of my sight."

The corners of Esmeralda's wide mouth danced. "Perma-boner?"

"It's a new word. I just made it up."

She snorted with laughter, which made her laugh harder at his horrified expression. "I'm sorry, I didn't mean to snort." Then she did it again, involuntarily and really lost it.

"I'm glad you can laugh about boners and snorting… I don't think they are funny at all," he teased.

She relaxed, safe in his arms.

On guard above them, Uriel smiled.

October 23, 998 ME

Petitions

"Miss ben Claude, do have a seat," Sir Preston ben Worley said, gesturing to a wingback chair positioned in front of his enormous desk. "Thaddeus, it is good to see you, my boy." He did not rise or offer his hand, but Esmeralda calculated that was due to his age, not his manners, as he appeared to be well into his nineties.

She felt a queer flutter in her stomach as she settled into the seat, as if Sir Preston was about to interrogate her, a foolish notion, but the entire business made her uneasy. Thaddeus gave her a reassuring shoulder squeeze and took the chair at her side.

She glanced around, not having visited his office before, communicating via phone with his various secretaries and assistants. The elegant space smelled of leather, paper, and the peculiar tang of antique wood, half furniture polish, half mildew. Stacks of legal briefings were scattered around the room, occupying the desk's corners and the entire credenza behind him. A stained china teacup rested on a delicate saucer, and a heavy old-fashioned pen created an odd shaped blotch on the desk pad near his blue-veined, mallet-sized hand.

She could not get a read on him, his aura veiled and shifting, which was sometimes the case with the elderly, as if the vigor of youth faded not only the body's physical abilities, but the energies pulsing out of their spirits.

"Yes," Sir Preston mumbled, giving a cursory review of the open legal folder. "I must say, from the very beginning, this case was highly unusual. When Thaddeus first contacted our office, it became apparent that a major miscarriage of justice had occurred. Your case has considerable merit." He leaned back in his palatial black leather chair, its gold tacks bronzed with age. "It also happened to dovetail with another we are handling, the details of which are confidential, but I can convey that Dr. Allison ben Whitaker is well known to my office," he said, studying Esmeralda from beneath his outrageous gray eyebrows.

Esmeralda balled her fist at the mention of her former doctor's name. That she once trusted the woman made her treachery a betrayal of the highest order. Guilty of twisting Esmeralda's reasoning, planting triggers, and subjecting her to mind control and manipulation, Dr. Allison and her ilk stole five years of her life. She loathed them all.

Sir Preston took the measure of the unusual looking young lady who snared Thaddeus ben Todd. The society matrons went into a tizzy when they learned of his engagement. Though not the rising star he once was, he remained one of New York's most eligible bachelors. The matrons reasoned he simply lacked the proper wife to relaunch his political career and bring him back into society. They scratched his name off their lists, but they were not pleased about it.

Esmeralda met his gaze, but held her silence, waiting for him to continue. He recalled another young woman who sat across from him wearing just such an expression, though he doubted Esmeralda was contemplating how many ways she could kill him.

"As you know, we have filed a number of petitions, the first, a restraining order against Dr. Allison ben Whitaker, her associates, and anyone from the Pennsylvania Department of Health and Human services." He looked down, referring to his notes and continued, "The second, was a civil complaint against the aforementioned parties for medical malpractice and malfeasance. The third, against the Commonwealth of Pennsylvania, for negligence, mental anguish, false imprisonment, and gross violations of your civil rights. In that petition, we focus primarily on denial of due process and legal counsel. In conjunction, we petitioned the court to have your record expunged. Finally, we are presenting evidence to the Eastern Alanthian District Attorney's office and hope they will pursue criminal charges."

"What have the outcomes been?" Esmeralda asked, rocked by the recitation of the crimes committed against her.

Sir Preston rifled through the stack of papers, murmuring under his breath. He found the document he was looking for and said, "As I am sure Thaddeus explained, we got the restraining order approved, which prohibits any party in the named action from contacting you physically, via mail, or other electronic means. They may not appoint a proxy or engage a third party on their behalf, which means that anyone from their legal teams is barred from reaching out to you. All correspondence will run through this office."

Esmeralda turned with a pained smile toward Thaddeus, while outwardly stoic, he pulsed silver light from his comfortable leather chair.

He folded his hands and said, "I read the complaints, the deadline for their responses was two days ago."

Sir Preston's old eyes glimmered with anticipation. "They are fighting us on all counts. We are in for a battle."

October 31, 998 ME

Samhain

Angelica ben Omri collapsed onto the sofa, surrounded by her treasured possessions, in utter defeat. The Book of Power seemed to taunt her from its holy place on the lectern. For three weeks, she battled the force that kept her at bay, but nothing she did broke the spell. She blamed it on her six days of torture at the hands of the Nephilim. It had done her no good. Currently out of favor with the Dark Master, she could not call on him for assistance, though she suspected even he might not be able to prevail upon the magic that barred her from the book.

She heard Charlotte triumphed on the final night of Maban and had taken the mantle of High Priestess. Angelica scoffed at the notion of Charlotte taking her place. She was the Witch of Endor and knew more of the dark arts than any human living, yet she was cast out, hiding in her own library.

Rapha grew increasingly impatient, but like his brothers, he was still bound to his territory. She shuddered to think what would happen when he was not. She stalled, placating him with excuses and promises.

Reasoning her power would be at its zenith on Samhain, she prepared every ritual known, hoping she would finally prevail upon the impenetrable shield. The time was upon her, and still, she could not even approach it. Who had cast such a powerful spell? The book was hidden from all, in a library protected by dozens of enchantments and spells. The house itself was obscured from natural eyes, so who did this? Her mind ran through the possibilities, but there was not a witch alive who wielded that kind of power, certainly not Charlotte, and Keyseelough would not dare. If Charlotte discovered the book, she would have taken it, not kept Angelica from it, not in this manner. Angelica stormed out of the house, burning with frustration.

By the light of the moon, she walked the ruins of Endor, remembering it as it was, not how it lay now. Teeming with activity, her subjects bowed as she strolled by. Young and beautiful, at the height of her power, she commanded respect and reverence, operating openly, unafraid and unashamed of who and what she was. It had been glorious. She loathed the turn of her mind, remembering days when she controlled kings and the lives of millions. Now, she was reduced to this, a lone witch haunting her forsaken village, doomed if she could not fulfill her vow, her glorious future nothing but a ditch digger's dream, out of reach, impossible.

She stopped in front of one of the abandoned stables, as an elusive thought flited across her mind. She paused, concentrating on the fleeting image, feeling the answer lay on the plot of land where her feet tread. She closed her eyes and became very still, "What? What occurred here that I need to remember?"

It hit her like lightning. "The girl! This was where I confronted that girl from Rephidim." Outside her protected village, she had proven so easy to defeat that Angelica went years without recalling her. Yet last month the little bitch broke bonds.

The timing added up.

It started with that disastrous encounter outside Pepperwood with the Dark Master. They argued bitterly over its undertaking and even more viciously when it ended in defeat. It was *his* obsession with that little horse woman that drove them there. *He* insisted they attack. She would have never picked a fight while the enemy was firmly entrenched, yet they followed *his* orders. They were repelled, scattering in defeat, and nearly wiped out by those filthy white angels. Afterward, the Dark Master brazenly lay the shame of their defeat squarely on her shoulders. It was their last argument.

Seething with anger toward Marduk and Korah, blinded by her own fury over their betrayal, and focused on new alliances and a path forward, she failed to make the proper connections. It was the girl, the so-called White Woman, who thwarted her.

Dozens of rivals, who wished her downfall, spewed prophecies that never came true. With forty years of history behind her, Angelica summarily rejected them as mere words and destroyed those who dared speak against her. Yet, Zuzite was no bumbling idiot or jealous rival, nor did he have a discernable ulterior motive for prophesying Angelica ben Omri, the Witch of Endor, would fall by the hand of the White Woman.

Spinning on her heel, Angelica determined this would be the latest in a long line of false prophecies, because she planned to annihilate her enemy.

November 1, 998 ME

Released

Esmeralda stumbled into Thaddeus' bedroom, weeping. "His treasure... He was protecting his treasure," she cried softly.

Thaddeus sat up, glancing at the clock on the nightstand which read 1:12 am. "Esmie, what's wrong? What happened?"

She stood by his bedside; her hands pressed over her face, muffling her words. "David and the giant... he's dead."

"What?" Thaddeus croaked, confused and still half asleep. "That was thousands of years ago, Esmeralda. Why are you crying?"

"No, you don't understand," she sobbed, her voice going to a high squeak. "I just saw it. I was there."

"Come here." Thaddeus reached out and pulled her forward. "Get in bed." Esmeralda rested on his chest, and he felt her shaking. "It's all right. It was just a dream."

"No, a vision," she clarified. "It killed him. He was protecting his daughter. The giant was coming to kill her."

He held her as she wept, not understanding but offering comfort and support.

At length, she succumbed to exhaustion and whispered, "I was in a tent and heard the Lord call a man named David. And it wasn't thousands of years ago, they looked like modern pilgrims. I saw his wife and daughter sleeping."

She rested her head on his chest and poured out the drama she witnessed in the Greek desert.

At length, she said, "The man's death was horrible, but I saw his spirit rise. He went with the angels to New Jerusalem. It was beautiful."

She covered one eye, very weary. "Thaddeus, the giant? It was not the same being, but it had a presence around it, an evil signature if you will, like what attacked me in Louisiana." She cleared her throat. "I saw its spirit rise, too." Her breath came in sharp pants, "It was vile and ugly, and it screamed the most horrible things. It was intent on the girl, even after it was dead, it wanted her. But the angels thwarted him, sending him away." Profound distress marred her features as she murmured into his chest, "Thaddeus, the giant is now a demon, and it's loose."

November 9, 998 ME

For One This, For Another That

Ian spurred his horse beside Esmeralda as they rode toward Rephidim. "I spoke to Joanna last night, and I think we are all in agreement. The Murray Hill location is ideal for the new Center, though if we can't come to terms on the lease the Chelsea property is a good second choice."

Esmeralda beamed. She'd spent the last month scouting potential sites and was pleased they agreed with her assessment. Thaddeus and Mack rode ahead, leaving them to discuss Center business in private.

"She wanted to come herself. But she will fly out and look at the property before we sign the papers. She hates delegating," Ian said with a wink.

"How is she doing?" Esmeralda asked solicitously.

Ian shook his head. "Joanna is an amazing woman. To the outside world nothing phases her, but her father's death affected her more profoundly than she lets on."

Esmeralda gave him a knowing smile. "I can understand that. We show the world a face, don't we? The truth about what is really going on is often quite different."

His dark brows drew to a point as he lowered his voice, "Is everything okay with you and Thaddeus?"

She held up her palm to stop him. "Of course, we are fine. I was speaking in general terms. I think strong people have a greater propensity to present a face to the world that says everything is all right, when it isn't."

Ian rested his hand on the pommel of his saddle and thought of James, who was the epitome of what Esmeralda just described. "By the way, how did your visit to Pepperwood go?"

Esmeralda pulled a white curl between her fingers and showed it to him, her expression ironic. "Eventful. I got this when I was there."

Ian's eyes widened. "I just came from there. They didn't mention anything."

Esmeralda shook her head with rueful humor. "You sent me on quite a tour, Ian ben Kole."

Ian glanced ahead, making sure Thaddeus and Mack were too far away to hear. "I'm so sorry about what happened to you down in New Orleans, but I thought the Pepperwood visit went well."

Esmeralda stretched her neck, sudden tension taking up residence. "It's an extraordinary place. I'll say that for it."

"What did you see?" Ian asked, vibrating with intensity. But he was like her, with no definable color, like a drop of oil in a puddle, shimmering and changing. The sense she got off him now was a fusion of his brother and sister-in-law, a deep sea green.

"Nothing that I could mention."

Ian tensed. "I understand that completely." He gave her a speculative look and asked, "And Beau? Do you have leave to speak?"

"They were two very separate and wild encounters." Esmeralda held up two curls in the back of her head to demonstrate.

"We are going to be twins, pretty soon," he joked.

"I felt you that night in the bayou." Esmeralda looked at him sidelong. "I sensed your prayers. Thank you."

"You are welcome." Ian nodded solemnly. "I am just sad that it happened, that we put you in danger."

Esmeralda inhaled, her breath ragged and weary. "I was not in danger from Beau. Everyone thinks that, but it's not true."

"I spoke with him." Ian kept his voice low. Beau Landry was a touchy subject with Thaddeus, but he thought Esmeralda might want to know.

Esmeralda pressed her lips in a grim line. "How is he?"

"He actually sounded pretty good, but you never know with Beau. He has become a master at putting on that face you and I were just talking about." Ian shifted in the saddle, unused to riding. He rubbed away a twinge in his skinny behind. "I have to admit, when I hung up, I had hope. He has suffered for a long time."

"Prayers," Esmeralda said with absolute certainty. "They are working. I feel it, too. I pray for him constantly."

"You are an amazing woman, Esmeralda. After what he put you through... most people would be cursing him."

Esmeralda covered an eye with the palm of her hand, shaking her head. "Nobody understands what happened that night. Honestly, even I don't, and I was there. But I want you to hear me, we were attacked, he and I, together. He did not cause that calamity, and he is not delusional. Ian, Beau Landry is not crazy."

Ian stilled, his voice grim. "I know he's not."

"No more than you and me. We've all seen things we can't explain. I think the only difference is we have been given guidance on how to process our experiences, but for the Lord's own reasons, Beau has not."

"That is the burden, Esmeralda, to know things and not be able to share. Like what happened at Pepperwood. Is there anything you can tell me?" Ian asked carefully.

Esmeralda sent up a quick prayer, then smiled. "There is a golden hedge of protection around the place. It is one of the most beautiful things I've ever seen."

Ian shot her a Kole Brother's toothy smile. "You saw it?"

"I did, it's wondrous and encompasses the entire property. I can just see a glimmer of the one over Rephidim ahead, do you see it?"

Ian narrowed his eyes, looking down the valley, the Thyatira Woods beyond the slope. "I don't see anything gold."

"Different gifts, for different purposes, I suppose," Esmeralda said philosophically.

"Esmeralda, I see black smoke."

Part 7 - Endor Rising

November 9, 998 ME

Unholy Assembly

Angelica ben Omri looked out at the assembled faces, the faithful. But only a third of those she summoned were in attendance, the rest threw their lot in with Charlotte, swearing their allegiance to the 'new' Ba'alat Ob. The bitch. Angelica bristled under the humiliation of it all. They would pay for their disloyalty when she resumed her throne. She planned to take it back by aligning with a power greater than Marduk. The caliber of her remaining servants made her task more difficult. They were a motley crew of castoffs, misfits, and unstable goons. Yet her core supporters remained true, many with her for decades, a few since the very beginning here in this house and in this place: Endor.

"I called you today, because the time has come to seek vengeance on the place and the power that breached this stronghold!" Angelica cried, raising a jeweled staff above her head.

A shout erupted from the crowd, their energy surging around her, malevolent and confident.

"For our memories are long, and we do not forgive! We do not forget! We never surrender!"

Black swirling smoke blasted from their wands into the Heavens as they cheered.

"Our Master, even now, awaits the time for his glorious second coming. What will he find when he returns to us? Have we been faithful or are we defeated like dogs?"

The crowd grumbled, but a few stalwart souls shouted, "Faithful!"

"In your hearts, I know you are, but there remains a blight in our own territory—Rephidim!" she snarled. Murmurs of disgust and loathing ensued, though some shuffled their feet, ashamed they had not prevailed upon the enemy's stronghold. She met the eyes of the Bezetha delegation, who bore primary responsibility for this travesty. Angelica reserved special contempt for Allison ben Whitaker, who failed her completely. They looked away, demeaned and contrite.

"I, myself do not want to face our lord and master to recount our failure." A hush fell over the crowd. "For he is more fearsome than the one who came before him, the usurper who has sought to rule and dominate us to this day. It was not Marduk we called forth. He is an imposter!" Angelica screamed as fire shot from the end of her wand. "We serve a new master, and in his name, we shall be victorious!

"How many of you fought against the enemy in the usurper's name?" The crowd exchanged looks, agreeing Marduk's power was not strong enough to overcome Rephidim. "We failed, not because of our own will, or desire, but because the power of the usurper is not enough. Today, we seek a higher power, a higher authority, and dedicate ourselves to none other," she paused, watching them, their anticipation palpable. "I declare, before you now, that our only master is Lucifer!"

A roar exploded from the crowd. They became giddy, dancing with their arms waving over their heads, shooting fire into the sky in celebratory glee. Great tremors of lust surged through the coven, as they trembled, anticipating true power, at last.

Angelica raised her arms to quiet them. "Our enemy prepares for a celebration, but we will cut them down before it even begins!"

Cheers cascaded through the trees, as Angelica poured blood into the massive cauldron at her feet. Black, billowing smoke exploded like a volcanic eruption into the sky. "Four riders approach Thyatira Woods, our woods! On foot, on horseback, and in the air, I command you now, destroy them!"

Hell Bent for Leather

The words were no more out of Ian ben Kole's mouth, before Esmeralda rose in her stirrups and screamed, "Thaddeus, they are coming!"

Thaddeus and Mack swung around on their horses. Esmeralda pointed to the sky. "Black smoke!"

Hundreds of wisps of smoke broke the canopy.

Mack whipped his head around. "Bloody Hell!"

Ian gave a mighty war cry as the cavalry officer surged back to life. "Come on!" he commanded, spurring his mount.

Esmeralda needed no entreaty. They galloped, Thaddeus and Mack falling in as they rode breakneck toward the cover of the woods. The earth trembled under the pound of the horses. The open plain offered no cover. They were vulnerable.

At a walk, they were at least an hour from Rephidim. Flying on horseback, she could not surmise how far they were from safety. But she recognized that black smoke and knew what and who came after them. With every strike of her horse's hoof she prayed, "Please, Lord. Please, Lord."

They reached the cover of the trees without incident. Ian's sharp command cut across the air, "Thaddeus, you take the lead. Mack, fall in. I'll cover our retreat, Esmeralda, stay between Mack and me."

Esmeralda shook her head. "I know these woods! You all do not! If we are going to make it," she pointed to each hard, strong, godly man and declared, "then you have to follow me!"

She saw the battle raging across Thaddeus' features. He held her gaze, then shook his head. "The Lord commanded me to keep you by my side, Esmeralda! You may set the course through these woods, because you know them better than me, but I will not abandon you to face the enemy headlong. Where the path is too narrow, I will take the lead."

The racking of a bullet broke the silence. Mack holstered his weapon inside his jacket. "If it comes down to hand to hand, Thad, you give her over to me. I know a bit about protecting high value targets."

Thaddeus nodded once, scanning the woods, calculating and pulling his service weapon. "I've got one clip."

Ian pulled his knife. "This is all I've got."

Esmeralda looked up at the sky with an expression of dread and dead certainty. "There are more than men coming after us."

Mack grinned. "I'll fight them sons of bitches, too."

"I'm not the rider my brother is, but he taught me, and there is nobody better. They won't take us while I sit this horse," Ian declared.

"Endor is twenty minutes east from where we are now."

Esmeralda turned to Thaddeus. "How do you know that?"

"Fishing. Ernst," Thaddeus answered succinctly.

Ian shook his head, looking grave. "Rephidim is at least 40 minutes northwest."

Mack snorted, "Then I suggest you lead the way, Curly. We are in for a hell of a fight."

Thaddeus reined his horse around, holding Mack's eyes and said, "Literally."

In the Wind

Ernst ben Otto would never admit it, but he was excited about the wedding. He liked the bride and the groom, and deep down a romantic heart beat in his chest. As a sucker for happy endings, he often wondered why anybody read sad or disturbing stories. Only Eve knew that about him, and if he went to her place to borrow a book she would sometimes say, "Oh, you won't like that one." But for all her yammering, she never gossiped, so he felt certain his softer side remained a secret.

After his mid-morning tea, he stepped outside and in-haled deeply, appreciating the crisp autumn air, the smell of hay, and horses. He stopped mid-stride, catching a faint whiff of something rotten—sulfur. Fleeting, yet unmistakable, it was the scent of death, the scourge of Endor. He inhaled again and swore in German.

Thirty-five years had passed since he fled his home and the fresh graves of his wife and daughter, but he would never forget that stench. The Witch had returned. With grim de-termination, he strode toward the center of town, rushing to raise the alarm.

Controlled Gait

"Too fast!" Ian barked at Esmeralda. "Post up, take her down to a trot, or these horses will give out before we reach Rephidim."

Not an accomplished horsewoman, Esmeralda turned, blood pounding in her ears. "What?"

Mack shouted, "Raise your ass, sweetheart, and slow it down!"

Esmeralda nodded and slowed the pace, trying to control the adrenaline that demanded she gallop to safety. She noted the time on her watch, 10:10 am, seven minutes since they spotted the smoke. "Oh, God, please help us!" she panted between breaths. Leaning forward in the stirrups, she let Thaddeus take the lead.

Church Bells

Rexum looked up from the order he was studying. He put a gnarled finger in his ear to quell the clanging in his head. When it did not stop, his eyes widened behind his thick glasses. He was not hearing things. The Rephidim alarm, silent for thirty-three years, raised goose flesh on his arms. He rose on quaking limbs, walked to his office door, and shouted, "They have raised the alarm!"

One of the young secretaries rushed forward. "What's happening?"

"Shut down the plant! Everyone to the center of town, we have an emergency!" He grabbed his basketball whistle from the lanyard by his door and blew. "Do it now!"

Rexum set off toward the weaver's room. It was by far the noisiest. They would not have heard anything over the racket of the looms. "Jacob, get to the dye house! Sandra, to the spinning room!" Blowing his whistle, he marched off, mustering his troops, ready to lead Arachnid Weaving to war.

Eve stood in Thaddeus' empty room, making a final inspection before he arrived. She always called it Thaddeus' room, even though two tenants lived in it since his time. There was something about the gentle giant with his sad brown eyes that tugged at her heartstrings. She never had a more wounded man under her roof, though she boarded the occasional drinker, brawler, and loudmouth, heaven knew she still had Olaf the grump. But most of her tenants were like Krish and Barton, solid steady men who only required a clean bed, good food, and a place to relax at night.

She knew from the first, Thaddeus required something different. Rather than a bed, he needed shelter. No home-made pie could fill the emptiness in his belly. And even the most comfortable chair would not induce him to relax. He needed a friend, but he also needed time. She gave him both. In exchange, she watched him heal, saw wry wit and teasing humor spice his serious, thoughtful personality. Tomorrow, he would take the last step toward restoration, living again.

She understood why he left and missed him almost as much as Esmeralda. But unlike Esmeralda, Eve understood. Her heart overflowed when she learned of his upcoming nuptials. They waited so very long to be together. And these last five weeks, planning with Julianna, she felt like the mother of the groom. He treated her as such and extended her the great honor of sitting in the first pew on his side of the aisle tomorrow, the mother's place.

The church bell confounded her, incongruent for Friday mid-morning. "Oh, dear heavens," she whispered in the quiet of Thaddeus' room. The alarm meant one thing; Endor was rising. They were coming after Esmeralda, again.

Julianna sat on the edge of Esmeralda's bed, crying happy tears, admiring the gorgeous gown hanging on the back of the closet door. Her baby girl was getting married tomorrow. She dreamed of this day since Esmeralda was a toddler and emerged from her bedroom with a pillowcase over her head, showing off her 'veil'. Until she was five, that was her favorite dress-up, Esmeralda the bride.

Julianna feared this day would never come for her shy and unusual child. But from the moment Thaddeus ben Todd ducked through their door, Esmeralda set her mind and heart on him. After he left, Julianna fretted Esmeralda would waste the rest of her life on a fantasy because he never took her crush seriously. While she was hospitalized, marriage was out of the question. The best Julianna could hope for during those dark years was recovery and restoration, but in the wee hours of the night, she wept for the loss of Esmeralda, the bride.

Alas, the Lord heard the desperate prayers of a mother and a young girl's cry of the heart. Tomorrow their prayers would be answered. Julianna bowed her head in thanksgiving and grateful tears.

At first she thought she imagined the church bells ringing, picturing how they would ring in celebration tomorrow,
but as the sound penetrated her daydream, she bolted off the
bed with a cry, "No, Lord! No!" She fled the house, running
toward the center of town.

Deep in the Thyatira woods, Esmeralda drew up straight
in the saddle, her thigh muscles screaming after holding the
post position for so long. "They are sounding the alarm,
Thaddeus! The Rephidim alarm!"

Thaddeus nodded, so focused he became incapable of
speech, glowing molten silver.

She fell back, riding beside Mack, not surprised to see
him shimmering red. "They've raised the alarm in Rephidim.
Men will take up arms."

"That's good, sweetheart, because I've got less than thirty
bullets."

At Ian's side, she noted he shimmered midnight blue, the
exact color of his brother. For a brief instant, she saw him as
a young man with auburn hair, astride his mount, rawboned,
thin, and deadly. "Ian, they've rung the church bells in Rephidim. We won't be alone out here."

He turned, fierce, ready for battle. "We are not alone
now. Never forget that, Esmie."

Their eyes met and held for a second, then she pushed
forward and joined Thaddeus in the lead.

Elders

Every resident of Rephidim gathered in the town circle
as Rexum mounted the steps to stand beside Eve, Ernst, and
the reverend. He looked out at the faces of his workers, his
family, his friends. As an old man, he remembered Thyatira before the Witch of Endor destroyed the tranquility of
their woods and their federation. Rephidim stood alone, an
island amidst a sea of rebellion, sheltered from the maelstrom
sweeping the kingdom. But he smelled the burning sulfur
and recalled with cold dread where that stench came from.

Claude guided a weeping Julianna up the steps. He passed her to Eve, who pulled her into a hug. Looking pale and stricken, Claude turned to the crowd. Ernst laid a hand on his shoulder, offering his silent strength. When Claude spoke, his voice rang strong and true. "Thirty-six years ago, our sister village, Endor, welcomed a witch into their midst. She poisoned the village and most of its people. Her lying tongue and seductive promises deceived them. She held Endor for three years and brought eternal destruction to the town and those who followed her. The young among us did not live through her reign of terror." He met the eyes of Leo and Simon, so alike with their red-hair and ruddy complexions. They nodded in encouragement, standing in solidarity with him.

"The Witch of Endor waged war against Rephidim, assaulting our people physically and spiritually. That church bell," he pointed skyward, "rang fifty times in three years. Without fail, the great and godly people of Rephidim warded off Endor, in the woods, in the streams, and on our knees! We defended each other and our land. She did not prevail against us. The Iron King is faithful and true, He defended us then, and He will defend us now. In the end, He judged Endor with fire and pestilence!

"Esmeralda, Thaddeus, Ian ben Kole, and Thaddeus' best man, Mack ben Robert, were scheduled to arrive this morning at 11:00 am." He looked at his watch and turned to Ernst. "When did you smell it?"

"Within two minutes of ringing that bell."

"It's 10:20 am. We have little time if they are coming in from the south. The Endorites will cut them off before they make it here. Mount up men! We are going into battle!"

Rexum's whistle pierced the commotion. "Women and children inside the church, you know what to do!"

With those words, the godly people of Rephidim marshaled their courage and went to war.

Dark Sky

Esmeralda pulled back on the reins, bringing her winded mount to an abrupt halt.

Thaddeus whipped his horse around. "What do you see?"

The moment he asked, a black cloud obscured the sun, and a cacophony of shrieks erupted overhead. The four riders raised their faces to the sky in mortal dread.

Mack grunted, "I haven't missed that smell."

"Astrals," Esmeralda pointed, "they've found us."

Ian rose in his stirrups and declared. "For the word of God is living and active, sharper than any two-edged sword, penetrating soul from spirit, rending marrow from bone. This abomination is anathema to Him, and those who practice wickedness shall not stand!"

Mack's nose flared. "Through His name we trample those who rise up against us."

"For You have girded me with strength for battle!" Thaddeus shook his fist. "And by His name, we shall be victorious."

Esmeralda watched in great wonder, as a sword appeared in each man's hand as they cried Scriptures. Her dread evaporated. She was a veteran, and this was her territory, her home. She closed her eyes and lifted her hands to Heaven. "I can do all things through Christ who strengthens me."

Darkness fell across the land, and thus began, the great and fearsome battle of Thyatira Woods.

Teams

No one planned it, but the Rephidim men congregated with their teammates. Rexum took note of it, and it made organizing their impromptu army simple. "Opies, you are the messengers. One of you ride out with each company and bring back news of the battle. Weavers and Spinners, two of your own are under attack, cover the southern road."

Claude led them forward in one accord, heading into the heart of the woods.

"Dyers, take the western road. Cut the Endorites off."

Olaf bellowed a war cry as his band of hulking dyers beat a hasty exit riding their draught horses.

"Woodworkers and Smiths, take the high ground to the east."

Barton and Matthew barreled past Rexum, riding like the wind.

"Bakers and Rovers, secure and guard the perimeter."

As the troops sped away, an eerie silence descended on the empty square. Rexum turned to Ernst, two old men, wily and intelligent, but no longer suited for physical battle. "It's been a long time since we did this."

"I have not missed it." Ernst took a deep breath and said, "Now, we wait."

Spooked

The riders were prepared for the onslaught; their horses were not. When the first black shadow hit Esmeralda's mount, it reared and bolted in panic. She kept her seat, but the terrified animal shot off like a cannon. Esmeralda heard nothing except pounding hooves and otherworldly screeching. Two more shadows attacked the horse, causing it to go berserk, spinning, thrashing, bucking. Thrown from the saddle, her foot barely cleared the stirrup as she sailed through the air. A fourth astral hit the horse, and it sprinted away.

Esmeralda landed hard, her body singing an agonizing song of pain. She rolled to her back, gasping, the breath knocked out of her, her shoulder and ribs on fire. The sky above turned black, plunging the woods into darkness. Waiting for her lungs to recover and her eyes to adjust, she scanned her surroundings, searching in vain for Thaddeus. A lichened rock protruded out of the ground, blocking her view to the east, and she was thankful she had not brained herself on it. Gingerly rolling left, she saw nothing but the forest floor, slender trees, and a blanket of old leaves. Groaning, she tried to use her uninjured shoulder to rise, but her ribs screamed in protest, and she fell backward, out of breath.

"Thou art hurt, child," said a voice over her head.

Esmeralda froze in terror. She recognized that voice, the Butcher of Bezetha, Doctor Nephel. Adrenaline shot up her spine, and she scrambled to her feet, holding her side, protecting her shoulder.

He licked his lips.

"Go away!"

"I am here to offer succor as a doctor, Esmeralda," he crooned her name with sinister lust. "I told thee that cheek would scar, and it did. Come hither."

He was no astral spirit. Flesh and blood stood before her. She had no weapons, no clear idea where she was, or how far off the trail the bolting horse carried her. The screaming chaos around them made it impossible to think, improbable anyone would hear her if she could find the breath to call out. "I didn't let you touch me then, and you'll not touch me now." She backed away, her eyes darting.

He narrowed his thin brows and pulled a scalpel. "I did not exactly have touching in mind."

Esmeralda's vision shifted, and she saw him for what he was, a wicked murderer, an abortionist whose hands dripped blood, his heart nothing but stone. She rebuked him, "Thy detestable practice is before the Most High, who sees all that is done in secret. The blood of babes cries out to Him, demanding justice. Now, He calls you to the pit, Doctor." She raised her hand, palm flat, and he froze where he stood.

Esmeralda watched in detached fascination as he brought the scalpel to his neck. His eyes widened in horror, as he slashed. She turned away, repulsed by the arterial spray, and gurgling horror as he died in the dirt.

Limping away, she left Doctor Nephel to his fate.

Her breath came in shallow, desperate pants, her ribs burning with every gulp of sulfur poisoned air. The stench invaded her nose, coated her tongue, and made her gag, which sent sizzling pain down her side.

Blending into the woods, she disappeared amongst the trees. Her mind raced, torn between locating the men and making her way to Rephidim on foot. But they would not seek Rephidim without her, and all three men would sacrifice themselves searching. Even with her extensive knowledge of these woods, the pervasive darkness disoriented her, the lack of sun compromising her sense of direction. It would be difficult for her to find Rephidim, impossible for the men. She could not leave without them.

Flattening herself against a boulder, she peeked around. Above, the astrals screeched, and she heard a shot to the east. Would she cause more harm than good barging into their midst? She was safe for the moment, undetected in her camouflage. But a hiss inches from her ear shattered the illusion of safety and sent a bolt of lightning down her spine. She leapt away an instant before a monstrous snake struck at her neck. It fell, coiling and writhing at her feet. Esmeralda took off, tearing through the underbrush, heedless of the noise, terrified.

The stitch in her side cramped, delivering punishing agony with every step. She struggled for air but kept running. A warrior bellowed to her left, and she changed directions, recognizing Mack's voice. She ran, clipping her good shoulder on a tree trunk. It arrested her momentum, spun her in a circle, and she caught herself against the trunk of a huge oak. Through the darkness, she watched as Mack gave a live demonstration as to why Prince Peter chose him as his head of security. Surrounded by bodies, he dispatched his assailants with ruthless, brutal efficiency without firing a shot. He turned, his eyes blazing fire, and two of his would-be attackers fled.

Esmeralda scanned the shadows, thought the way was clear, and bolted. "Mack!"

With agile grace, he leapt over the bodies, took her around the waist, and covered her head as they escaped the killing field. Crashing through a row of mountain laurel, he yelled, "I've got you now!"

The words shattered her brain, throwing her into an alternate realm. Yet, unlike the past, she kept her faculties. The world simply slowed down. Instead of screaming, she heard talking and knew what the enemy was planning. "Mack," in her mind, her voice was low, hollow, drawn out, "they are coming up from the rear, four of them."

He pushed her behind a rock, covering her with his body, aimed, and fired four shots. Esmeralda heard the bullets make impact, splitting skin, shattering bone, and exploding brains. In arrested slow motion, the bodies fell. Mack lifted her off the ground by the back of her shirt, running again.

Pounding hooves came from the right, but Mack's sheltering grip prevented her from turning her head to see who approached.

"Hand her up!" Ian yelled.

Mack catapulted Esmeralda into the saddle in front of Ian like a shot put. The pommel gouged her pelvic bone, and she gasped. Ian grabbed her around the waist in a python's grip.

"I've got her! There's Thaddeus, a hundred yards, eleven o'clock!" Ian kicked the horse and shot off.

Esmeralda turned and saw Thaddeus covered in black shadows. In slow motion, she lifted her hand and pushed, exhaling deeply, rebuking, praying. The astral spirits exploded under the assault. The world sped up again.

Thaddeus shook himself and stood upright, dazed.

Mack barreled toward him, shouting, "Behind you!"

Thaddeus turned, and a shot rang out. Just as Esmeralda lost sight of them, Thaddeus fell.

"No!!!" she screamed. "Ian, go back, go back!"

Ian ignored her cry, tightened his arm around her waist, and urged the galloping gelding faster. Gunfire erupted around them. Ian pushed her low and leaned over her, covering her with his body as they flew through the woods. The pommel gutted her with every footfall, the sweat of the horse bathing her face as its mane tangled in her nose and mouth. She gasped, struggling to sit up, crying for air, silently weeping.

Wind Knocked Out of Your Sails

When they breached the hedge of protection, the cater-wauling stopped, daylight returned. Ian did not slow, nor did he let her rise. Esmeralda watched the ground fly past, detached and strange, on the edge of consciousness.

He reined up, dismounting with a shout, "I need a fresh horse and a weapon!"

Esmeralda clutched her midriff and cried, "Find him, Ian! Go back. They shot him!"

Ian mounted the horse Ernst offered, accepted a rifle, and nodded. "You'll have your wedding, Esmeralda. I promise." He rode off, praying he had not just lied to her.

"Come on, let's get you to your mother." Ernst took the winded horse's bridle, walking the beast and Esmeralda toward the town's center.

"Ernst... he's been shot," Esmeralda gasped.

He stared at his feet, nodded once, and said, "We will pray."

Esmeralda curled into herself, covering her face, reliving her last glimpse of Thaddeus as the bullet made impact, animating his body in an odd, jerky contortion of arms and legs as he fell. "No, Lord, please."

A chorus of shouting came from the church as the women and a few children burst through the door.

"Esmeralda! Are you okay? Are you hurt?"

"Mom?" Esmeralda raised her stricken face, streaked with tears and grime. Convulsive sobs choked off her words as she dissolved completely at the sight of her mother.

"It's all right, baby. It's going to be okay," Julianna soothed. "Help me get her down, Ernst."

Gentle hands pulled Esmeralda from the saddle, but her knees buckled. Ernst held her tight, keeping her upright.

"Come on, baby. Can you walk? Let's get you home, so you can lie down," Julianna soothed.

With Ernst on one side, Julianna on the other, Esmeralda stood at the center of town, enduring the horrified stares of the women and children. Their men were in the thick of it.

Death Comes to the Woods

Branches whipped at Ian's face, blood drumming in his ears. He too had seen Thaddeus fall and knew the reality and horror of war, had buried many a friend shot in battle. He urged the horse faster, the rifle gripped in his right hand.

The moment he cleared the Rephidim hedge, the woods grew dark. Black powder and gore polluted the air, underlain with sulfur. He recognized the sounds of men locked in mortal combat, heard the disconcerting whiz of bullets. Horses screamed; men shouted, grunting in pain, calling to comrades. The ground shook beneath thundering hooves and running feet. It coalesced and harmonized, composing war's lethal song of carnage and death.

Ian was no fool. The former First Lieutenant flanked the action, not flying headlong into a firefight. A black robed Endorite leapt from a boulder to his left, intending to unhorse him. Ian blew the man out of the sky and wheeled around. Three more combatants materialized, leering in the blackness, crazed with bloodlust. Ian fired in rapid succession. Two fell where they stood. The third bolted.

"Ian!" Olaf cried. "Over here! The Spinners are under heavy fire!"

Ian flattened himself against the saddle, keeping the white stocking feet of Olaf's draft horse in sight. They careened through the uneven terrain, toward the fiercest fighting, near the spot where Thaddeus had fallen.

Revelation Song

Esmeralda felt the town's eyes upon her, strange Esmeralda once again an object of their curiosity and pitying stares. The realization that she had always been separate from them cut her to the quick. They loved her, but they never understood her. There was only One who did, and He could stop the battle raging in the woods.

She raised her face to the sky, tears pooling in her ears.

I was there. I will never leave you or forsake you.

The day she left Rephidim, she prepared three songs to sing in church. She often wondered if life would have turned out different if she had chosen another. Afterward, drowning in despair, one sustained her. She remembered King Jehoshaphat's faith, how he trusted the Lord and sent his musicians ahead of his army into battle. There was power in worship, power in song. When her tormentors in the mental hospital were coming for her, she would sing. More often than not, it turned them back, and they left her alone. It was the only weapon she had inside that horrible place, just as it was now.

Groaning in agony, she eased her arms above her head. Alone in the Spirit, surrounded by her hometown, and gripped with foreboding, Esmeralda sang.

Hairbrained Folly

Angelica realized moments after launching the attack their efforts were futile. Until they released Lucifer, merely invoking his name carried no more power than if they battled under the name of Santa Claus. Worse yet, the same impenetrable force that kept Angelica from the book surrounded the girl. After weeks of fruitless toil, she knew the mission was doomed. She would not sacrifice herself in some hairbrained folly, even if it was her idea, but that mattered little.

There would be no witnesses to tell the tale.

She came back into her body. Her coven, those talented in astral projection, lay in pentagrams across Endor's sacred square. Angelica moved among them, many dead already, victims of the sword. She paused over the prone bodies of the Bezetha delegation. This was their fault. They should have destroyed Rephidim long ago. At the very least, they should have maintained control over the girl. Angelica stared into the pale face of Allison ben Whitaker. Her eyes were blank, but unlike many of her comrades, she still lived. Not for long. Angelica began with her, driving her ceremonial dagger straight into Allison ben Whitaker's heart.

She killed them all, without thought or compunction. Dead witches told no tales. Barely pausing to wipe her hands, Angelica ben Omri fled Endor.

Step Back

Ian witnessed some of the most horrific battles of the Civil War, his regiment in the thick of them, embedding the stench of blood and gunpowder permanently in his brain. Unlike Beau and James, he recalled the final battle with vivid clarity, and Thyatira Woods had the same distinct, other-worldly element to it. That terrified him.

He rode with Olaf and six other dyers toward the fighting. The sound of battle lessened as they approached. Ian did not know if his mind filtered out the noise, or if the chaos had in fact lessened. They crested a hill and pulled their horses to a halt.

"Scheisse!" Olaf cursed, seeing his friends caught in a trap.

In a clearing below, the Endorites surrounded a group of Rephidimites. The Rephidimites were boxed in.

Ian clearly saw it was a massacre in the making. "Yeshua," Ian whispered and aimed his weapon.

There were seven of them against a force of fifty men.

The cries of the astral spirits fell silent, though the sky remained black. An eerie quiet crept through the woods, broken only by the sound of men and horses moving through the leaf covered ground.

"We kill them now!" shouted an Endorite, raising a knife, preparing to charge into the dell.

Ian placed the man's black clad chest in his crosshairs and with infinite slowness, pulled the trigger. The man spun and fell to the ground.

The Endorites howled in rage. Spurred into action, they rose en masse, aiming their weapons at the trapped Rephidimites below. Before they could fire a shot, a fierce battle cry erupted deep in the woods. It caused the hairs on men's arms to prickle, sent chills down their spines, and arrested them where they stood.

Previously unseen by human eye, unheard by human ear, the magnificent horses of Endor materialized out of the gloom. Their hooves shook the ground as they surrounded the evil men of Endor. Their leader stepped forward, a golden mare, her tail and mane like the hair of a beautiful woman, her coat shimmering with tresses of purest gold. She tossed her head, giving a loud cry, and with that the legendary horses of Endor entered the Battle of Thyatira Woods.

The trapped Rephidimites surged up the hill, as the animals charged. Caught between the horses and the charging men, the Endorites found themselves trapped. Chaos ensued. No one broke the perimeter the horses set, trampling and kicking any foe who tried to break their line. Ian heard one man's skull crack like a pumpkin as he died in the dirt. Olaf and the Dyers cut through the terrorized Endorites, wielding the heavy batons they used in the mill with brutal efficiency. The Endorites panicked. Surrounded by the lethal fury of their foes, they ran down the embankment, seeking escape.

Those who survived the onslaught, converged as one, falling into the valley. A fight broke out among their ranks. The horses withdrew and watched the wicked brutalize each other with guns, knives, and fists, not a single Rephidimite among them. The Witch of Endor's men turned on one another in savage barbarity. When the last man stood, surrounded by his dead comrades, he turned with a snarl directed at the golden mare. His eyes blazed hellfire, hate, and madness. With blasphemy on his lips, he drove his knife into his own heart and died.

The sun peeked through the tops of the trees, beams of light piercing the darkness in glittering shafts. Bridles jingled, as men shifted in leather saddles, staring in awestruck wonder at the carnage below. The golden mare lifted her head and cried out in victory. Her fellows joined her, stamping their feet, and rearing on their hind legs. Then, as if blown away in the mist, they faded into the Thyatira Woods.

Krish, the Opie, crashed through the forest, riding furiously back from Rephidim, shattering the stunned silence. His dark eyes grew enormous at the sight of the slaughtered enemy. Then he raised a fist and pumped it three times, declaring, "To God be the glory!"

His words broke the spell, and a mighty cheer erupted. They leapt from their horses and embraced, jubilant with relief and victory.

Ian's voice ripped through their celebration. "Men, tend the wounded, search for the fallen." He scanned the men still on horseback. "Claude, Barton, Olaf come with me. Thaddeus ben Todd went down." Ian raced away, toward the last place he'd seen Mack and Thaddeus.

Ben Todd Brothers

A quarter mile away, Mack guarded the entrance to the stone enclave like the angel at the tomb. No one was getting past him to Thaddeus, no one. He stood amid a massive firefight, yet he did not fire. Mack had fifteen bullets left, and every damn one of them was going to count. He killed that son of a bitch who shot Thaddeus, but not before the wicked bastard got off his shot. Mack dropped the man's two companions, then pulled Thaddeus away from the action, and took cover.

Scanning the woods, Mack fought down an eerie sense of déjà vu. Richard… First Lieutenant Richard ben Todd, his best friend, his son's namesake, and Thaddeus' brother, was killed in action by one of those black hearted cowards.

Their mission that fateful day had been to eliminate the group responsible for attacking the Palace and murdering Princess Alexa. They received intelligence that twelve jihadists were hiding in a house on the outskirts of the New City. Mack's unit surrounded the property and moved in. But the enemy knew they were coming. Someone had tipped them off, and they were ready.

When they breached the door, they came under immediate fire. But crazy zealots, even with guns, were no match for the well-trained soldiers, who rained fire and death on them. In the last room, Mack and Richard found a teenage boy huddled in a corner, crying.

Richard shouted, "Hands against the wall!"

A closet to their right cracked open, and Mack saw something roll across the wooden floor, then the world exploded in a blinding flash as an X420 gas concussion grenade detonated in the small space. He had a vivid memory of sailing backwards with his weapon still in his hand. A shot rang out, and he felt the impact as a bullet tore through his shoulder. He cracked his head on the corner of a wall, and it knocked him unconscious for a few seconds. Gagging from the gas and concussed, he tried to raise his gun, but his arm would not move. Half blind from the smoke, gas, and falling ceiling plaster, he saw the teenage boy emerge from the bedroom, wearing a gas mask and aiming a small handgun at Richard, who took the brunt of the grenade and lay unconscious on the floor.

"No!" Mack screamed. In his mind, it had been a howl to reach the heavens, but in reality, it came out barely more than a wheeze. He lay in a puddle of his own blood, paralyzed and helpless as he watched his best friend shot, and there was not a damn thing he could do about it.

Mack shook off the memory and melted into the shadows of the stone enclave, determined that would not happen again.

"Son of a bitch, this hurts," Thaddeus groaned, leaning against the stone wall, pressing a field dressing to his wounded shoulder. "What's going on out there?"

"Fighting's moved off to the east. I reckon we'll hunker down 'til it stops."

Thaddeus tried to get up. "If it's stopped, we need to go. I need to make sure Esmie is okay."

"Don't move!" Mack barked. "You won't do Esmeralda any good if a bone fragment pierces an artery. I am sure Ian got her to safety. That dude was not kidding when he said he could ride, I've never seen anything like it." Mack shook his head ruefully. "His brother is a sanctimonious pain in the ass, but Ian was not bullshitting when he said he learned from the best." Mack crouched on his haunches, checking Thaddeus' bandage. "How you doing?"

Thaddeus let loose a string of cuss words but managed to articulate, "Hurts."

Mack rolled his shoulder in empathy. "Shoulder wounds suck. They take forever to heal. Dangerous as shit, too. You got all kinds of arteries and nerves running through there."

"Aren't you a ray of sunshine," Thaddeus said through pale lips.

"No sense lying. That bitch is going to hurt for months. Took me nine weeks before I could wipe my ass with my right hand. Tell you what, I never thought I'd celebrate something like that, but I did. You're about to find out exactly how useless your left hand really is."

Thaddeus made a half-hearted snort of disgust. "I'm supposed to get married tomorrow, wiping my ass had not even occurred to me... thanks. I needed something else to worry about." He groaned through a painful chuckle and added, "Perhaps I'll ask my new bride, 'Come here, Vixen. I need a wipe.'"

Mack laughed. "Sounds like a hell of a way to spend a honeymoon. She better get used to it though. You're old as hell. Young girl like that will be wiping your ass before long."

A wave of dizziness crashed over Thaddeus. "I am approximately nine months older than you."

"My wife could tell you exactly how many days apart we are." The corner of Mack's mouth lifted in a smile.

"They liked each other, didn't they?" Thaddeus closed his

eyes. His breathing became shallow, as he struggled to get air in his lungs.

Mack scanned the woods. Nothing moved and the gunfire grew sporadic. He wished it would end. Thaddeus needed a doctor. Blood was seeping through his makeshift field dressing at an alarming rate. "They did. Lavinia wanted to come. Gah... I'm glad she didn't."

Thaddeus shook his head, feeling disoriented and groggy. "Me, too. What the hell was that, Mack?"

Mack dug the heel of his boot in the dirt. "Some kind of Halloween shit."

"What's... Hallo... ween?" Thaddeus' tongue felt thick, like it was swelling up in his mouth, choking him.

Mack snorted, "Another perk of living with a genius. She tells me all about these archaic holidays. Why do you think I call her Valentine?"

"Never thought to ask, thought it was her name... or something." Thaddeus' vision waivered, his breath coming in shallow pants.

"No, it's an old lovers holiday. We actually celebrated it this year. It happens to be the day we got back together, so it's worth celebrating."

Thaddeus groaned, "I won't... the night... Esmie came..." He tried to moisten his lips; they were so dry. "I'm a dog, Mack. Bad... man."

"Oh, I think I could put up some pretty good competition there." Mack scanned the woods again. They were still quiet. "You didn't let her run off and have a baby without you."

"You have... beautiful son," Thaddeus murmured.

Mack saw Thaddeus' eyes flutter shut. He checked the pulse in his neck. It was there, rapid and thready. He walked to the entrance of their enclave, checking his phone. Still no signal. He cursed and put the useless thing back in his pocket. It was 10:56 am. Thaddeus needed medical attention, and Mack had a sick feeling Rephidim was not the ideal place for it.

Don't Move

Mack heard Ian calling and swore in blessed relief. He stepped out of their enclave and drew the rescue squad's attention. "We need a doctor!"

Barton wheeled his horse around. "I'll go!"

Ian spurred forward and dismounted in a single fluid motion. His extraordinary horsemanship struck Mack again. "Is it over?"

"Yep," Ian said, looking grim.

"You got the girl to safety?"

Ian nodded. "She's fine. How is he?"

"He's alive, hit in the shoulder, and it's bad." Mack's nose flared. "That bullet fucked up his arm. He's going to need surgery, fast."

Claude pushed past Ian, stalking inside. He gasped when he saw Thaddeus, leaned against the stone wall, ghostly white, his lips turning blue. "This is not good. We've got a doctor here, but he does little more than treat scratches and the occasional broken bone."

Mack's jaw worked. "I need a fresh horse. I'll ride out to get a cell signal." He pointed at Claude. "Don't move him. I think that bullet may have nicked an artery. It's clotted now, but the least jostling could kill him."

"Claude, we should get Esmeralda." Ian checked his phone on the off chance he had a signal.

Claude scowled, not wanting his daughter anywhere near these woods until he was certain the danger was over. But he did not like the look of Thaddeus, and Esmeralda would want to be by his side. "You men, give me your coats. Olaf, go get Esmie. Ian, get this man a horse."

"We need one of those glowing horses. I have never seen anything like it," Ian said, sprinting away.

Claude and Olaf exchanged a serious look, and Claude nodded. "Bring Ernst back with Esmeralda."

Mack ignored the two Rephidimites, waiting for Ian to return with a mount. Claude draped coats over Thaddeus' unconscious form and asked, "Do we need to put a tourniquet on this arm? He is bleeding."

Mack shook his head. "Tourniquet is dangerous, last resort with a wound like that. I got a pressure dressing on it and loosened all his clothes. But he's going into shock, his heart's not pumping enough blood and oxygen. That's why his lips are turning blue. Unfortunately, the treatment for shock runs counter to care of an arterial injury, which requires his blood to clot. Either way, shock or blood loss might kill him."

Mack's severe assessment shook Claude visibly. "We cannot let that happen."

"I don't plan to." Mack searched the woods and said, "Dammit, where's Ian with that horse?" He checked his phone again, still no signal, 11:12 am.

SOS

Mack reached the plain outside the Thyatira Woods at 11:30 am, fighting off the sick feeling Thaddeus was not going to make it. He caught a weak cell signal and made the distress call. "This is retired Agent Mack ben Robert of the Royal Guard, service number 347859, requesting medevac. Location, approximately fifteen miles north of Easton PA, village of Rephidim, Thyatira Woods. FBI Director Thaddeus ben Todd, in critical condition, gunshot wound. We've taken fire in a localized skirmish. Approximate casualty count, one hundred. Need full scale medic, Joe's on the ground, and Sherlocks. Attack launched east of Rephidim, insurgents from an abandoned settlement called Endor. Situation is critical."

Mack's next call was to the Palace. "Nathan, it's Mack. Got an emergency. Put Golden Boy on the line."

Agent Nathan ben Henry, Prince Peter's head of security, dropped his breakfast burrito and moved out of the service kitchen. "What's the situation?" Mack relayed the events, Nathan whistled low and asked, "Damn, Mack, what do you need?"

"I'm calling in a favor with the Prince, and he might need your help."

"You got it." Nathan knocked on Peter's bedroom door and entered without waiting for leave to do so. "My Esteemed, Agent Mack ben Robert is on the phone for you."

The Prince sat up; his blond hair disheveled with sleep. The bedroom reeked of wine and sex, a naked woman beside him.

Peter reached for the phone, his mind running through possibilities, every one of them dire. "Mack?"

"I need your assistance." Mack quickly debriefed him, then said, "Use your influence, make sure no red tape gets in the way of this rescue. You'll recall, he was my best man."

"You relayed the details to Nathan?"

Nathan nodded.

Peter cradled the phone on his shoulder, pulling on his boxer shorts, and ignoring the mewling protest from the woman in his bed. "Consider it done. I will engage the best surgeons in the kingdom, so let me know where they take him."

"Will do, thanks." Mack disconnected the line.

"Sorry, sweetheart." Peter shrugged apologetically toward the bed. "Duty calls." He dressed in a pair of jeans, grabbing a shirt that stank of last night's cigarettes and what's-her-name's perfume, and without a backward glance called, "Thanks."

Prince's Study - New City, Alanthia

"That is correct, Commander, I am designating the situation in Rephidim top priority," Peter said into the phone. "Thank you, sir."

Walking by Peter's study, Korah came up short, doubled back, and loomed in the doorway.

Nathan came to attention and said, "Good morning, my Esteemed."

Korah dismissed him with a wave of his hand. "Leave us."

Nathan looked between Korah and Peter, the hair on the back of his neck prickling. The two royals never spoke. In the year and a half since Nathan took over as Peter's Head of Security, he could count on one hand the number of exchanges he witnessed between father and son, and all of those had been in official settings.

When he first joined Peter's detail, Mack pulled him aside and said, "The biggest threat to the Prince's safety comes from inside this Palace. You watch Korah like you would a haji. Korah is the more dangerous of the two."

Nathan bowed and addressed Prince Peter, "My Esteemed, I'll be just outside."

Korah glared at Nathan, catching the undercurrent, and shut the door in his face. Cutting his eyes to Peter, he asked, "What are you up to?"

Peter lifted the lid on the lacquered case on his desk, lit a cigarette, and took a leisurely drag, knowing it would irritate Korah, who could not abide the smell of smoke. "Merely enjoying a morning cigarette, and you?" He blew several smoke rings, then added, "What are you up to?"

"I am here to ascertain exactly why you think you have the authority to designate anything top priority without clearing it with me first." Korah's hazel eyes bore a hole in Peter's skull.

"Darn, you have spoiled my surprise. I was planning a military parade for your birthday next week."

"I will not be in residence." Korah took a menacing step forward. "And we both know that is not why you were on the phone."

"You will not be here?" Peter's voice dripped with feigned disappointment. "Oh, what a shame. It promises to be quite a celebration. I am certain everyone will be so disappointed. Perhaps we will hold it for you in absentia? I am happy to stand in. The troops do love when Prince d'Or shows them his support." Peter smiled as the barb found its mark, knowing his popularity with the media and the military was a growing concerned to Korah. "I can give a nice speech, a little hoorah. Think of the PR, they will eat it up."

Korah pitched his voice low and said, "Whatever you are up to, call it off, or I will."

Peter frowned, oozing mock concern. "Oh?" He took a long pull on the cigarette and shook his head. "Now that would be exceedingly bad press, not advisable."

Korah scoffed, unsheathing a tried-and-true weapon, wielded with devastating skill throughout Peter's life. "You do not advise me on anything. High level briefings, sadly, do not come illustrated with cartoons, and I do not take advice from illiterate drug addicts."

Peter put a hand over his heart, pretending to be crestfallen. "Does this mean I am out of the inner circle, Father? You wound me to the core."

Korah's lip lifted. "That can be arranged."

Peter snuffed out his cigarette and came around the desk, invading Korah's personal space. The challenge was unmistakable, a lifetime in the making. When the twenty-year-old Prince faced the fifty-four-year-old King, the tables turned for the first time. There was no doubt, in either of their minds, who held the advantage in a physical confrontation.

"Not this time," Peter growled. "Never again."

When Korah moved to the door, the Prince's dimple, identical to his father's, made an appearance. The smile disappeared at Korah's parting shot.

"Do you think your whores protect you? There are other ways," Korah laughed. "Don't try me, Son, you will lose every time."

Peter's nose flared. With an angry exhale, he pulled out his secure phone and said, "Miss Pink, we have a situation."

King's Study - New City, Alanthia

"Get the Minister of Defense on the phone," Korah barked to his secretary and slammed his office door.

Rephidim...

That could only mean one thing, one person—Angelica. That blasted woman, he knew they had not heard the last of her. And now Peter was involved, and he did not want his son poking around Thyatira, wanted no one digging up the ashes of Endor.

Why was the crazy bitch meddling back there?

Pain rose like a specter out of the depths of his mind, and he collapsed into his chair with a ragged sigh.

Endor, where it all began, and where it all ended.

Korah rubbed the bridge of his nose, swamped with old memories. He never let himself think of her any longer, but the ghost came for a visit, and he saw her face—his wife. For a fleeting moment, he felt the intense and powerful love they once shared... before everything fell apart.

"I am so sorry, my darling. I never meant for it to happen, for it to end like that. I never meant for you to be hurt. Please... forgive me?"

He buried his face in his hands and closed his eyes, but Korah's plea was met only with deafening silence.

What's for Lunch - New York City, Alanthia - Paul

Sitting at his desk in New York, Agent Paul ben Casper's stomach growled. He looked up at the black and white institutional clock, 11:50 am. Having skipped breakfast, no wonder he was hungry. He blew out a long breath, contemplating the stack of files that would still be here whether he ate lunch or not. "Ken, I'm going to get something to eat. Do you want anything?"

"What are you thinking?" his partner, Agent Ken ben Clifford asked, digging in his back pocket for his wallet.

"I'm thinking bahn me or pho."

"Again?" Ken pulled out a ten.

Paul shrugged. "What do you want then, if Vietnamese doesn't sound good to you?"

Ken smacked his lips considering, "I don't know, pizza?"

"We live on pizza. I'm sick of it."

"I'm broke, pizza."

"Uff da," Paul said with a rueful shake of his head. "I'll pick you up a slice, but I'm getting something else. I got spoiled down in New Orleans. They've got some amazing food there. I ate like a king."

As he pocketed Ken's money, Agent Delores ben Edward shouted, "Director ben Todd's been shot."

All noise and movement in the bullpen stilled.

"The call just came in from the DOD. They are responding to a request from," Delores checked her notes, "from retired Agent Mack ben Robert of the Royal Guard. They were involved in some sort of altercation in eastern Pennsylvania. The Director is in critical condition."

"He's getting married tomorrow," Ken exclaimed in disbelief.

"Everyone, in the conference room, now!" Operations Director Juan ben Geraldo snapped.

He did not have to ask twice.

Deep Water

Ernst drove his best sprung wagon into the woods, following Olaf's lead. Esmeralda sat on the bench beside him, looking grim, her lips moving in silent prayer.

Julianna patted her daughter's thigh, trying to reassure her. "It will be all right, baby. I know it."

"Ernst, hurry."

"Esmeralda, it will not do Thaddeus any good if I get this wagon stuck." As if to prove his point, he angled the team off the narrow path, skirting a large rock.

"We need to go! Olaf, give me your horse!" Esmeralda called, half rising.

"No," Julianna said, pulling Esmeralda back into her seat. "You cannot ride with your arm in a sling, and I think you've broken at least one rib, which could puncture a lung. You should not even be out here."

"Mom… please? Please stop." Tears leaked out of the corner of Esmeralda's eyes.

Julianna's chin trembled. "I don't want you hurt."

"It's a little late for that." Esmeralda swallowed thickly. "Hurry, Ernst."

Ernst grunted.

Ten minutes later, they came around a bend and spotted a group congregating near a shelter of large rocks, their faces ashen. Claude came forward, coatless, his shirt stained with blood. He helped Julianna down, allowing his wife to hug him, assuring her the blood was not his own. Turning to Esmeralda, he offered his hand.

Her legs quaked, as a wave of dizziness overtook her. "Dad?"

"He's alive. Come down. I'll take you to him."

Esmeralda balled her fists. That was not what she wanted to hear. She wanted to hear that Thaddeus was all right, but her father's face, more than his words, conveyed how serious the situation was.

The crowd parted as he guided her over the uneven terrain.

Ian met her in the clearing, his face stained with gunpowder and sweat. "Mack's ridden to get help, but the doctor is with him."

Esmeralda closed her eyes and prepared herself.

The enclave was crowded. Perched on a small ledge, Eve held an IV fluid bag with visibly trembling hands. Beside her, Reverend ben Heinz suspended an ominous looking bag of blood. Bolstered by Barton on one side and Krish on the other, Thaddeus sat upright, his back to the stone wall. An oxygen mask obscured the lower half of his face, and rolled towels on either shoulder kept his head upright, his airway clear. Doctor ben Hagen knelt, pressing a stethoscope to

Thaddeus' bare chest, marred by trails of blood. The crimson created a ghastly contrast against his bluish, white skin.

"How is he?" Esmeralda asked, unable to move.

Doctor ben Hagen rose from his haunches and shook his head. "Not good, I am afraid. His friend's quick action saved his life, but I have been unable to conduct a thorough examination here. The bullet appears to have exited through the underside of his armpit, damaging one or more of his arteries, the subclavian and subscapular both residing near the injury. As a result, his blood loss has been extensive, and I fear he is going into Hypovolemic Shock. We are administering oxygen, IV fluids, and giving him transfusions, but he needs surgery."

"Then do the surgery!" Esmeralda demanded as she fought down panic. Claude tightened his arm around the uninjured side of her waist, holding her close.

Doctor ben Hagen shook his head. "I can't do surgery here. This is an extremely delicate procedure. We do not have the capability in my office, let alone a dirt floor. He would not survive if I tried. The best thing we can do right now is replace his lost fluids and blood, provide ample oxygen, keep him warm, still, and alive until a rescue team gets here."

A gray blue aura surrounded Thaddeus. She could see his life ebbing away while his body screamed for the oxygenated blood his heart was so desperately trying to pump. "How long does he have?"

The doctor looked down. "I can't say, Esmeralda."

His expression told her not long. She pursed her lips, gathering every atom of strength she possessed and turned to her father. "Dad, help me down."

Claude eased her to her knees at Thaddeus' side. Esmeralda felt under the coats for Thaddeus' hand. It was frigid. "He's cold."

"His body is redirecting blood to his vital organs," Doctor ben Hagen informed her.

"Shouldn't he be lying down?" Esmeralda asked.

Doctor ben Hagen shook his head. "No, his friend did the right thing by keeping him upright and still."

She smoothed Thaddeus' hair; he'd run a bloody hand through it at some point during his ordeal. "Someone bring me a cloth and some water."

"He cannot drink, Esmeralda," Doctor ben Hagen warned.

Esmeralda's gentle touch did not leave Thaddeus' face. "It is to wash away this blood. He cannot abide being grimy. It makes him anxious," her words faltered as she added, "and he does not need to be anxious."

"All right," the doctor nodded and turned to Ian. "Have it warmed."

Ian exited the enclave, shouting, "We need a basin of warm water."

Several men volunteered to fetch the water, still more built a fire, antsy for something to do. Ian glanced up at the sky, now a cheery blue, clear and quiet, as if nothing had happened. The stench of battle lingered, blood, gunpowder, the tang of male sweat, and testosterone. He scanned the trees, looking for Mack, listening for the thundering blades of a rescue helicopter. Had Mack made it safely out of the woods? Were they waiting in vain for help to arrive while Thaddeus died by degrees?

"Ernst, is there a clearing near here where they can land a helicopter? I am afraid even if they get here in time, transporting Thaddeus back to Rephidim might kill him."

Ernst's forehead wrinkled in concentration. "How large an area will they need?"

"I'm no pilot but it needs to be flat, probably a hundred feet in all directions, clear of trees and debris. Anywhere around here like that?"

"Not that comes to mind, but we will find one, even if we have to cut down every tree in these woods." Ernst moved to the center of the men and called, "We need a landing zone, empty and flat. Search the area, call out if you find such a place. Someone needs to go to town and bring back every saw you can find. We may have to cut trees." The remaining men moved.

Their absence left a void, an eerie quiet, like a death vigil. Ian's shoulders slumped, and he hung his head, dejected. In constant prayer, he found no peace. The fragility of life became all too apparent, fleeting and delicate under the assault of bullet to bone.

Through the trees, Mack rode in on a horse lathered and winded. Ernst took the mare, soothing and encouraging her. Mack's steps were purposeful, eating up the distance between them. "I got through, made the call forty-five minutes ago. How is he?"

Ian shook his head, grim. "He's not good, Mack. The doctor is doing everything he can, but he needs surgery, and he's gone into shock. Esmeralda is with him."

Mack looked up at the sky. "I'm sure it's running through channels, but I called in a favor to expedite matters. They should be here any moment."

"The men are scouting a suitable landing site. I don't think he will survive transport in the back of a wagon."

Mack let a series of foul expletives loose. "I will burn down this whole forest if I have to because we are not losing another ben Todd brother, not today!"

Rexum's whistle broke the tension. "We've found a site!" Men's boots kicked up leaves as they rallied to the whistle with renewed hope.

"Does it require clearing?" Ian barked.

"One tree, and it's a monster," Rexum called. "Men, follow me we will make the site suitable. Send the Opie with the tools!"

Direct Orders

Ian wanted to fall to his knees in thanksgiving when he heard the medevac helicopter approach. A great cheer rose from the woods two hundred yards away.

"They are flying over us to land in Rephidim!" Mack barked. "Someone with a fresh horse, meet them and redirect them to the landing zone. Rexum, make sure the men have that site ready!" He abandoned his water warming duty and ran inside the enclosure.

Esmeralda looked up through the gloom with expectant hope, her white curly hair as wild as her eyes. "Are they here?"

"Yes, ma'am. We'll have him out of here in no time." He directed his statement to Thaddeus, "You hear me, ben Todd? Hang on!"

"Mack!" Esmeralda called after him. "Thank you."

Mack said over his shoulder, "You thank me when we get him on that bird and safely to the hospital."

He tore through the woods, prepared to lift the fallen tree by himself if he had to, then arrested where he stood, his mouth dropping in shock, unable to believe his eyes. The medevac flew over them at an altitude too high to land, its nose pointed east, back toward New York.

"What the—?" Mack pulled out his pistol and fired three shots, the reverberations echoing in the haunting stillness as the helicopter disappeared.

"Where are they going?" Ian cried, coming alongside Mack. "This has got to be a mistake!"

Mack's face contorted. "Somebody called 'em off!" He turned to the west, toward the New City, shaking his fist. "You wicked son of a whore! One of 'em wasn't enough for you, was it? You gotta kill 'em both? I will fucking destroy you for this, Korah. I swear to God!"

Then Mack ben Robert fell to his knees, silently weeping, his tears, like Thaddeus ben Todd's blood, seeping into the dirt of the Thyatira Woods.

Ian turned, resolutely striding back to the enclave. "We have to move him. We do not have a choice."

"What happened?" Esmeralda demanded.

Ian shook his head, unable to form the words. "I don't know, but the helicopter turned back."

"No." Esmeralda denied it, her hand covering her mouth. "They couldn't have! He is going to die, Ian."

Ian swallowed hard. "The Lord has Thaddeus in his hands, Esmeralda. We will do this—on faith."

In a helicopter, twenty miles outside of Rephidim, Agent Paul ben Casper heard the transmission: "Mission abort. Stand down. All units turn back."

Over the headset reserved for the inflight crew, Paul said, "Pilot, do not acknowledge."

"Sir, that was a direct order!"

"I am the lead agent on this mission. Proceed to our destination."

"You can't do that," Ken growled.

Paul turned. "Somebody has been trying to kill Director ben Todd and his fiancée for months, and this smells like a cover-up. Proceed to our destination, Pilot."

The agents on the aircraft stared at Paul in disbelief.

"Paul, you are putting all our asses on the line, not just yours."

"We're talking about a man's life here, Ken. My career, and yours, should be of secondary importance at this moment."

The pilot shook his head. "Negative, Agent. I can't put this bird on the ground. I've got a wife and two kids, and for all we know Director ben Todd's dead already, which is why they ordered us to abort. The best I can do is get you there."

"It will not do him any good if he is alive and you fly off and leave us in the middle of the woods," Paul snarled. "Are any of you men with me?"

All heads turned away.

Medic

In the enclave, Doctor ben Hagen bandaged Thaddeus' right arm to his body, securing it with Arachnid Weaving's finest, strongest cloth. The dressing would guard against jarring, and he hoped, prevent exsanguination during the treacherous transport back to town. Thaddeus' color, while still stark, lost some of its blue tint as the transfusions did their work.

"Wait!" Mack called, running in from the woods. "There is another bird in the sky."

"Oh, thank heavens!" Eve fell against the side of the rock, sagging with relief.

The doctor looked up, harried and sweating. "We've got him stabilized, but it's tenuous."

"You done good, Doc." Mack bobbed his head.

Out of stubbornness and the need to do something, the men of Rephidim had continued preparing the landing site, which was now clear of debris. A ring of fire marked the spot, and green wood billowed smoke signals into the sky. As the chopper hovered, sparks and ashes drove them backward, but they called down encouragement as the pilot descended.

A rappel line flew out of the side of the helicopter.

Mack swore at the top of his lungs, but his curses were lost in the operation's chaos. A lone soldier took his place on the seat of the aircraft, loaded with double packs. In a smooth practiced motion, he leapt from the helicopter, and rappelled to the ground.

Mack resisted the urge to fire as the helicopter took off, once again heading east. "What the hell is going on?" Mack shouted.

Paul removed his helmet and snarled, "They aborted. Command came in from the top, but I convinced them to drop me off. I'm a medic. Where is he?"

Mack gritted his teeth and growled, "This way."

"Are you Agent ben Robert?" Paul asked, handing Mack a pack, and tucking his helmet under his arm.

"I am."

"I've heard of you, sir." Paul followed Mack past the stunned and confused faces of the Rephidimites who could not believe a second helicopter just abandoned their friend. "I'm Paul ben Casper."

"We'll play nicey-nice later. Come on, the doc will appreciate an extra hand. We're moving him to town, and the two of you will need to keep him alive while we do it."

"That's why I'm here."

"Paul!" Esmeralda cried when he walked into the enclave.

Paul gave her a curt nod, taking in the scene with quick assessment. "What's the prognosis, Doc? I was a combat medic, here to assist."

"Do you have plasma in that pack?"

"You betcha!"

"Good, we need to get a unit in him before we do anything."

Paul unpacked his kit and handed the plasma to the doctor, who replaced the second depleted unit of blood.

"Let's step outside, so we can review."

In hushed tones, the country doctor confessed he had not performed surgery since his residency twenty-five years before. "I could not examine the actual wound, not in the field. The bleeding is currently under control, which allowed us to stave off imminent death from Hypovolemic Shock. That fresh plasma will help in coagulation, but with the least jostling, he could throw a clot."

Paul exhaled deeply. "At which point, he bleeds to death, strokes out, or has a heart attack."

Doctor ben Hagen eyed the wagon with distaste. "Exactly. If that happens on the back of that wagon there won't be a thing you or I can do about it."

Mack turned from his place near the entrance. He'd been listening. "We're not going to let that happen. Just tell me what I need to do."

Ian came by his side, silently concurring with Mack.

"Ernst, bring that wagon around. We're moving him," Doctor ben Hagen said, then went back inside to ready his patient.

Esmeralda sat beside Thaddeus, holding his uninjured left hand. "Doctor ben Hagen, can I have a moment before you move him? Mom, Dad, you stay. Hold the bags. Barton, stay put. I don't want him toppling over. I just need a second, okay?"

The doctor nodded.

Eve kissed her fingertips and pressed them to Thaddeus cold face. "I love you," she whispered, then accepted the reverend's arm and allowed him to escort her out of the shelter.

"Hey?" Esmeralda whispered near Thaddeus' ear, "I don't know if you can hear me, but I want you to know how much I love you, how much I have always loved you."

Her voice faltered, and she closed her eyes, willing herself not to weep. "It was supposed to be a surprise. I planned to tell you tomorrow night, but I think you need to know." Tears rolled down her cheeks, as she pressed her lips to his ear. "We're going to have a baby, Thaddeus. And our baby will need his father. You stay strong. Don't give up. You owe me a wedding night."

She was not sure if it was a trick of her eyes, or if it actually happened, but it did not matter because she held it close to her heart. Thaddeus ben Todd smiled beneath his oxygen mask.

One Accord

Half the village gathered in the clearing, holding hands and praying, as they watched the slow process of preparing Thaddeus for transport. His height complicated matters, so they fashioned two stretchers together to keep his legs stable. Dozens of blankets and quilts lined the bed of the wagon to provide the necessary cushioning during transport. Paul brought a portable oxygen generator that was far less bulky than the standard unit retrieved from the doctor's office.

With a final kiss, Esmeralda relinquished her place, leaving the men to accomplish the delicate task of conveying Thaddeus onto the stretcher. Claude stayed, suspending the critical IV fluids. Paul took charge of the transfer, having the most training and experience. Mack and Ian, also veterans, had done their share of lifting wounded men onto stretchers, but never one as delicate as Thaddeus. They recruited Olaf as the fourth man.

Paul took his place at the most critical area of the lift, Thaddeus' right arm and shoulder. He squinted at the fabric wrapped around Thaddeus' torso. "What is this? I've never seen anything like it."

Claude cleared his throat. "We make it here. I wove that piece, it will hold."

"Extraordinary..." Paul fingered the cloth. "Okay, men on the count of three. One, two, three!"

In concert, they lifted Thaddeus onto the stretcher. The doctor swooped in, checking his vitals, watching for the lethal river of blood.

All was well.

A collective sigh of relief echoed in the silent cave.

"All right, let's load him up," Paul directed.

Mack set his jaw and met each man's eyes. Unified in purpose, they lifted Thaddeus and made their way to the wagon where Hans and Barton waited to receive him.

Esmeralda pressed her praying hands over her lips, watching the careful progress. She could scarcely breathe; a falter or a misstep could kill him. By the grace of God, they loaded him without incident. In the light, his pallor was even more ghastly. Esmeralda choked off a sob and let Ian lift her into the back of the wagon.

Doctor ben Hagen and Paul shared a look, knowing they faced the impossible, saving Thaddeus' life in a country doctor's office. "Ernst, we're ready."

With Mack and Ian on either side of Thaddeus holding the IV bags, Esmeralda at his feet, and Doctor ben Hagen and Paul at his head, the wagon began its laborious trek through the woods.

"Wait," Mack breathed, soft and low. "Do you hear that?"

Paul looked up, a grin splitting his face. "That's a bird flying in."

Esmeralda held onto the side of the wagon, beseeching the sky.

Like an angel from heaven, a white helicopter appeared overhead and began its careful descent into the makeshift clearing. A cheer erupted from the crowd and a mass of humanity ran forward to wave them in. Ian exhaled a prayer, echoed by all.

Within moments, two medevac techs rushed from the helicopter which was blessedly on the ground. All of Rephidim cheered and escorted them toward the wagon amid jubilant praise and thanksgiving.

"Ernst," Doctor ben Hagen shouted over the noise, "get the horses to the edge of that clearing. Don't let them shy!"

"Blinders! Olaf, Barton, use your neck cloths!" With quick efficiency Barton and Olaf completed the task, and the nervous horses calmed.

The two medics reached the wagon just as they began moving. "Which of you is Agent ben Robert?"

"That'd be me." Mack looked between them. Before he loaded Thaddeus on that helicopter, he needed to make sure this wasn't more of Korah's shenanigans. "Where y'all from?"

"Prince Eamonn's Memorial Hospital, dispatched here to pick up a VIP."

"Who sent you?" Mack had his hand on his weapon, prepared to take out these two characters and highjack that helicopter.

The blond rescuer grinned. "The call came in from Prince Peter ben Korah himself. He said to give Agent Mack ben Robert a message when we arrived."

Mack looked at them warily. "What's the message?"

The Hispanic rescuer shook his head. "Didn't make any sense to me. He said to tell you, 'Happy Valentine's Day.'"

A thick knot lodged in Mack's throat. Valentine's Day was the day Mack rescued Peter from the Palace infirmary and drove him to safety at Pepperwood. It was Mack's last official act as Peter's head of security. "Well, enough."

"Prince Peter sent a helicopter?" Esmeralda's chin quivered. "He sent a rescue squad for Thaddeus?" She covered her mouth, overcome.

"Looks like he did. It sure does." Mack squeezed his temples with his free hand.

"Sir, not only did he send us in, but I understand specialists are coming in from all over the kingdom."

Ian closed his eyes and smiled.

Doctor ben Hagen looked like a thousand-pound weight had been lifted off his chest as he reviewed Thaddeus' vitals, recapping the treatment he administered in the field.

As the wagon closed in on the clearing, Mack took charge. "I'm getting on that medevac. I'll escort Esmeralda."

Paul nodded, and a silent understanding passed between them. They both recognized she should not be left unprotected.

"Ian, you stay here with Agent Paul. Get him settled in with the locals. Paul, I'm leaving this investigation with you. I guarantee the Palace will try to cover it up. Don't let 'em."

He shook Doctor ben Hagen's hand. "Thanks, Doc. Curly, kiss your Momma and Daddy. Let's go."

A brief goodbye, a careful loading, and they were off. With one major obstacle behind them, they all knew several more were yet to come.

Part 8 - Turning Point

November 9, 998 ME

Fear of Flying

As the helicopter lifted above the trees, Esmeralda had the absurd thought that Thaddeus was afraid of flying. It seemed critical to tell someone, but with her head spinning like the propeller, she could not seem to get enough air in her lungs to say anything. Her stomach clenched, as she grabbed Mack's knee and wheezed, "I'm going to be sick."

"Bloody Hell!" Mack exclaimed as she vomited crimson down the front of her tunic.

Warm blood and bile soaked her, and she pawed at it helplessly, wiping her mouth, bewildered

"Hey there!" the Hispanic paramedic said, going into action. "It's all right, miss. I've got you now."

Triggered!

Esmeralda slumped and the world slowed down. She heard her lungs struggling for air, felt flames of agony race up her side and explode in her chest. Frantic, she managed to say, "Baby… don't hurt the baby."

Mack looked at her with dawning horror. So focused on Thaddeus, no one noticed Esmeralda's ghostly pallor or shortness of breath, but bloody vomit was a sure sign of internal bleeding. When the paramedic lifted her tunic, Mack stifled a gasp. Her entire torso was distended and swollen, massive bruising covering the left side of her body.

"She was thrown from a horse," Mack said, watching in impotent fear as the paramedics worked.

The pilot radioed the hospital. They were bringing in not one, but two critical patients. ETA thirty-five minutes.

Waiting Room

The helicopter arrived with both patients alive. As they rushed Esmeralda and Thaddeus into surgery, Mack collapsed. A young nurse found him slumped in a chair. "Come with me, sir. Let's get you checked out."

Mack scowled, suspecting they were covering their asses and did not give a crap about their procedures or their liability risks. "I'm fine. Go away."

A few minutes later, another nurse came in, a hefty, middle-aged woman carrying a hand mirror. "Take a look at your face," she challenged in a thick Brooklyn accent.

He took the mirror, surprised to see crusted blood running from temple to shirt collar.

Nurse No-nonsense crossed her arms and said, "Your hands aren't any better. If you hit somebody in the mouth, those knuckles will get infected." She raised a thin, tweezed eyebrow at him. "Do you like your hands? You want to keep them?"

Mack examined them, detached. They were scraped, filthy, and cut. "I didn't even notice."

She shrugged. "Happens all the time, adrenaline." Then her voice softened. "There is nothing for you to do here except sit and worry. You may as well let us have a look at you."

"All right then," Mack capitulated, resigned to a bit of poking and prodding.

As he sat in the exam room, having his wounds debrided, he realized of the four who rode into Thyatira this morning, only Ian ben Kole escaped without a scratch on him.

Later, Mack fumbled with his phone, clumsy with his hands bandaged and sore. There were people to update, so he made the most difficult call first. Esmeralda left her phone with her parents, who were on their way to the hospital.

Claude answered, "Esmeralda, how is Thaddeus?"

"Sir, it's Mack ben Robert. We've made it to the hospital and Thaddeus is in surgery. However, while we were in the helicopter, Esmeralda also became ill. It appears she broke a rib in her fall, and it punctured a lung. She is also in surgery."

"Oh, my heavens. Is she all right?" Claude asked.

Mack could hear Julianna's frantic questions and 'I told you so's' in the background. He paused and let Claude relay the information.

"They took good care of her in the air ambulance, sir. I don't know anything further and won't until she comes out of surgery. I will send you the address of the hospital. I'm in the surgical waiting area on the fifth floor. I'll call you if I get any news before you get here."

When Mack hung up, he decided if Lavinia ever had a mother's intuition about Richard, he was going to listen to her. Julianna knew Esmeralda was hurt, and no one took her concerns seriously, including Esmeralda.

Mack dialed the second number.

"Greetings." Peter came on the line.

Mack sighed, "Thank you."

Peter laughed without humor.

They both knew who called off the first rescue team, but neither would mention it over an unsecured line, and Mack could not be certain if Peter was alone.

Feigning an ordinary exchange, Peter asked, "How is New York?"

"Iffy, but we'll see. They are in surgery, the bride and the groom, a hell of a thing." Mack fell back in his chair, spent.

"I have been contemplating a particular penthouse in Manhattan. They say it is a buyer's market, so I need to move fast," Peter said off-hand.

"If you're in danger, get out of there," Mack hissed.

"A change in scenery may be in order. It has grown warm here."

"Be careful. Don't let Nathan leave your side."

"Oh, indeed. I find the New City has lost its appeal at the moment. I hear there is a club opening in Manhattan that looks promising," Peter drawled, affecting the ennui of the ultrarich and bored. Then he disconnected the line without saying goodbye.

Mack stared at his phone, ashamed he ever bought into the false persona of Prince d'Or. His call for help inadvertently put Peter in danger, again. There would be fallout from the attack.

But in the helpless hours, watching his friend die by degrees, Mack vowed that Korah was going to find out exactly who he was messing with. Mack ben Robert was not about to let this incident pass without maximum retribution.

Following that train of thought, Mack dialed a number he had not called in a year and a half. After a series of transfers and a long wait, he said, "Sir, it's Mack ben Robert."

"Mack ben Robert? How is the wine business?" Sir Preston ben Worley asked.

"Quite well, and considerably less hazardous than my previous line of work." Mack's voice dripped with irony. "Though we have a situation. I understand you've taken Esmeralda ben Claude's case?"

"Indeed," Sir Preston affirmed.

"I was with Thaddeus ben Todd, on our way to his wedding, we were attacked in the woods outside of Esmeralda's hometown."

"Attacked?" Sir Preston asked.

"This has Korah's stink all over it."

Sir Preston made a low growling noise. "Where are you?"

"Prince Eamonn's Memorial. Thaddeus and Esmeralda are in surgery."

"How seriously are they injured?"

"Damn serious, Sir," he said, closing his eyes and filling Sir Preston in on the pertinent details, pleased Korah's greatest adversary was on their side.

After disconnecting, he contemplated the phone with mixed emotions. He longed to hear Lavinia's voice but could not force his fingers to dial her number. He preferred giving her upsetting news in person, tried to shelter and protect her as much as possible. In the muted quiet of the waiting room, he held the phone for a long time, then put it in his pocket and decided to wait until he had something concrete to tell her.

Esmeralda came out of surgery first.

"Are you Miss ben Claude's relative?" the surgeon asked.

"No, sir. I am a family friend. Her parents are on their way, and her fiancé is also in surgery." Mack pulled out his wallet, showing the surgeon his credentials. "What can you tell me?"

The surgeon glanced at the ID, pretending not to see the expiration date. The entire hospital buzzed with the news that Prince d'Or personally requested their assistance, hinting he may attend their next fundraiser should they grant his small request. The doctor had his eye on several pieces of very expensive equipment, so he decided to be as accommodating as possible. "The surgery went well. She sustained two fractured ribs, which we stabilized with titanium plates, and repaired a tear in her left lung. It was fortunate her lung collapsed while in the air ambulance, where they were able to treat the injury."

"How is the baby?" Mack asked with a sick foreboding.

The doctor shook his head. "It's too early to tell. The ultrasound revealed the fetus is six or seven weeks, but even under normal conditions a heartbeat at that gestational stage can be difficult to detect, so we cannot ascertain with any degree of certainty whether it survived. Her breathing and oxygen levels were severely compromised, and she sustained significant bruising to her pelvic and abdominal area, consistent with injuries from a fall."

Mack covered his mouth and closed his eyes, recalling that he boosted Esmeralda onto the saddle with Ian and remembered her gasp of pain when she landed on the pommel.

"There is spot bleeding, but that is to be expected. Time will tell, and I am not an obstetrician, but I suspect she may be on extended bed rest if the baby survives."

"Oh," was all Mack could say.

"Babies at that age are extremely resilient by design. We are monitoring them both. Unless infection kicks in Esmeralda will be fine. The baby is in the Iron King's hands."

Mack sent up a solemn prayer, his thousandth of the day. "May I see her?"

"She's in recovery now, where we will monitor her until she comes out of the anesthesia. If all goes well, we will move her to a room in a few hours, and you will be able to see her."

"Any word on how the other surgery is going?" Mack was half afraid to ask.

"I'll see if I can get someone to give you an update." The surgeon patted Mack's shoulder. "Hang in there, Agent. I understand they have flown in Dr. ben Sterling, the best vascular surgeon in the kingdom. And our team deals with gunshot wounds every day, so he's in good hands."

Mack closed his eyes and exhaled a shaky breath. At least now Thaddeus had a chance.

The Spider's Web

"Thank you for coming so quickly," Sir Preston said, accepting a glass of brandy with a brief nod.

"I was bored and thought perhaps you might have some interesting entertainment for me." Kayah ben Samuel raised her glass in salute before settling in her customary chair beside the ever-present fire burning in his study.

"Entertainment? Is that what you call it these days?" Sir Preston asked, narrowing his bushy eyebrows at her.

Kayah grinned. "It is preferable to conjugating French verbs, which I trust is not why you summoned me tonight."

Sir Preston scoffed. "There are eight-year-olds in the ghetto who have a better grasp of French than you."

"Hmm," Kayah studied her manicure idly, "I've told you before, if you wanted language skills you chose the wrong girl."

"Speaking of Lavinia," Sir Preston began, trying to illicit a reaction from Kayah, knowing she hated when he mentioned her friend, "I visited her husband in the hospital today."

Kayah frowned. "And why is Mack in the hospital?"

Sir Preston swirled his brandy, then took a fluttery sip, deliberately making her wait. "He was involved in an altercation with FBI Director Thaddeus ben Todd."

Kayah ran her tongue over her upper teeth, remembering a charged encounter with said FBI agent in a narrow hallway. "I thought they were friends."

"No, you misunderstand me, Kayah. They did not attack each other. They ran into trouble outside a small village in eastern Pennsylvania."

Kayah raised an eyebrow, knowing he misled her on purpose. Sir Preston never misspoke. "What sort of trouble?"

"The unsavory sort."

"Perpetrated by whom?" she asked, recognizing his mood, familiar with this particular game. She would have to pull every scrap of information out of him a piece at a time.

"An old adversary," Sir Preston replied.

"One of yours, I take it?" Kayah surmised half the people in Alanthia over the age of fifty were Sir Preston's adversaries, his long tentacles stretched everywhere.

He put his brandy snifter on the side table and folded his knobby, age-spotted hands. "I have a particular interest in the situation."

"I have no doubt," Kayah chortled. "Do tell, though, I find you have piqued my curiosity." Drawing her into an intrigue that involved a member of law enforcement deviated from their norm. Police officers came into the picture after she completed her assignment, never before.

"I would like you to kill Angelica ben Omri."

Kayah looked at him aghast. First, that he had spoken so forthrightly, and second that he suggested she assassinate the former Chief Justice of the Alanthian Supreme Court. "You have lost your mind, Old Man."

"Have I?" he countered, twirling the end of his moustache theatrically. "Don't accept, if you believe it is beyond your skill level."

"Please. You taught me better than to rise to such juvenile baiting. We both know my capabilities." She cocked her head, considering him. The assassination of such a high-ranking official was no ordinary job. He might be setting her up for a fall, perhaps cutting her loose as punishment for her little side activities and machinations. However, the challenge intrigued her. "I will consider it."

Sir Preston nodded, knowing how her mind worked. He rose on creaky bones, signaling an end to their meeting. "Agent ben Robert is at Prince Eamonn's Hospital... in the surgical waiting room."

Kayah walked to her car, considering that since she was twenty-three-years-old every time she left Sir Preston's townhouse, she felt like a butterfly who managed to escape the spider's web.

Macaroni and Cheese

Kayah found Mack, a bit worse for the wear, slumped over with his bandaged hands supporting his forehead. "Rough day?" she asked in a voice, sarcastic and droll.

Mack dropped his hands to his lap and turned. "What the hell are you doing here?"

"Visiting the sick." Kayah strolled into the empty waiting room.

Mack scowled, in no mood for Kayah's cat and mouse games. "You didn't call Lavinia, did you?"

Kayah shook her head. "No, a mutual friend mentioned you were here, so I figured I would come and offer some moral support."

Despite his weariness, he laughed at the absurdity of Kayah and morals in the same sentence.

"What's the news?" Kayah asked, pretending to care.

Mack yawned, loud and masculine, full of fatigue. "The surgeries went okay, and they are both in recovery. They are transferring Thad to ICU."

"Better than the morgue." She took in his pale complexion, caught a slight quiver in his hand. "Come on, you look like you need something to eat."

"It's been a hell of a day, Kayah. But you are right, I haven't eaten since breakfast." He looked down at his clothes and added, "Nowhere fancy, somewhere they won't mind that I'm covered in blood. I'm sure you know just the place."

She lifted her lip in a bratty sneer. "As a matter of fact, I do. I live about three blocks from here, and there's a place around the corner where everything is southern fried and dripping in grease. They serve something called collards, which look vile and smell even worse. I'm sure you'll love them."

"Collard greens are good, Kayah." He rose from his chair, groaning after sitting for so long. His ribs hurt, his hands stung, and at the mention of food, his stomach started trying to eat a hole in his backbone.

"I'll take your word on the collard greens. I get their macaroni and cheese, it is divine." Kayah winked.

"You don't strike me as a macaroni and cheese kind of gal."

"Oh, I ate my share of it growing up. I am somewhat of a connoisseur, and Ms. Mabe makes the finest in New York City. If I call her, she will save me a corner piece. I like the crispy edges."

"Kayah and edges, why does that not surprise me?" Mack drawled.

Before they left, he checked in with the nurses and learned there were no further updates on Thaddeus. He left a note for Esmeralda's parents, explaining that he stepped out for a bite and scribbled his number down with instructions to call if anything changed.

Thirty minutes later, Kayah unlocked the door to her townhouse and said, "The kitchen is through there." She motioned with her head, disarming the alarm.

Mack shifted the heavy takeout bag, smelling lemongrass cleaning products and diffused essential oils. As expected, the house was tastefully decorated, fashionable, and utterly sterile. Motion activated lights illuminated the floorboards and ceilings, accenting expensive silk plants and pottery. He felt as if he had stepped inside a model home, that at any moment an overly made-up real estate agent would appear, offer him a homemade chocolate chip cookie, and invite him to look around.

Setting the food on the counter, he noticed the only personal touch in sight, a painting of Kayah, Himari, and Lavinia at Himari's wedding. The artist was unmistakably Filippo ben Vincente. It pulled him across the room, like iron to a magnet.

With his body aching, covered in dried blood, and starving, he allowed the memory of that night to surround him, recalling just how beautiful his wife looked wearing that red dress, strolling down the hall at the RMA like a vision.

And later, he had laid her down and loved her, conceiving their precious son. Of all the days in his thirty-eight years on Earth, that one ranked in the top five.

Kayah moved to his side. "We had fun that night, or rather, you did."

"I don't suppose I ever thanked you." He turned to face her. "In retrospect, tonight isn't the first time you've sought me out on the orders of that wily old bastard, is it?"

"I wouldn't have done it, either time, if I didn't want to." Kayah did not bother to deny it. "He has his reasons. I have mine."

Mack wandered back to the food. "Lord have mercy, let me eat before we go digging around in either of your brains."

Kayah took down two plates from her cabinet and offered Mack one. "He knows Lavinia's value, and he has had his eye on her for years. I figured she might have some fun with you that night." She pointed a finger at him, quirking an eyebrow. "I've done my best to keep her out of his clutches. I know you've done the same."

Mack bit into a chicken leg and moaned. "You're damn Skippy. I don't want him anywhere near her. Lavinia does not even know his name, and I plan to keep it that way."

Kayah dished up her plate and said, "Good policy. She's not suited for Sir Preston's sort of games."

"Alas, what does it say about us, that we are?" Mack gave her a dreamy smile, savoring his mashed potatoes.

Kayah shrugged and cast a dubious eye at the double container of collard greens. Taking a tiny bite, she grimaced. "Those are as disgusting as I thought they would be."

"Oh, you just don't know good food." To prove his point, Mack shoveled a gloppy bite.

"Not true," she said, raising a fork loaded with a crispy edge of macaroni and cheese, "this is fabulous."

He dug into her container and helped himself, nodding with a grin.

They stood at the island, eating in companionable silence. While not enemies, they were not friends. However, they shared a love of Lavinia, and in that, Mack supposed, they were united. Kayah did not come around often, and tonight was the first time he said more than a dozen words to her, but he appreciated the food and could not deny it was nice to step away from the hospital.

"Where are you staying?" Kayah asked as she rinsed their plates.

Mack rubbed his forehead. "I haven't even thought about it. We stayed at Thaddeus' last night, but all my stuff was in a saddle bag, which I suppose is lost somewhere in the Thyatira Woods."

"You're welcome to stay here. You are going to need some clothes, though. You've got so much blood on you, you look like a murderer."

Mack raised a brow, stifling the immediate smart-ass comment that she would know. But in the face of her generous offer, that seemed rude, and he had been raised better. "I might take you up on that. Those plastic chairs leave a bit to be desired, and I have no idea where Thaddeus' keys are."

"There's a souvenir shop around the corner. I think they have t-shirts, hats, that sort of thing. I'll go pick you up a couple of things while you shower. The washing machine is through there, and there are towels in the spare bedroom upstairs." Kayah picked up her purse. "Make yourself at home."

"Why are you doing this, Kayah?" Mack asked.

She shrugged a shoulder. "Lavinia."

Mack let out a long slow breath as the exhaustion of the day caught up with him. "I need to call home, and she's going to freak out."

"Then don't tell her, not until you get home."

Mack hung his head. "That's just it. I won't be going home for a while."

"Then I suggest you do it sooner rather than later. I'll be back in a bit, then you can tell me what happened." There was an edge to Kayah's voice that Mack did not understand.

Mack watched her leave, struck anew by what a complicated woman she was.

What's the Deal?

An hour later, Kayah curled her legs under her rump and tucked a soft throw over her lap. The night had turned chilly, but she could not abide central heat, so she kept her townhouse on the cold side.

Mack laid on the sofa, sporting a new hoodie and sweats, looking like an advertisement for New York City. As he relayed the events of the day, she could not fathom why Sir Preston took such an interest.

"What about Endor? What was that place?"

"I don't know, we're going to have to ask Esmeralda. Her momma and daddy can probably shed some light on the subject, but I did not want to interrogate them as soon as they walked through the door. They were shook up."

Kayah plumped a pillow behind her back and settled in. "No doubt, it's not every day a war erupts in your backyard, especially for a bunch of bumpkins. I bet they freaked out."

"That's the thing, Kayah, they didn't, and they aren't bumpkins, not like you'd expect. There are still a few of these isolated communities around. They live a different life, but I'm not inclined to say it's bad. The way they hung together and got the job done reminded me a lot of Shechem, the place I grew up. And we would have been in a world of hurt if they hadn't come out to fight." Mack shook his head, looking grim. "I was down to fifteen bullets."

Kayah pressed her lips into a smile. "I'd take you and fifteen bullets over a bunch of jihad assholes."

Mack acknowledged the compliment with a nod of thanks.

"But why did they attack, and why would Korah intervene?"

Mack narrowed his eyes. "I don't know, but I aim to find out."

November 10, 998 ME

Not the Wedding Day We Imagined

Esmeralda swam to the surface of consciousness, aware her parents were in her room. Her mother alternated between crying, soothing Esmeralda's forehead, and lamenting she had known something was wrong and everyone ignored her. With nowhere for her anxiety to settle, she fixated on Claude, who promised a dozen times that he would never dismiss her woman's intuition again.

"I'm okay, Mom. How's Thaddeus?" Esmeralda asked. Through the veil of lingering anesthesia and pain medication, Esmeralda rejoiced at the news—all three of them survived.

When she woke again in the wee hours of Saturday morning, she saw her mother had fallen asleep. Turning to her father, she said, "Take me to see him."

It took quite a bit of cajoling before Claude relented, but he knew her well enough to realize that she would not rest until she saw for herself that Thaddeus was alive.

As Claude wheeled her down the corridor, she sensed the desperation flowing out of some of the rooms. To Esmeralda, their fear smelled musky, pulsing putrid green energy that reeked of industrial antiseptic and sickness. But in others, she sensed life, hope, and healing. She prayed as they went that the latter was what she would find once they reached Thaddeus' room.

"He's stable," the night nurse reassured them. "That's good news."

Esmeralda looked down the hallway at the open door, suddenly afraid to see him. It was irrational, but it felt safe outside. "Has he awoken?" Esmeralda asked.

"No, not yet, but that is not unusual, especially after a six-hour surgery. You can go in, but just for a few minutes."

Claude placed a hand on her uninjured shoulder and squeezed.

All fear evaporated the moment she saw him, precious Thaddeus. Mindful of the lines, IV's, and monitors, Esmeralda slipped her hand underneath his. His skin felt blessedly warm, the blue hue gone, yet his face remained pale. "Hey there, Tin Man," she whispered. "How are you feeling?"

The monitors beeped with monotonous regularity, lights flashed, and numbers changed with each heart beat and breath, but he was alive and that was all that mattered. "You gave me quite a scare. I thought getting shot in the shoulder was no big deal. They use it in books all the time, I guess you showed us." She sniffed back a tear and gave him a watery smile. "Mom and Dad are here and so is Mack, but he's gone to get some sleep which I think we all need." Her insides shook, fluttery with fatigue. "I just wanted to come and see you, to make sure you were okay. It was supposed to be our wedding day." Esmeralda's voice caught.

Thaddeus' hand twitched over hers, then he curled his fingers for just an instant. Their connection sparked, and Esmeralda knew everything was going to be all right.

Ghost Town

Agent Paul ben Casper followed Ian ben Kole and Ernst ben Otto through the Thyatira Woods on a reconnaissance mission. Instead of celebrating a wedding, the residents of Rephidim fortified their village, armed themselves, and buried the dead. Most believed the imminent danger from Endor had past, others were not sure, but no one harbored a false sense of security. They knew how evil operated; it never stopped.

Once they got Thaddeus on the helicopter, Paul worked with Doctor ben Hagen, tending the injuries of the men involved in the battle. The stories that emerged curled Paul's toes. The residents did not parse words about who or what attacked them, nor did they stammer, hedge, or otherwise sugarcoat the power and wickedness that resided in Endor.

Paul rode out early that morning to obtain a cell signal, and when he spoke to Mack, he realized the former Royal Guard did not mince words either. "Paul, there is one thing you can be certain of, the Palace will do everything possible to bury what happened yesterday. Conduct your investigation, but don't be surprised if your report never sees the light of day."

As they crept through the underbrush, Paul came to terms with what this was probably going to cost him. If Mack's prediction came true and they scuttled the investigation, it would not matter what he found down here, and jumping out of a helicopter, against direct orders, was going to carry consequences. He hoped delivering the plasma that saved the Director's life would mitigate whatever disciplinary action faced him back in New York, but he had a sinking feeling it was not going to go well for him.

He now understood Thaddeus and Esmeralda's reluctance to tell him what happened when Esmeralda was attacked in New York and New Orleans. Spoken aloud, it seemed crazy that a witch had come after a librarian from a small rural village. Yet, she sustained injuries in all three attacks, the violence and severity escalating, the undertones becoming more sinister.

Even after speaking to the villagers, he could not pin down exactly what happened, but he planned to follow the evidence, no matter where it led him or how many enemies it made. That was the oath he took when he joined the FBI, to seek the truth and uphold the law. And even if he was the only one who believed he did the right thing, he slept with a clear conscience.

The trio did not talk as they rode. Paul was not sure if it was his imagination, but the closer they got, the thicker the woods became. The trees looked old and ominous, and he imagined faces contorted in torment in the swirling bark of the live oaks. Shadows seemed to move and lengthen without a source, pressing in with malevolent doom. He kept looking over his shoulder, unable to shake the disconcerting feeling they were being watched, though they never encountered anyone, and any noise they investigated turned out to be nothing more than a bird or a squirrel.

Tying their horses at a safe distance, Ernst led them to the edge of the burned-out village. At first, Paul thought the noise coming from Endor was a chainsaw. He scanned the area, expecting to find felled trees, evidence of a fortification being built. But the town lay still, and the sound was not coming from a chainsaw, rather a massive swarm of flies.

Dozens of dead bodies littered the abandoned square.

They moved closer, and Paul swore, covering his nose with a borrowed Rephidim knit muffler. The stench was vile. "It does not look like anybody is here."

"It smells like a battlefield." Ian took his cue from Paul and pulled his turtleneck over his nose and mouth.

Ernst grunted. "The perfume of the devil. I know it well. *Ist* not the first time I have smelled that stench in Endor. We buried the bodies, all those years ago, after the fire." With a nod, he indicated an open field, taken over by tall weeds. "But we did not put them in the cemetery. They did not deserve to be buried with—" His face clouded with old pain, and he swallowed hard. "They did not deserve to be buried with the righteous."

"How long ago was that?" Paul asked, noticing the cemetery was tended, unlike the rest of the overgrown village.

"More than thirty years." Ernst looked down at the ground, a defeated slump to his shoulders. "This has her fingerprints all over it. I know the way she works. She used these people to do her dirty work, and when the wrath came down, she fled as she did the last time. I can guarantee, we will not find Angelica ben Omri's body among the dead."

Paul choked back a cough. "Did you just say, Angelica ben Omri?"

Ernst turned with his eyes blazing, daring Paul to contradict or argue with him. "I most certainly did. I have firsthand experience with that evil witch. It has been a long time since she ruled here, but I know her true face. This was her… the Mistress," he snarled. "That is the name she went by, but I know her true name."

Dawning understanding crashed in on Paul, and he shook his head, realizing just how much trouble he was going to be in back in New York. "That is why the Palace is covering this up."

Ernst frowned, shaking his head. "There are other reasons, though they are hidden and dark. Prince Korah ben Adam is no stranger to Endor. He will not want anyone digging here, literally or figuratively. I realized that the moment the helicopter turned back." A haunted look passed over his features, and he said, "You boys can investigate. I have seen enough."

Ian turned to Paul, his eyes narrowed to slits. "There is great evil emanating from this place. I'll go up with you, but we don't need to linger, and I'm not touching anything."

Paul nodded, staring at the black cauldron in the center of the square. "Nobody is going to believe this."

Ian looked at the ground, his tone resigned. "I know exactly how that feels. Come on, Agent, let's get this over with."

Campfires and Canvas

In a dusty camp, four thousand miles away, darkness began to fall. A pilgrim girl wove her way through the tents, counting as she went, two rows over and five back. She paused outside a patched beige one and called a tentative greeting, "Hello? Is anybody home?"

The flap opened and a girl smiled. "Hello."

"Hi. I'm Astrid. Your mom asked me to come by and introduce myself. She said we were about the same age and that you needed a friend." The corner of her mouth lifted as the two girls shared an embarrassed grin about meddling mothers. "Would you like to come and listen to some music with me?"

"Music?"

Astrid gestured toward the community campfire. "Sure. Every night we hangout before meeting. Ethan and some of the other guys play. He's great, the rest of them…" she shrugged. "Do you like music?"

"I do," the girl said, extending a hand. "I'm Davianna ben David. It's nice to meet you, Astrid."

November 12, 998 ME

Private Room

Thaddeus decided no one ever slept in the hospital. Between the constant carousel of nurses, doctors, orderlies, technicians, food service personnel, and housekeepers, he barely found a ten-minute stretch where someone was not coming in his room. Even when they gave him a half hour of peace, the incessant beep of the monitors drove him mad. "This is not exactly the honeymoon suite I had in mind."

The corner of Esmeralda's mouth lifted. "Don't knock it, you have no idea how much effort it took to get us in the same room."

Thaddeus swallowed painfully, his throat still raw from the intubation tube. He felt like shit. "How did you manage it?"

Esmeralda yawned, wincing at the stab of pain in her ribs. "You can thank Mack for that. I think he pulled some strings."

"He is my best man," Thaddeus said dryly. "Remind me to thank him."

"Don't thank me," Mack said, materializing in the doorway, "thank him."

Prince Peter ben Korah entered the room, wearing a superbly tailored charcoal suit and his famous smile.

Esmeralda gasped, her uninjured hand flying to her wild mass of curls. Half in love with the Prince for the last five years, she was mortified to meet him while lying in a hospital bed, dressed in an abominable mint green gown that made her look ghastly. Her cheeks flamed, and she fought down the urge to pull the covers over her head and hide.

"Director ben Todd, it is a pleasure to meet you." Peter bowed formally, then turned to a crimson faced Esmeralda. "Miss ben Claude, please accept my sincere apologies for dropping in unannounced and disturbing your evening."

Mack nodded to Peter's contingent of bodyguards and closed the door.

"My Esteemed," Thaddeus cleared his throat, "thank you for coming. I understand I owe you a great debt of thanks."

Peter inclined his head, acknowledging the sentiment. "Director, I believe the debt is still mine to discharge for the brave sacrifice your brother made in the service to my family and the kingdom."

Their eyes met across the hospital room, and an understanding passed between them, unspoken but concrete. There was one person to blame for Richard's death, the same person who abandoned Thaddeus and left him to bleed to death in a stone enclave—Korah.

Esmeralda watched the interplay, recovering by degrees from the shock of finding Peter ben Korah in her hospital room. She mustered the courage to look at him, expecting Prince d'Or to shimmer gold but was shocked by the reality. He radiated green, like burning copper, bright and hot, but there was darkness in him, a black stain, as if he had been tainted and touched by evil, similar to what she witnessed in Persa and Beau. Knowing what she did of the attacks on him, it should not have surprised her, but it did. Somehow, it made him seem more human, though he was still magnificent. And up close, he was truly the most beautiful man Esmeralda ben Claude had ever seen.

"My Esteemed," to her horror, her voice squeaked as she stuttered, "thank you... for, for what you did, s-s-sending the helicopter." She blinked back a sudden rush of tears.

Peter did not bat an emerald eye at her stammering. "You are most welcome. I simply regret the circumstances of your rescue."

Esmeralda offered her free hand, fortifying herself for the onslaught.

Peter took it, and Mack watched with a knowing expression. Thaddeus was not quite sure he liked the Prince holding Esmeralda's hand, knowing she had a crush on him.

A spark of electricity crackled in the air, the hospital room faded away, and she felt the vision take her to the dark chamber below the Palace. She knew this place, knew what they did here.

"Seize him!" the Witch ordered.

Black-robed figures fell on the Prince. He fought and cursed them, but through sheer force of numbers, they overcame him. Through his eyes, she stared straight into the face of her enemy, her nemesis, and his.

"Angelica ben Omri did this, my Esteemed." Esmeralda's voice seemed to echo in the sterile hospital room.

Peter's face turned thunderous, and he squeezed her hand. "How do you know that?"

"I have seen her. I know what she does." Esmeralda felt a surge of his power run up her arm. It was deadly calm, determined. Fortified, she stared him straight in the eyes and said, "And we are going to destroy her."

"Which is why I brought the Prince here today." Mack looked between them, lying in hospital beds instead of the Hamptons, enjoying their honeymoon. "Thaddeus, Esmeralda, welcome to The Resistance."

Part 9 - Epilogue

January 27, 1000 ME

Better Than Crunches

Ensconced in the master bedroom of the Lenox mansion, thirty hours into their long-anticipated reunion, Beau Landry toyed with a strand of Alaina ben Thomas' damp hair, twirling it around his finger, admiring the play of light on the strands of gold, pale yellow, and brown. He brought it to his lips and said, "It's darker than it used to be."

Alaina harrumphed. "It happens. I stopped coloring it last year when I semi-retired."

"Retired?" Beau chuckled. "What are you now, twenty-five?"

Alaina rolled to her side, a half-smile on her freshly scrubbed face. "Flattery will get you almost anything." He knew good and well that she turned twenty-eight last month.

Beau growled low and deep. "I must remember that."

"Good." She kissed his cheek. "What do you say we sneak off to the kitchen? I'm hungry."

"It's from all that exercise, *chèr*," Beau said, flashing her a riverboat pirate's grin.

"Better than crunches." Alaina snuggled into his arms, their skin still dewy from the shower. "I hate crunches, I did five hundred a day, six days a week, more the weeks I shot swimsuits or lingerie."

Beau ran a hand over her flat stomach and murmured, "It shows. Your body is so beautiful, Jolie Catin." Her muscles quivered under his touch, and she made a faint mew of pleasure. Her lips parted as his hand continued its slow drift, skimming over her blonde curls, landscaped and manicured for swimsuit modeling. "Can I touch you?"

She answered, pressing into him. "Yes, touch me."

Beau traced a single finger down the golden path, gently coaxing. "So nice," he crooned, watching her face grow hazy with desire. "You like that?" He petted her in long, slow strokes as Alaina moved, responding with a feminine sound of affirmation. Beau grinned at her rapturous expression and added a second finger, circling the sensitive apex. Her breath caught, her gorgeous lips parted, eliciting little panting noises as he teased

"*C'est bon, ma chère fille,*" Beau said, enraptured and aroused. He slid a finger inside, and she arched. "*Ma belle fille,* that's right."

He felt the spasms begin. She threw her head back, exposing her lovely, long neck. He did not take his eyes off her as he brought her to climax, reveling in the slick wetness of her soft quivering folds, perfect and precious under his hand.

"Beau," she gasped, laughing as she finished. "That is definitely better than crunches."

He chuckled. "Unlike the runway, *Bébé,* I'll feed you. *Allons,* let's get you some food."

A slow, lazy smile of contentment spread across her face. "Sex and food… I have died and gone to Heaven."

He gazed upon her beautiful, sated face. "*Comme je l'ai,* Jolie Catin." As have I, pretty baby doll.

As they walked together through the darkened house, Alaina stifled a giggle. "I feel like a teenager, sneaking around a mansion we have no business being in."

"I think your style was grand theft auto, not breaking and entering, right?" he teased.

"Shut up," she laughed. "I wonder if they ever found that car."

"I'm sure somebody found it, whether it ever made it back to it's owner, I can't say, but they never came looking for you."

The corner of her mouth ticked in a smile. "I've somehow managed to avoid being arrested."

"You're too pretty to go to jail."

She looked down, sadness crossing her face. "I've known a couple pretty girls who went."

"Ugh, *mon Dieu*, that's depressing."

She shrugged but changed the subject. "This house is amazing," she said, admiring the carved Spanish archway they passed through.

"*Grandpere* bought it in the 50s for a song, but that's his way. It's where the family stays when we come to the New City. *Maman* spent the most time here in recent years."

"She has?" Alaina eyed him with intense speculation. "I did not know that."

Beau glanced at the ceiling, avoiding Alaina's eyes. His mother had been here the night he and Alaina disappeared into the bayou. She was in town attending Joanna ben Luke's pitch to start the Center for Street Kids of Alanthia. In the intervening years, her absence that night haunted mother and son as they wondered if he would have lapsed into such impenetrable darkness if Sarah had been on hand. Would Ian and Joanna have met, if his mother was not here, if Lenox had not given the grant? They were questions Beau pondered more than he ever admitted, and in his darkest hours he wondered, if given the chance, would he trade the lives and futures of hundreds of kids the Center saved in exchange for the years he lost? He liked to think he would, but he was not entirely certain.

Exerting a strength of will and a firm determination not to let the past intrude on the present, Beau shook off the tangle of "what if's" and answered Alaina's question. "Yes, she's been here often through the years, mainly on Foundation business. She attends fundraisers and charity auctions, though she and Grandpere have passed most of those responsibilities on to me."

Alaina took his arm. "You are running the Foundation?"

He shrugged, gauging her reaction because there were still things he had not told her. "I have been involved for several years, but I am transitioning into more of an official role lately."

"So, you spend your days giving away money?" Alaina asked, charmed.

Thoughts of the difficult meeting he had with Ian and Joanna yesterday came to mind, but he quipped, "For the most part, but I'm good at it, chèr. I enjoy giving it away, though it always seems to come back. Money has a way of finding me." He gave her a rueful smile and added, "I started with the veterans."

"A worthy cause," she said, tilting her head, her expression soft.

"It is."

Alaina froze as they rounded a corner. "Look! That's a Filippo ben Vincente."

Beau followed her gaze. "One of many, chèr. Maman took a liking to his work some years ago." He walked with her toward the huge oil, studying it.

Alaina grinned, reaching out to touch the wooden frame. "I know where he painted this. That's the view from the balcony of our first apartment." Her expression became wistful with remembrance. "He doesn't paint this way anymore. But even if I did not recognize the scene, I would know this is some of his early work. You can tell by the colors."

"They're dark," Beau observed.

The corner of Alaina's mouth lifted. "He used a lot of purple."

He wrapped his arms around her waist and rested his head on her shoulder. "Something significant about purple?"

"Yeah. He was falling in love with Himari, but he didn't know it, neither did she." She snuggled in his embrace. "I did though."

"They were good to you? Filippo took you in."

"He did," Alaina laughed. "Himari was our neighbor, and we were all sort of a mess. Those two got me drunker than I have ever been, and we went dancing a lot. Himari taught me how to hack, and Filippo," she sighed and swallowed hard, "changed my life. He's the best friend I ever had. You know he took Serendipity?"

Beau turned her in his arms. "I do know that," his lips hovered above hers, "because I have it."

Alaina drew back. "You have what?"

Beau raised an eyebrow, his mouth turning up at the corner. "The original."

"What?" She stared at him aghast. "Beau, the original sold for two million shekels! The buyer purchased it anonymously."

He smiled, slightly chagrined. "It's hung in your study these last nine years. It kept your presence there... at home."

Alaina covered one eye with her delicate fingers, her chin trembling. "You've had it all these years, and I never knew."

"I looked at it every day," he whispered.

"I hoped," she sniffed. "I hoped you had not forgotten me."

He gave her a rueful, sad smile. "Not for a moment, Jolie Catin. Never."

Tracing his eyebrow with her fingernail, she said, "Jorge wrote to me over the years. Did you know?"

"No. He didn't tell me."

She patted his cheek, and they resumed their slow stroll toward the kitchen. "He took me to dinner, twice, the last time about eighteen months ago."

Alarm bells sounded in his brain. "Eighteen months ago?"

She gave him a sidelong look, her expression inscrutable. "He popped up every time I was about to lose faith."

Had it been his mother, that was in character, but his father surprised him. The timing of their last visit made him cringe. Eighteen months ago... his last bad episode. "Well then, I suppose I owe *Papa* a debt of gratitude." Beau squeezed her hand and confessed, "Our years apart were not pretty for me."

"He told me." Alaina looked down at their bare feet, her pink toenails glimmering in the shadows.

Beau cleared his throat and ran his fingers through his hair, still damp from the shower. "Not necessarily something I'm terribly proud of."

"I'd have come. I wanted to." Alaina took his shirt in her fists. "But your father, convinced me not to." Tears pooled in the corners of her eyes. "He promised me, though, if you ever started to fall in love with someone else, he would call me." She hid her face, crying for the loneliness, the wasted years, and the invisible prison that kept her away.

Bone deep shame swamped him. He had caused her so many tears. *"Mo chagren."* He stood with his arms hanging loosely at his sides. "Alaina, there was never going to be anyone but you.

"I kept a calendar where I marked off the days. I told myself, six months, pull it together for six months, then I'd call you. I almost made it... several times. Then it would find me."

She met his eyes, her own were red with tears.

"It would drag me back, and I wouldn't know day from night, reality from delusion, and I'd be lost again. How could I ask you to live like that, Jolie Catin? I couldn't," he sighed. "I just couldn't."

Alaina did not break eye contact, as she said, "In sickness and in health, 'til death do us part." She cupped his cheek. "Beau, I love the whole man, all of you. If it was your body fighting a chronic disease, I would not leave. I would stand by your side, but you have to let me stay."

Beau wiped his eyes and glanced away. She was right. It was a disease, a weakness of the mind that found and attacked him. However, something changed after his last bad episode, culminating the night the Devil dropped by.

He had clarity.

For more than a decade, he battled hidden memories, but now he knew the truth, and indeed, the truth set him free. He might even be cured. He managed to pull together eighteen months of check marks, triple the number he originally held himself to. Only then did he have the strength to try, to trust himself. "I'll let you stay. I promise."

February 8, 1000 ME

A Lagniappe - Mill House Beach

Beau led Alaina from the Mill House Beach living room, her Uncle Boudreaux tale spinning in his brain like a top. Employing his customary sardonic bravado in front of their housemates, he held it together. But her bombshell left him feeling exposed, as if insanity waited around the corner, ready to pounce if he made one wrong move, and if he snapped, he wanted to do it in private. But he promised he would not banish her if it came after him again, and tonight, right now, was the first real test.

He thought he was done dealing with the fall out. But walking down the hall with Alaina in tow, he feared he had only scratched the surface. The last bad episode, the one he tried to convince himself was simply a delusion, came roaring back with vivid clarity, and he realized there was truth in that night because he had reenacted large parts of he and Alaina's kidnapping with Esmeralda ben Claude by his side. In some ways that night with Esmeralda had been more terrible than the battlefield, worse than the night Charlotte kidnapped he and Alaina, because he was too weak to defend himself.

He closed the door behind them, praying for strength.

Alaina shivered and moistened her lips, looking frightened as the blood drained from her face. "I shouldn't have told you. I knew it!" She took him by the shoulders. "You are not okay. I can see it."

Beau drew in a ragged breath, closed his eyes, and willed his body to calm. With a lifetime of practice, he ordered his heart to stop pounding and overcame the shaking in his limbs.

When he opened his eyes, she saw he was still present. He had not lapsed into that catatonic nightmare she feared above all else. She would rather fight that damn witch and her evil spawn, naked and unarmed, than see that blank look on his face again.

"I remember now." Beau looped his hands behind her back. "I'm all right. Don't be afraid. We just kicked down a door, and a few skeletons spilled out."

"Skeletons," Alaina laid a gentle hand on his cheek, seeing a flash of the witch's evil makeup, "are scary."

Beau's lips pressed in a grim line. "They are dangerous, too. I been all full of piss and vinegar 'bout how I was going to take those two out, like I would just march in there with guns blazing, and that would be the end," he scoffed and gestured toward the pair of armchairs. "Let's sit down."

Alaina settled in her chair, and he moved to open the sliding glass door a crack. The air was frigid, but the sound of the vast Pacific reminded him there was a power greater than himself. He turned and asked, "Do you remember what a *lagniappe* is, *chèr?*"

Alaina drew her brows down, thinking. "It's about shopping, isn't it? Like ordering a dozen eggs and getting thirteen?"

Beau nodded. "It means a little extra, something more than you were expecting." He rubbed his hands over his face, controlling the urge to straighten the quilt on the bed or move the lamps into perfect symmetry on the matching nightstands. The compulsion scared him almost as much as what he was about to tell her.

"What's a *lagniappe* have to do with anything, Beau?" Alaina asked, on the edge of her chair. His demeanor frightened her.

Beau forced himself to relax and sat down, resting his arms loosely on the chair. "I suppose, I got one with your story." He met her eyes, feeling resigned, but lucid. "A bit of a surprise, a little something extra."

"I don't understand." Alaina brought a knee up to her chest and turned sideways in her chair, facing him.

"When we first got back together, you told me my father came to see you eighteen months ago." Beau looked down at his lap. "What did he tell you?"

Alaina blinked, knowing she walked precarious ground here. Jorge's visits and calls were done behind Beau's back, so she chose her words carefully. "He called me one night and asked me to pray. A couple weeks later, he took me to dinner."

Beau leaned forward and straightened the comforter, then stopped himself. "Did he tell you I was back in the hospital?"

Alaina nodded.

"My last bad episode... I suppose I went out with a bang," Beau quipped, though there was no dancing humor in his eyes. "I spent six months in the hospital, and it wasn't entirely voluntary. Our lawyers cut a deal... to keep me out of jail."

"Your father didn't tell me that." Alaina kept her voice steady, refusing to shy away. If he was going to open up, she would not hide. Sarah Landry wouldn't.

Beau tilted his head, appreciating his father's discretion. "According to the law, I assaulted my *maman*, threatened an officer with a deadly weapon, and abducted a woman. Unfortunately, she was the fiancée of an FBI Director, who is the man I threatened to kill, before throwing his wife into Uncle Boudreaux's boat, and driving off with her."

"Mon Dieu." Alaina's eyes widened. "I suppose you did get in trouble."

Beau chuckled ruefully. "In some ways yes, but in others?" He shook his head. "They didn't have much of a case, and they knew it, not in criminal court. Now the doctors… they did. That's why we agreed to the six months of inpatient rehab. In a strange way, it saved me. I wouldn't be here if it wasn't for that night."

"How?" Alaina could not comprehend how something that terrible could have led to their reunion.

Beau rubbed the stubble on his jaw, suddenly missing his beard. "It was the catalyst for my recovery. Up to that point, it was a daily struggle. I called it white knuckling because I held on through sheer force of will, but it was always looming in the background. That night, it came out of the shadows and attacked."

"What attacked, Beau?"

Beau sighed through his nose and said, "For the last eighteen months, I did what I always do, I took an experience I could not explain and pushed it away. I told myself it was just a delusion, a figment of my imagination."

He tapped his temple and smiled. "There are some scrambled eggs in here. But when you were telling what happened to us in the bayou, I remembered all of it. But I also realized it happened a second time."

"She took you again?" Alaina covered her mouth in horror.

"It was different," he said with a frown. "You gonna think I'm crazy." He rose from the chair, went to the nightstand, and adjusted the lamp.

Alaina did not comment but noticed when he got agitated he organized objects. "Beau, in the last few months,

I have seen things and learned things I can't explain. On screen, I watched a car disappear right before my eyes, twice. We fought a computer that could think, speak, and learn. I know for a fact, Peter and the rest of them were at your house, and the next moment were in New York. There is not much you can say that will make me believe you're crazy because, *mon loup*, if you are, then so am I."

Beau turned, the corner of his mouth twitching, "Damn, *chèr*, we are crazy."

Alaina snorted, "We live in a crazy time and do our best to deal with it."

"Apparently, I haven't dealt with it too good. The rest of you didn't end up in the hospital."

"The rest of us did not go through what you went through," she countered.

He nodded, thinking she sounded very much like his mother. "So back to the *lagniappe*. I'm just going to tell it, stop dancing around, face the giants as they say."

"Go ahead."

"The first time Charlotte came after us, she took us physically. It happened in this world, in the dimension we are standing in right now. The second time she came after me, she did it in the spirit world, which, based on that night, seems to run parallel with this one. I don't understand it, but it is the truth. It's something I've never been able to wrap my head around, that I've stepped through the veil into that place and seen things I couldn't explain. The strange thing is, in my last bad episode, I was not in there alone."

"All right," she said slowly.

"I was up at Landry's for Sarah Beth's birthday. Ian and Joanna sent their operations manager for the New York Center down to meet with us, that's the FBI Director's wife, Esmeralda. I was having a bad day, but I promised Ian I'd introduce them, and *Maman* was all over me, so I went. I suppose it saved my life, though I couldn't see it at the time or even in the months after, because from the outside looking in, the evening was a disaster."

Alaina remembered that night, keeping her voice steady, she said, "Go on."

Beau settled back into the armchair with his elbows resting on his knees, remembering. "The band played our song." He gave her a sidelong look. "And I had to get out of there. But Esmeralda asked me to show her where the bathrooms were. She was so shy. I think my family overwhelmed her, and she looked like you did that first day when I pulled you off Betty Jean's porch. I figured I had done my duty and was planning to make my excuses and leave. Then the world went haywire."

He stood up and started pacing. "One minute, I was walking down the hall, the next I was back at that witch's camp. I swear to you, Alaina, it was real, and I had you in my arms."

Alaina shivered. "What time was it?"

Beau narrowed his brows. "Why does that matter?"

"What time was it?" she asked again, insistent.

"I don't know, about 22:00, give or take." Beau felt a surge of impatience. He wanted to finish his story. Now that he'd begun, he needed to get it out.

Alaina paled. "Which would have been 8:00 pm for me... At 8:03 pm that night, I had a spell or something."

"*Mon Dieu*, what happened?"

"I don't know, but something went very wrong. At first I thought I was sick, so I called Ellen and asked her to come over. I thought I fell asleep and had a nightmare. I have them periodically about the bayou." Alaina rubbed her temple. "I kept going in and out of it. One minute I was with you, and the next, back in my bedroom. When Ellen got there, I was delirious. She thought I had a fever, but when she took my hand, it felt like something split me in half."

"Like you existed in a place you can't explain, being hurt by things no one else can see, hearing voices... going mad?" Beau shook his head.

"I saw you! We were back there." Her face clouded. "But it was different, like a dream where things don't look like they should, but you know what they are."

"Exactly," he said with a nod. "So, I really was not alone. You were there, and so was Esmeralda."

"You were dying!" Alaina cried. "That's the last thing I knew. I saw you. You were bleeding, and I could feel you laying on top of me, protecting me." She wiped her eyes with the back of her hand, shaking. "Then just as suddenly as it came on, it was over, and Ellen was there. I grabbed her hands and prayed. I prayed so hard, Beau."

Beau opened his arms, "Come here."

They held each other for a long time, rocked by the revelation that part of Alaina had joined Beau for a second night of bayou terror.

Beau sniffed and bit his bottom lip. "Little Esmeralda was dying, too. Something hit her hard, and her eyes rolled back in her head. I remember urging her to hold on, not to die. Then, out of nowhere, she blurted out this scripture, and the black spirits started howling and shrieking. Then I got pissed. I would not let them kill me, curled up on the floor, crying."

A fierce light sparkled in his eyes. Beau Landry, the warrior stood before her, dangerous, wild, bloody. The enemy had been mistaken if they thought that man would die lying down.

"That's when we fought. It was the most magnificent thing I have ever seen. And we took them out, Jolie Catin. They could not stand under the assault. The Lord saved my life, but I heard your voice telling me to fight, so I could come back to you. I held on to those words. They were the only part of that night I refused to let go. For months, I pretended, even to myself, that I didn't remember, but I did. I couldn't forget because it was different this time. I knew what I'd seen. Somehow after that night, the torment stopped, and I began to heal." He sagged, all the energy sapped from his limbs, and he pulled her down to the bed with him. "Esmeralda knew it was real."

"What do you know about her, Beau?" Alaina asked, drained.

Beau rested his cheek on his outstretched arm. "I know she is somebody we want by our side when we take on Charlotte and her nasty ass, bucktoothed son."

February 15, 1000 ME

Should You Tell Him? - Pepperwood

Prince Peter's words echoed in Alaina's mind, "We will no longer tolerate wickedness, nor allow it to prosper in Alanthia. One of Prince Josiah's first orders of business will be the complete eradication of subversive and dangerous groups operating inside the Kingdom. Mr. Landry, we would like to give you the opportunity to take part in the investigation and subsequent action against them. We will authorize the full force and power of the Federal Investigative and Armed Services to act with extreme prejudice."

When the initial jubilation passed, Alaina gestured to Beau, communicating without words the need to speak with him in private.

He followed her upstairs, his eyes brimming with ironic humor as he closed their bedroom door. "I know what you are going to say, *chèr*. I should tell him."

"When he first made the offer, all I could think was that we wouldn't be going in there with Uncle Boudreaux and an ancient shotgun, but now that I think about it…"

Beau grinned. "You're thinking Director Thaddeus ben Todd might have a problem with me becoming an honorary FBI Agent? I expect I'll let him take that up with the Prince." He waved away her concerns. "Besides, as of yesterday, I'm a certified giant killer, and there ain't many that can list that on their resume."

Alaina laughed out loud.

"And those New Yorkers don't know the bayou, *chèr.* Thaddeus ben Todd can't dispute that I do." His expression turned to one of absolute mischievous chagrin. "Considering I disappeared in the dark with his wife, not to mention that I did it while I was half out of my mind, being attacked by the very evil we are going after, he ought to thank me."

Alaina draped her arms around his shoulders. "He might still fight this."

Beau shrugged. "I'll appeal to a higher authority."

"I'm sure Peter will stand behind you. He gave his word." Alaina ran her finger over his jaw.

Beau shook his head. "Not that authority… his wife."

Alaina pressed her body against his. "We are a higher authority."

"Talk about it," he pulled her tight, "only one higher, but I don't kiss Him."

End of Book Notes

The process of writing M4-Sword of the Spirit was a departure from my previous novels. Typically, I have a detailed outline of the major events and structure the novel around the outline. Thaddeus and Esmeralda's story simply would not adhere to structure, so I ended up following them around and recording what happened, a scary and exciting process.

Tackling a May-December romance was also a challenge because their relationship began when Esmeralda was just a child, and Thaddeus was in his late twenties. It took a delicate hand, but the characters and their stories blossomed on the page, and I think it became something special.

In the timeline, I discovered 997 ME and 999 ME were well fleshed out, but 998 ME was unexplored, which gave me a lot of freedom to move the characters around and orchestrate events. It also created depth and background, filling out details we did not get to see in previous novels. And while this is Esmeralda and Thaddeus' story, we get to explore Beau Landry's dark years and got to attend Mack and Lavinia's wedding.

The battles in this novel, internal and external, physical and spiritual, were heart pounding and heart breaking. For me, the saddest part of the entire story is the scene in Beau's office when he says to Alaina's portrait, "I'm not better, *Bébé*."

Millions of people struggle with mental illness or love someone who does. I tried to portray their stories with dignity and tackle a subject shrouded in shame. I felt it was important to show the day-to-day courage it takes to get out of bed, to face the world, and to try to act normal. Loving someone who battles mental illness takes fortitude, especially when the world condemns or writes them off. Sarah Landry's confrontation with Thaddeus on the dock was particularly powerful in that regard.

As an author, I scripted the final battle quite differently than it unfolded. I realized as I wrote that to orchestrate the ending the way I plotted it, I would have had to make Angelica ben Omri do something stupid, something out of character that would get her killed. The wily old witch was just too darn smart to do it, and it would have been disingenuous to force that in the text. So, she got away, and she wasn't supposed to. I was mad about it. But the integrity of the work demanded I be true to characters that I so painstakingly create, and I could do no less.

I fought my own battles as I neared the close of this novel. And while I continued to write, I was overcome with self-doubt. So, I did the best thing I could have done, I flew eleven-hundred miles to see 'Astrid'. This whole thing began because she said to me, "Staci, you have to write our story." Now Davianna and Astrid's story is not Susan and Staci's story, but our friendship inspired the two characters, and where would Davianna go if she was in trouble? To see Astrid, obviously. For four days, she barred me from 'book talk'. I only wrote a few hours. It was the first time in ten months that I'd taken a day off, and I desperately needed the rest. I needed my friend. I finished M4 sitting on her couch while she was at work. Instead of being joyful, satisfied, and excited, I was uncertain. Truly, in a writer's crisis.

Something happened while I was doing the first hard edit of M4-Sword of the Spirit; I resettled. I took the tough love I had been given, kept the parts I felt were valid, and discarded the rest. I studied up on my punctuation, which was abhorrent, and committed to my style and my stories. But best of all, I stopped wondering and worrying. I grew, I changed, and like the M4 characters, came out on the other side stronger.

I hope you loved the book. I hope it entertained you, made you laugh, cry, and think. I hope you enjoyed visiting with old friends, and I hope you are ready for the next installment because we have all the players in place now. The Resistance is complete, and there is a lot more to come.

Thank you.
Staci Morrison
October 10, 2018

CPSIA information can be obtained
at www.ICGtesting.com
Printed in the USA
BVHW052145290422
635743BV00002B/106